THE LESBIANA'S GUIDE TO CATHOLIC SCHOOL

THE LESBIANA'S GUIDE TO CATHOLIC SCHOOL

SONORA REYES

BALZER + BRAY

An Imprint of HarperCollins*Publishers*

Balzer + Bray is an imprint of HarperCollins Publishers.

The Lesbiana's Guide to Catholic School
Copyright © 2022 by Sonora Reyes
All rights reserved. Printed in the United States of America.
No part of this book may be used or reproduced in any manner whatsoever without
written permission except in the case of brief quotations embodied in critical
articles and reviews. For information address HarperCollins Children's Books,
a division of HarperCollins Publishers, 195 Broadway, New York, NY 10007.
www.epicreads.com

Library of Congress Cataloging-in-Publication Data

Names: Reyes, Sonora, author.
Title: The lesbiana's guide to Catholic school / Sonora Reyes.
Description: First edition. | New York, NY : Balzer + Bray, [2022] | Audience:
    Ages 13 up. | Audience: Grades 10–12. | Summary: Sixteen-year-old
    Mexican American Yami Flores starts Catholic school, determined to keep her
    brother out of trouble and keep herself closeted, but her priorities shift when
    Yami discovers that her openly gay classmate Bo is also annoyingly cute.
Identifiers: LCCN 2021053154 | ISBN 978-0-06-306023-4 (hardcover)
Subjects: CYAC: Brothers and sisters—Fiction. | Self-acceptance--Fiction. |
    Dating (Social customs)—Fiction. | Suicide--Fiction. | Lesbians—Fiction. |
    Bisexuality—Fiction. | Mexican Americans—Fiction. | Catholic schools—
    Fiction. | High schools—Fiction. | Schools—Fiction. | LCGFT: Novels.
Classification: LCC PZ7.1.R483 Le 2022 | DDC [Fic]—dc23
LC record available at https://lccn.loc.gov/2021053154

Typography by Jessie Gang
22 23 24 25 26   PC/LSCH   10 9 8 7 6 5 4 3 2 1
❖
First Edition

To my mom. Mi otro yo.

AUTHOR'S NOTE

This book deals with issues of racism, homophobia, immigration, and the suicidal ideation and hospitalization of a character. I have done my best to depict these topics with sensitivity and care. If these are difficult subjects for you, please take care of yourself and know that your mental and emotional well-being comes first.

1

THOU SHALT NOT TRUST A
TWO-FACED BITCH

Seven years of bad luck can slurp my ass.

It's been way too long since I punched something, and that vanity had it coming. Stupid mirror. Stupid *Yami*.

Whatever. Mirrors are overrated, and punching them is underrated. I've never liked looking at myself anyway. Not because I don't think I'm cute. I mean, I *am* cute—objectively—but that's beside the point. I like this new reflection better. It's cracked enough that I'm hardly recognizable. Splintered in all the right places. *I* did that. With my fist. Who says I'm not tough?

I don't run from a fight—as long as it's with an inanimate object. I didn't punch the mirror hard enough to shatter it, but the pulsing in my knuckles tells me I hit it pretty hard. My chest swells at the accomplishment, and so does my hand.

Shit. That's a lot of blood.

Okay, maybe I shouldn't have done that. My hand is shaking and starting to drip, but I'm stuck. All I can think about is

Bianca, and the other thing I *really* shouldn't have done.

Who quits their job just to avoid the possibility of running into an ex? Not even an ex. An ex-traordinarily two-faced bitch. An ex–best friend, who I'm ashamed to have ever had feelings for.

Bianca's never been good at keeping secrets, so I don't know why I thought she'd keep this one to herself. It's my own fault for trusting her. Last time I saw her was when she outed me at the end of sophomore year. I was happy to never see her again, but today she just *had* to walk right into the coffee shop I work at. *Worked* at.

She has some nerve trying to confront me at work. It's not like I could defend myself. I never could, against her. Because of her, I couldn't even make it a couple weeks into my summer job.

So you're running away to Catholic school now? Are you that desperate to avoid me?

Yes. Desperate enough to quit my job, too. Anything to keep from seeing her. Anything.

"Yami?" Cesar knocks at the door but doesn't wait for a response before cracking it open and peeking inside. "I'll call you back," he says to whoever he's on the phone with. He must have heard the mirror break. His eyes widen slightly at the sight of my fist, so I jump in before he can say anything.

"Was that your *girlfriend*?" I tease.

"Something like that." He shrugs.

"You're such a player," I say, shaking my head.

"*Anyways*, you okay?" My brother stares at my bloody

knuckles and the mirror, waiting for an explanation I don't give. I should be the one worried about him, not the other way around. His knuckles are freshly scabbed like mine are about to be, and he has a black eye. Just another variation of the usual.

"Are *you* okay?" I throw the question back at him. His eyes flick to the mirror and back at me before he walks in. He hops over the dirty clothes on the floor and onto my bed, grinning.

"I got all As!" he says. Okay, so I'm not the only one deflecting. Cesar and I have an unspoken rule: you can ask personal questions exactly once. If the question is avoided, you don't pry. That's how we keep the peace. I give Cesar a high five with my good hand, then go to our shared bathroom to wash off the blood, leaving the door open so he can hear me.

"¡Eso! No wonder you got a scholarship to Slayton."

Cesar is definitely the better student between us. He skipped a grade, so we're both about to be juniors. A lot of people assume we're twins, which I don't mind. It makes it slightly less embarrassing that my younger brother is so much smarter than me. I'm not in all honors classes like him, but I do all right.

Without a scholarship of my own, I'll need to get another job ASAP to pay my half of tuition. It's the only way Mom could afford to send us both to Slayton Catholic, and I'm more than happy to do the extra work. I would probably die of embarrassment if I had to go back to Rover High after what Bianca did. Catholic school and another job will be worth it if I never have to see her gorgeous, backstabbing face ever again. Goodbye, Rover, can't say I'll miss you.

I make sure all the blood is gone and dab some of Cesar's

superglue on the cut before going back to my room. By the time I'm done, you can barely tell I hurt myself. If nothing else, hiding my pain is one thing I'm good at.

Cesar's lying on my bed, staring at the ceiling, fidgeting with the cross at the end of the chain around his neck. "Do you really want to go to Slayton?"

I shrug and fall onto the bed next to him.

Bianca isn't the only reason I need to go to Slayton, but I can't tell Cesar that. As far as he knows, Mom's forcing us both to go because we need a "better education," with the best teachers and more advanced classes. It's also Mom's way of making up for the fact that she doesn't have time to take us to church anymore.

At least, those are the reasons we tell Cesar. We don't tell him it's also because of all the trouble he's been getting into at Rover, and that Mom thinks Slayton will be safer (because of the Catholic values). We don't tell him I insisted on going with him to keep him out of trouble. It's a fancy-ass Catholic school, but it's a fresh start, for both of us. And at least now I'll know to keep my mouth shut about any crushes. This time, I'll be stealthy gay. Like Kristen Stewart.

Cesar rolls on his side to face me. "I heard it's nothing but white people there."

"Probably." The students at Rover are mostly Black and Brown Chicanes, but Slayton's on the north side of Scottsdale, about a forty-minute drive from where we live. Let's just say there's not a lot of melanin over there. I could probably pay my tuition selling sunscreen between classes.

"And the football team sucks," he says.

"You don't even play football."

"And now I never will." There's a sad gleam in his eye, as if playing football was once a dream of his. I swear he's the most dramatic guy I know.

"Aww, pobrecito." I try to pinch his cheek but he swats my hand away. He's only ten months younger than me, but I'll never let him forget he's the baby.

"I heard they make you do, like, ten hours of homework a day. That's called child abuse. When will we sleep? When will we eat? We're gonna starve!" He throws his arms in the air.

I laugh and hit him with my pillow. "We'll live." I don't mention that he's the one who'll have the excess homework, with all the AP and honors classes he's in. "Besides, it's better than the alternative, right?"

"What alternative?"

"You know"—I gesture to his bruised eye—"getting jumped?" His jaw clenches, and I immediately feel bad for bringing it up, so I keep going. "Or eating moldy chicken nuggets for lunch. *That's* child abuse. At least Slayton can afford to feed us real food."

"I guess." He doesn't sound amused. Cesar has no self-preservation instincts. It's almost as if he *wants* to keep getting his ass kicked at Rover.

I throw my arm around his shoulder. "Don't worry, if you ever miss Rover food, just lick the bottom of your shoe. You'll feel like you never left."

He lets out a little snort and throws one of his legs in the air.

"Excuse you, my shoes are clean AF. This is five-star dining right here."

"The *bottom* of your shoes, tonto." I go to flick his ear, but he sees it coming and flicks mine first. "Ow!" I rub my ear. Damn you, slow reflexes.

It's fine, though. I'd rather have a flicked ear than a mad-at-me little brother.

My phone buzzes, and Mom's picture lights up the screen. I don't know why she calls my phone when she could call my name. Our house isn't exactly big enough for me not to hear. I answer anyway.

"Hey, Mami."

"Ven pa' acá, mija."

"Coming." I hang up. My mind is racing, trying to come up with some excuse for how the mirror broke.

"Tell her I broke it." Cesar must have read my mind, even though he's not even looking at me. He's good at that.

"Why?"

"She'll believe you, and I won't get in trouble." He's right. Cesar is Mom's little baby. He breaks a mirror and she'll want to know if his hand is okay. I break a mirror and I'm grounded, at the very least. Still, I'm not throwing him under the bus.

I roll my eyes and head to my mom's room. In the hallway, I avoid looking at her collection of crosses and the gallery of Jesus portraits on the walls. Because apparently one Jesus isn't enough holiness to literally scare me straight—not that Mom knows she needs to. I wish Cesar didn't buy into this stuff so hard, so I could at least complain to him about it. The biggest portrait makes me particularly twitchy. Jesus is staring directly at me—no, *through* me—and his eyes are all sad like he knows I'm going to hell. I can't shake the feeling that it doesn't matter if I'm in the closet or not. Mom's voice nags in my head: *Jesus sees everything.* There's a burning in my gut, like the crosses are trying to exorcise the gay out of me. I keep my eyes on the carpet and speed-walk the rest of the way down the Hallway of Shame and into her room.

I almost step on a half-made beadwork earring on my way in. The angular design looks like it's going to mimic a red-and-orange flower. As usual, the floor is littered with beads, strings, wires, and other side-hustle supplies. Mom makes jewelry and Mexican beadwork to sell in her spare time, and she does a damn good job of it. As if she isn't already busy enough with her full-time call center job and two kids. I check to see if she saw me almost step on the earring, but she doesn't react.

She pats the space on her bed next to where she's lying. Her hair is in a messy bun, and she's wearing sunglasses—the ones she wears when she has post-crying eyes. I don't know what's wrong, but I don't think it's the mirror. I'm the one she calls when she's wearing her sunglasses. She's always too worried about Cesar to put her problems on him.

I hop over the mess on the floor and up on the bed to assume our usual cuddling position. Her bed is way comfier than mine, and no matter how old I get, I'll always feel safer in it. She pulls me into a hug and strokes my hair. I close my eyes, and we're both quiet for a moment.

She doesn't say anything about the mirror. She must not

have heard me break it. I know I'm supposed to be comforting her right now, but I feel so guilty. I have to come clean.

"I quit my job," I blurt out, better to rip off the Band-Aid. She would have figured it out anyway. "But I'll get another one, I promise."

"Ay Dios mío . . ." She sighs and gives herself the sign of the cross. "Don't tell me Bianca convinced you to quit. She's a bad influence on you." Bianca's name makes my body go cold for a moment.

"No, Mami. We're not even friends anymore." I try not to let it get to me that she hasn't even realized. It's only been a few weeks since Bianca outed me, so maybe Mami's just been too busy to notice.

"Ay, ay, ay . . . Then we'll talk about a new job later." For some reason she doesn't sound mad about me quitting. Not the reaction I was expecting.

"Okay . . ." It takes a while for her to say what she actually *does* want to talk about.

"I need you to do me a favor. Okay baby?" Her voice is hoarse.

"Yeah, Mami?"

"You know I want what's best for you and your brother."

"I know."

"I don't know what to do with that boy." She rolls onto her back. "Your dad was always so good at getting through to him."

I don't say anything. Dad got deported back to Mexico when I was ten. We talk on the phone and video-chat sometimes, but

I haven't actually seen him in years. After he left, my mom went through hell trying to get him back and spent all her savings on legal fees. But the system failed us, and he's not coming back.

Papi and Cesar are the only two people who I feel like really get me. It sucks I only get to talk to him on a screen for short bursts at a time.

"I talked to him today. He misses you. And Cesar." She wipes her eye under the glasses. "Cesar just . . . he doesn't listen to me like he listened to your dad." I can breathe a little easier knowing she's upset about Cesar, not my job, or even the mirror. But I know she'll eventually make this about me. She always does.

"Cesar's gonna be okay, Mami." I squeeze her hand. Cesar will always insist he's fine and play tough guy, but just because he hits back doesn't make it a fair fight. Mom and I have tried to ask why he keeps getting into fights and what's wrong, but he lashes out or retreats when he feels like he's being questioned. The best I've been able to do for him is keep an eye out, but I'm even failing at that. It seems like every time I look away he's either picking a fight or getting jumped, so I feel powerless to stop all the black eyes and busted lips he keeps coming home with.

"He listens to you." Mom's lip is quivering, and I don't know what to do. I shove my wounded fist into my hoodie pocket. If she figures out I punched something, she'll think I'm the reason Cesar's been fighting. One misstep always makes things my fault. It's a lot of pressure, having to be the perfect role model for my brother when I can barely keep it together myself.

Since Dad's been gone, there's been this unspoken rule that I'm supposed to take care of Cesar the way he did. According to Mom, anything bad that happens to Cesar is on me.

I'm tired.

"What do you need me to do?"

"I need you to set a good example. Tell him this will be a good opportunity for the two of you. Look out for him. This new school is small, so you won't have a problem." It feels like she's saying I haven't *been* looking out for him. As if the whole reason I got a job in the first place wasn't so I could follow him to Jesus School *to* look out for him. I want to tell her it's not my fault what happens to him, but she wouldn't buy it if I did.

"Okay, Mami."

"Oh, and you're grounded."

"What?" I sit up. How can she ask me a favor, and ground me, *while* she's cuddling me? I'm surprised my neck hasn't broken from the whiplash.

"Until you find another job. You know I can't afford to send you to that school."

"I'll find another job," I say. I was already planning on that. Being grounded doesn't matter anyway, since the only person I have to hang out with now is Cesar.

"And you'll look out for your brother."

"Yes, Mami," I say as I crawl out of her bed.

I'll let Cesar think we talked about the mirror.

2

THOU SHALT HAVE NO OTHER GODS
BEFORE CAPITALISM

I *should* be working on the summer assignment I got in the mail for my language arts class, but finding a job takes priority. What kind of school gives homework on VACATION, anyway? If I end up finding a job, maybe I'll do my presentation on how unethical and life-draining homework is.

No matter how busy I keep myself filling out form after form, being grounded is lonely. Usually I'd have Bianca over for moral support or to give me advice. But now I know she wasn't really my friend in the first place.

Part of me wants to be grateful she only told a grand total of three people about me being gay—our other friends Stefani and Chachi, and Bianca's mom—but that part of me is way too naive. She shouldn't have told *anyone*. I guess, looking back on it, I was never really close with the other girls in our friend group. They just tolerated me because I was friends with Bianca. She was the "leader" of the group, the rest of us her dutiful followers.

But she was more than just a leader, and I wasn't just a follower. She was the superhero, and I was the sidekick.

Okay, maybe the sidekick is a little generous. I was more like the fangirl in distress who the hero constantly has to save. No one cares about that character. So really, I'm glad Bianca shattered that illusion, so I don't have to play that role anymore. I'm my own hero now, and she's the villain.

I guess I was pretty naive back then. I had *seen* Bianca's mean side. How she would talk shit about anyone and everyone just to do it. How she looked down on anyone outside our little group. Under Bianca's glow, I felt special. I should have known how easy it would be for her to turn and make me the target.

For a while, job hunting is a convenient distraction from Bianca. I don't have to think about how much I hate her while I'm busy filling out applications and compulsively rewriting my résumé. I spend the rest of June and all of July job hunting, but after getting nothing but soul-sucking rejections, I'm still not having any luck. My résumé isn't exactly impressive, no matter how I twist it. I've only had one job working as a barista, and I couldn't even hold it a couple of weeks. And there's only so many job openings within walking distance from our house.

Technically, I'm only supposed to use my phone for job hunting and emergencies, but I *am* allowed to stare at my notification-less screen between applications. My phone background makes me feel slightly better about not having any texts. It's a picture of me and my dad doing our best *America's Next Top Model* poses. I was eight, so Papi's on his knees to match my height, and we're both doing that weird pose with our hands on our hips and elbows inverted. I grin at the picture and consider calling my dad, but since I'm grounded, I just keep staring at my lack of notifications.

I hate myself for hoping to see Bianca's name. I shouldn't miss her. I should be pissed. I *am* pissed, and yet . . .

"Ugh!" I wander into my mom's room and leap over all her jewelry onto the mattress to take comfort in her bed. She'd kill me if I stepped on any of her stuff. I pull the comforter over my face and think.

Since Mom can cover only half my tuition, if I can't get a job to cover my part, I'll have to go back to Rover. Alone. I'd have no way of looking after Cesar like Mom expects. She's already annoyed that I couldn't get into his genius classes—if he gets himself in trouble and loses his scholarship, it'll be on me.

That's what this is about. It's not about me "running away" from Bianca. Never seeing her again is just another perk of this whole situation, *if* I can make it work by getting another job. But no one wants to hire a sixteen-year-old with no car and no experience. I have to think outside the box. I sit up and let the comforter fall off me. Think. *Think.*

The bed is too comfy to get any real thinking done, so I hop off and sit on the floor. But I can't concentrate there because Mom's jewelry is a mess. She leaves bits of half-finished pieces scattered all over and doesn't even bother separating her finished pieces from her works in progress. I start organizing her mess to clear my head. Frankly, she could make a lot more money off this if she set it up a little nicer and actually put any inkling of energy into marketing her Etsy store. Out of curiosity, I pull up her online store on my phone.

It's pretty embarrassing, honestly. The pictures are frickin' blurry, and the jewelry is posed against the washed-out dark blue carpet in my mom's room instead of literally any other backdrop. It hardly does the vibrant colors any favors.

Mom doesn't know the first thing about social media or technology of any kind. That gives me an idea. . . . Maybe I can surprise her! Revamping her Etsy store and making an Instagram for it could be exactly what she needs. I carefully sift through all her work and pick my favorite of each style. She has some basic jewelry she sells for cheap, like beaded earrings or necklaces with a crystal on a chain. Her handwoven bracelets are always a hit at the farmers markets. But my favorite is her beadwork.

The colors she chooses grow more vibrant when they're woven together, like the design gives a life to them that wasn't there before. Her beaded necklaces, earrings, and bracelets all remind me of Mexico. I haven't gone since I was little, but I always felt more at home across the border.

I smooth out the white sheet on the bed and lay Mom's finished pieces on top. They look nice, but the sheet does no justice to how cute they look on. Good thing I'm always down for an excuse to give myself a makeover. After doing my nails, face, and hair, I'm ready to model some jewelry.

"Cesar! ¡Ayúdame!" I call out.

"With what?" he calls back.

"Just come here!"

"Ugh, fine." Cesar comes in and stares at me and the jewelry on the bed. "Uh, what are you doing?"

"Making Mami rich." I smile. "You're my photographer."

"Only if you come with me to get Takis."

Hmm. I swear I just heard him tell some girl on the phone he's sick and can't hang out. Cesar's definitely using Takis as an excuse to get me out of the house. He never even shares with me, which I would be annoyed about if I actually liked Takis. I think he might be passing up opportunities to do stuff to make sure I'm okay.

He doesn't know what happened, but he has to know *something* happened. I'm sure the broken mirror and Bianca's absence tipped him off. I used to spend almost every day with her, either at my house or hers, ever since we were little, but summer's almost over and she hasn't been to our house once since before school let out.

"But I'm grounded," I whine.

"Mom's at work." He winks, which he apparently doesn't know how to do without turning his entire head and opening his mouth to get his eye to close. "Besides, she wanted us to bring Doña Violeta tamales anyways. She doesn't have to know we *also* went to get Takis."

It doesn't take much convincing because personally, I don't feel like I deserve to be grounded anyway. I'm sure she'll un-ground me the second I tell her about my Etsy idea. Frankly,

I don't want Cesar walking to the corner store by himself. And Mami wouldn't either. The guys he's always fighting with don't live far from us, and I swear he's jinxed when I'm not around. I'd rather not risk it, even if it's hot enough to fry an egg on the street. "Fine, but we're taking pictures first."

I hand Cesar my phone, and he starts snapping pictures before I'm ready.

"Not yet!" I rush to put on a bracelet and show off my wrist for the picture, but he shakes his head.

"Put those on, too." He points at a pair of brown-and-blue earrings that were made as a set to match the bracelet.

I put them on and strike a pose with my hand touching my ear, so you can see both.

"You don't have to do all that. Your mouth isn't even in the picture," Cesar says, and I relax my puckered lips.

Cesar's a bossy photographer, but a good one. He keeps directing my poses and what jewelry to wear with what. It doesn't take long for him to get bored, though, and he ditches me while I agonize over choosing the right shop name and Insta handle. After about an hour of deliberation, I end up going with JoyeriaFlores for both Etsy and Instagram. The previous Etsy name was Maria749, which obviously needed to change. Next, I need money to put up some listings. I delete all the current listings, since it's hard to even tell what she was trying to sell with those. And according to the app, she hasn't made a sale on here in quite some time, which is about to change. I want to be able to prove to Mami that the shop is a success *before* I show it to her, so I have my work cut out for me.

Only problem is, I already gave her all the money I earned from my last job to pay for tuition. Luckily, I have someone else I can ask. I shoot a quick text over to my dad, telling him all about my plan and sending him some of the pictures I took and letting him know what the listing fee is. It's only a couple of minutes before my phone buzzes with his response.

Papi: Ay, que linda ♥ Your mami is going to love this. I can't wait to hear about her reaction.

And then I get a notification from PayPal. He sent me enough money to pay for the listing fee for the first twenty items, plus an extra twenty bucks and another heart emoji.

God, I love my dad.

With the listing fees paid for, I'm careful to account for the listing fee, transaction fee, and processing fee in each price so we don't lose money on anything. With this kind of money-making magic, how could anyone resist hiring me? Their loss.

As soon as I'm done listing all my favorite pieces, I share some pictures and the links on my Twitter with a caption about how hard my mom works to provide for us and how much I love her and her jewelry, blah blah. It's cheesy but people eat that shit up.

"Taki time." Cesar slides back into the room with a straight face.

I read over the caption several more times before finally hitting post. By the time I get downstairs, Cesar is waiting at the door with the tamales from the freezer. He's wrapped them into paper plates to bring to Doña Violeta. She's been real depressed since her husband passed last year and hasn't been looking after herself, so the block pretty much keeps her fed. She used to be the neighborhood nanny and took care of all the kids on our street, since none of our parents could afford day care. It was at least eight of us in her little one-bedroom house, and she somehow made it work. She took care of us then, so we take care of her now.

As soon as we're out of the house, the sound of sad mariachi music echoes through the neighborhood, coming all the way from Doña Violeta's porch. She used to play folk songs you could party to, but now it's always depressing. She just sits out on her porch all day, playing funeral music on repeat that bums out the whole block.

I can't stop checking my phone on the walk over. Nothing. I guess it's only been a couple of minutes since I set up the shop and Insta, so I really shouldn't worry yet. I shove my phone back into my pocket, hoping for better luck the next time I check it. We only make it past two houses when the sidewalk burns like a comal through my shoes. Five feet from the door and this Phoenix heat already has me sweating. The sacrifices I make for this family.

Bianca's house is on the way to Violeta's, but I keep my eyes peeled forward. I don't want to look at the flower garden we never finished planting together. The empty talavera pots we painted by hand would risk reminding me that being Bianca's friend was *fun*, and I need to think of her as an evil, heartless bitch right now. But Cesar stares at her house as we get closer, and I can't help but look.

The pots aren't empty. The flowers aren't dead. My stomach gets all tangled, and the sun feels twice as hot. She finished planting them without me.

"So what happened with you guys?" I hoped he wouldn't say anything but knew it was going to come up eventually.

I wipe the sweat from my forehead. "Nothing. She's dead to me."

Cesar laughs. "If she's dead to you, how is it nothing?"

"Because I don't want to talk about it." I can still feel the ache from the stab wound Bianca left not in my back, but in my chest. But I can't talk about that with Cesar. If Bianca is dead to me, I don't have to think about how different things would be if I'd never come out to her. If Bianca doesn't exist, I can move forward with my life. I'm grateful for the "only ask once" rule, so I don't have to think about it too much.

I'm also glad Rover was big enough that rumors only ever really spread within a single friend group. Whatever rumors there were about me, Cesar never got wind of, and vice versa. I like it that way.

I pull out my phone again to distract myself from any Bianca thoughts. The Instagram is getting a few likes and follows, but nothing too noteworthy. I groan. I know that realistically it won't blow up right away, but it's hard to be patient.

"Stop checking. You're just gonna make yourself mad," Cesar says, and Doña Violeta's pit bull puppy starts yapping at us from a few houses away. It's enough to distract Cesar from nagging about my phone. He's right, though. I make it a point to stop checking, at least until we get home. I turn the phone on silent so I won't be tempted to look.

Cesar goes to the chain-link fence, where the pit greets him and licks his hands through one of the holes. The poor dog is never allowed inside, so she's stuck in Doña Violeta's shaved-down front lawn all day. Most of us stop to bring her food, but there are a couple of kids who volunteered to do her landscaping, since her lawn was getting out of control. Now the grass is always cut, but the poor dog doesn't have a lot to entertain herself with.

Cesar always makes it his mission to give her attention whenever we walk by. Aside from the efforts of the community, the puppy is the only thing holding Violeta together. She's only about a year old, and cute enough to distract Cesar from my problems. It's obvious he's trying to fill the empty space Bianca left, but he doesn't need all the details. I love that about my brother.

Doña Violeta doesn't seem to notice us until we're right in front of her, hugging her and kissing her cheeks. She smiles at us with watery eyes but doesn't say anything.

"We brought you tamales," Cesar says over the music, gesturing to the plates in my arms. She doesn't answer, so we go inside to heat them up for her. Otherwise she might never eat. While Cesar heats the tamales, I straighten up her sitting room a bit. Her furniture has those clear plastic coverings to keep it from being comfortable. I always hated that as a kid and still don't understand it. The covering on one of the couches still has faded permanent-marker drawings on it from when Bianca and I tried to "decorate" when we were little. My face heats at the memory. It's like no matter where I go, Bianca is right there taunting me.

When the food is ready, Cesar and I sit on the floor of Violeta's porch while she eats, telling her any stories we can come up with to lift her mood. The longer we stay, the less sad her eyes get. We wait to say bye until her smiles aren't forced, and we can trust her not to spend the rest of the day crying.

"Thank you for this. Los quiero muchísimo," she whispers as she kisses my forehead, then repeats with Cesar.

"Love you, too," we both say as we give her a big hug before heading to the corner store for Cesar's Takis, then back home. The childish orange paint job makes our house stand out from the others. Dad, Cesar, and I painted it one summer while Mami was out of town. Orange is her favorite color, and he wanted to surprise her, but since we were eight and nine, we weren't experts. Mom says she doesn't want to repaint it because of the money, but really I think she's holding on to that piece of my dad.

When we get inside, sweaty and Taki-less (in my case), I finally privilege myself with a glance at my phone. JoyeriaFlores is by no means viral, but it's got a few hundred notifitications on Twitter and Instagram, with plenty of people excited in the comments. I quickly check Etsy.

Half the items have already sold. I throw myself onto my bed and happily convulse, squealing loud enough for Cesar to come in all concerned.

"Okay . . . I don't wanna know." He backs away slowly from my squealy frenzy.

Once I calm down, I type up a thank-you post for everyone's support, promising to restock some of the favorite items soon. Then I get to work trying to get the rest sold. I go back in my mom's room and put on some jewelry, then take some videos for TikTok. I only post one and save the rest in drafts to post later. Hopefully one of these videos hits everyone's For You page so it can blow up. When the front door opens, I rush over to greet Mami, preparing myself for a swift un-grounding.

"Mami, I have a surprise for you!" I say, hugging her.

"A surprise?" She raises an eyebrow.

I grab my phone from my pocket and pull up my Twitter post, then I hand her the phone. I hold my breath while I watch her every expression, trying to calculate how far into the post she's read. Her expression doesn't change, but her thumb moves to click on the Etsy link.

"Do you like the name? Look at the sales! Isn't that amazing? *This* will be my new job! I can help you with your workload and I'll take care of all the online stuff." I feel like I'm about to cry from pure joy. Mami must be so proud of my entrepreneurial genius. She hands me my phone back.

"Take it down."

I blink. "What?"

"Take it down."

"Why?" I can't help the crack in my voice.

"Because I said so."

I stare at her with my mouth hanging open. Does she not realize how good this could be for her? For all of us? She's the one who wants me to make more money. She's the one who grounded me *because* I'm not making money! Why is she so damn stubborn? This was the perfect idea, and I honestly don't know what else to do. It seems like I can never do anything right with her.

"Listen, mija, I've had a long day. I can't deal with this right now." She walks past me into her room without another word. I storm into mine, fall back into my bed, and groan into my pillow.

If it was up to Dad, he'd let me do it. He *loved* this idea. Maybe he can help me. Or maybe I just need to vent. I send him a voice message.

"Paaaaaapi, I miss you. Mom is being a huge dick," I start, then delete it and start again.

"Papiiiiiii. Tell your wife to stop being such a *huge dick!*" Delete.

I've recorded seven different messages by the time I get my anger out. I finally send a tame one, calmly explaining the situation to him. Maybe he'll work his magic and talk some sense into her.

My phone keeps buzzing with notifications, and eventually the background of me and my dad's model poses fades to black as my phone dies. I don't have the heart to charge it, because that would mean I'd have to break the very embarrassing news that the shop is closed after only one day.

When I finally put my phone back on the charger in the morning, the notifications are still blowing up. Which pisses me off, because it was such a wasted effort. But then I see I have two texts. One from Mom . . .

Mami: Leave it up . . .

And one from Dad.

Papi: I talked to her 😏

3

THOU SHALT NOT COVET THY NEIGHBOR'S BUTT

By the time the first day of school comes around, I still can't use the mirror in my room. Luckily, Mami's been so busy and distracted the last month that she hasn't found out about it yet, and I intend to keep it that way. She rarely comes into my room, so I shouldn't have a problem. Unfortunately, it means I have to let Cesar stink up the bathroom before I get ready, since he always manages to get in there first. I turn on the fan so I don't die from toxic fumes.

The mirror in the bathroom is much bigger than my broken vanity, and it makes me uncomfortable. There's something unsettling about seeing your whole reflection looking back at you. If the eyes are the windows to the soul, then I guess I feel like I'm invading my own privacy. My eyes wander to the corner of the glass, where Cesar has the Mayan Code of the Heart taped up: In Lak'ech Ala K'in, with the famous poem underneath.

✦ ✦ ✦

Tú eres mi otro yo / You are my other me.
Si te hago daño a ti / If I do harm to you,
Me hago daño a mí mismo / I do harm to myself.
Si te amo y respeto / If I love and respect you,
Me amo y respeto yo / I love and respect myself.

It's kind of ironic how much he loves that poem, considering how often he gets into fights. Maybe it's because it was basically our dad's mantra. Dad was always outspoken about our roots, and he wanted us to be too. He used to sit us down at random times and give us lectures on things like immigration, colorism, our Indigenous history—all that good stuff. I hated it at the time, but now I kind of miss it.

Mami's always had other things going on, especially now. She's just too busy to carry on that tradition.

Without Dad here, I feel like I'm less Indigenous somehow. Cesar wears his indigeneity on his sleeve, though. He says "in lak'ech" instead of "same," and always wears both a cross necklace and a chain with the jaguar symbol on it—for facing fears, I think. Maybe it's his way of compensating for the fact that we haven't had a solid connection to our ancestry since Dad left.

I have my own way of facing my fears—sharpening my winged eyeliner. A perfect wing makes looking at myself more bearable. And if I get it just right, it'll make me less nervous about today. My hand trembles a little, and I have to clean off the first line.

This will be fine. I have a foolproof game plan:

1. Find a new best friend.

2. Don't be gay about it.

My hand steadies at the thought, and the line goes on smooth. I woke up late today, since Cesar was up late talking to some girl on the phone like he always does, and our walls are paper thin. Because of my fuckboy brother, I don't have time to do my whole face. I'll just have to wing it. Heh.

"Yamilet, ¡apúrate!" Mom's shouting almost makes me smudge my eyeliner again. Good thing it didn't, or she'd be waiting another five minutes for me to fix it. We're not even close to late. She's just hell-bent on taking us early so we have time to find our classes.

"Almost done!" I call out as I slip into my blue uniform shirt and plaid skirt. The dress code says the skirt is supposed to go to your knee. This skirt would go past the knee of a life-size Barbie doll. On me, it's almost to my ankle. I roll the top of the skirt until it's at my knee, and it makes me want to gouge my eyes out a little less. I tuck in my shirt, also part of the dress code. The tucked shirt emphasizes my belly, so I tug at the fabric until it hangs over the top of the skirt. Satisfied, I grab my bag and make my way to the kitchen to get some toast.

Cesar slides in front of me before I can eat, blue shirt tucked into his khakis. He reaches out his hand like we've never met and shakes mine hard enough that he could dislocate my shoulder.

"Hiya there. Good golly gosh, the weather sure is nice, isn't it?" He's talking in a nasally voice and switching between, like, three accents that aren't his. Still shaking my hand, he adjusts the invisible glasses on his nose with the index finger of his free hand.

I straighten up and shake his hand back. "Oh, it's just splendid! Simply wonderful. Cheers!" My accent comes out British.

I do my best curtsy, pulling the sides of my skirt out. He bows. Mom smacks the backs of our heads. Her smack doesn't sting, but the glare burns.

"Be serious," she scolds, then lets the tiniest smile crack. "You both look nice."

When we go out to the car, Bianca and her mom are walking out of their house across the street. I hide my face by making a visor out of my hand and book it to the car, praying my mom won't notice them.

But, of course, she does.

From the front seat, I can see Mami wave enthusiastically as she walks toward the car, but Bianca and her mom kind of just ignore her.

"That was weird," Mami says when she opens the car door and steps in, Cesar sliding into the back seat behind her.

"I *told* you, we're not friends anymore," I say, slouching in my seat so Bianca won't see me when they drive past us. Not that she was looking.

"Well, that's no reason for them to be rude!" Mami frowns.

"Sorry," I mumble, as if it's my fault.

Thankfully, she changes the subject and spends the rest of the car ride gushing about how proud she is of us and how she's excited for us to "start this new chapter in our lives." She's actually made it a point to mention how proud she is of *both* of us, not just Cesar, since the Etsy store is a lot more successful than either of us predicted it would be. Still, I wish she wouldn't tell me she's proud of me. I don't want to disappoint her. I ignore her and post another jewelry video from my drafts to TikTok.

When we pull up to the school, I'm surprised at how much space five small buildings dare to take up. There's a chapel and a gym across the student parking lot, and a huge courtyard separating the cafeteria from the office and the building where most of the classrooms are, all the room doors accessible from the outside. The lockers are outside next to the courtyard. Lovely. More time to be out in this Satan's ballsack heat. When we get out of the car, I sneeze from the smell of real, freshly manicured grass wafting past my nose on the hot breeze.

Despite how spaced out they are, it seems like I'll be able to see every building from just about anywhere on campus. On one hand, I feel like I'm burning under a microscope because this school is so much smaller. But at the same time, it seems like it'll be a lot easier to look out for Cesar here. There's nowhere he can get jumped at this school without me knowing.

After Mami leaves, Cesar and I are glued at the hip. We say it's so we can help each other find everything, but I'm pretty sure we both know that's BS. Being alone is scary. I'm supposed to be replacing Bianca, but I have no idea where to start. There's already a bunch of kids in the courtyard, so I'm playing this game in my head called "spot the person of color." So far,

I've only seen a handful of Asian kids, one Black guy, and a few Brown kids. Total, there's like a dozen kids out of a couple hundred. Including Cesar and me. I hate how *visible* that makes me feel.

I notice my skirt is the only one rolled up. Somehow, no one else's skirts are reaching their ankles. I bet they have them hemmed that way. Mom wouldn't let me "deface" my skirt. She said they were too expensive to risk altering, in case there were mistakes.

When the bell rings, Cesar and I are forced to go our separate ways. Cesar to smart-people classes. Me, language arts. I speed-walk through the courtyard so I'm not alone in the open for too long. As quick as I'm going, a couple of kids still pass me. Since all the classroom buildings are outside, it takes me less than a minute to get to my class, room A116, and it's already more than half-full. It makes me feel like a cool kid for once, strolling into class without a care in the world, with only four minutes to spare before the next bell.

The second I'm in the door, the cool air from the AC washes over me. The AC at Rover was spotty sometimes, and the number of students packing their body heat into each classroom didn't help. That's not an issue here, but I still find myself sweating. Between the bloody crucified Jesus, judgy Virgin Mary, and the tortured saints on the wall, this room is worse than my mom's Hallway of Shame. I'm glad I stayed up last night doing that bullshit assignment now. I have a feeling this teacher wouldn't have been forgiving.

I sit in the first row, but on the corner seat. It's the perfect spot because teachers think I care, but I'm far enough to the side that they don't notice me. Genius.

There's a cute blond girl walking straight toward me. My mind immediately goes back to my plan. She might make a good Bianca replacement. She has this bounce to her walk that makes her ponytail sway. She's wearing a blue ribbon in her hair and a huge, adorable grin that makes me nervous. I think I look at her a millisecond longer than I should. I have to be more careful. I don't see her two friends following her until they take the other seats near me and I feel like I'm being cornered. There's still three minutes left before the next bell.

"Hi, I'm Jenna!" says the cute blonde. "This is Emily and Karen." She points to her friends, who smile as she introduces them. Karen has strawberry-blond hair and a ton of freckles. Emily's short brown hair barely fits into her ponytail. While they're all white, Karen has a pretty obvious spray tan, and Emily's dark brown hair contrasts with her vampire-looking skin, which looks to have never seen the light of day. All three of them have matching blue ribbons as hair ties.

"I'm Yamilet." I hold my hand out to shake Jenna's before I realize this is not a business meeting. I don't know. It feels like everything should be formal when you're in uniforms.

"Oh my God, she's so cute," Jenna says.

"What?" I feel like I'm blushing.

Emily giggles. "It's cute that you do handshakes."

It's cute that you think I care you're leaving. I remember how

Bianca's laugh salted the wound. How I froze up in front of my boss and the customers, who all seemed to be enjoying the show. *We're not friends anymore. Go ahead and run away to Catholic school.*

"What?" I swallow. I know I missed something.

"How do you pronounce your name again?" Jenna asks.

"Yah-mee-let," I repeat phonetically. But the look on their faces tells me they'll never be able to pronounce it. "But if you want, you can call me Yami."

"Yummy, that's adorable," Karen says, scooting on top of my desk.

"Thanks." I try not to sound annoyed that she couldn't even pronounce my nickname.

"So where are you from?" Karen asks. All three of them lean toward me like it's some kind of secret.

"Rover . . . it's a public school. You've probably never heard of it. It's kind of far."

"No, I meant, um, like, I like your accent. Where are you *from*?" She squints and cranes her neck. Emily's face goes red.

Oh.

"Phoenix." I force a smile. I don't want to give her the satisfaction of telling her what she really wants to know. Who does that?

"Oh my God, Karen, you can't just ask people where they're *from*!" Emily scolds.

The next bell rings, and I take a deep breath. This is going to be a long day.

The teacher, Mrs. Havens, is tall, overly fake-tanned, and platinum blond. After running a quick roll call, she turns the TV on, and the script for the Pledge of Allegiance is displayed on the screen. Everyone stands, puts their hands on their hearts, and starts chanting.

My dad always told me I don't have to do or say anything I don't believe in; he only stood for what he felt was right. "Liberty and justice for all" never applied to people like us. The last time I saw him in person was at a protest. There was this anti-immigration law getting passed that would make racial profiling legal and my dad wasn't having it. I thought his green card would keep him safe, but I was wrong. He got arrested at the protest, and I haven't seen him since.

After that, I stopped standing for the pledge.

I was never the only one sitting at Rover, but things are different here. Richer. Whiter. Here, sitting like I used to would be admitting what an outsider I am. I stand but don't say the words. It's the closest thing to protesting I can do without causing a scene. My dad would be ashamed.

Mrs. Havens notices that my mouth isn't moving, and she gives me a look. I want to stare deadpan back at her and continue to say nothing. But I'm too chickenshit for that level of confrontation, so I start mouthing the words "watermelon, watermelon, watermelon."

What's worse than making us do the pledge every morning at school? Making us *pray* every morning. It's not that I have anything against prayer, but it's weird that it's a required activity at school. Everyone mumbles the same prayer, some of them with closed eyes. Something about God's love for us and our duty to serve him? It's nice that so many people feel loved like that, but I can't relate. If the God I grew up learning about is real, I seriously doubt he loves me. Why else would he make me gay and then send me to hell over it? I left that abusive relationship a long time ago. I would have left it earlier if Mom let me, but it wasn't until Dad got taken away that she had to really hustle by selling jewelry on top of her full-time call center job. Even though she still believes harder than anyone I know, that's when she stopped having time to take us to church. That's probably why I've never heard of the prayer the class is all reciting from memory, so I just stand there looking like a dumbass.

"All right, welcome to Grade Eleven Language Arts. I hope you've all had a productive summer. I want to get right down to it, since you were all already sent your syllabi. Who wants to present first?" Mrs. Havens doesn't waste any time.

The summer assignment was to do a persuasive presentation on a topic of our choosing. I did mine about how much of a buzzkill homework is. Only one person volunteers to go first. From what I can tell, she's one of, like, four East Asian kids at the school. I hear a couple of murmurs and hushed laughter when her hand shoots up, and I'm intrigued.

The teacher doesn't seem happy, either. She looks around the room, as if trying to find another raised hand. The girl smiles victoriously when no one volunteers.

"All right, Ms. Taylor. What've you got for us?" Mrs. Havens sighs out loud.

Damn, tough crowd.

"Careful not to stare. Bo always notices," Karen whispers at me. I guess I was staring. "Her peripheral vision is better, because of the eyes." She stretches the corners of her eyes with her fingers, then stifles a giggle. Jenna rolls her eyes but doesn't say anything.

"What?" My face gets hot. She can't be serious.

"Karen!" Emily slaps Karen on her orange-tinted wrist. She makes wide eyes at me as if to say, *Can you believe her?*

"I'm just saying!" Karen giggles.

Mrs. Havens shoots us a glare, quickly ending the conversation. I rub my temples. It's easier if I pretend I didn't hear anything; I don't have the energy. I want to say something, but I don't want to make a scene and get painted as *that* person, I already stand out as it is. I can't get in trouble on day one. I focus on Bo instead.

When she stands, I notice she's the only girl I've seen so far who went for the khakis instead of the skirt, and she's wearing rainbow Vans. I have to remind myself we're at a Catholic school, so I shouldn't read into it. Not everyone who likes khakis and rainbows is gay. Maybe she's just desperate to wear any color that isn't our uniform's blue and beige.

Bo walks up to Mrs. Havens, chin up. She hands her a flash drive, then stands in front of the class, waiting for her presentation to show up on the projector.

The title slide states in huge letters: CHOICE VS. LIFE.

Bo flashes a smile and stands up straighter.

"Abortion is a human right. A right that, when legally stripped away, doesn't actually prevent the procedure from taking place. It only prevents *safe* abortions from taking place."

I must be staring with my mouth wide open, because Bo looks at me and grins, as if this is the exact reaction she was going for. She then goes on to argue why abortion should be legal everywhere. I almost laugh. I'm completely baffled that someone has the balls to do this at Catholic school. Her presentation is complete with statistics and sources from scientific journals. She even quotes the Constitution. Bo's a badass. I like her. I make a mental note to try and make friends with her later.

There are a few girls nodding along in agreement every now and then, but for the most part, everyone looks monumentally uncomfortable. Especially Mrs. Havens. I don't know why, but I absolutely love that.

Once Bo is done, Mrs. Havens looks fully unimpressed. "I expect better from you, Ms. Taylor."

Damn, is she going to publicly shame everyone like this?

"Why? Because I'm Chinese?" Bo snaps back. "Sorry for not living up to your model minority BS."

"And not everything is about race, Ms. Taylor. You may have a seat."

Bo rolls her eyes and sits back down. Mrs. Havens asks for another volunteer, but since no one raises their hand, she chooses me to go next.

After seeing Bo's presentation, I'm not as nervous. Mine

might get me a side-eye from Mrs. Havens, but it's not the most controversial topic today. Bo gave me an extra boost of confidence.

I get up and walk to the front of the room. Deep breath.

"Ms. Flores, unroll your skirt, please. That's against the dress code."

I look down and realize my shirt isn't pulled out far enough to hide the rolls in my skirt. Dammit.

"I'm too short for these skirts. It's way too long," I say under my breath, but I know Mrs. Havens heard me, because she sighs. Some kid coughs while I'm unrolling my skirt.

"Bet money she's the next one at the abortion clinic." A few hushed snickers.

"Excuse me?" My eyes dart around to try and find a guilty face. The voice came roughly from where my new "friends" are sitting. They aren't laughing, but Karen looks like she might be trying not to.

"Ms. Flores, please go ahead with your presentation," Mrs. Havens says, probably trying to keep me from losing my shit. I ignore her. I've heard too many stereotypes about teenage Mexican girls to let it slide. My face is burning too hot to remember my bullshitted presentation anyway.

"Why do I look like the type of person who would get an abortion? Is it because I'm Mexican? Because I don't want my skirt to reach the floor? Because I have to *work* to pay my tuition? Did you even listen to that girl?" I say, gesturing wildly at Bo. "People like me are *less* likely to get abortions. We can't afford it!"

"That's enough, Ms. Flores. Your presentation, please." Mrs. Havens tries to stop me, and my brain is telling me to shut the fuck up and do the presentation I stayed up all night preparing, but I can't stop.

"You know what, *this* is my presentation. You know who's most likely to get an abortion at *our* age?" I stare right at Karen. I'm only like 40 percent sure it was her who said it, but she deserves a talking-to either way. "Rich white people. Rich white people with the *privilege* of having the choice of what to do with their bodies and the rest of their lives. And you know who's most likely to *lie* about getting an abortion? People who grow up in a religion that gets off on shame and guilt, who can't safely carry proof of their 'sin' on their bodies or risk being shunned by their families and excommunicated by their church."

"Ms. Flores!" Mrs. Havens's face shakes as she shouts my name. She takes a breath to calm herself down before continuing. "Sit down, please."

So . . . bashing the Catholic faith on my first day may have taken it a *little* too far.

"I—I'm just saying." I mumble it like an apology and go back to my desk. Karen, Jenna, and Emily all stare at me like I shot someone.

"Mr. Baker, you're up." Mrs. Havens says, walking toward my desk. When some kid steps up to the front of the class, she nonchalantly places two pieces of paper on my desk, then walks back to hers.

A lunch detention slip, and my grade. Zero.

There's a fifteen-minute break between second and third hours—religion and chemistry—which isn't something we had at Rover. You can buy cookies and soda if you want. I so badly wish I had the cash—I could really use a pick-me-up right now, considering the way my morning has gone.

I wander the courtyard, trying not to sulk about detention, and almost eat the pavement when Cesar jumps on my back without warning. I think it's supposed to be a hug. I turn around and push him off me, but I don't even care he made me trip. It's nice to see a familiar face. That is, until he starts giving me puppy eyes.

"Yami, my beautiful, flawless, beloved sister. Your eyebrows look spectacular today. Your hair is lovely. Have I mentioned that you—"

"What do you want?"

"Buy me a cookie?" His grin is exaggerated so all his teeth show.

"Do I look like I have cookie money?" I'm fully aware I sound like Mom.

"Hmm . . . good point." He rubs his chin and scans the courtyard. "Yo, Hunter!" he calls out.

Some guy—Hunter, I'm guessing—approaches us. He looks like he actually conditions his wavy brown hair, and he has what Bianca would have called "smoochy white boy lips." Which basically just means he's a white boy with an upper lip.

"What is *up*, Flores?" he says, and gives my brother dap with unnatural enthusiasm.

"You got a dollar for a cookie?" Cesar asks. I try not to roll my eyes. He couldn't have known this guy for more than an hour and he's already asking for money. He is so shameless. Though I have to admit I'm a little jealous of how quickly he's already gotten comfortable here. I'm happy for it, though. Pretty sure he only had one real friend back at Rover. Some guy named Jamal, but they didn't hang out together at school too often.

"Yeah, I got you, bro! I only have a card, though. I'll just buy you one." He smiles at me. "You want one too?"

I want to be offended, because why would I want some rando to buy me a cookie? What makes him think I can't afford one myself? But then I see Bo getting in the cookie line.

"Sure." On second thought, I do want a stranger to buy me a cookie.

"This is my sister, Yami, but you can call her Yamilet," Cesar says, and I laugh. I kind of ruined it today, but Yami is supposed to be an earned nickname.

"Hi, Yamilet, I'm Hunter." Hunter makes an effort to say my name right, and he's a little flushed for some reason. He leads us to the line.

I told myself I would be super straight at this school, but I can't help it. Bo has a cute butt. I look away and ask myself my new motto, WWSGD? What Would a Straight Girl Do? I can acknowledge a cute butt straightily, right? Maybe I'm looking out of jealousy, and not attraction—maybe I just want to know her workout regimen. I want to be friends. I should talk to her.

She's right in front of us. I should just . . .

"Bo, right?" I say. I don't know what it is, but I'm feeling bold today. Bo turns around and smiles when she sees me. Up close, her lips are way smoochier than Hunter's.

"Yeah, hey! I like you." *She likes me.* "Sorry, I don't know your first name, though, Ms. Flores." She says "Ms. Flores" in what I assume is an exaggeration of Mrs. Havens's voice, but it sounds flirty and it makes my cheeks get hot.

"Yamilet." I smooth out my skirt so she doesn't notice my blush. When I look back up, her friendly dark brown eyes meet mine. She tucks a strand of her messy black shoulder-length hair behind her ear.

"Bo," she says, cheeks pink and round. "Oh, I mean—you already knew that."

I laugh. "I liked your presentation. It was super ballsy. I thought you were gonna get paddled or something."

"*I'm* ballsy? You practically had Mrs. Havens in the fetal position! And as much as they wish they could paddle us, they can't do that anymore." She grins. "Best way to piss them off is by protesting their shitty views while still getting an A. It's my only talent."

I snort-giggle and my hand shoots over my mouth. Cesar laughs at me.

I introduce Cesar and Hunter to Bo to get her mind off the fact that I just honest-to-God snorted.

"Yeah, I know Bo." Hunter chuckles.

Of course I managed to make it more awkward. Obviously

everyone at this tiny school already knows each other. I bet they are so sick of being stuck with the same people every day. Maybe that's why Cesar and I seem to be getting so much attention. No one here probably ever gets an opportunity to meet a new kid.

We barely have time to get our cookies before the bell rings for the next class. One nice thing about being in such a small school is that all the classes are pretty close together, so I don't have to rush between them. Another perk is that most of my classes have at least one familiar face, even though I've only met a grand total of four juniors, plus Hunter, who's a senior. Of course my genius brother would have classes with seniors. I can easily gravitate toward people I've already met, instead of having to make new friends in every single class. My favorite so far is art, right before lunch. Bo and Hunter are both in that one with me, and the teacher seems super chill. She pretty much gives us free rein to do whatever we want for an hour, as long as we produce some kind of "art."

After fourth hour I have to go to room C303 for lunch detention. I take my time walking there, but it's too short a walk to take more than a couple of minutes, so I'm still there with a few minutes to spare. When I walk inside, the first—and last—person I want to see greets me.

"Hey, detention buddy." Cesar laughs.

"You too? *Already?*" I was supposed to be keeping him *out* of trouble.

"*You* already!" He throws it back at me, and he's right. I'm not setting a great example.

"What'd you do?" I ask.

"Chewed some gum. You?"

Bashed Catholicism and called my classmates racist . . .

"I don't want to talk about it," I say. Then the teacher comes in and hands us all green mesh "detention" vests. Apparently, lunch detention here means public shaming and picking up trash.

Once we get out into the courtyard, I wander around searching the ground for fallen trash. I decide against going inside the cafeteria and walk to the outside lunch tables looking for something to pick up. All I see is a wad of dirty napkins lying near one of the trash cans, like someone shot and missed from a distance. There's not much work to do unless I lurk by tables waiting for someone to have trash for me to take—which I'm not doing.

Whenever no one is looking, I check my phone to see how our Etsy orders are going. As of this morning, sales were slowing down a bit since I first got involved. But when I check, it looks like we're fully sold out! I quickly open up TikTok to see that my video from this morning went semi-viral, with thousands of likes and comments! We'll definitely have a backlog of orders to fill now, but that's a good problem to have. I shoot Mami a quick text, updating her about the sales, then put my phone away. She agreed to give me the extra money I make for her after my half of tuition is paid, so I plan on getting to work as soon as I get home. I could really use the extra money. Who knows what Mom would do if she found out I was gay? It'll be good to have some savings, just in case. Mom's been teaching me the art of jewelry making since I was a kid, so I'm more than prepared to make some cash.

Before long, Jenna, Emily, and Karen find me. It's like they thought someone else might snatch me up for their friend group. They're all happily linking arms, with Karen's borderline brownface spray tan in the coveted middle position. When Jenna grabs my arm to link with hers, I jump. I hate that I jumped, because Jenna's adorable, and I do like her. It just surprised me that they don't all hate me for being confrontational with Karen.

"Oh my God, you're so *cute*, Jumpy!" Jenna says, and her voice squeaks a little on the word "cute." *No, you're cute*. God I'm so gay. Stop being so gay, Yami. Stop that shit right now.

Jenna guides me to their usual lunch table inside under a massive crucified Jesus statue in the corner of the cafeteria. It's staring me down. I can feel it—lording over us all, judging me for ditching my detention duties. I avoid looking at it the best I can. I don't know how anyone has any fun around here with overlord Jesus watching.

I don't like Karen, but Jenna and Emily seem nice, aside from the fact that they choose to hang around someone so openly racist. Besides them, there's one other guy at the table. I'm assuming he's Karen's boyfriend, based on the fact that they're sucking face instead of talking to the rest of us, which is fine. Karen might not have been the one who made the abortion comment, but I'm still not cool with anyone who asks where I'm from as if I don't belong here. Maybe I don't belong *here*, but she can go and choke for pointing it out.

I don't have many options yet as far as friends go, so I pretend to pick up their trash in case the detention monitor walks by while I'm with them. Before I know it, they're all interrogating Jenna about her mysterious crush.

"Come *on*, who is it?" Emily nudges Jenna's shoulder.

Jenna shakes her head, pretending to zip her lips shut.

"We're just gonna keep asking," Karen sings. Her boyfriend's eyes glaze over and he checks out of the conversation by staring at his phone.

I know there are plenty of reasons to be tight-lipped about a crush, but I can't help but wonder if it's a girl. Either way, I can relate to Jenna for not wanting people to know who you're crushing on.

"If she doesn't want to tell anyone, she doesn't have to," I say, possibly overstepping the New Friend boundary.

"Thank you!" Jenna says emphatically, squeezing my arm.

"What about you, Yummy? We saw you talking to *Huuunter*! Do you like him?" Karen taunts.

"That boy is a *whole* meal," Emily says, fanning herself. "He was talking about you in trig. Pretty sure every girl in that class is jealous of you."

"Really?" I ask. I don't want to be making any enemies, but I guess it's good everyone thinks I like a boy. Still, it makes me want to squirm away from the conversation. "I mean, he's cool, but we just met."

"*Guys*, leave her alone. Emily's just exaggerating. No one

hates you." Jenna comes to the rescue like I did for her.

"Ugh, fine," Karen says before turning to her boyfriend, back to ignoring the rest of us. The subject finally changes, and I go to turn in my vest.

I only get ten minutes to eat after detention, but I could definitely get used to Slayton's food. There are sections of the cafeteria that have their own cuisines: Mexican, Chinese, Italian, burgers, fries, milkshakes. . . . You could eat something different every day of the month without repeating.

Karen might not notice me, but to Emily and Jenna, I'm still the center of the universe. They walk with me through the lunch lines and spend the rest of lunch asking me questions about my old life. I tell them I like it better at Slayton. Here's the thing. I don't particularly feel like thinking about Rover, or anything that happened there. I'd much rather think about how cute Jenna is and how they all keep calling *me* cute. I'd rather think about Bo, and how she *likes* me. I want to think about anyone but Bianca.

But that's the problem, isn't it? I'm not supposed to be thinking about Bianca. Or Jenna. Or Bo. Not like that. I'm supposed to be thinking about Hunter, and how he says my name right and buys me cookies. Hunter, who blushes when I talk to him. Hunter . . . who is not a girl.

And then Jenna calls me cute again, and she really needs to cut that shit out because she is most definitely straight and I am most definitely Not Gay. Not here.

4

HONOR THY LINER AND THY HOOPS

I spot Mami's car in student pickup as soon as I walk out of my last class. She's waving frantically with a huge smile on her face. The second I get in the car, she bombards me with back-to-back questions, not leaving me enough room to answer any of them.

"How was your first day? Did you make any new friends? Did Cesar get in any trouble?"

"It was good, I made a few . . . and no." Unless you count lunch detention as trouble, but there's no way I'm telling her about that. "First day wasn't so bad, but I—" I start, but she cuts me off with a hand gesture when Cesar climbs into the back seat.

She proceeds to ask him all the same questions, like I'm invisible. I was *going* to tell her about my new friends and complain about Karen, but my time is up.

Cesar spends the ride complaining about his physics teacher, who I'm guessing is the one who gave him detention. Thank

God he doesn't mention that part. When we get to our driveway, Mom lets out a deep sigh and her whole vibe changes.

"God give me the strength." She gives herself the sign of the cross, then rushes inside.

"What's with her?" Cesar asks, and I shrug. I find her in her room. She's sitting on the floor, making necklaces. I didn't think the mess on the floor could get *this* bad. I feel a little guilty since she's probably stressed about having to restock after everything sold out.

"I love that you put this together, and that it's successful, but this might be too much work for me to keep up with, mija," she says, and I sit on the floor next to her and start helping.

"You don't have to do it alone," I say, taking note of the strings and beads she's using and preparing my own. "You have me to help you now."

She loosens up a bit at that, but still looks a bit tense. "We're almost out of materials already. I'm not used to running out this fast."

"That's a good thing! That means more money for us." I give her an encouraging smile, hoping she's not *too* stressed out because of me. I'm about to flat-out apologize when Cesar walks in and sits next to us.

"Don't be stressed out, Mami." He leans over to kiss her cheek, then follows my lead and gets to work, too.

"You're so helpful mijo, thank you. How did I ever get so lucky?" She ruffles his hair, and my face gets hot. She never thanked *me*. I guess I am the reason she's stressed, but still. I kind of wanted this jewelry thing to be *our* thing. Something Mami and I could bond over, I don't know. She asks Cesar more questions about school, giving me shortish answers when I try to include myself in the conversation about the school we *both* just had our first day at. Maybe when my Etsy shop makes us rich, she'll stop picking favorites.

After a while, Cesar asks me about my day. He sometimes shares the attention when he notices Mom sidelining me. I appreciate it, but Mom doesn't seem as interested when I talk.

"You know what, I'm not really built for this jewelry thing. My fingers hurt." Cesar shakes his hands out. "I should probably start on my homework." He gives me a pity smile and leaves us. It isn't until he's gone that she asks me a question.

"So, your brother's doing good now?"

The next morning, I obsess over the details I can control. I pull my shirt out enough to hide the rolls in my skirt. I wear my best Jordans. I think about curling my hair, which I never do. But it's so long it would take all morning, so I braid it. I put on my favorite gold hoops. They're not real, but they look it and I like the way the gold frames my face. I feel like Selena Quintanilla. Cute and elegant at the same time. I put extra love into doing my makeup. The hoops and J's and makeup show all the me the uniform hides. I'm ready.

When we get to school, I steer clear of the cop patrolling campus, just in case. All the students seem to be friends with him, but still. He gives them high fives and dabs at them when they pass by, as if anyone still dabs. I've never seen a cop act all buddy-buddy like that. My experiences with cops haven't exactly been pleasant. I've only had two close interactions, and I'm not trying to have a third. Once freshman year, when I saw my friend Junior get his head bashed into the cement floor of his own garage by a cop. And once when my dad was taken away. They both ended in deportations. My dad, and Junior's mom. The cop at this school seems safe enough, but I'm not getting close enough to find out.

The first familiar faces I find are Emily and Karen in the courtyard, so I go to them.

"Yummy!" Karen calls out when she sees me.

"Becky!" I say, and go in for a hug. Karen frowns.

"Karen," she corrects, and Emily changes the subject before it gets awkward. She and Karen start talking about volleyball tryouts, which I have zero interest in, so I zone out.

My eyes wander, and I find Jenna walking toward us. When our eyes meet, she smiles like I'm important, and her walk becomes even bubblier. She hugs me first, then Karen and Emily. I almost forgot how nice hugs are. After Bianca outed me, I went all summer without a single hug from anyone outside family.

Jenna cups one of my earrings in her hand. Her fingertips brush against the side of my neck and make the baby hairs stand up. One of the perks of brown skin is she hopefully can't tell I'm blushing.

"You look so ghetto today!" She giggles. So does Karen.

I blink. They're my favorite earrings. I thought it was going to be a compliment. But I look "ghetto." What is that even supposed to mean?

Karen gives me a sympathetic look. "Yummy, I love you, but yeah, you kind of look like a cho-la." I hate how casually she says she loves me. She doesn't even know me. And I doubt she even knows what a *chola* is, but I know what she meant by it. That I look too Mexican. Too "ghetto."

I look to Emily. Her cheeks are cherry red and her eyes wide. She tries to touch my shoulder, but I take a step back and push her hand off me. I use my stink-eye to punch all of them, since I'm too much of a wuss to do it IRL. They don't seem to notice the mental punching.

"If you loved her, you'd be a true friend, like me, and let her know how she looks," Jenna says to Karen.

"Guys, that's—" Emily starts, but my ears are ringing too loud to hear what she's saying. I want to go off on them, but I don't even know how to put into words why I'm angry. All I know is I don't want to be near them. I turn around and walk away.

First hour is my least favorite class right now, because all three of them are in there.

I sit at the desk closest to the door, in the back of the room. Jenna, Karen, and Emily didn't get the hint, and they sit by me like they didn't just call me ghetto. I get up to move seats, but Jenna grabs my arm.

"Chill out, it was a joke!"

I yank my arm away and make my way to the farthest empty seat without saying a word. I can feel their questioning stares on me, but I ignore them. I don't care if they think I'm overreacting. I like my hoops, and eyeliner, and J's. I look good, okay? I do. I'm a fine-ass elegant beast. They're wrong. They're *wrong*.

If I'm going to go back to having no friends, it's going to be my choice, no one else's. I can't do this with them. I get my phone out and pretend to be texting. I want to look cool and aloof, like I have friends I can text. Really, I'm staring at my screen thinking about how it's two days in and I'm back to square one. Worse than square one. The only person I want to text is the person posing with me on my phone background. So I do.

Yami: I hate it here.

Dad is the only one I'm willing to admit that to. I'm surprised at how fast he responds.

Papi: Hang in there, mijita ♥

I smile down at my screen. I may be alone, but at least I have a texting buddy.

Yami: Come rescue me . . .

I sigh. Maybe I shouldn't make jokes like that when he can't physically come and do anything. No one is going to rescue me today. I'm about to start having Rover flashbacks about being alone after Bianca outed me when Bo takes the seat next to me. She doesn't say anything, since Mrs. Havens is already starting her lecture, but her sitting by me makes me feel a little better. Bo and I might not be close, but I'd rather sit with an acquaintance than by myself.

She gives me a little wink before getting out her binder, leaving me to self-destruct. Was that a flirty wink? Or was she just being friendly, since I was sitting alone? Does she somehow know about the "ghetto" comment? What does it *mean*?

I can't focus on Mrs. Havens's lecture to save my life. I'm too busy trying not to overthink Bo's wink, or how "ghetto" my earrings make me look. I spend the entire class *telling* myself to pay attention instead of paying attention.

When lunch rolls around, I don't know where to sit without Becky and her minions. Cesar is sitting at a table full of seniors, since most of his smart-people classes are with them. I think they're jocks. Honestly, it's hard to tell, with the uniforms. They're acting like loud fools, though, so I'm just guessing. Cesar is talking with his hands, his expressions all exaggerated, and everyone around him is laughing at whatever it is he's saying. He fits in so well here, unlike me. I'm glad he found his people, though. At least it doesn't seem like he'll be getting jumped here anytime soon.

Then I see her. I *hear* her. Bo's laugh is like music among the bustling traffic of the cafeteria. Her friends are laughing, too, and all I know is that *I* want to laugh. I have a couple of classes with the other people in her group, but we haven't talked. Bo would probably let me sit with them. I'm a little nervous, though. She's gay, I think. The rainbow Vans and khakis are pretty convincing. I don't want to be tempted and I definitely don't want anyone thinking I like Bo like that. Besides, my metaphorical closet is safe and I have no intention of coming out. Not here.

I look around one last time. Even with only four hundred students, I somehow feel smaller standing alone in this cafeteria than I ever did at Rover. All the classroom buildings are outside, so there are no internal hallways for me to hide in. The art teacher says her room is always open for lunch, but I don't want to spend lunch alone with a teacher. Not quite that desperate. I think about going to the bathroom to eat in one of the stalls like a lonely new girl in a movie. But let's be real. That shit is disgusting.

Instead, I go out to the courtyard and sit at one of the tables. This gives me time to review our jewelry orders on my phone. I'm happy to see that some new orders have already come in since this morning. I confirm them, then look around to see I'm the only one sitting alone. There aren't really any loners at this school. It seems like all the quiet kids have their own group. It makes me miss Rover. There were tons of loners there, so at least I wasn't alone in being alone. But I can't go back. I can't even reminisce about the good times without remembering how it all ended. . . .

When I told Bianca I loved her, it made her cry. Like it was somehow harder for her than it was for me. Why did I do that?

It all makes sense now, she said. She told me it creeped her out. That if only she had known, she would have avoided all of it. All of me. As if she wouldn't have cried on my shoulder when her parents got divorced, or let me cry on hers when my dad got deported. As if none of it mattered because I'm gay.

When I told her I loved her, she made me feel like a leech, like I took advantage of her by being her friend. Like it was only for my benefit. It didn't matter to her that I wasn't ready to come out until then. The years we spent as best friends didn't matter because I must have had ulterior motives, and everything I had done now seemed creepy. She told our friends and they ghosted me.

If Bianca and I met today instead of ten years ago, I don't think we'd be friends. Besides our mutual love of makeup, we don't have much in common. She was always a pretty judgmental person and liked to gossip about things we had no business knowing, while I preferred to mind my business. But we grew up together, and that should count for something. Even her *mom* hates me now. I had to block both their numbers from my mom's phone so they couldn't tell her. Luckily, my cooties seemed to have spread to Mami, and Bianca and her mom are ignoring her, too. Losing a best friend is one thing, and it sucked. It still sucks. But I won't lose my mom.

So I take it back. I don't miss Rover, or anyone who goes there. I'm doing fine by myself at Slayton, thank you very much.

I jump when someone reaches for my fries.

"Jesus!" I put my hand over my heart and laugh when I realize it's just Cesar. "Why aren't you with all your friends?" I doubt Slayton's social butterfly is in a similar position to my own.

"You weren't eating, so I came to help you out." He grins.

I smack his hand away from my fries and stuff a handful of them into my mouth. "Happy?" The words are muffled by the fries.

"Yeah." He smiles and sits across from me. "So, you too cool to sit with your friends now?"

I take my time chewing before I answer. "Yup."

He raises an eyebrow but doesn't pry. For once, though, I want to talk about it. I want to scream about it. I take a breath to keep myself from actually yelling.

"If I sit with them, I know I'll hit someone, and I don't want to get suspended."

"Right. *That's* why you won't fight them." He looks like he's trying not to smile, and I hate it. I'm not in the mood to hear about my inability to stand up for myself. I just want to be mad right now. Is that so bad?

"Shut up."

He shuts up and takes another one of my fries. I know I shouldn't be mad at Cesar. He's trying to help. And if anyone at this school would get it, it's him.

"I do *not* care to sit with ignorant rich folk who think hoop earrings on brown skin makes me ghetto."

Cesar's eyebrows shoot up and he shakes his head. "The cau-cacity!" I shush him and look around us.

"Cesar, read the room!" I say, but I can't help but laugh. No one was listening.

He ignores me and glares at Karen and them through the cafeteria window, not that they can actually see him. "You want me to handle them for you?"

"Really, Cesar." I know it's an empty offer. There's no way he's fighting Jenna and Karen for me. Still, I don't like him talking like that. Slayton Cesar should not be entertaining the thought of getting into fights.

"I got you." He looks me dead in the eye without blinking

and puts a hand on my shoulder. "Just say the word and I'll ding-dong ditch 'em." The weirdo winks at me.

"You're too much!" I laugh, and he grins.

"I know you'd do the same for me."

"Damn right I would."

"In lak'ech," he says, and I think I get what he means. We're the same, Cesar and I.

The setup in first hour is different the next day. Six desks sit at the front of the room. Three on one side, three on the other, all facing each other. I take my usual spot in the front corner.

"Do you know what we're doing?" Bo says as she sits next to me.

"It's my third day ever. I know nothing." It comes out snappier than I meant it to, and Bo looks a little thrown. I guess the stress of not having friends is getting to me. I'm actually glad she's still sitting with me. I smile at her to let her know I'm 100 percent approachable and talk-to-able. I look down to see a pin on her backpack that has *Homophobia is GAY* in rainbow letters. I have to actively stop myself from clutching my chest to keep my heart in place. I want that pin. I want the unapologetic self-confidence that comes with having a pin like that.

Of everyone I've met here, Bo's my favorite. Rainbow Vans, rainbow pins, khakis. I think it's safe to say she's one of my people. I shouldn't make assumptions, though. Not when everything at this school is as weird as it is. Maybe she's an "ally"?

I want to comment on the pin, but I can't bring myself to

do it. I'm not supposed to feel any kind of solidarity based on that pin. So *maybe* she's gay. That's great for her. Not me. As far as Bo is concerned, I'm straight as a pencil. Straight, straight, straight.

We don't have time to talk about gay pins anyway, because Mrs. Havens is ready to start.

"We're going to be practicing our debating skills this week!"

She picks six people and has them debate random subjects, on the spot. Bo is in the first debate group. Karen happens to be debating the opposite side of Bo. So, naturally, I'm all about the US abolishing daylight savings time, or whatever it is Bo is supposed to be arguing for. I don't understand half of what they're saying, but that doesn't mean it's not entertaining.

Bo claps her hands with each word. "Daylight. Savings. Is. Arbitrary!"

"It saves energy!" Some guy slams his hands on his desk to emphasize his point. People get *into* it, and I don't blame them. I'm as competitive as anyone, so I'm sure I'll be the same way. I'm pretty sure this isn't the "right" way to do an academic debate, but Mrs. Havens didn't give any instruction, and she's not correcting anyone.

I'm in the next group, and honestly, I'm a little pumped. Bo killed Karen on that daytime savings shit. At least, I'm pretty sure she did. Emily's in the group I'm arguing against, so I'm about to follow Bo's example and go in on whatever topic Mrs. Havens gives us. I sit tall in one of the desks in the front. Let's go.

"This group's topic is"—Mrs. Havens drumroll-slaps her

thighs—"should gay marriage be legal?"

I try not to visibly flinch. This is a topic I refuse to get up in arms over. Not here, where they'll clock me over it.

"Are you serious? It's already legal." Bo stands from her desk before I know which side I'm supposed to be arguing.

"Ms. Taylor, sit down, please." Mrs. Havens sighs, like this is a normal occurrence.

Bo stands firmly in place. "I'm not going to sit down while you argue about what rights should or shouldn't be denied to an entire group of people. There are more appropriate topics to debate."

"Speaking of what's *appropriate*, Ms. Taylor, sit *down*." Mrs. Havens is glowing red, instead of her usual orange. It's glorious.

"Choose a different topic." Bo crosses her arms.

Please, please choose a different topic.

"It seems to always be you who has a problem with the way I teach my class, Ms. Taylor. I don't see anyone else complaining." Mrs. Havens gestures to the rest of the class, but I feel like she's pointing directly at me. I can't look at her, or Bo. "If you refuse to participate in class, you can go to Principal Cappa's office." She points to the door.

"Fine." Bo grabs her bag and storms out. I want to leave with her. I'd rather go to the principal's office than stay here, but I still can't seem to move.

The other side is arguing for separation of church and state. Like the only way they can accept me is through excommunication. The Catholic church has no problem taking all my money, but they don't *really* want me. I'll never be able to get married through the church, like my mom's always wanted.

I don't know if I even want to get married. I mean, I'm only sixteen, so I don't exactly spend a lot of time thinking about it. But one day, who knows? I'd like to think it could at least be an option. Today, I'm supposed to be arguing against that.

If I'd eaten breakfast, it would be making its way back up my throat. I feel like everyone's staring at me. Like they all know I want to run away. Like they *know* I'm gay.

I'm hyperaware of every part of my body. I have to look unbothered. I stay sitting upright and try to focus on breathing without looking like I'm trying to focus on breathing.

Chill, Yami.

My throat is unusually tight, which makes that a little difficult. Is it normal to be able to feel your pulse in your ears? It doesn't matter. I'll take hearing my pulse over hearing my peers argue about whether I'm an abomination. Somehow, I'm hearing both.

Homosexuality is sin.

It's not natural!

A child needs a mother and a father!

What's next, we legalize bestiality? Pedophilia?

I don't want to think too deeply about what that last comment means. That they see me as an animal. A predator. Even someone who I called my best friend felt that way. I can't think about it, or I'll crack in front of everyone. I let the argument fade to the background and focus on the corner of my desk, where someone drew a bunch of little hearts. They make my face hotter. If I had my pencil, I'd scribble over them until the whole corner was nothing but a vortex of gray.

I wipe my sweaty palms on my skirt. Dammit, is my face sweating too? I can't look upset right now. This is not personal. No one can know how not personal this is for me.

Bianca, say something . . .

It's not personal. I just think it's best if we go our separate ways.

"Yamilet, anything to add?" Mrs. Havens asks. That crusty-looking bitch. I'm the only one who hasn't said anything yet. I was doing fine pretending to be fine until now.

"I think . . ." I swallow. *I think I'm gonna be sick.* "I think my group has made their point." They've more than made their point.

The bell rings, and I'm the first one out the door. I'm not so good at breathing without looking like I'm trying to focus on breathing anymore. The best I can do is keep from hyperventilating until I get somewhere private. Everything is blurry, so I blink back tears before they fall. Instead of going to my next class, I power-walk to the bathroom before anyone has a chance to notice me.

I swing the first stall door open and slam it behind me. But stall doors don't like to slam, no matter how close to a panic attack you are. I have to shut it twice before it stays closed long enough for me to lock it. A quick glance under the stalls tells me I'm alone.

I reach for some toilet paper to blow my nose. The roll is empty.

"Are you kidding me!" I don't mean to shout, but the lack of toilet paper is enough to make my vision blur again. It's infuriating.

Okay, slow breaths. In . . .

I close my eyes, and the tears start falling.

Don't cry. Breathe out . . .

A whimper escapes with my breath. I hate that sound.

Breathe in . . .

It's shaky, but it's getting better.

Out . . .

The bell rings, and it drowns out the sound of my sobs.

5

MAKE UNTO THEE NON-RACIST FRIENDS

I cry as hard as I can until the bell stops ringing. It's not enough time. When the sound stops, I cover my mouth and cry into my hand to stay quiet. The only noise I let myself make is to sniffle. The lack of toilet paper is killing me. I don't want to get snot on my shirt and I'm not ready to leave the stall, so for now I'll live with the runny nose.

From the stall next to mine, the sniffle echoes.

I almost get whiplash from jerking my head to the left. Someone else is in here. I freeze and hold my breath, but I can't hide now. How could I not notice another human person right next to me! They must have had their feet up so I couldn't see them. I didn't put mine up, which means they probably know who I am. Unless someone else has the same Jordans as me. Which they don't, because I would have noticed and made friends with them.

Perfect. Now someone knows I'm crying in the bathroom. I'll probably end up getting blackmailed or something. But I'm not the only one ditching class to have a bathroom breakdown. Which is good. I mean, it's not *good*, but at least this way I'm less likely to be blackmailed. I mean, I still could, because this person most likely knows who I am, and they could be anyone. Maybe Bo? She did seem to have just as rough a time as I did last hour. . . .

A hand (Bo's hand?) reaches under the stall, offering me a wad of toilet paper.

I just stare at it. Now it's weird. I was fully prepared to leave and never acknowledge the awkwardness of this situation. But now there's a hand full of toilet paper reaching under my stall. If I take it, I'm admitting I'm in here, crying in the bathroom because I couldn't handle a little debate.

But if I don't take the damned toilet paper, my nose will keep running.

I give in.

"Thanks." I say, then blow my nose.

Instead of responding, the stall door next to me opens. Quick footsteps, and she's gone.

I wipe my nose one more time, then flush down the toilet paper and head to class. As soon as I open the bathroom door, Bo crashes into me.

"Sorry, sorry!" Bo says, then her eyes soften when they meet mine. "Are you okay?"

So it wasn't Bo who handed me the toilet paper. The thought makes me deflate a little for some reason. It was wishful thinking that she, of all people, would be my bathroom savior.

"I'm fine," I say. Maybe I should hang out in the bathroom

a little longer. At least until you can't tell I was crying by look-ing at me. But I can't follow Bo into the bathroom right after she saw me leave, so I walk across campus to the bathroom by the cafeteria. Then I wait it out until my eyes go back to their normal color.

My mom works late on Wednesdays, so instead of waiting for her to pick us up from school after sunset, Cesar and I take the light rail home. It's a straight line almost all the way to our house, but it's a long trip. I stare out the window at the clear sunny sky, ignoring the horns honking and cars whirring in my peripheral vision. If Cesar notices I'm quieter than usual, he doesn't say anything. I don't want him to, either. I don't know what it is, but I can never hold it together when he asks what's wrong. I just want to be home so I can forget about today and sleep until tomorrow. Crying is exhausting. I'm about to fall asleep when Cesar pokes my arm.

"Yaaaaami."

I bat his finger away without opening my eyes.

"I'm bored." He pokes me in the belly this time.

On a reflex, I swing my arm and smack him on the forehead. It's an accident, but he deserves it. He's dirty for going right for my tickle spot.

"Damn, you got some quick hands!" He rubs his forehead, but he's half smiling. Actually, hearing that is weirdly reassur-ing coming from Cesar. Makes me feel tougher than I am. Like I can handle myself.

"Yeah, catch some of these!" I do a couple of little air jabs by his stomach so he knows I'm not to be messed with.

"Hey, careful! You could break your hand on these abs of steel!" He flexes, and I snort. Cesar has a bit of a pancita, like me. He's not exactly buff.

"*Any*ways"—I roll my eyes—"can I take my nap now?"

"No. I need you to entertain me."

"You're the one keeping me up. You entertain me."

"You're so difficult. Fine. Umm . . . hmmm . . ." Cesar throws his head back, making a show of how he can't think of what to say. I almost expect him to ask why my eyes are puffy, but he goes for a joke instead.

"So are you still digging Satan Catholic?" I let out a huff of air from my nose in amusement. I'm actually a little mad I didn't come up with that myself. Still, I don't want him to know how much I don't love our new school.

"I like it, yeah." I sit up a little straighter.

He squints at me, and I know I'm not selling it hard enough.

"I mean, it's a lot to get used to, but it's a good school, right?" I say. Cesar seems like he has everything going for him now, and I don't want to ruin it by complaining. No one's picking on him. He's made lots of friends. He hasn't gotten in any fights. It's only been a few days, but I'll take that win.

"Yeah . . ." Cesar chews on his lip, and I give him a look. I have this theory that Cesar and I can telepathically communicate. My eyes say the things I don't have the emotional capacity to say out loud. *Are you okay?*

He's quiet for a while before he says anything. "Why aren't

you pissed at me? It's my fault we got sent here. I know you don't like it."

"What are you talking about? I like Slayton." The downside of telepathic communication is my eyes don't lie very well.

"Okay." He gives me a half-hearted smile. "Yeah, I like it too." His eyes lie even worse, and I feel like I already failed him.

Our stop cuts the conversation short, and he doesn't bring it up again.

I don't even bother doing my homework or working through the backlog of jewelry orders tonight. All the crying I did earlier completely drained my energy, but I can't sleep. My dad would know how to make me feel better, so I FaceTime him. It rings.

And rings.

And rings . . .

I hang up and walk outside to get my mind off things. Doña Violeta must be in bed already, because the funeral music isn't bumping down the street right now. For once, I miss her sad mariachi music. It would give me an excuse to cry right now. I cry anyway.

Without thinking about where I'm going, I let my feet carry me down the street and I find myself standing in front of Bianca's house. She left the flourishing talavera pots out to mock me, I'm sure. I wonder if she finished the garden alone or if she already got someone to replace me. The openmouthed flowers look like they're laughing at me, and I don't blame them. I look desperate being here.

Before I came out to Bianca, this was where I'd come in times like this. She was the one I'd go to. I wipe my tears and knock on the door before I can talk myself out of it. I don't know what I'm expecting. If I can fix this one part of my life by working things out with Bianca, then maybe everything else will hurt a little less. I can hear chattering inside, and Bianca laughing. I miss that.

It's her mom who answers the door. She cracks it open, so I can barely see her full face.

"Hey, tía." I call her "tía" out of habit, and immediately regret it. She was always like an aunt to me. A second mom, even, before she found out about my crush on Bianca. Now she keeps herself at arm's length.

"Sorry, Bianca's not here," she says, and starts to close the door, but I block it with my foot.

"Who was that laughing just now then?" I cross my arms. I may be upset, but I'm not letting her off the hook that easy. Then I hear Chachi's voice.

"Bianca, is that your *giiirlfriend*? I thought you said you weren't friends anymore."

"What? No! And we're *not*," Bianca insists, then takes her mom's place at the door. She looks pretty, like always. She has her long black hair in a messy bun, and her tank top strap is falling off her shoulder. Her eyeshadow bunches at the crease of her eyelid from a day's worth of wear. But the thing that catches my eye is the friendship bracelet on her wrist. She made that at my house.

"Hi," I say.

"Yami, what are you—wait, are you crying?" She lets the door hang open just enough so her friends can see me. Like this wasn't already embarrassing enough.

"I'm fine." My eyes are dry, but Bianca knows me too well. And the fact that she bothered to ask . . . maybe she still cares? "I just thought—"

"Look, I told you I don't like you like that. Stop *stalking* me." She's projecting her voice so Chachi and Stefani can hear, like this is some kind of performance.

I process that for a second, then start laughing. She fidgets under the sound of my laugh, giving me a confused look. I was a fool to think she cared about me. Not just now, but ever. If she cared, she wouldn't have done what she did.

"Okay, well, bye," she says, and shuts the door.

Once it's closed, I kick over the talavera pots and stomp on the flowers over and over again. I don't discriminate between the ones I planted and the ones she did without me. I came here for closure, but all I feel is a hole in my chest. I fill the void by stomping on the potted soil until I can't feel my foot.

The next day, I still feel lost. I would have gone outside for lunch, but it's a hundred degrees and I'm not trying to go into class all sweaty. I could probably sit with Cesar and Hunter and their other popular senior friends who are somehow both nerds and jocks at the same time. I know he would try to get me to make friends with them. Everyone here seems to love my brother, so I'm sure they'd welcome me. Hunter's nice, too, but I can only handle so much testosterone at one lunch table. And I don't want Cesar feeling bad for me that I can't make my own friends.

Looking around, I have to consciously avoid looking at Jenna's table, because I don't want to slip up and make eye contact with any of them. Then I'd have to give them stink-eye to make sure they know how I feel about them. It would just be awkward, and I don't have the time or energy today.

Then there's Bo's intoxicating laugh from across the cafeteria. She throws her head back from the powerful force of her own laughter. And I find myself drifting closer, but I stop myself. I'm almost positive she's gay. If I sat with her, would everyone else be positive *I'm* gay?

No, gaydars don't work like that. Besides, I have a terrible one. I was sure Bianca was into me before I came out to her, and I couldn't have been more wrong. So maybe Bo isn't even gay! It's not like I'm crushing on Bo or anything, though she could be potential crush material. If I was going to be catching any crushes here. Which I'm not.

Shit. How long have I been staring? Judging by the fact that she's smiling and waving at me, she probably isn't too weirded out. There's no turning back now, so I walk over.

"Hey, Yamilet! Do you know David and Amber?" Bo asks me. She says my name right.

"I know you, we have religion together!" Amber says. I've seen her, but we haven't talked. She's a thick white girl with curly blond hair. The teacher in that class doesn't give us a whole lot of time for socializing. Honestly, religion class would actually be cool if we learned about any religion besides Catholicism.

"You're Cesar's sister, right? Everyone says he's my long-lost twin." David laughs, throwing his hands up in a *who knows why* kind of gesture. He has art class with me, Bo, and Hunter, so I've seen him before. Cesar told me about his "twin." I *guess* I can sort of see how they maybe look a little bit alike? I mean, they're both shortish Brown guys with similar body types. Other than that, though, there's not much of a resemblance.

"I guess that makes us family!" I'm sitting next to him, so I give him a little side hug.

"Sister!" He hugs me back like we've always known each other.

"People say that? I don't see it," Bo says, squinting over at Cesar's table.

"It's racism," Amber says through a cough.

I'm kind of relieved someone else said it. It's much safer when the white girl is the one to point it out.

"Well, I'm Amber. Bo's *best* friend since kindergarten." She throws an arm around Bo, who flinches at the contact. Now I see what Jenna meant about jumpiness being cute. I shun the thought. I don't want to think about Jenna . . . or Bo being cute.

But something tugs at my chest, and I think I'm a little jealous? Because Bo is gay—probably—and she has a best friend since kindergarten who stuck with her.

"David is our other best friend, since freshman year." Amber puts her other arm around David. "You can be our best friend, too, if you want." She smiles. And I know I'm supposed to be more careful about getting too close to Bo, but I can't help but like her and her friends. Especially after the way she stood up for me in class yesterday, whether or not she knew that's what she was doing by protesting that gay rights debate. I feel the need to show my gratitude.

"So, Bo . . . I just wanted to say thanks for yesterday. For what you said in class."

She gives me a weak smile. Like she gets that a lot. Like she's disappointed I didn't back her up. That no one did. I can't help but feel guilty about it.

"So, you're not friends with Jenna and them anymore?" Bo changes the subject. She's looking at her food instead of at me.

"Come on, Bo, I thought you were over her!" David playfully nudges Bo's shoulder, but she doesn't laugh.

"I am! I mean—I was never *under* her!" Bo's cheeks are turning a blotchy red. I wouldn't blame her if she had a crush on Jenna. I could have almost caught one before she revealed her whole self with that "ghetto" comment.

"I'm not buying that for one second," Amber says. Jeez, they're putting all her business out there for me.

"Just because I'm gay doesn't mean I like Jenna." Bo whispers Jenna's name so no one outside our group hears. So Bo is gay, and she's okay with me knowing. Hearing Bo say it out loud sends me into an existential crisis. My heart beats quicker, trying to catch up with my racing thoughts and internal squealing. Inevitably, I miss the rest of their argument.

Not being the only gay girl at school should make me feel

better, but it doesn't. What if Bo knows? I feel like she knows. Because gay people have the most solid gaydars, right? Besides me, I guess. Maybe it works better when you're not in denial.

If I had a better gaydar, maybe I could have avoided all this to begin with.

That gives me déjà vu. Bianca said that to me—that she would have avoided being friends if she'd known. The thought makes me sick. No, I *wouldn't* have avoided it. I *want* to be friends with Bo. Lord knows I need some decent friends. I'll just have to throw off her gaydar somehow.

"No, I'm not friends with Jenna and them." I cut into the conversation before Bo implodes, or I do. "I can't stand them, to be honest."

"Right?" Amber says. "They're the *worst*."

"Karen is a bitch, but they're not *all* bad. I used to play volleyball with them, before I quit," Bo says to me, her face still all blotchy. "Jenna and Emily were always nice to me."

"So anyways," Amber says, seemingly eager to change the subject. "Tell us about yourself, new best friend!"

"Um, I . . . ." I can't think of anything. "I . . . uh—"

"Well, don't put her on the spot like that." David laughs at my brain malfunctioning, then leans forward, rubs the small patch of stubble on his chin, and proceeds to tell me all three of their life stories. They all seem weirdly open about their personal business.

Bo is adopted, and her parents are white. Her family is "Catholic," but they never go to church. Bo and Amber have been going to Catholic school their entire lives. David went to public school like me until his freshman year, when he got a scholarship to Slayton, and his mom jumped at the opportunity for him to get a better education. He says "better education" in finger quotes, like he's not convinced. He has to drive even farther than me and Cesar to get here, since he lives on the res. The entire time, he and Amber sit super close together and kind of give me couple-y vibes, but they're supposedly Not a Thing (yet?), according to Amber.

"Almost everyone here is Catholic," David says, "but I'm an atheist." I watch him in awe. "What?" he asks, and I realize my jaw dropped.

"Just waiting for you to burst into flames in front of the Jesus statue."

Amazingly, he laughs without catching fire.

I grew up Catholic, but I don't exactly agree with everything the faith preaches. As far as a higher power goes, I have no idea what I believe in. That Catholic guilt still messes me up, though. If there's a hell, I'm definitely going there. I'm actually pretty terrified of that.

Seeing how open they are with me makes me feel a little more at ease. And as long as I ask a question every now and then, I keep the attention off myself. I usually do a lot more listening than talking, and I don't intend to change that. I like this group. So far. It's cool getting to know them, but they don't need to know me like that. Bo being out doesn't change the fact that I can't slip up here. I'm not Bo, and it would be naive of me to think I could be myself the way she can and get the same treatment.

The next week, Mom has her usual Wednesday late day, and Cesar has after-school detention, so we'll get home even later than usual. I was annoyed but also a little relieved when I found out his detention was just for sleeping in class again. I'm guessing he was up late talking to some new girl again, which is preferable to the alternative. If he was getting into fights already, all this would be for nothing.

I really wish he wouldn't get detention on Mom's late days, though. We get home so late as it is, and I don't appreciate having to wait out in the Arizona sun for an hour. I would wait in the library, but Karen and her boyfriend are in there, and I'd rather choke on a Cheez-It than deal with her. Cesar said I could leave without him, but Mom would kill me if she ever found out I left him here. Who am I kidding, she'd kill me if she found out he got detention in the first place. I'd get in more trouble than Cesar, but what am I supposed to do? March into his class banging pots and pans to wake him up?

I sit at a table in the courtyard and do homework while I wait for him to get out. It's September, which is basically June part four here, so it's still hot as balls. I guess it's better today than on a day Mom would actually notice. I'll just tell her the rail was delayed. Believable, honestly.

Emily walks up to my table and stands awkwardly.

She clears her throat and nervously brushes a piece of dark brown hair behind her ear. "Hi . . ."

"Hey," I say flatly, with stink-eye.

"I want to say sorry for what Karen and Jenna said last week.

About your earrings. It was rude and insensitive." She clasps her hands behind her back and leans forward, like she wants me to say something.

"And racist," I add.

She nods. "And racist, yeah. It really shouldn't have happened. I talked to them, though. And I think they get it now."

"Oh, um, thanks," I say, relaxing the stink-eye.

She smiles and walks off to the parking lot without another word. I'm not used to people apologizing to me, so I don't know how to feel. I guess I can be cool with Emily. I don't need to be cool with Jenna and Karen, though.

I confirm some more jewelry orders before getting back to my homework. We sold two friendship bracelets, a beadwork necklace, and a pair of traditional gold earrings since the last time I checked. Before I get a chance to move on to my homework, someone else sits down next to me.

"Hey, you need a ride?" Bo asks. It's three thirty, so Cesar should be out any second. I'm surprised Bo's even still here.

"Trust me, you don't want to give me a ride. I live far."

"I don't mind. I don't feel like going home yet, anyway."

"Really, it's okay. I don't have any gas money or anything." I don't want to take the light rail home, but I really don't want to make Bo drive forty minutes out of her way and then make the drive back home.

"Don't worry, my parents pay for my gas, so that's not an issue."

Someone squeezes between me and Bo and throws arms around both our shoulders.

"My sister is incapable of accepting acts of kindness. We would *love* a ride," Cesar says.

"We're fine taking the light rail, seriously." It's not that I don't want Bo to know where we live. Or maybe it is.

Cesar glares at me so hard I can almost feel the daggers stabbing me.

"Okay, what if you just drop us off at the light rail?" That's about all I'm comfortable with.

"Sure!" Bo seems happy for a field trip to the light rail.

"Shottie!" Cesar shouts. Dammit. I don't usually care about sitting in the front seat, but I kind of wanted to sit next to Bo. I file into the back seat instead.

"Hey, since our mom works late on Wednesdays, you think you can drop us off at the light rail every week?" Cesar asks as soon as the door closes.

"¡Sinvergüenza!" I whisper-yell, but I'm laughing. I reach forward to push him. He pushes me back. That boy has absolutely no shame.

"Yeah, of course." Bo does her cute little eye-smile thing at me through the mirror, and I want to die.

Mom joins me filling jewelry orders in the living room when she gets home. We have a system going. Mom's much faster, so I make the earrings first while she does the beadwork necklaces. I take my time beading an intricate flower design into a pair of earrings. Even considering how delicate and slow my hands are moving, my fingers are already starting to cramp. I push through the pain, because I'll never reach my mom's level if I don't. By the time I finish beading one tiny set of earrings, she's finished a whole necklace. We eventually meet in the middle and work on friendship bracelets together.

Her telenovela plays on the TV while we work. Instead of watching, I pay close attention to Mom's hands. If I wasn't seeing this in real time, I would think it was sped up. I don't know how her fingers move so quick. She's not even looking at what she's doing. Somehow she's going this fast without taking her eyes off her telenovela. I take a short video of her quick-working hands and post it to Instagram and TikTok to fish for more orders. Then I try to keep up with her speed making my own, but I keep messing up the patterns when I go too fast. Instead I have to take my time and thread my bracelets with love.

"¡Cierra los ojos!" Mom gasps at the TV and throws a hand over my eyes, all dramatic.

"Ay, Mami, stop!" I push her hand away to see two women kissing on the screen. Something swirls in my stomach at the sight. I'd be happy if it wasn't for the fact that my mom didn't want me seeing it.

"She just murdered her good twin and *this* is what you're shielding me from?" I don't know why I'm bothering. This isn't a battle I'll win.

"I won't have that ungodly crap in my house." She clicks off the TV, cementing my refusal to ever tell her about myself. No ungodly lesbians in her house. Maybe she didn't mean it like that. Or maybe she did. It doesn't matter, since I'm saving all my extra earnings so I can get by on my own if she finds out about me and kicks me out.

She replaces the telenovela with cumbia music, then dances her way into the kitchen to make dinner.

Woosah.

I shake it off and take a moment to admire the bracelets I've made so far. If I stare at them too long, the colors might put me in a trance and make me forget. It's easy to get lost in the vibrant angular patterns. My bracelets look just as good as Mom's, even though I took longer and finished fewer. I let myself appreciate my handiwork before I move on to making miscellaneous stuff. But I don't get much done before the smell of frying tortillas wafts through the room. After an excruciating and barely productive wait, Mom finally comes back in with a plate of chicken flautas and beans for us and kisses my forehead.

"Oh, I love this, mija. Me and you take care of things now, and your brother will take care of me in my old age." I hate how despite her homophobia, my chest still warms at her attempt to bond with me. Still, I can't help but read into it.

"I can still take care of you then, Mami." I prick my finger with the earring wire I'm shaping, and she chuckles.

"Oh, I don't think you'll have to. Your brother's going to be the next Bill Gates. He can take care of us both!"

I start eating so I don't have to talk. I wish she wouldn't be so obvious about how much more potential Cesar has than me. Yes, he's a prodigy and a genius, but I'm the one staying up late doing homework and working, while he stays up talking to girls. I'm the one working 24/7 to pay my own tuition, while Cesar doesn't even have to *try* for her approval. She's right, though. If one of us is going to "make it," it's him.

My phone buzzes, and I let out a childish squeal and happy-flap my hands when I see my dad on FaceTime. *Finally* he calls me back.

"Pues stop screaming and answer it!" Mami waves at my phone.

I'm still squealing when I finally pick up. He has a huge smile on his face that stretches the bags under his eyes, and his eyes get twinkly when he laughs at my reaction. I've never seen my dad "cry," but he gets a little misty-eyed sometimes when we talk after longish gaps. We FaceTime as often as we can, which lately hasn't been very often, since he's working like a million hours a week.

"Ahh, look at my two favorite ladies! So beautiful you both are." He smiles and runs a hand through his hair. He's usually wearing a work hat with the logo for his cab service on it when we FaceTime, but he's not today. It makes me realize that he now has a few streaks of gray hair combed back with the black. "How are my girls doing?"

"Great! Yamilet is a little entrepreneur, did you know?" Mami shakes my shoulder.

"Of course I knew. She's going to take care of our retirement. Isn't that right, mija?"

I have a hard time hiding my blush. At least *someone* believes in me. I feel myself getting choked up. It feels terrible to say, but I wish someone *here* believed in me. Someone more tangible.

Dad must notice something's off. "Maria, mi amor, can I have a minute with Yami?"

My mom puts a hand on her heart. "What about your *beautiful* wife, eh? You got something to hide from me?"

"Yeah, we're going to talk shit about you," Dad says.

"Emiliano!" Mom gasps like she's never heard him cuss before. She's always a stickler about cursing, and she only does it herself when she's *pissed.* I don't wait to get scolded, so I hop over the back of the couch and trip on my own feet on the way to my room with the phone.

"Sorry, Mami, love you!" I call out before I close my door.

I kick my chanclas off and flop belly-down on my bed, leaning on my elbows with my phone propped up in my hands.

"So, tell me one good thing about this new school before you tell me why you hate it," he asks once the coast is clear. The camera shifts as he adjusts himself to lie back on the love seat in his studio apartment. He's always making me recount the positive before diving into the negative. But he still always gives me space to vent when I need to.

"Um . . . I made some friends?" I mean Bo, Amber, and David, *not* Karen and them.

"That's amazing! Tell me about them."

I proceed to gush a little about how nice they all were to me, and how they are so open about their lives even though they barely know me. Honestly, I spend most of the time talking about Bo.

"That's what I love to hear, mija. So, if you have such good friends, why do you hate this school so much?"

"It's Catholic school. Why do you think?" My dad isn't

religious like my mom. He went to church with us when we were little, but he was like a third child, being dragged there just like us. He always said he thought it was bull, and he made me promise not to tell Mom. She knows anyway.

"That bad, huh?"

"That bad. They're almost as strict as *Mom*." I groan.

He chuckles. "I know your mami can be a little intense, but you know she wants what's best for you." His eyes soften at the mention of my mom. They love each other so much it's sickening.

"Not for me. For Cesar," I blurt out, then cover my mouth. "Don't tell him I said that."

"I won't." Dad's always been good with secrets, even if he disagrees. He's good about staying in his lane.

"Don't tell Mami either." I point my finger at the screen as a warning.

"You know I won't. That's a conversation for you and your mother. Where is this coming from?"

I swallow. Where do I even start?

If anyone can make me feel better right now, it's my dad. He's always made me feel like I'm tough enough to get through anything. I don't know if there's such a thing as unconditional love, but I think my dad loves me and Cesar as close to unconditionally as possible. My mom has always loved God unconditionally, and my dad always loved *me*. When he left, he took a lot of the strength he helped me build up. For the past six years, I've been a little more fragile.

"Mija, what's going on?" When I see the concern on his face, I realize I'm tearing up. I don't think I understand what's wrong until it comes out of my mouth.

"Papi, I'm so tired of having to take care of everyone." I wipe my eyes.

He's quiet for a while, and I almost start to think he'll be disappointed in me.

"Oh, mija . . ." He closes his eyes. "That's supposed to be my job. I hate that I can't be there for you." The camera is angled down now, so I can only see his chest and the old oversize (supposed to be) white T-shirt he's wearing, adorned with a a jaguar chain that matches Cesar's. All I want to do is fall into one of his hugs, but it's been so long I barely remember what they feel like. I want to tell him it's not his fault, and I know it isn't. But I'd be lying if I said part of me didn't blame him in some way. I want him to be *here*.

"It's not fair," is all I can say.

"I know it's not. You're doing a better job than I ever could, and that's not fair at all."

I laugh because it's so ridiculous. I'm doing a terrible job. I'm tiptoeing between eggshells, trying not to let everything fall apart.

"I'm just tired. I'm so tired."

"Talk to me," he says. His voice is like a hug. The closest I can get. I close my eyes and embrace it.

"I feel like I have to be happy about everything because if I tell Cesar I don't like Slayton, he'll say he doesn't like it either and Mom will blame me. And I know I'd rather be at Slayton than Rover . . . and I know it's better for Cesar, too, and I *know* there's no solution. But I just want to be *honest* about how I feel for once." I take a deep breath because I feel like I emptied my soul from my lungs.

"You're allowed to be honest," he says, shifting the camera so I can see his soft eyes boring into mine. "Especially with me. You know this, right?"

"I know."

I think I'll be honest with him one day, about everything. I'm not about to come out to him right now—I'd feel almost selfish doing that when I should still be focused on Cesar and earning money for tuition. But it's good to know he'll be there when I'm ready.

It's late when I hang up with him and start working on my homework in bed. Now, whenever I do my homework it's always late, since earning tuition comes first. I fall asleep on top of the comforter with my textbook and binder to keep me warm.

Luckily, I have time for a nap after school the next day, since Cesar (unluckily) has detention. That boy apparently only knows how to sleep when he's in class. Part of me worries there might be something deeper going on with him, but it's not like he'd tell me if there was. All the other signs point to him being okay, though, so I don't let the worry consume me.

Mom calls me a half hour after school lets out.

"I'm here. Where are you?" Not Good.

"Um, one second." I hang up and run to the pickup area. I assumed Cesar told her he had detention, or at least made up some kind of excuse, like an after-school club or something. But no, he left me to cover for him, as usual.

I climb into the car and improvise.

"So, Cesar joined Mathletes. It'll be another half hour." I text him as I tell her so he knows to play along when he gets out.

"Ay, ay, ay . . . and you didn't bother telling me this before I left to pick you up?"

"Sorry, Mami. I thought he told you," I say, sinking into the passenger seat.

"He did not." She rolls her eyes.

"Are you sure? I could have sworn he mentioned it. . . ." I try to sound surprised.

"So, Mathletes, huh? How'd you convince him to do that?"

I blush a little. It's kind of nice that she automatically assumes I was the reason he joined. I guess I can't *just* take credit for the bad stuff. Even if the good stuff is made up. She doesn't wait for me to answer.

"So he's doing good, then?" There's a hint of concern in her eyes when she looks at me.

"Yeah, he's great." Lie. Detention is not great. But at least he's not fighting.

When we finally see him, he's jogging to the car in his gym clothes, sweating more than should be humanly possible. It actually looks like he poured a water bottle on his head. Cesar is usually keeled over wheezing when he's this sweaty, but his breath is fine. He gets into the back seat and wipes his forehead, like he's doing it for effect.

"Excuse me, I didn't realize math club was so physically demanding." Mom raises an eyebrow at him.

"Yami, you don't have to lie for me," he says.

I whirl around, about ready to tackle him out of the car. Mom's glaring at me and I'm glaring at him, and between the heat of our stares and Cesar's body heat, this car is about to catch fire. Cesar, of course, is unbothered.

"I made football tryouts!"

"And why would Yamilet lie to me about that?"

"Um, I thought you wouldn't approve," I mutter. Football, really? Football tryouts were *weeks* ago. I made a perfect lie for him. What is his problem?

"Of course I approve!" Mom reaches back and kisses Cesar on his fake-sweaty forehead. "Gracias a Dios. You need an outlet for all that aggressive energy. This is good."

"Well, *I* think *Mathletes* would have been a better choice," I say. It's a more believable lie. Am I going to have to teach him how to throw a football now? If he wanted to choose his own lie, he shouldn't have made me cover for him.

"Why? Just because I'm smart I need to be thinking about math all the time? I'd rather play *football*."

"But you never played before! It makes no sense!"

"That's what practice is for." He smirks. "I mean, come on. Mathletes? Pfft."

"You ungrateful little—" I lunge back at him.

"¡AUXILIO!" He kicks and calls for help like he's being murdered. Mom swats at my back until I drop it.

"Yamilet! That's enough. Let your brother choose his own path."

"Fine." I put on my seat belt with all the attitude in my body.

6

THOU SHALT PROCURE A PSEUDO SUITOR

I guess I don't actually hate Slayton. I don't love it either, but after about a month, I've gotten used to it. It's not even October yet, but it feels like I've been here longer. I like the food. I like my friends. Cesar isn't fighting. He even has tons of friends who would probably defend him if anyone tried to put a hand on him, which is a comforting thought. Plus, his grades are up despite his constant sleeping in class. I guess if I was that smart, I'd get bored enough to fall asleep too. I try not to let it get to me that he sleeps in class every day and still gets better grades than I do.

I can't keep him from falling asleep in class, but the football lie is working out better than I expected. Mom's more than happy to take the extra hour of work and pick us up after he's done with practice—aka detention—and she's way too busy to catch on. She'll eventually want to come to a game, but that's a problem for future Yami and Cesar.

As usual, Bo and Amber join me at a table in the courtyard

and get out their textbooks. We make it a habit most days to sit here and do homework or draw after school. Since Cesar's in detention almost every freaking day, I spend a lot of time here. I tried asking him why he's always sleeping in class, but he shrugged me off. In accordance with the unspoken rule, I didn't pry. I guess he has insomnia or something. With all the time I spend waiting outside for him (since Karen and her boyfriend are *always* in the library after school), I know I'm starting to get a gnarly T-shirt tan.

After a while of failing to understand my math homework, I switch to an art assignment that requires less thinking. The prompt is "insecurity." Whatever that means. Ms. Felix says art is subjective, so as long as I have something to turn in, I'll be fine. I could make a freaking earring and bring it in if I wanted to. But I don't want to waste Mom's supplies.

A fourth guest joins us. He doesn't get any homework out.

"Hey, mind if I sit with you guys?"

"Hey, Hunter. Sure," Bo says. She gives him a questioning look as he walks around the table to sit by me, even though there was an empty space next to Amber.

"Cool drawing. You're really talented, Yamilet."

"Thanks!" I grin. I'm not the most talented artist in the world, but I'm getting the hang of things. I'm sketching a picture of myself as a secret agent, Men in Black style. I love the idea of being a secret agent or a spy. I sort of feel like I already am one, with all the lying I do. Being a spy is a cooler way of living that life, though. I can present compartmentalized versions of myself to each person I know, and no one needs to know about my undercover identity.

Amber leans toward Hunter with her elbow on the table, resting her chin on her hand. "What did we humble peasants do to deserve your company?"

Hunter blushes for a second. I wouldn't have noticed it if he wasn't so white, since he gains his composure real fast. He gives me a subtle half smile.

Bo raises her eyebrows at Amber, then winks at me when Hunter isn't looking. I guess Karen and them aren't the only ones who think Hunter and I are a thing. Still, I wish she'd stop winking at me, because it gives me *feelings*.

"Um, so Yamilet . . ." Hunter wrings his hands as he talks. "I like hanging out with you in art. I thought maybe we could hang out, like, outside of art sometime. Maybe you could come watch football practice instead of hanging out here? You know, if you're bored." Did I hear that right? He invited me not to watch a football game, but to watch him *practice*? That counts as hanging out? I swear I don't understand straight people.

"Um . . . wouldn't that be kind of boring, too?"

He laughs. "Oh, I mean, did I say practice? I meant home-coming."

"What?" This is not happening.

"What? Shut up." He's red again.

"Did you just tell her to shut up?" Amber snaps.

"No! I meant, me shut up. I was just kidding about home-coming. Unless . . . you want—"

Bo covers up her laugh with a cough. I don't know how this happened. It's not like I know Hunter that well, though I guess that never stops guys from making moves.

Actually . . . maybe this is an opportunity for me. If Hunter is my date, no one will think I'm gay. But then again, wouldn't it be messed up to use him like that? I can't imagine how pretending to like someone who likes me could end well for anyone involved.

"Sorry, she's got plans," Amber cuts in. I must have taken way too long to answer, because she's giving me a *you're welcome* kind of look.

"Right. Yeah, I have plans. I'll watch the homecoming game, though?"

"Oh, no problem! Sure, sounds awesome." He bounces back from the rejection real quick with the promise of an audience for the game. In fact, I can almost feel his spirit's fist pump. "Well, I'll see you guys later."

He salutes us and then literally runs away, but I'm hoping that's just because he's late to practice. I swear I don't understand how he's popular. Catholic school is a trip.

Cesar jogs out to us right when he gets let out and jogs in place by our table, probably trying to get sweaty before Mom gets us. Amber and Bo laugh. I already filled them in on Cesar pretending to be on the football team, so his random exercising is more entertaining than confusing.

"So Bo, I don't need a ride tomorrow," Cesar says, still jogging in place.

I cock my head. There's an art to telepathic communication. Cesar and I are on the same wavelength, so he gets my secret message: *huh?*

"I got plans." There's mischief in his smile as he switches to jumping jacks. Telepathic code for *mind your business, Yami, you nosy piece of shit, get your own social life.* Or maybe I'm reading into it.

"Okay, cool." Bo shrugs.

"That reminds me, can I come over after school tomorrow?" Amber asks Bo.

"Sure. You want to come too, Yamilet? I can drop you off at home after. Or the light rail, or wherever."

"Yes!" I know my answer comes a little fast and I look way too excited, but I don't care. I'm just excited to be entering friendship level two: hanging out outside of school.

"If you could change one thing about the world, what would it be?" I ask my dad in our FaceTime call. We've been talking for over an hour now, ever since I got home from school, and I'm not ready to hang up and start filling jewelry orders, so I've been asking random questions. I adjust myself so I'm lying sideways on my bed, propping my head up with my fist and holding the phone in front of me.

Dad sighs. Something almost sad flashes across his eyes for a moment. "Of course I'd make the world more immigrant-friendly."

"Maybe you can one day," I say, offering a hopeful smile. I used to believe he'd make it home someday and do just that, but

I've learned my lesson since then. He's not coming back, and I just have to live with it.

"What about you? What would you change about the world?" he asks, adjusting his work hat.

"Um . . ." I think about telling him I'd rid it of homophobia, racism, and all other forms of bigotry. But I know if I get into that I'll be tempted to just come out to him, and I don't think I'm quite ready for that yet. "Female priests?" I really don't know where that came from. It's not even something I really care about, but it's true that I find it unfair that only men can be priests, even if I myself would never want to be one.

Dad chuckles and playfully rolls his eyes. "Okay, Yami."

I roll mine right back. Even for the activist he is, Papi can be a little old-fashioned about some things. I can't tell if he rolled his eyes because my thing was so insignificant compared to his, or if he actually thinks the concept is stupid.

"Not that I don't love talking to you, mija, but I got to get to work."

I make a pouty face, and he mirrors it. "Fine. Yeah, I should probably get to work, too. Te quiero mucho, papi."

"Te quiero muchísimo, mijita." Then he blows me a kiss. The call ends, and I spend the rest of the evening working with my mom, wishing she cared enough to talk to me the way Dad does.

The next day goes by too slowly. I want school to be over so I can hang out with my soon-to-be level-two friends. Is it sad to be this excited to go to someone's house? I chalk it up to being deprived of social interaction outside school, since I haven't been to anyone else's house since the Bitch-Who-Must-Not-Be-Named fucked me over.

We stop at the gas station for snacks before going to Bo's. Cheetos, mini donuts, and soda. The houses in the hood are all different from each other, so I was expecting Bo's neighborhood to be all cookie-cutter houses, but it's not. All the houses on the block look like they were custom-built, and they're all so far apart they could fit a small apartment complex between them. There's a brick pathway to one house, stones paving the way to the next, and then there's Bo's house. Several sets of ornamental dwarf maple trees stand on either side of the cobblestone path leading to the entryway, where two Chinese dragon statues frame Bo's front door.

Seems like our whole house could fit in her living room. Twice. My mouth hangs open as I take it in. It's a good thing I never let Bo drive us home. That would have been embarrassing.

This is the biggest house I've ever been in, but not the biggest one on her street. A hideous animal greets us when we walk in. It's the funniest-looking mutt I've ever seen, but it seems like it loves me already, so I kind of melt.

"Down, Gregory!" Bo laughs as the dog—Gregory—gives her slobbery doggy kisses. When some older white guy in a sweater-vest walks in, the dog gets distracted and leaves Bo alone.

Amber goes over to the white guy and gives him a superlong

handshake complete with finger guns and pattycake.

"You guys are so embarrassing." Bo covers her face with her palms, then turns to me. "This is my dad."

"You must be Yamilet?" Bo's dad asks.

I give my sweetest smile and nod. He knows my name, so that means Bo must have talked about me. I don't know why that makes me so nervous.

"Nice to finally meet you!" He gives me the Vulcan salute from *Star Trek*. Bo's dad is a huge dork. I guess Bo is kind of a dork, too.

Wait, *finally*? How much has Bo talked about me? What does she say about me? I feel like a frozen computer. But Bo starts toward the stairs, so I shake it off and follow her with Amber.

Decorations cover so much of Bo's house; statues of lions, dragons, and Buddha are everywhere. There are fans and paintings with writing I don't understand on the walls between family portraits. I'm almost surprised to see in the pictures that both of Bo's parents are white, even though she'd already told me they were, because of all the Chinese decorations.

Bo sees me looking at a Chinese painting, and it's as if she just read my mind. "I know what it looks like, but my parents aren't *those* white people. The orientalist kind who adopt a kid from China so they can be closer to "the culture." Not that I was adopted from China. My birth parents were, like, second or third generation, I think." There's something in Bo's voice that doesn't quite match what she's saying about her parents, though. Like maybe she's a little insecure about the subject.

"Oh." I nod, not really knowing what else to say. Her parents may not be *those* white people, but I wonder if Bo is cool with the way they plaster her heritage to any surface it fits.

Another dog greets us when we get up the stairs. I recognize him as a Mexican Xolo dog—gray and hairless, with big ears and a fluffy tuft on top of its head. They're kind of known for being funny-looking. There's another living room up here, plus Bo's room, a guest room, and a study.

"Dante!" Amber squats down to scratch the dog's ears. It seems Bo might be a fan of the movie *Coco*. That definitely gives her points in my book, since it's one of my all-time favorites.

The vibe in Bo's room is totally different from the rest of the house. There's an abstract rainbow mural covering two of the walls, while the other walls are littered with drawings and paintings. Some are framed and some are just tacked up, a few of them overlapping. They all have Bo's signature in the bottom corner, even the ones that were clearly drawn when she was, like, three. She's really talented. The paintings she's done more recently look like they could be straight-up photographs. Among all the images, she has portraits of Amber, David, and both her dogs. But what I can't stop staring at is the mural. It's not neat like the other pictures, but it somehow feels . . . happy? It's like an army of rainbow bombs going off in front of the sun.

"Sorry for my super-gay room," Bo says when she realizes I'm staring at the mural. "You'll have to get used to that."

I laugh. The things I would give to have a super-gay room. Seems like the dream.

Amber and Bo sit on the bed. Sitting on someone's bed is at least a level-three friend privilege, so I take the desk chair.

"So, your parents are pretty supportive, huh?" I wish I didn't say that. Gay stuff is the number one topic I should be avoiding.

"You mean about me being gay? Yeah, they're cool."

Amber and Bo keep talking, but I'm in my feelings. I can't help the pang of jealousy in my gut. I couldn't imagine ever coming out to my mom. At least not anytime soon. Maybe if I ever move out of the country, I'll tell her then. She's just so old-fashioned. The epitome of an Overprotective, Old-School, God-Fearing Mexican™.

Gregory interrupts the conversation when he pushes the door open with his nose and struggles to hop onto the bed. The dog has great timing, I'll give him that.

"What kind of dog is that?" I ask.

"He's a pit-bull–basset-hound mix. Isn't he ugly?" Amber says while absentmindedly stretching out one of her blond curls until it's straight.

Gregory has a big pit-bull head, but his face is a little droopier than your usual pit. And he has short but buff legs, and a long basset-hound body, complete with floppy ears.

Bo covers Gregory's giant ears. "Shhh, he's beautiful."

"I guess he's kind of cute," I laugh. "In a so-ugly-he's-cute kind of way."

Amber cups her hand around the side of her mouth, so Bo can't see her lips, like it would prevent her from hearing. "Bo likes to rescue ugly animals."

"Ugly animals deserve love too!" Bo kisses Gregory's

forehead. I can't lie. That is the cutest shit I ever saw.

"So, Yamilet, what is Cesar gonna do when your mom wants to go see one of his games?" Amber asks.

I shrug. "Who knows? He'll probably come up with some overly complicated scheme and pull me in on it at the last minute." Cesar doesn't admit to his lies, even if he's about to be caught up. Instead, he comes up with elaborate ways to cover his tracks.

"His twin is on the team." Bo puts finger quotes on "twin." "Maybe she won't notice he's not there if David has anything to do with it!" She laughs.

"Don't be giving him ideas." I know it's a joke, but I wouldn't put it past Cesar.

"You know who else is on the football team?" Amber wiggles her eyebrows at me. "Your not-so-secret admirer."

"Oh my God, my soul literally departed from my body out of secondhand embarrassment." Bo shudders.

"I thought it was kind of sweet," Amber says. "Sorry for butting in. You kind of looked like you needed some help. If you want to go to homecoming, you can tell him your plans got canceled."

I think about it for a minute. School dances when you're in the closet are a nightmare. You're expected to have a "straight date." And if you dance with another girl, it's supposed to be for attention. Attention is the last thing I want if I'm doing gay shit like that.

"That's okay. I didn't want to go anyway," I say.

"Well, I didn't want to pressure you, but we usually don't go, either. Want to ditch together?" Bo asks, and Amber claps her hands.

"Sure, yeah, I'd like that." I feel myself blushing and I don't know why.

It's about an hour before we finish the entirety of the junk food we bought. If I don't leave soon, I'll be walking home from my stop in the dark. I know the logical solution would be to let Bo drop me off at home, but after seeing this house, that's definitely not happening. I ask her to drop me off at the light rail again. On the way home, I distract myself from thinking about Bo and my not-crush on her by finishing my homework for the week. Who knew denial could make me a star student?

When I get to the corner of our street, I see there's a car in our driveway I don't recognize. And when I get inside, some-one else's backpack is on the kitchen counter. It doesn't sound like anyone is in the house, though, so I drop my bag on the stool next to the mystery person's bag. Then I see them through the window.

Cesar is standing in the backyard with Jamal, his friend from Rover. It gives me an uneasy feeling to see someone from our old life here. I never really got to know Jamal, but we were on a "nod when you see each other in the hall" basis. I liked him because he always seemed to have Cesar's back when I wasn't around. I know of a few times Cesar got jumped and Jamal hopped in to help. A lot of girls liked Jamal, but he never paid any of them any mind. He's tall and thin, and he stands all proper, always tucking in his button-down shirts. If he wasn't Black, he'd fit right in at Slayton.

I hear my mom's car pulling in the driveway. Jamal should leave soon, because Mom doesn't like when people she doesn't know come into the house. Especially when she's not home. I start walking to the back door to warn them. Before I get to the door, Jamal hands something to Cesar. I squint and lean forward, but I can't make out what it is. Takis? Money? Something worse?

I'll ask Cesar about it later, but now I need to warn them about Mom, or she'll kill all three of us. When I reach for the handle, Jamal reaches for Cesar's hands, and they kiss.

Wait.

Did I see that right? They *kissed!*

I may have seriously misjudged this situation. New diagnosis: GAYYYYYY!!!!

It takes every ounce of willpower in my soul not to shout that shit out loud. My brother! And Jamal! For a second, I feel like that meme of the white lady with all the math equations behind her. Is *Jamal* the person Cesar has been up late talking to every night? God, I hate that I of all people assumed it was always a girl. But obviously I'm not upset about this discovery. I know I shouldn't be this excited, but goddamn I cannot contain myself right now.

I hear a car door shut in the carport outside the laundry room just before the door opens. I turn around so fast I almost fall back against the screen door I was about to open.

I can't let Mom see them.

"Mami!" I rush over to the laundry room and give her a hug, putting all the lingering giddiness into my "distract Mom" performance.

"I didn't bring you no food." She laughs.

"Dang, Mom, can't I just love you?" I say, leaning to the side when she tries to sidestep me.

She gives me a look, then walks right past me. This is why I could never actually be a secret agent.

I run in front of her and stand on the opposite end of the screen door, so she doesn't see Jamal. She does, however, see his backpack.

"Yamilet. Who is in my house?"

"Mom, don't be mad—" The screen door opens, and Cesar and Jamal walk in. Cesar freezes when he sees Mom. Both of them look like their lives are flashing before their eyes. She didn't see anything, though. All she knows is there's a stranger in her house. A much easier problem to solve.

"Uhhhh . . ." It sounds like Cesar's brain broke. Real nice.

"Mom, I, um, I want you to meet my boyfriend!" I step between Jamal and Cesar and hold Jamal's hand. It's clammy and gross, but I guess I'll forgive him for being sweaty, considering my mom is about to murder him. "Don't worry, Mom. Cesar was just giving him the protective-brother talk, so he's got you covered on the whole 'scaring my boyfriend to death' thing."

Jamal lets go of my hand and wipes his palms on his pants. Then he reaches out a hand to my mom. "It's nice to meet you, Mrs. Flores. I'm Jamal."

She doesn't take his hand, instead crossing her arms over her chest. Jamal waits a moment before awkwardly clearing his throat and putting his hand down.

"Jamal." She nods. "I'll give you a pass, since Yamilet clearly hasn't taught you the rules yet." The venom in her voice is directed at me, not him.

"Thank you, Mrs. Flores." His voice is so soft I can barely hear him. He looks down and rubs the back of his neck.

"Rule number one: no boys allowed when I'm not home."

"Yes, Mrs. Flores." He swallows. "Sorry, Mrs. Flores."

"Next time you come into my home, I expect you to do it right." She points at the door, telling him to leave.

"Yes, ma'am." He grabs his backpack and rushes out the door. I'm surprised he didn't shit himself. *I* almost shit myself. Mom can be scary when she wants to be.

As soon as the door is closed, she laughs. "Oh, I *like* him!"

Cue record scratch.

"Really?" Cesar and I say at the same time.

"*Yes*, Mrs. Flores, *thank you*, Mrs. Flores. I could get used to that!"

Cesar looks like he's holding his breath.

"What, Cesar, you don't like your sister's boyfriend Steve Urkel?" She has this ugly-ass hyena cackle whenever she tries to clown on someone. The laugh is always funnier than the joke. But it's contagious, so I can't help but join in against my will. Cesar doesn't.

"Mami, don't be mean! He's nice," I say, trying to stifle my giggling for Cesar's sake.

"He is. I think—you'll probably like him, I think." Cesar stumbles over the words. "I have homework." He grabs his backpack and disappears to his room.

Ooh, Cesar *would* leave me alone to have the Talk with Mom about *his* boyfriend. I mean, I think it's his boyfriend? Who knows, maybe they're just casual. I definitely deserve to get some answers after putting myself on the line like this.

"You're right, mija, he seems nice."

"So you're not mad?"

"I'm just happy you finally got a boyfriend! After all these years, I was starting to think you were gay!" She does the sign of the cross and another hyena cackle. The words knock the air out of me, but I push out a laugh anyway. If she finds out about me and Cesar, she'll probably have us exorcized.

She spends another couple of minutes clowning on Jamal's outfit before she tells me she wants me to invite him over for dinner on Friday. As soon as she lets me off the hook, I go to Cesar's room. He's pacing back and forth, fidgeting with his hands. I thought I was going to tell him off for leaving me alone with Mom, but I find myself rushing into a hug. He stiffens up like he was expecting anything but. The way he's breathing feels like he might be crying, but it's hard to tell. After a minute, he pulls away.

"Um, what all did you see?" His hands are shaking, but no tears.

"What do you mean? Y'all weren't getting busy out there, were you?"

"Oh my God, Yami! No!" His cheeks darken. "But you

saw . . . um . . . you know . . ."

"I saw you kiss, yeah."

"I . . . I was gonna tell you." He lets out a shaky breath.

"You don't owe me shit. It's okay, really." I want to reach out and hug him again, but something tells me I should wait.

"I'm just gonna say it, okay?" he says with a quivering lip, but doesn't continue.

The room is completely silent while I let him build the courage. We're both holding our breath. I find my lip mirroring his as it starts to tremble. Whatever Cesar is about to say could change everything. We can be in this together.

"I'm bi," he says, finally wiping his eyes and nose, which were both starting to leak.

"Cesar, noooo, don't cry. . . ." I pull him back into a hug. I expect him to tense up again, but he goes weak, like the hug is the only thing keeping him on his feet. I don't know what to say. He just came out to me, and I know how big of a deal that is. Oh, do I know. I don't know if he's crying from relief or if he's scared or what, but I just want him to stop because he's about to make *me* cry.

"Thanks for covering for me." He gives me a look that probably just means exactly that, but it maybe also means *hurry up and say you're gay so we can bond over it*. Not that he knows. Yet. I open my mouth to tell him, but nothing comes out. He starts fidgeting again, and I know I need to say *something*.

This should be easy, since he did it first, but I'm holding my breath again. The longer it takes me to respond, the more he'll start to think I'm biphobic. I know I'd be overthinking it if anyone took this long to respond to me coming out. Okay, I can do this. I finally let myself breathe and try again.

"I'm . . . I'm g—" I start again, but the words are trying to claw their way back into my throat. I can only push them out through a whisper. "I'm gay."

It's not just me anymore, and the thought makes me tear up.

"Yami, noooo!" Cesar's voice cracks, and now he's the one hugging me. I start laughing. We really can't stand seeing each other cry.

Cesar takes a step back and gives me the world's cheesiest smile. "You know what that means, right?"

"What?" I wipe my eye.

"In lak'ech, baby!"

I spit out a laugh-cry, and Cesar starts Fortnite dancing. He's chanting between moves.

"In . . . la . . . keeeeeech!"

He's twerking now, and how could I not join in? I jump on his bed and floss dance while he attempts to wall twerk. We laugh and sing and twerk. It's so gay.

7

THOU SHALT DIVERT THY MOTHER'S GAYDAR

"I should have known," Cesar says after wearing himself out with all the twerking.

"Why? How could you have known?" I am a little relieved he didn't catch on. If my own brother didn't, other people must not know either.

"I heard you turned Hunter down for homecoming."

"So? He could have just not been my type." It's not like I don't know Hunter is conventionally attractive. Just because I'm gay doesn't mean I can't *see* him.

"I mean . . . if I was single, mmh! He could get it."

I roll my eyes and change the subject. "Remember that guy who is apparently my boyfriend? Mom wants him to come over for dinner Friday."

"Oh . . ."

"I got you. I'll pretend to be your boyfriend's girlfriend, but only if you tell me everything." I sit cross-legged on his bed and rest my face on my palms, ready for story time.

"You can't just put me on the spot! I don't know what I'm supposed to say. Ask me a question or something."

"Fine. What did he give you?" With Cesar's track record, I'm still not 100 percent convinced it was something innocent, but I'll give him the benefit of the doubt.

"Seriously? How long were you watching us?"

"Like two seconds, chill! I was trying to warn you that Mom was coming."

"Yeah, thanks for the heads-up," he mutters. Ungrateful little asshole.

"Excuse me, I just saved your ass. You're welcome." I get up to leave, hoping he'll stop me before I have to commit to pretending to be mad. I want details.

"Wait, no, thank you. It was a promise ring." He sucks in his bottom lip to hold back a grin. I drop my jaw in a wide smile, hopping back on the bed.

"Let me see! Are you gonna wear it?"

He pulls a ring out of his pocket. It's a black-and-silver band with a jaguar symbol on it. Perfect for Cesar.

"I can't wear it. I'm not out. . . ." He rubs the ring between his thumb and index finger and looks down.

"Did you tell him?"

"He knows. He said he wants me to have it anyway, and I can wear it whenever I'm ready. He'll be waiting a good minute for me to put it on, though."

"Aww!" I hold back an excited squeak. Jamal is a sweetheart. "How long have you been together?"

"A year today." Cesar doesn't do so well hiding his grin this time.

"A YEAR?" I never pictured Cesar as a committed relationship type, but a year is a long time. I can't believe how oblivious I've been. Or how good at hiding it *he's* been.

"It's an anniversary present." His cheeks flush.

I resist the urge to pinch them because I want him to know I'm taking this seriously. Inside I'm all rainbows and happy squeals. "What's he like? Is he good to you?"

Sheesh. I sound like my dad.

"*Yes*. Don't be weird."

"Okay, okay." I throw my hands up in surrender. "Just know if he hurts you, I'll tell Mom he hurt *me* and we'll tag-team him for you."

"Yeah, I'm not worried about that." He laughs.

"You should be! I'm serious, I will fight him." I know Cesar thinks I'm a weakling because I've never been in a fight. But he's wrong. I could kick some serious ass. Probably.

"No, I mean that wouldn't happen. You don't have to worry about Jamal."

"I better not." I give him my best *I love you but I mean business* look.

"You're too much." Cesar rolls his eyes.

I want to keep joking with him, but now I'm getting this sinking feeling in my gut.

"Cesar, is that why you got . . . um, picked on?" I don't want to say "jumped," because it feels too heavy for the moment. "Because of your sexuality?"

Cesar sighs. "I mean, I'm not out, but some dudes got ahold of a note I wrote for Jamal. Thankfully, they didn't know it was to him. But I don't want to get into it right now. It's really no big deal. It's not like the whole school knew or anything." He looks away, avoiding my eyes.

I can't believe Cesar and I both got outed at Rover, and neither of us had any idea. I guess it's nice that rumors die fast there, but at the same time, I wish we could have been there for each other. I want to shake him and tell him it is a big deal. I want to yell that it's not fair, and he deserves better. Instead, I say something I rarely ever say.

"I love you."

"That's gay," Cesar whispers. Touché.

School on Friday goes by way too fast. All I can think about is Jamal coming over for dinner. Now that I'm home, I'm even more nervous. Mom has to buy it.

She makes me clean up all our jewelry supplies before he gets here. I guess having wires and beads and crystals everywhere is too messy for guests. She turns on her cumbia playlist while I clean and she cooks. The smell of chicken and the slight hint of chocolate in the mole feel as much a part of the music as the drum.

It's just Jamal, but Mom always wants to have background music when we have people over. I like having the music to loosen the mood a little. Jamal shows up at six p.m. on the dot. Mom gives me an impressed look before she dances over to the door, then goes into scary mom mode. She stares at Jamal for two excruciatingly long seconds. He pretends not to be fazed, but he has to be. He holds out his hand and smiles.

"Hi, Mrs. Flores. How are you?"

"Mijo, we don't do handshakes in this house." She pulls him in for a hug. So much for the tough mom act. She tries, but she can't resist letting all her love overflow. She's not the best at pretending to be hard. I take after her like that.

Jamal keeps giving Cesar goo-goo eyes whenever my mom isn't looking. I try not to notice that they're playing footsie under the table. It's almost like they *want* Mom to catch them. Jamal is the worst at pretending to be straight. They're in luck, though, since she has a notoriously terrible gaydar, with a very low success rate so far.

"So tell me, Jamal, are you Catholic?"

"Mom!" I say.

"No, I'm Christian."

"Okay. That's acceptable. Do you go to church?"

"Mom!" This time both Cesar and I cut her off.

"Fine, fine. I just want the best for my daughter. You understand, don't you, Jamal?"

Jamal nods. Then Mom changes the subject, thank God.

I guess I never really talked to Jamal before, or I would have probably clocked him. Something about the way he holds himself screams "gay" to me. I must not have that gay of a vibe, considering Cesar didn't figure it out and Bianca tried to ruin my life when she found out. But now I am in a happy fake relationship, so I'm doing fine without her.

After dinner, I walk Jamal to his car like a fake girlfriend should. As soon as the front door closes, he lets out a huge sigh.

"Don't worry, she likes you," I say. He called Mom "Mrs. Flores" and always said please and thank you. She ate that shit right up.

"Really?" He grins and gives me an enthusiastic high five, then gets into his car. Cesar comes out before he drives off, so Jamal rolls his window down.

"You both did terrible," Cesar says.

"What? What was I supposed to do?" I throw my hands up.

"Sell it. You should go on a fake date or something. Get to know each other, so you don't look so stiff next time."

"Whatever you say, amor," Jamal says.

"Okay, fine, but you're paying." I poke Cesar. It's only fair, considering we're both doing this to save his ass.

"With what money?" he says.

"Use your puppy eyes on Mom. She'll give you some."

"So, lunch tomorrow?" Jamal asks.

"Sure." I won't complain about a free lunch and getting to know Cesar's boyfriend.

"Cesar! YamiLET!" Mom's muffled shout from inside rings loud enough to hear from the driveway.

"Úfale, gotta go." Cesar leans through Jamal's window to kiss him on the cheek.

I wave, and we both hurry inside to do the dishes before my mom has a chance to loudly and passive-aggressively do them herself. Which it looks like she's already started. Ugh.

"We got it, Mami," I say as I gently coax the soapy plate from her hands like it's a bomb only I can defuse. Cesar grabs a towel and starts drying the one she already washed. She sighs and relinquishes control before sitting on the barstool on the other side of the sink.

"Mami, can I have some money? For football?" Cesar asks with those big puppy eyes. He doesn't even have to specify why he needs football money. She's already reaching for her purse. She places two crisp twenties on the counter. More than enough for Jamal and me to get lunch.

The next day Jamal shows up right on time, and his car looks cleaner than it did yesterday. Did he clean it for me?

"What do you want to listen to?" he asks when I get into the car.

"Play whatever you want." It's his car, so he should get to pick the music.

"Do you like Saul Williams?" he asks.

"Who?"

"He's my favorite poet." Nothing wrong with poetry, but I was sort of expecting music. "I'm listening to *The Dead Emcee Scrolls: The Lost Teachings of Hip-Hop*. It's good, I promise." He smiles as he plugs in the AUX, all excited.

I'm not that into spoken-word poetry, but I see the appeal. The rhythm of the words feels like music without having too much going on. Deciphering meaning from the words is hard for me without being able to read along, though. I've never heard poetry like this.

Jamal seems to have the whole thing memorized. He chants along, not missing a beat. Some of the lines really resonate, so I snap my fingers along to Jamal's voice, and I find my head bobbing with the rhythm of the words. There's not a whole lot of time to listen, since we're only going down the street. I barely have time to unbuckle my seat belt before Jamal jogs over to my side to open the door for me.

"Thanks," I say, stifling a laugh. It's a little cute how quick he got here just to open the door when I could have opened it myself. I think he's trying to make a good impression.

"Are we supposed to, like, hold hands or something?" Jamal fidgets with his pockets as we walk into the diner and down the tiled floor to a table in the corner.

"No, probably just around my mom."

"Okay, sorry, that was a stupid question." He's wringing his hands on the table now.

"Hey, chill. I'm not my mom. You don't have to impress me or anything. Cesar trusts you, so I know you're good people."

"Thanks," he says, and pulls his hands under the table. I think he's still nervous, though.

"Sooo . . . I guess we're supposed to get to know each other." I try to come up with the kinds of things a girlfriend should know about her boyfriend. "Do you have any siblings?"

"Two sisters. They're five and three. And a stepbrother. He's older, like, in his twenties, I think."

"Cool. You probably know everything about my family already, because of Cesar."

"Not *everything*."

"What do you want to know?" I ask.

"Well . . . I don't want you to tell me anything he wouldn't tell me. But he doesn't talk about your dad much, just says you're the favorite."

"Oh, poor Cesar, there's *one* person who likes me as much as him. I'm definitely *not* the favorite." I don't know why I get so defensive. I guess I am closer to Dad than Cesar, but Cesar's *everyone's* favorite. Is it so bad for me to be Dad's? "Sorry, I don't know why I snapped at you."

Then Jamal looks so deeply into my eyes I feel like he knows all my secrets. "I know it's hard living under someone else's shadow. But you're your own person, too, with your own talents and passions. I'm glad you have someone like your dad to see that in you." His eyes don't leave mine the whole time he talks, so I cave and look down.

I open my mouth to respond, but nothing comes out. I'm just surprised at how seriously he's taking me. I was just venting. It's not like I was expecting him to get all deep about it. It makes me wonder how he and Cesar work out, since Cesar is the opposite of serious. I guess they probably balance each other out in that way.

"If it makes you feel better, I'm barely anyone's favorite either. Except maybe Cesar's." He gives me a sad little smile.

"Why not?" I ask.

"I guess I don't fit into their box. I'm not exactly the most masculine guy. My stepdad says I'm an embarrassment." He's looking down, not touching his food.

"Do they know about Cesar?" I ask.

"They will soon. I'm gonna come out, I just don't know when's the right time."

"You're not scared to tell them?"

"I'm scared either way. Might as well get it over with," he says.

"Well, good luck. I hope—oh my God . . ." I better be seeing things, or I'll kill my mom. And Cesar. Because if my eyes are correct, they're both here spying on us.

"What?" Jamal asks.

"Don't look," I say before he has a chance to turn around. "Cesar and my mom are here."

I get out my phone to virtually chew Cesar out, but it looks like he tried to warn me while we were on our way.

"Okay, so *now* should we hold hands?" Jamal asks. I swear he started sweating as soon as I mentioned my mom.

"Yeah." I reach a hand across the table, and he takes it.

It's weird trying to eat with one hand while someone's holding the other. Do couples even do this? I wouldn't know.

My phone buzzes, and I already know who it is.

Cesar: you're not selling it

I fake-laugh loud enough for them to hear, and Jamal joins in.

Cesar: there you go

Jamal and I spend the next half hour pretending to be all smitten. We fake-laugh and hold hands and eat off each other's plates, even though I don't like his food. You're welcome, Cesar.

But pretending to be in a relationship makes me wonder what it would be like to be in an actual one. Maybe one day I'll do it for real. But I hope it's easier than this. I want to able to hold someone's hand whenever I want. Or talk to someone on the phone until we fall asleep. Or kiss someone that I'm actually attracted to.

I want to kiss a girl. I want to hold a girl's hand. I want to cuddle with a girl. I want a girlfriend. But Cesar has a boyfriend, and he can't even do all those things. My mom isn't like Bo's parents. We don't have the privilege of being ourselves. It doesn't work like that.

Not for us.

8

THOU SHALT MIND THINE OWN BUSINESS. BITCH.

I always look forward to art class. Like usual, today Ms. Felix just gives an assignment and lets us go at it for an hour. She never cares if we're goofing off, as long as we have something to show at the end of class. She just floats around doing her own art and complimenting everyone else's for most of the time.

It's like therapy for me. I can decompress from the tension of having to be around Jenna and Karen in language arts. It might be the borderline toxic fumes from all the markers and dirty paint-water, but I find it hard to worry too much when I'm in here. Bo and David are both really talented, while Hunter and I try our best and usually miss the mark. After working on landscapes and still lifes, we're onto portraits, and we have to partner up to draw each other.

Bo and Hunter both ask to be my partner at the same time. They share a look, then Bo shrugs. "No worries, I'll work with David," she says, and my heart sinks to the pit of my stomach. Hunter grins at me, showing off both dimples and those smoochy white-boy lips.

"Wait! I don't know how to draw . . . um"—Hunter looks at me with bright, hopeful eyes, and my mind races, trying to come up with an excuse to be partners with Bo—"white people."

Hunter just stares at me and blinks. I hold eye contact, waiting for him, or anyone, to say something. We both just stare at each other while I slowly die inside, my soul floating away into the next plane of existence, screaming into the abyss.

"She's right." Bo finally cuts the silence. "White people are hard to draw. It's like, whaaaat? How?" She turns her face to me so Hunter can't see her wink. She probably thinks I'm avoiding him after he asked me to homecoming. My knight in shining khakis.

"I can draw white people, bro," David says to Hunter, who looks disappointed.

"Okay, cool." Hunter turns to David and they get to work.

Bo grins at me. I blush and get started.

The thing about art that no one tells you is that almost anyone can do it. There are rules, and as long as you follow them, you can fake skill until you actually have it. Regardless of skill level, drawing every inch of Bo's face makes it really hard not to get caught up admiring her, so I take my time drawing the lines and circles that make up every generic face before I finally have to really look at her. She's giving me a straight face, which is smart so her facial muscles won't get tired while I draw. She's not wearing any makeup, but she doesn't have dark circles under her eyes like I do. I imagine her sleeping peacefully for a full eight hours. She probably wears rainbow pajamas. I wonder if she puts her hair up to sleep. She would look so cute in a messy bedtime bun.

Focus.

I move on to Bo's eyes, framed by short, straight lashes that almost make it look like she's wearing eyeliner. Maybe I'll draw her eyes later. I probably look too dreamy drawing those. Her lips aren't any easier, though. Too smoochy.

Whew, I feel like I'm sweating.

I end up rushing the drawing so no one can see my heart eyes.

"Can I keep it?" Bo asks when I'm done. I nod, but I want to disappear. For once I'm grateful not to be an expert at drawing. That way the portrait won't quite give away how cute I think she is.

Bo takes much longer to do her portrait of me. She keeps asking me to look at her. I don't know what it is about eye contact that makes me feel like I'm completely naked and on display. I guess she's not really looking into my eyes, though. Just trying to draw them. Somehow that's worse?

"Don't look, it's not done yet!" Bo scolds when I try to sneak a glance at her page. She's hyperaware of every bit of my face right now. I just want to know what she thinks I look like.

"Don't make my nose too big, okay?" I didn't know I was self-conscious about my nose until now. Or my wide-set eyes, or big mouth, or squarish jaw.

"Trust me, okay? I'll do your face all the justice it deserves."

What does that even mean? "Okay, just make me look good. My life is in your hands."

"No pressure, though," David adds from across the table as he grins and scratches his chin patch while studying Hunter's face.

"You'll show me as soon as you're done, right?" I ask.

Bo grins. "There's a student art show in March. Maybe you'll see it then."

Well, that was cryptic as shit.

Three guys come into the room, stealing Bo's attention and everyone else's. They're singing a cappella. Some song they clearly made up specifically to ask someone to homecoming. The one in the middle has roses in his hand. He gets down on one knee.

"Sarah, I'm on my knees, will you go to homecoming with me, please?" he sings.

She takes the roses and they kiss. Bleh.

Ms. Felix doesn't let them soak up the moment too long. The boys go back to whatever class they're supposed to be in, and Sarah gushes to her friends about what just happened.

"I would die if someone tried that with me. It's so embarrassing," I say.

"Are you kidding? That was so cute!" Bo stops drawing to comment.

"I don't like the idea of asking someone publicly. Then you're trapped into saying yes, or you look like an asshole." I can't imagine if Hunter had asked me publicly instead of just in front of Bo and Amber. I would have spontaneously combusted on the spot.

"Yeah, that'd be pretty embarrassing for everyone," Hunter

says, rubbing his neck like he read my thoughts.

"I don't know, I feel like that's what makes it a big romantic gesture, right? Putting yourself on the spot. It's like 'I like you so much I'm willing to get publicly embarrassed for you,'" David adds, almost defensively.

"But you're not just embarrassing yourself, you're embarrassing the person you're asking, too," I say.

Bo nods. "I think you're right if it's not a sure thing. But Sarah and Ryan are together, so obviously she'd say yes. I think it's cute, but only if you're sure the person would already want to go, you know?"

"Oh . . . I never thought of that." David looks way too bummed out for what the situation calls for.

"Wait, were you planning on asking Amber?" Hunter asks.

My eyes shoot to David. I didn't even put together that that's why he was stressing it, and now I feel kind of bad.

"Well, now I'm not. I don't want to embarrass her." David slumps his shoulders.

"As her best friend, trust me on this. She won't be embarrassed." Bo winks at David, and his cheeks get darker. Knowing I'm not the only one she winks at is somehow both a relief and a disappointment.

Bo doesn't make any sense to me. She usually ditches school dances, so I figured they weren't her thing. And that made me think she wasn't much of a romantic, or someone who would even *want* to go to a dance. But she's apparently a fan of the public proposals. Maybe she would want to go, if she had someone to go with. . . .

Bo snaps a picture of me, which erases whatever was in my head. Class is almost over, and she hasn't finished the portrait, so I guess she wants the picture to finish later. I try peeking one last time, but she slams her sketchbook shut. Ugh. Looks like I'll have to wait until whenever she decides to let me see it. Hopefully before the art show all the way in freaking March.

Once October is in full swing, the only two things anyone cares about are homecoming and Halloween. The uniforms take the fun out of Halloween, so the hype for homecoming is a million times stronger. Public homecoming proposals are now a regular occurrence. So far, Hunter is the only one who's asked me, which isn't a surprise, because I don't talk to that many people.

You can always expect at least one proposal to happen at lunch. It seems like almost everyone who goes to homecoming here makes a huge spectacle of it. There were a few public prom and homecoming proposals at Rover, but never this much. I wonder how Bo can stand to see so many proposals and still feel all mushy about it. It's not like she—or I—can ever have that kind of cutesy public display at this school without getting tomatoes thrown at us.

Bo and Amber are huddled together across the lunch table on Bo's phone, and I feel a little left out. At least David's left out, too. I pull out my phone and confirm a few more Etsy orders to keep my mind from wondering what they're talking about. We sold a wave of friendship bracelets, which I'm glad for, because they're my favorite to make.

"What are you guys doing?" David finally asks, and I look

up from my phone. I have to admit I'm curious.

"Trying to find Bo a girlfriend." Amber says it like it's no big deal. I shouldn't feel jealous, especially because I already told them about Jamal. I needed to keep my lies straight. I don't know why it felt so much worse to lie to my friends than my mom. I guess I feel like with my mom, it's out of necessity, but with Bo, Amber, and David it feels selfish. Especially since Bo is one of the only ones at this school who might actually understand my situation. Still, I can't risk the truth getting back to Mom.

"Don't you have to be eighteen to use dating apps?" The thought of Bo getting a girlfriend gives me a weird sinking feeling.

"No need to call the cops, we're just browsing!" Amber waves away my question. "What do you think of Jamie? She's cute, right? She's studying social and cultural analysis at ASU! Which we all know is basically queer studies. Sounds like Bo's type of girl." Amber shows me her screen, with a picture of a girl with blue hair and a lip ring.

"Yeah . . . she's cute." I force the words out of my throat.

"Hey, have you guys ever wondered how many people at this school are actually closeted?" David asks. I was *almost* glad for the subject to change. I think he's just trying to be included in the conversation, but the question makes me queasy. "Like, statistically speaking, Bo can't be the only one who's not straight." I almost choke on my food.

"It's none of my business, so . . . ," I say. Hopefully he'll change the subject.

"Bo wasn't the only one last year. Remember Elaina?" Amber says. Bo rolls her eyes.

"Yes, I was. Elaina's not gay, she's trans. It's two different things," Bo says flatly.

"I meant, like, you weren't the only LGBTQ+ person here," Amber says. "But David, I thought about the gay thing before, too. Jake Jeffrey is definitely gay. His girlfriend has to be a beard. I bet she's in on it." I don't like this at all. If I wasn't here, would I be on their list? I feel like Jesus's eyes are judging me. "Hot Jesus," as Cesar calls him (only to me). It's the abs.

I look to Bo. If anyone has the guts to call this stuff out, it's her. But she sits quietly without looking up from her food.

"And Ms. Felix, the art teacher? Definitely gay," Amber adds.

"You can't be sure about that kind of thing, though. Didn't everyone think you were gay last year?" David asks Amber.

"That was only because Bo came out, and she's my best friend." Amber tosses a tater tot in the air and catches it in her mouth. Like she could care less that everyone assumed she was gay.

"Yeah, Yamilet, you might want to brace yourself for that. People assume all Bo's friends are gay like her," David says. Amber shoots him a glare on Bo's behalf.

"Run while you can if you're not cool with that," Bo says. She's not smiling.

"No, I'm cool," I say. But I don't know if I am.

Jenna and Karen are staring at us from across the room. At Bo, specifically. Karen giggles behind her overly tanned hands, and Jenna looks weirdly shy compared to normal. Karen pushes her toward us and trails behind.

"While we're talking about who's gay, Jenna might actually have a little crush on you, Bo." David nudges Bo to get her attention.

Bo turns to look at them, and Jenna makes a little squeal and hides behind Karen. Bo gives Jenna a cute little smile, and I try to shove down the wave of jealousy before it shows on my face. Is *Bo* Jenna's secret crush?

Jenna finally gets pushed in front of Karen, and she puffs out her chest and walks straight toward Bo. "Um, hi . . ."

"Hey, what's up?"

"Sorry, I know we haven't talked in a while. I was wondering . . ." Jenna takes a breath. "Are you going to homecoming?" Her face is completely red. People are starting to stare. Amber and David drop their jaws.

"Are you asking me to homecoming?" Bo's smile grows, and I notice now that when she smiles with her whole face, the right side of her mouth tilts slightly higher. It's the cutest crooked smile ever, and I want to see more of it—though preferably not because of Jenna. Bo's whole face lights up, and mine goes hot. I don't know, I guess I was looking forward to not going to homecoming. With Bo.

Karen bursts out laughing, and Bo's face twists in confusion.

"I'm sorry, I'm sorry! It was just a dare!" Jenna giggles uncontrollably. "Holy shit, I think she was gonna say yes!" She laughs. Everyone laughs. Bo's face goes red, and so does my vision.

"You think that's fucking funny?" I stand. It takes a lot to get me to stand up for myself. But when you mess with my friends? I can't just sit there. I march straight over to Jenna and Karen. Amber is right behind me. They run away, giggling. They actually run away from us as we walk over. I guess I was kind of hoping that would happen, since I don't know what I would have done if they actually squared up.

Bo stands up, too, but goes in the other direction. She's gone from the cafeteria before she can hear the nasty things people are saying. Amber and I chase after her out into the parking lot. David calls after us, but we're not turning back. Not without Bo.

"Bo, wait!" I call out, but she doesn't stop. She walks straight to her car, and we have to run to catch her before she opens the door.

"Where are you going?" Amber asks.

"Home." Bo gets into her car. She's not getting away that easy, though. I hop into the passenger seat. Amber climbs in the back.

"If you want us to stay with you, we will," I say, and Amber nods.

Bo doesn't look at us.

"We don't have to talk about it. We can get ice cream, or go to the movies or something. I'm buying." Amber reaches forward to put a hand on Bo's shoulder.

Bo half smiles, and the air is a little less tense.

"Movies." She starts the car, and we drive off.

✦ ✦ ✦

One thing I can't stand about Halloween season is the horror movies. I hate them with a passion; action movies are more my thing. But Bo likes horror. And today is about Bo, so I suck it up. Big, deep breaths—I don't want to look like a total baby. It's lunchtime, so we're the only ones in the theater. There's still popcorn littering the floor in front of our seats, since the staff probably wasn't expecting anyone to show up.

"Oh my gosh, we're still in our uniforms. We're going to get caught." Amber squeezes my and Bo's arms.

"Shh, we'll be fine," Bo says.

"I'm so nervous. This is great. I love you guys," Amber whispers.

"I love you guys, too," Bo whispers back.

"Why are we whispering?" I say in my outside voice, to remind them we're alone in the theater. They laugh.

Within the first ten minutes of the movie, Bo clasps my hand hard. I jump a little because I wasn't expecting it. It's good for me to think about anything other than the movie to keep from getting too freaked out. So Bo holding my hand would be a nice little distraction, if it wasn't for the fact that I'm freaking out over that, too. Eventually I notice she's also holding Amber's hand. It's not a Thing, I guess. Still, she's *holding my hand.*

Bianca used to hold my hand.

She did it all the time, and it was never a big deal until I came out. She made it seem like I was some kind of monster for letting her hold my hand without telling her I'm gay. Since she wouldn't have done it if she knew, apparently. At the time,

I didn't think anything of it. Friends hold hands sometimes, and I didn't realize I wasn't allowed to do that. Is it so bad that I wanted to give and receive the same level of affection from my friends as everyone else? But since I like girls, every bit of physical contact is taken as sexual. It's lonely.

So when Bo holds my hand without apologizing, I feel like it's a slap right in Bianca's big mouth. Because Bo doesn't give a shit about Bianca's unspoken rules, at least with me and Amber. Gay friends can hold hands, too.

When the movie is over, I realize I've been squeezing Bo's hand so hard I can barely straighten my fingers.

"Oh, sorry," I say as I try to get my hand to look less like a clump of disfigured tentacles.

"It was a team effort." Bo opens and closes both her palms, laughing.

Ditching school for the movies was a good Band-Aid, but I'm guessing the wound is still there, because the next day, Bo isn't in the cafeteria at lunch. She didn't respond to my text asking where she was, so David, Amber, and I go looking for her. She's not out in the courtyard or in any of the bathrooms.

We finally find her in the art room, working on a drawing she hides as soon as we walk in. I take the seat next to her, and Amber and David sit on the other side of the table.

"What are you doing in here?" Amber asks.

"Hiding," Bo says matter-of-factly.

"We'll hide with you." David pulls out his sketchbook and starts drawing. I get mine out too.

Bo smiles, but the air around her is so heavy it's hard to breathe.

"This is why I stopped playing sports, you know," she says. Amber touches Bo's shoulder.

"School dances, too. It's exhausting always having to be aware of whether you're being too much yourself for other people's comfort. People can be such assholes sometimes. I always had to be so conscious of how I came across after I came out. Like, never look at anyone in the locker rooms and stuff. Every girl thought I had a crush on them. It's like, I can't possibly be crushing on every single girl I've ever met, right? I might have liked Jenna, though. I think she knew." Bo puts her head down. She has no idea how real that is for me. Jenna is Bo's Bianca, I think.

"In lak'ech," I say without thinking. I hang around Cesar too much.

"What?" Bo asks.

"Um, it's kind of like saying 'I understand you.'" I don't want Bo to know it's basically my and Cesar's way of saying "same." It's a simplified explanation, but it's not exactly a lie. Just like my whole existence at Slayton.

9

THOU SHALT NOT SELF-SABOTAGE

Up until now, Cesar has managed to convince Mom not to go to his "games." The lie has worked seamlessly the last few weeks. Mom's usually pretty busy with work, so she's been fine not going, but she still cheers him on and wishes him luck on game days. She even goes so far as to make him game-day breakfasts with chorizo chilaquiles and papas with a spicy aroma that smells like guilt, for me at least.

Usually when Mom shows interest in actually going to a game, I remind her how many orders we need to fill, and we get to work. But this is the homecoming game, so jewelry making isn't going to get us out of it. Of course, that means Jamal wants to be there, too. Who knew watching your real boyfriend crash and burn could be a romantic activity with your fake girlfriend?

Tonight's game will be the first time Bo—and the rest of Slayton—will see me wearing my own clothes, so naturally I've been planning my outfit for weeks. Black sandals, a red off-the-shoulder romper, and one of my mom's handmade necklaces. The black, yellow, and red beads hang from the base of my neck, covering my clavicle with an angular pattern, almost making the necklace look like it's a part of the romper. I look cute as hell, if I do say so myself. I wonder what Bo wears when she's not in her uniform. . . .

As my mom and I drive to the game, I still have no idea what Cesar is going to do. He's been really hush-hush about his "plan," which means either he doesn't have one, or it's so brilliant he wants to surprise us. I convince Mom to let us sit at the back of the bleachers, since there's fewer people. Really, it's because I needed an excuse to have a worse view of not-Cesar playing football, just in case. I'm probably more anxious about it than he is, considering my mom's track record. If he doesn't sell it, she'll kill both of us. But especially me. I pretend to be jittery because of the late October wind, and not for fear of my mom's wrath. Still, I have to admit it's kind of nice spending time with her without having to worry about jewelry orders for once.

Bo and Amber find us when the band comes out, drums and trumpets blaring.

"Yami, hi!" Amber yells over the noise, hugging me. She steps aside, revealing Bo's fine self behind her. Bo's hair has been tamed into a low ponytail that shows off a single cross earring, and she's wearing a floral button-up shirt tied off at the waist with cuffed jeans. Eleven out of ten. I can't help but notice her taking in my outfit, too. I yell over the music before anyone notices me checking Bo out, or her (maybe?) checking *me* out.

"Amber, Bo, this is my mom and Jamal, my, uh . . . boy-friend." I still don't like lying to them about Jamal, but I can't explain the situation without outing Cesar.

My mom hugs Amber and Bo. Bo stiffens at the hug like she wasn't expecting it, but Amber isn't fazed. The two of them sit on my right, with Jamal to my left and my mom to his. Two separate worlds that need to stay that way.

When the team comes out on the field, I scan them, looking for Cesar. I can't see faces because of the helmets, but there are only two non-white players. We spot David right away. Number twenty-one. My mom stands up and starts singing.

"Dale, dale, dale! Dale, veintiuno!" She thinks he's Cesar. Looks like he told her that was *his* number. Jamal and I follow my mom's lead and cheer along.

David doesn't take his helmet off at any point, but he does turn around and wave at us a few times. I can't even focus on the game, I'm so anxious. Amber and Bo know to let my mom think what she thinks, since they're in on the lie. Well . . . one of the lies.

"So how do you guys know each other?" Amber asks me and Jamal at halftime.

I hesitate, and Jamal saves us. "We went to Rover together." It's not even a lie. I don't know why I couldn't have just said that.

Before anyone has a chance to ask more questions, I go get nachos. I know I'm dirty for leaving Jamal alone with my mom and friends he doesn't know. Oops.

I weave my way through a group of shirtless guys with our school colors painted on their torsos and faces. One of them taps my shoulder. "Hey, Yamilet, right?" I don't know this guy, and he kind of mangles my name. I've seen him hanging around with Cesar and Hunter, though.

"Yeah, hi," I say.

"Hunter wanted me to invite you to the homecoming after-party tomorrow, in case he missed you after the game."

"Oh, thanks, but I don't know. I probably won't know anyone there," I say, even though I'm sure Cesar will want to go.

"It's fine. You can bring a friend if you want." He shrugs, hands me a folded-up piece of paper, and walks off.

I unfold it to see an address and a smiley face. I stuff it into my pocket, then get my nachos and leave. I'll have to see if Cesar was invited. I wouldn't want to go by myself.

After we win the game, Cesar is the first one out of the locker rooms. He's in David's uniform, sweating profusely. He probably did jumping jacks for the last ten minutes to pull this off. That boy can really sweat. I wonder if he was hiding in the locker room the whole game. . . . My mom ignores the sweat and gives him a huge hug.

"You did so good, mijo! I'm so proud of you!" A few more sweaty kisses. Gross. Cesar and my mom don't seem to mind.

Cesar goes back to change, and Mom goes to wait for us in the car while I wait for him to come back. Hunter comes out first, and comes straight for me, picking me up in a hug. The noise that comes out of my mouth when he lifts me off the ground is something between a gremlin screech and a shrieking pig. Not exactly the cute squeal he was probably expecting. He puts me down.

"What was that noise?" Jamal says, and Bo and Amber giggle, which isn't good for our cover. He's supposed to be acting jealous or something. Good thing Mom went to the car, otherwise she'd definitely grill me over that hug later.

"I was just surprised." I hit Jamal's arm, and then Hunter's. "You scared me!"

"Just wanted to say hi, and thanks for coming." He blushes.

I'm about to introduce Jamal to Hunter as my boyfriend so he's in the loop when David and Cesar walk back out together. David must have been waiting in the locker room for Cesar to give him his uniform back. He's a real one—going an entire game without taking off that helmet couldn't have been too fun. I wonder what Cesar bribed him with. . . .

"Gotta go!" Hunter says, then rushes over to David and Cesar. Cesar slaps Hunter's hand, then jogs over to us like he was tagged in. Weird.

"Coach J wants to give the team a pep talk, so David said not to wait for him," Cesar says. Amber looks disappointed, but Bo gives me a wink.

"Guess we should head home, then," Bo says, linking arms with Amber and leading her toward the parking lot. Cesar and I follow.

Before we get past the food stand, a line of football players blocks our way, Hunter among them. They start lifting up their jerseys one by one, revealing the letters *H-O-M-E-C-O-M-I-N-G-?* underneath. Then they split down the middle and David walks to Amber with a bouquet of flowers.

Amber has a huge dopey smile on, and she's flapping her hands near her face.

"It took you freaking long enough!!" she shouts, then they hug. I guess that's a yes?

I knew David was going to ask her, and I'm happy, but it's just now hitting me that it means Bo and I will be ditching the dance together, just the two of us. The idea of hanging out one-on-one with Bo makes my stomach feel all tight.

Everyone around us cheers for David and Amber, and I let out a sigh of relief. The hardest part is over.

Cesar is going to homecoming with his football friends while I hang out with Bo, but I promised him I'd go with him to the after-party. It's sweet that Jamal trusts Cesar to party without him. I mean, it should be a given when you're in a relationship to trust your partner, but I don't know a lot of people who do. Maybe one day we'll mature and stop feeling jealousy, but for now, Cesar and Jamal are ahead of the curve.

Bo's ugly-cute dogs jump on me as soon as she opens the door, and they follow us upstairs. Bo and Amber have a tradition of watching horror movies with one-star ratings instead of going to dances. Even with low ratings, I get scared easily. If there's blood or monsters or demons or serial killers, it's scary. Period. I find myself staring at Bo's hand, waiting for her to get scared too and reach for mine.

To my disappointment, she doesn't. I guess it's not "scary" enough for Bo to want to grab my hand for comfort. And I'm not about to make that move. I'd rather Bo not think I'm as squeamish as I am. Without Bo's hand, I have to get creative to keep from pissing my pants at every low-budget jump scare. I imagine all the bone cracks and flesh-cutting are sound effects made by biting into carrots and crunching lettuce. It's a sort of comforting thought. I try to distract myself by thinking about how I'll convince Bo to come to the party. I'm happy to get my mind off the movie, so I bring it up the minute the credits roll.

"I got invited to the after-party," I say, trying to sound extra casual.

"Are you gonna go?" Bo asks through a mouthful of popcorn.

"Yeah. You should come, too! They said I could bring someone. . . ." I don't know if it sounds like I'm asking her to come as my date. It feels like it does, but I don't mean for it to sound like that.

"Amber invited me, too. But I don't really want to go. Besides, I'm pretty sure they meant a boy."

"They didn't specify gender. Come on, it'll be fun!"

"It's not my crowd." Bo sinks into the couch. I frown. It's my shitty version of a puppy face. She's unaffected. I can't blame her, since there's a good chance Jenna will be there. And there's no way I'd go to a party Bianca might be at.

"Okay, well, if you change your mind, it'd be awesome if you came."

Bo sits up and smizes at me. Maybe she's a little affected.

"Why do you want me to come so bad?" She leans toward me. It's a subtle lean, barely an inch, but I notice it.

Because I like hanging out with you. Because you'll make me feel more comfortable. Because you can make any situation more fun. Because I think you're pretty, and cool, and fun to be around. Because I'm gay, and I think I might like you.

"I don't know . . ." is all I manage to say. Bo tilts her head, and I think she's onto me. For all my reservations about eye contact, her eyes are hard to look away from. Her irises are dark and big, like black holes. They're sucking me in, and I don't know what will happen if I let myself get pulled in too close. There's no turning back once you're caught in a black hole. I find myself leaning in. Is she leaning, too? I can't tell. We're way too close.

"I'm straight," I blurt out. *Real smooth, Yami.*

". . . Okay?" Bo crosses her arms. Yeah, I don't think she was leaning, too.

"Sorry, I thought . . ." Fuck, why would I say that? She already knows I "have a boyfriend." It was completely unnecessary.

There's a pause, then Bo throws her head back and laughs.

"You thought what? That I liked you? Not every lesbian is going to have a thing for you just because you're a girl. Are you serious right now? Get over yourself."

"No, I know! I shouldn't have said that. I'm sorry." I try not to let my voice crack. If she did like me, I've clearly sabotaged that now. But obviously she didn't. I know that's supposed to be a good thing because I am Not Gay. But it sucks.

"What did I do this time? Was I supposed to sit on the other couch? Should I have canceled when Amber did? Am I not supposed to even *look* at you? Why am I always the one to have to walk on eggshells to keep everyone from thinking I'm some kind of creep?" She's raising her voice now, and her eyes are starting to get shiny.

"No, I . . . you didn't do anything wrong, Bo." My voice shakes, and I hate myself for making her feel how I feel all the time. Like a predator.

"Whatever. I have a girlfriend anyways. Thought you knew." For some reason those words burrow into my ears and make my vision blur.

"Oh . . . that's . . . that's great. Who's your girlfriend?" I shouldn't be asking about that right now. I should still be apologizing.

"Her name's Jamie. Not that it's your business," she says coldly. Then I remember the girl with blue hair from that dating app Amber showed me.

I shake my head to get back into the moment. I fucked up. Focus on that. "I'm sorry, Bo. Seriously, I don't know why I said that. You didn't do anything wrong," I plead.

"Don't you have a party to go to?" It's a not-so-subtle way of telling me to get out.

"Um, yeah, I should go pick up Cesar. . . . Are we good?" It's selfish, but I just want her to tell me she doesn't hate me. That I won't be alone again after this.

"We're good." She gets up and walks to her room instead of walking me out like she normally would.

I don't think we're good.

10

THOU SHALT NOT DRINK AND CALL

Even though I didn't want to come earlier, I could use a party right now. Anything to forget about how Bo hates me. How I totally fucked up our friendship. About how Bo has a girlfriend who probably never made her feel as bad as I just made her feel. The bass of the party music pulls me out of my wallowing. We can't even see the house yet, but the music is *loud*. Parked cars line the street, so we have to park on the next street down. When we finally get inside, it's obvious that a good number of people are already tipsy or completely drunk. Some of them must have pregamed at the dance. Even sober I could get lost in this house—it's like Bo's on steroids, with super-high ceilings, huge rooms, and winding double staircases.

"Take a shot with me! It'll help loosen up that stick in your ass." Cesar grabs my arm, and I jump. I guess I've been a little stiff since I left Bo's.

"I can't, I'm *driving*!" I shove his shoulder. Still, I let him drag me to the kitchen, where we run into Hunter.

"AYYYEE!" Hunter shouts, raising a glass at us and almost

spilling it. Then he gives Cesar his usual enthusiastic dap.

"What up, what up," Cesar murmurs while pouring himself a shot.

Hunter nods to me. "I thought you wouldn't be able to make it, since you couldn't come to the dance."

"I had plans, but I'm free now." I give him my nicest smile. I hope he's not mad at me for not going to the dance with him.

"Well, I'm glad you could make it." He smiles back and touches my arm. I think we're flirting. Or at least, he is.

Hunter hands me a shot glass, and I wave it away.

"I'm the designated driver, unfortunately."

"If you want to drink, you guys can hang out here until you're sober. Stay the night if you have to. You won't be the only ones."

Cesar raises his eyebrows at me like Hunter offered us his parents' fortune, but I'm nervous. The only time I ever had alcohol was at Bianca's birthday party last year. I didn't even drink when I went to a *party* party freshman year. But it's hard to say no now, as long as Cesar's staying the night, too. It's a special occasion. Of the *I said something so stupid to Bo, I need to drink to stop thinking about it* variety. Real healthy, I know.

I send my mom a quick text.

Yami: staying the night at Bo's.

I ignore how the lie makes me feel guilty for more reasons than one. Hunter holds a shot glass of Vodka to my face, and I stick my tongue in it to see how bad it tastes. It makes me gag.

He laughs. "It tastes like shit. That's why you drink it fast.

Here." He tilts my chin up. It feels like one of those really forced Heterosexual Moments in every movie ever, where a guy makes unnecessary physical contact while teaching a girl something extremely simple.

And with that, I have an idea.

I'll try out being straight for tonight. Commit to the lie I told Bo, or try to. If I can prove I'm straight, I won't have to shout about it like an asshole. Secret Agent Yami on a mission.

I let Hunter tilt my head back, and he hands me the shot glass. He plugs my nose. I don't know if it's supposed to be romantic or whatever, but it's fucking weird.

"Okay, now just chug it like that."

I swallow the guilt down with the alcohol. I don't think plugging my nose even helped, because whatever he gave me was disgusting. Then he hands me a lemon, and I bite into it. He pours me a full drink in a red cup this time.

"This one will taste good, I promise." I take a sip, and he's right. It tastes like vanilla Coke.

"Ooh, teach *me* now!" Cesar claps his hands and flutters his lashes, all dramatic. It finally reminds Hunter I'm not the only one in the kitchen with him, so I'm grateful. Hunter blushes, then pours Cesar a drink, and we all clink our red cups.

I burp. Hunter burps back at me. How romantic.

I already feel a little lighter. Alcohol makes pretending to be straight a little less intimidating. I take a big swig of my drink before I grab Hunter's hand and pull him over to the living room, aka dance floor. I'm not a dancer or anything, but in my family, if you don't have rhythm, you learn real quick or you get clowned on. Some of my tíos are allowed to not know how to dance, if they're drunk enough. They'd fit right in with this crowd.

Hunter puts his hands on my hips and rests his head on my shoulder, as if we know each other like that. I almost feel bad for dancing with another guy while I have a "boyfriend," but Jamal isn't here, and I need to practice being straight with some-one. But Hunter isn't moving on beat with the music, so it's hard for me to work with him. And a minute in, I'm already bored. He must be catching on that I'm not feeling it, because he shouts into my ear over the music.

"I'll give you the tour!" He grabs my hand and pulls me away.

The music is loud enough to be bumping pretty much any-where you go. Some people are dancing inside. Outside they're chilling and smoking. Hunter keeps looking back at me like he wants my approval, like he's nervous I won't like his house or something. I smile awkwardly and keep following.

Before I know it, we're in Hunter's room, and the door is closed. Of course the tour would end here. I kick myself for not having seen this coming. He starts going through one of his drawers. My stomach tightens. Is he looking for a condom?

"What are you doing?"

"One second," he mumbles, and keeps rummaging. He starts pulling something out.

"I'm not going to have sex with you," I say before he has a chance to embarrass himself. He whirls around, with a deer-in-the-headlights look and a comic book in his hand.

"What? I'm not—I'm a . . ." He looks around as if there were other people in the room who could hear him. "Um, I'm a virgin. . . . I mean, I would want to get to know you first. I was just gonna show you this."

My chest gets heavy from embarrassment. It's a comic book. With spies.

"I saw that you like spy stuff, so I thought you'd like it. . . ." He holds it out for me with his eyes fixed on the floor. His face is still burning red.

"Oh . . . sorry. Thanks." First Bo and now Hunter. I really need to stop assuming people are coming on to me. Maybe I do need to get over myself.

"For what? You can take it if you want." Hunter's gaze slowly moves from the floor up to my eyes, and he smiles, then coughs. "The book! I meant the book, not my . . . um . . . I like you, but I'm not ready for sex."

I snort-laugh and take the comic to keep him from imploding. I put it in my bag and give him a quick hug. Except Hunter doesn't get the hint that it was supposed to be quick, and he holds on a few seconds too long. I start pulling away, but before I know it, his mouth is on my mouth. I let out a startled yelp and hop backward.

"I'm gay!" I say, then my hand shoots over my mouth. He rubs his head.

"Oh my God, I seriously misread this situation." He takes a step back.

My surroundings blur together, and I don't know if it's the

alcohol or that I just came out. I don't realize I'm hyperventilating until he puts a hand on my shoulder. "Hey, don't worry. I
won't tell anyone, okay? Your trust means a lot to me."

But I don't trust Hunter. I barely even *know* Hunter. What
the fuck is wrong with me?

"Thanks . . . I, uh, have to pee." I grab my drink, then chan-
nel my inner Hunter and run away.

I thought having to pee was an excuse, but I actually really
have to pee. I drink on the toilet, finishing off my cup before I
realize how hard the alcohol is hitting me. Something about sitting on a toilet makes me want to relive the cringiest moments
of the day. My brain runs wild and betrays me. I told Hunter
I'm gay. I told Bo I'm *straight*. He'll probably blow my cover. She
probably hates me. For some reason, I care more about the latter
right now. I get out my phone to text her.

"Hi, Dad!" I giggle at my screen saver before focusing on
texting Bo. In my head, my screen-saver dad moves to give me
a thumbs-up and says, *Go get her*. With his encouragement, I
send her two texts.

Yami: Heyy

Yami: I'm really really sorry

With my phone still in hand, I scroll Instagram for a bit, but
I can't help but think about Jamie, and how much I want to be
her. Maybe I should dye my hair blue . . . or was it purple? I
wonder if you're allowed to dye your hair at Catholic school.
Probably not.

What color was her hair again? I need to know. Not because

I want to stalk Bo's girlfriend on Instagram, but because . . .
I might want to dye my hair one day, or something. I start
scrolling through the 224 people Bo is following, looking for a
Jamie, but I give up when Jamie isn't one of the first fifty or so.

I get up and wash my hands. My reflection startles me, and
I knock the soap over. It's just me, though. Nothing to worry
about. I have to focus hard on the mirror to make any sense of
my face. I tug at my lip, sizing up whether I'd look as cool as
Jamie does with a lip ring. I poke the glass.

"You're gonna do such a good job." I don't even know what
I'm talking about. I giggle to myself, then go to find someone
I know.

Cesar is sitting on the couch, talking on his phone. I climb
over the back of the couch and fall onto the cushion.

"I looooove you," he mumbles into the phone. I'm guessing
he's talking to Jamal. I snatch his phone out of his hand and
hold it to my ear.

"Sorry, good sisters don't let their brothers make drunk
phone calls!" I say, and Jamal laughs on the other line.

"Okay, take care of him for me." Then he hangs up.

"Rude." Cesar pouts.

"It's for your own good," I say. And not because I think he'll
embarrass himself to Jamal, but because he might accidentally
out himself at this party if he's talking all lovey with his boyfriend.

Cesar rests his head in my lap, and I gulp some of his drink
since I ran out of mine. I absentmindedly start stroking Cesar's

hair like Doña Violeta did when I was younger. I really miss that sometimes.

"Do you think depression ever goes away?" Cesar slurs.

Whoa. It's like he read my mind about Doña Violeta. I think about it for a second before answering. "I don't know if it ever goes away . . . but I think it gets better. With like, coping skills, and support from other people, you know?" At least, I hope Doña Violeta will get better with time. It breaks my heart seeing her so sad every day.

Cesar looks thoughtfully into the distance. "Yeah, I hope you're right."

But before we go any deeper, he hops off the couch and runs over to play beer pong.

While I'm sitting alone on the couch, some guy I don't recognize takes the spot next to me. He must not go to Slayton.

"Hey, what are you doing over here lookin' all lonely?" He's close enough to my face that I can smell his stank breath. He licks his lips. I purse mine. Even if I didn't already fail my "act straight" mission, I still have standards, and this guy is not it.

"I'm Connor," he says.

I nod but don't say anything.

"Do you have a name?"

"Yamilet." *Please go away.*

"Ohhh, *Yamilet* . . . gorgeous name. So exotic. Do you speak Spanish?"

Here we go.

"Mhm," I say while I look over his head to see if I spot anyone I know.

"That's hot. Can you say my name in Spanish?"

Is this guy serious? I have to resist the urge to smack him. Instead I give him a deadpan stare so he knows he looks like a fool.

"Connor," I say, purposely sounding as white as possible. He laughs.

"You're funny. And you're pretty, too, you know that?"

"Yeah, I know," I mumble.

"Um, okay." He looks annoyed now.

I roll my eyes. It's like he's expecting me to disagree, but for what? Maybe he wants me to say thanks, but all he's done for me is make me want to break my nonviolent streak.

Finally, *finally* I see someone I know. Emily is dancing with Hunter, but I'd rather be around them than this guy right now.

"Okay, bye!" I ditch Connor and go to them. Emily might be friends with two of my least favorite people in the world, after Bianca, but I'm too drunk to care right now.

I almost feel jealous. I was supposed to be pretending to be straight tonight. If I hadn't ruined it, I could still be dancing with Hunter right now. Emily stops when she sees me and ditches Hunter to give me a hug. Her dark brown hair is curled in a bob instead of her usual barely-holding-it-together ponytail.

"I'm so happy you made it!" She pulls away from the hug and strokes my hair the way a straight girl does. If I was sober, I might not have hummed out loud. I can't help it, it feels *good*. If I was sober, I probably wouldn't have even let her touch me at all. Right now, though, it doesn't even matter. She grabs my hand and leads me to the kitchen.

"You're taking a shot with me, okay?" She pours two out as she says it.

I take it a lot easier this time. I must be a lightweight, because the room is spinning now, in a good way. Like the teacups at Disneyland. I would imagine, at least. I've never been there.

"I wanna go to Disneyland," I mumble. I don't think Emily hears me. I pour myself another whipped cream Vodka and coke.

"You know, I used to be intimidated by you. But you're really cool." Her words are slurring together a tiny bit.

"Really? I thought you thought I was cute?" Or was it Jenna who thought I was cute? Either way, I'm not the least bit intimidating. I try not to let it bug me that she maybe doesn't actually think I'm adorable.

"You *are* cute!" she squeals, and I sigh in relief. I knew it. I *am* cute. She doesn't elaborate on the "intimidated" comment.

"You know," I say after taking another swig, "I used to think you were cool, but now I'm intimidated by you."

"Why?" She frowns.

I shrug. I don't think I have the capacity to have a serious conversation about who Emily chooses to surround herself with.

"Well, I'm not scary, I promise." She smiles and grabs my hand, then pulls me back to the dance floor. She throws her arms over my shoulders and clasps her fingers behind my head. How is this not scary???

"Want to make Hunter jealous?" she whispers in my ear, and before I answer, her hips close the space between us and we're basically grinding. I wonder if Jamie and Bo dance like this. Probably not, since Bo doesn't like dances. This is straight-girl grinding, though. All for Hunter's entertainment, not mine. Hunter gives me a thumbs-up, like he's proud of me. I wish I could say I get any enjoyment out of dancing with Emily for attention, but I feel like I'm on fire the entire time. Like at any moment someone will realize what a fraud I am. If she knew I was gay, she would never dance with me like this.

Before I know it, Jenna comes up behind Emily and grinds with her. Karen gets behind Jenna, and Karen's boyfriend is behind her, and it's this whole grinding train I want no part of.

"I have to pee!" I shout, and escape to the backyard. I wonder if they think I'm about to pee outside. I don't think I'm quite that drunk yet, though.

As I'm walking out, I hear a chorus of boys cheering, and I turn to see Jenna and Emily *making out*. I can't name the feeling it gives me to see that. My head starts spinning again.

I find my way to the backyard and lie down on the grass to make the world come back into focus. Why do straight girls get to kiss in front of everyone but I can't? I close my eyes. I don't even care what's going on around me.

Last time I was this drunk, I was the one drunk-kissing a straight girl. Bianca didn't kiss like a straight girl, though. But I guess I should have known better, since it was spin the bottle. When the bottle pointed at me, Bianca gave me this *look*.

She licked her bottom lip and smiled with a slow blink. I don't know anything about relationships or sex or anything, but that was the most suggestive look anyone's ever given me. I don't know if the look I gave her back gave away how desperately I wanted her to kiss me. She didn't hesitate. She crawled over and open-mouth kissed me like she meant it. I really thought she meant it.

But no, Bianca's just one of those straight girls who kisses girls when there are cute boys around to see.

My phone buzzes and I realize I'm still lying by myself on the grass. It must take me a solid two minutes to get my phone out of my pocket. It's a text from Bo. I gasp in excitement.

Bo: I may have overreacted . . .

I put all my energy into sending a text that doesn't give away how drunk I am. It takes a few minutes, but I manage to send one with no typos.

Yami: You may not have.

I put my phone back in my pocket and close my eyes again, focusing on the blaring music from inside. I don't know how long I'm lying down when I hear two someones lie down on either side of me.

"Whoa, look at the stars," Amber says. I open my eyes. It's her and David. Pretty stars. Prettier here than back home.

"Well, that's bullshit," I say.

"What's bullshit?" David asks.

"Rich people even get better stars." My voice cracks, and I think I'm about to cry. It's not fair. I want pretty stars, too.

David nods like he knows exactly how I feel, and Amber holds my hand without saying anything. I know the rules say I'm not supposed to let straight girls hold my hand, but it makes me feel better, okay? The rules are bullshit.

The music stops, and I'm curious enough to sit back up. There's a chorus of shushing, then Cesar runs up to me and yanks me to my feet.

"Cops!" The adrenaline rush that comes with that word sobers me up enough to run with him. It's a huge yard, and it feels like we're running on a merry-go-round, but I don't let that slow me down.

The wall at the edge of the backyard is too high for me to jump in my condition. Cesar tries to give me a lift, but we both fall over. He's as drunk as I am. We scramble behind a bush near the wall and hide instead. I can see flashing lights over the wall, and I think I'm gonna be sick. I try not to think about what might happen next, or what happened last time we were in this situation. . . . I plug my ears and shut my eyes as if it'll make the cops go away.

As I catch my breath, I realize we're the only ones who ran. Everyone else is just quietly waiting to get breathalyzed and arrested. Not us.

After a minute, the music comes back on, just a bit quieter. People start dancing and smoking and drinking again. My head hurts.

"Guess they left. Perks of being on the north side, apparently." Cesar dusts himself off, then holds his hand out to help me up, but I don't take it. I lean my head back on the wall and look up at the pretty rich-people stars. Everything is so different over here. I don't even try to stop the tears from dripping down my face.

Cesar sits back down with me. I don't have to say anything. I know he gets it. I only went to one other "party" party before. He was there. Cops showed up there, too. They didn't have a warrant, but they broke the door down and came in anyway. I watched one of them bash my friend Junior's head into the concrete floor of his garage before I ran away. Not everyone was so lucky. Anyone who didn't get away got MICs, even if they weren't drinking. Junior's mom got deported, even though she didn't know about the party.

And here they just asked us to turn the music down. No one is getting arrested or deported. No kid is getting their head bashed into the floor. The party is still fucking happening.

"Yami? Where are you?" Amber calls out, jogging over in our general direction, with David right behind her.

I wipe my eyes and step out from behind the bush. So does Cesar.

"Here."

"We thought you left!" David says.

"Nope. But I think I'm gonna go."

"But you're drunk." Cesar's words slur as he points an accusatory finger at me.

"I'm fine. I'll come get you tomorrow." I enunciate as clearly as I can to prove my point, but he and Amber are both too messed up to stop me. I make my way straight through everyone without saying bye or acknowledging a single one of them.

"La mee-grah, la mee-grah!" Say My Name in Spanish guy calls out to me in a forced accent, and cracks himself up. La migra—immigration. As if it wasn't obvious to everyone else already that it was only the two Mexican kids who ran at the first sign of cops.

I turn around and walk straight toward him, fists clenched. If Cesar heard him, he would have clocked him in his throat. He didn't hear, but someone needs to punch this guy. I don't feel in control of myself right now. It feels like a dream, and I'm outside my own body watching myself march up to him and punch him right in the nose.

"OHHHHHHH!!!!" a bunch of guys yell when he falls to the ground and doesn't get up. Two of them bow down to me, like they're grateful I just laid out their friend. I turn back around and keep walking.

I think Hunter is trying to call out for me as I pass, but I keep going. I feel everyone staring at me. I don't stop, and they part for me like the Red Sea. When I make it to the privacy of my mom's car, I realize that if I drive right now, I might not make it home. I don't think I could walk a straight line, let alone drive in one.

I'll wait.

It's hard to sit and wait without getting in your head too much. I try focusing on the distant pulsing sensation in my hand, instead of thinking about the alternatives. Like Junior getting his head smashed into the cement. His mom getting deported. My dad getting deported . . .

I miss my dad so much. I miss his hugs, and his constant reassurance that I was going to turn out okay. When I was little, I could go to him about anything. He would build me up and turn me right back around to face whatever. I want to tell him about tonight. About the cops, and that I punched someone. I want to tell him about Bo, and our fight. And that I like her even though she has a girlfriend and thinks I'm straight.

What would I have to lose by coming out to my dad, anyway? Even if he hates me for it, it's not like I'm relying on him to survive like I am with my mom. He would never hate me, though. He'll probably make this whole thing a lot easier. He'll know exactly what to say to make me stop feeling like such a piece of shit. I send him two texts. Two things I wish I had the strength to say more often.

Yami: I love you.

Yami: I'm gay.

I know you're not supposed to call or text anyone when you're drunk, but I've been wanting to tell him for so long. I guess I'm worse at being straight than I thought. I couldn't even keep it up for one night. Not even a few hours. But I already feel better knowing I can talk to my dad about it soon.

While I'm making drunk confessions, I might as well call Bo. No way I'm going to regret this tomorrow. I get her voice mail, which sober me would have taken as an act of kindness from God himself. But drunk me doesn't give a shit about second chances from the universe. I leave a message.

"Um . . . hi." I pause for way too long. "I punched someone. It was cool, I guess. You may be surprised to hear it was my first time inflicting violence on another human." I don't know why I'm talking so proper. Maybe to make the idea of punching someone in the face sound less violent. It doesn't last, though.

"Am I a scary person, do you think? I think people assume I'm more scrappier than I am. Oh, the party sucked. I should have stayed with you. If I wasn't such a dick, maybe you would have let me stay there instead. That would have been better, I think. I just wanna say, you don't make me uncomfortable. I make me uncomfortable. You're a cool person. You're soooo cool and pretty and funny and way too good for me. Your girlfriend is soooooo lucky. Please, Bo, you need to stop doing your cute eye smile thing to me, because I'm literally dying inside. Fuck you, seriously, you're ruining everything. I like you a lot, do you know that? I don't think you get it. I *liiiiike* you! I like being with you. I mean, not *with* you, with you. Obviously. Because I'm straight, remember?" I start laughing, and I can't stop. My laugh is worse than my mom's right now.

"JUST KIDDING I'M GAY AS FUUUCK!" I'm practically screaming from laughing so hard. There are tears coming out of my eyes. She's gonna think I'm hilarious. I hang up.

My phone buzzes. It's not Bo or my dad, though.

Cesar: LUCHADORA YAMI!!!!!! He's STILL sleep! Didn't know you had it in you 😆

I grin and recline my seat all the way back so I can get

comfortable, then curl up on my side.

I respond that it's about time he put some respect on my name, but I only say it in my own head. I used up all my texting energy on Dad. How long does it take for drunkenness to wear off? Hopefully not too long. I feel like I'll throw up if I move, so I close my eyes.

It only takes a second for an overwhelming feeling of *what the fuck is wrong with me* to consume my entire being.

Suddenly I have enough texting energy to send both Bo and my dad one more. I text them the same thing.

Yami: LMAO JK

I text Bo again, because maybe she hasn't heard the voice mail yet.

Yami: I'm drnk please donnt listen to the message

Once damage control is done, I close my eyes again, and fall asleep.

11

THOU SHALT BEAR FALSE WITNESS AGAINST DRUNKEN VOICE MAILS

The buzzing of my phone almost doesn't wake me up. It takes me a second to realize I'm still in my mom's car. When the buzzing doesn't stop, I get a little annoyed before it hits me that it might be my dad calling. I have to squint to see the name on my screen. It's almost three a.m., which means I wasn't asleep more than ten minutes.

It's Bo. Beautiful Bo.

"Heyyyyyyyy, Bo . . . Bo-nita," I croak, then start laughing. Bonita. I'm so clever.

"Um, hi. Sorry I didn't answer. I was asleep. Are you okay?"

"Ummmm, no, I am not okay. . . . Have you ever seen poor-people stars, Bo? They suck. Also, I punched someone!" I gasp like it was my first time learning about the punch.

"You're not driving, are you?" She ignores my starry insight. And the other thing. How rude.

"Maybe, I don't know."

"No, you're not. Where are you?"

The next thing I know, I'm in the passenger seat of Bo's car. I'm pretty sure I'm a time traveler, because I just skipped whatever happened between that conversation and now. Dope.

Bo is asking me something, and I have to strain to make sense of it. I groan.

"Where do you live?"

I giggle. Nice try, sexy demon. No way am I giving up my secret identity.

Another time skip.

I'm hunched over a toilet, throwing up. It's not my bathroom. Someone is holding my hair back.

Time skip.

"Where is it?" I'm crawling around in Bo's room, looking under her bed.

"Where is what?"

"The portrait you made of me! I need it." Need to find that portrait. Need to . . .

Time skip.

Bo is helping me into a bed that isn't mine. It's not Bo's, either.

"You can sleep here. I'll be in my room if you need anything, okay?"

I'm in her guest room.

"I hope your girlfriend is the nicest to you ever. You deserve someone better," I mumble.

"Thanks . . ."

"Is she nice to you?"

"She is. It hasn't been that long, but I like her a lot," Bo admits, and I push down the jealousy. I should be happy for her.

"I'm glad. I bet she's a lot nicer than Jenna," I say, and Bo looks down. "And me. I'm sorry I wasn't very nice to you. Why are you so nice to me?" I don't understand Bo. She comes across as a stone-cold badass at school. But she adopts ugly dogs and takes care of her drunk friend who she has every right to hate.

"It's good karma." She shrugs, but I think she simplified it for me, like I simplified "in lak'ech." "Good night."

She starts to walk toward the door. But it's cold in here, and I don't want her to leave. What I really want is a hug.

"Noooo . . ." I reach my arms out toward her. "Cuddle."

She laughs a little. "Seriously?"

I do my best eye smile, hoping it will make Bo melt into my arms the way her smizes make me want to melt into hers.

"Do you have something in your eyes?" she asks. I stop smizing.

"I'm cold," I pout. Instead of cuddling me, she puts another blanket over me.

When I close my eyes, Dream Bo is right there in bed with me to keep me warm.

Dream Bo is a little stiff, so I grab her arms and pull them around me the way I want to be cuddled. I'm the little spoon, of course. I hum and hug her forearm, which is my pillow. Bo may or may not still think I'm straight, but Dream Bo knows everything. I let myself pretend for now that she's real, and doesn't have a nice girlfriend, and that cuddling was her idea. I pretend she likes me, too. And this gay thing. I think I could maybe get used to it.

I wake up alone with a headache that is straight-up supervillain, puppy-killing levels of evil. The sun creeping in from the cracks between the blinds is too bright. But this is the comfiest bed I've ever been in. I never want to leave it.

It takes me a minute to remember how I got here. To be honest, there's a lot I can't remember, which freaks me out.

I use all my strength to sit up. There's a water bottle and Advil sitting on the nightstand. Bo really thought of everything. I take a couple of Advil and gulp some water. Two seconds later, I've downed the entire water bottle. I don't think I had any water last night. Maybe that's why my hangover is so bad.

After soaking up a few more moments in the bed that I'm sure is meant for royalty, I get up. I can't avoid facing Bo forever. Especially being in her house. I open the guest room door to see her in the upstairs living room staring at her phone screen, blushing and grinning. Maye if I stop sabotaging myself, one day I could have a girlfriend that makes me blush at my phone.

"Hey," I say.

"Hey." She puts her phone down. "You feeling okay?"

"I'm a little sore, and I have a headache, but yeah, I'm good."

"That's good. Sounds like the party was fun?"

"Not really . . . thanks for getting me." I sit on the opposite side of the couch.

"No problem."

I don't say anything for a bit. She looks back down at her screen.

"So, you're not mad at me anymore?" I finally ask. She looks up.

"I was, but I got over it."

I sigh in relief. "I'm really sorry."

"I know. You told me a million times last night." She laughs. I don't remember that. I wonder what else I told her. . . .

"Shit. Did you listen to that voice mail?"

"What voice mail?" She unlocks her phone.

"It's nothing! Seriously, just drunk rambling. You should delete it. . . ."

"Ohhh, *this* voice mail?" She turns her phone to reveal my unlistened-to message, and she *presses play.*

I lunge for the phone, but she's too quick. She jumps off the couch and I have to chase her around the living room table, trying to get it. The message is playing in the background, and I'm yelling over it so she can't hear the voice mail.

"Um . . . hi. I punched someone. . . ."

"Oh, I *heard* about this! He deserved it." Bo laughs.

"Stop! Give it to me!" I hop over the table and she dives out of the way, laughing and throwing pillows at me like this is a game and not like my biggest secret is at stake.

"Oh, the party sucked. I should have stayed with you. . . ."

"LA LA LA LA LA!" I shout, trying desperately to cover the noise of the message. I finally tackle her and manage to pin her phone-holding hand to the floor. I keep shouting over the phone. I can barely hear my voice in the message. Maybe she can't. I grab the phone and scramble to delete the message before it's too late.

". . . I don't think you get it. I liiiiike—"

Deleted. I drop the phone and fall onto the floor.

"Jesus, what the hell?" Bo rubs her hand where I slid it against the carpet. I feel bad for giving her carpet burn, but it's the price I had to pay to keep her from finding out.

"Sorry. It's just embarrassing. You know . . . drunk talk . . ."

Bo snorts, then hops to her feet and reaches out her hand to help me up. I let out a sigh of relief and take it. When she pulls me up, the headache pulls down. A grunt escapes my mouth.

"Come on, I'm starving."

I can smell bacon grease. We go down to the kitchen, where Bo's mom is eating, and her dad is cooking. It's the first time I've seen Bo's mom at the house. Her dad serves us both bacon and pancakes.

"Good morning!" her mom says. "You must be Yamilet?"

I nod and extend my hand. "Nice to meet you."

"I'd like to talk to you about last night," she says with a hand on her husband's shoulder.

"Mom, really?" Bo starts, but her dad cuts her off with a hand gesture.

"Oh . . . okay," I say. Did Bo tell them what happened?

"You did the right thing, Yamilet. We're glad you called Bo to pick you up instead of driving home. It takes a lot of courage to ask for help." She squeezes my shoulder with her free hand.

"You're not mad?" So they know I was drinking. They know Bo left at three a.m. to get me. They know I stayed the night because I was too drunk to let Bo know where I live. And they're proud of me?

"We'd much rather you inconvenience someone than end up dead," Bo's dad responds.

"Oh . . . well, um, thanks. For letting me stay here. And for the pancakes," I say, trying not to let on that my face is burning right now from embarrassment. I don't mention that I actually had no intention of asking for help. I only called Bo to make that drunken confession. I'll let them think I'm responsible, though.

"We can't stop you from doing what you're going to do, but we hope you're doing it safely."

"She's fine, Dad," Bo interrupts, trying again to save me from the lecture, but her mom continues.

"Make sure you're always with someone you trust. And don't ever accept a drink from a stranger. Here." She takes my phone from where it was sitting on the table. I fight the urge to stop her. "I'm putting my number in here. If you ever find yourself in a situation where you need help, and you don't feel comfortable calling your own parents, give me a call. You won't get in trouble, but I'd rather an adult be the one to come get you."

"Thanks . . ." I don't know what else to say. Bo's parents are really cool.

I start eating so I have something to do with my hands, and realize how hungry I am. Probably because I threw up the complete contents of my soul last night.

After we eat, Bo drops me off at my mom's car at Hunter's house so I can pick up Cesar and go home.

"Sorry about my parents. They're a little much," Bo says, adjusting her grip on the wheel.

"No, they're sweet. If it was my mom, she would have killed me." I shudder, imagining my mom's reaction to finding out I drank at a party and needed to be picked up. "Wait, they're not gonna tell her, are they?"

"Nah, they're pretty committed to being the *cool* parents." Bo rolls her eyes at the word "cool." I let out an anxious breath. At least my mom doesn't have to know. And with the embarrassing voice mail gone forever, there's only one more piece of evidence to cover up. I need to talk to my dad.

Between brutal hangover naps, I must have tried calling him ten times. No answer. I had to tell my mom I'm sick because there's no way I can work like this. Seriously. Why do people drink? Luckily, she doesn't want me getting my germs on her jewelry. Lord help me if a customer gets "sick" because of me.

Dad's probably busy or something. It hasn't even been twenty-four hours, so it's a little too early to panic. My body and head hurt too much to really panic anyway. Maybe he hasn't even gotten my text yet. If I flood his texts with other things, maybe it will get buried? Maybe he never has to see it at all.

But part of me wants him to see it. He said I could always be honest with him, and I was. If there's one person I feel like I can tell everything to, it's my dad. I love Cesar, but he doesn't always give the best advice. I decide this is a good thing. The main thing that could make it all go sideways is if he tells Mom, but I doubt he will. He's always been good with keeping my business between us. He's never gotten me in trouble with

Mom before. Just to be safe, though, I send him one more text.

Yami: Please don't tell Mami. She wouldn't understand like you.

I feel relieved getting it off my chest. I just wish he would freaking *respond*. Maybe he needs some time to process it. I can be patient. I can be so patient.

"Yami, wake up. I need a favor." Cesar shakes my arm and I swat at him. If it was up to me, I would have slept the entire day and through the night.

"Cesar, *ya!* What do you want?"

"Jamal got kicked out. Come on." He pulls me out of bed before I can answer. And it sounds urgent enough that I let him.

Jamal and Mom are sitting at the table. He has a busted lip and a swollen cheek. I hear the end of a conversation between the two of them.

"I didn't know where else to go. . . ."

"Oh my God, are you okay?" I reach for his swollen cheek, and he flinches.

"Yeah, I'm good," he mumbles without looking up at any of us.

"He is *not* good." Mom sounds mad. "Mijo, who did this to you?"

Jamal keeps his eyes low and doesn't say anything. Cesar is standing back a few feet. He's shaking, like he's trying to hold himself back from getting too close right now. I guess he doesn't want Mom to see how upset he is.

"Answer me when I ask you a question," Mom says in her scary voice.

"It was my stepdad," Jamal mutters, looking at the table. Oh no . . . he must have finally come out. . . .

"Ay Dios mío." Mom does the sign of the cross, then puts a gentle hand on Jamal's cheek. "You're staying here for a few days, okay, mijo? I don't want you on the streets."

"Really?" Jamal finally looks up. His chin is quivering.

"Don't be getting so happy now. You won't be allowed in Yamilet's room, obviously."

"He can sleep in my room," Cesar offers. Even though I still feel terrible, it's hard not to laugh at that.

"Good. You keep these two out of trouble, all right?"

Cesar salutes her, and Jamal does a terrible job of hiding his busted grin.

12

THOU SHALT NOT COVET THY BROTHER'S LIFE

Jamal makes himself as useful as he can while he's here. He helps us clean, and since he has his own car, he offered to take Cesar and me to and from school while he's with us. Which is kind of a huge offer, since it's so far away. Sure, it means we have to get dropped off early so Jamal has time to make it to Rover, but it saves my mom the trip. She keeps saying she could get used to having someone so helpful around. And after a few days of riding with Jamal, I could get used to it, too. It definitely makes Cesar's day brighter, and hopefully that will translate to him getting in less trouble?

After class the next week, I can see Jamal's car waiting for me in the pickup area.

"Hey, Yamilet!" Hunter calls out. He keeps trying to talk to me after school. And in art, too. I know he wants to talk about what I told him at the party, but there's no way I'm letting that happen. It never happened.

At least in art, a quick glance at Bo and David is all it takes to shut Hunter up. He has the good sense not to say anything in front of either of them—he did say he'd keep my secret, after all—but he's persistent after school. I pretend I don't hear him and walk straight to the car, where Cesar and Jamal are already waiting. It's not the most sustainable method of avoidance, but it's working for now.

Avoiding Hunter is easier with Jamal picking us up. He's always right on time, so I can hide from Hunter in his car until we leave. The only downside is I kind of miss Bo taking us to the light rail. (Okay. I miss her a lot.) Even though I have two classes with her and we hang out every day at lunch, it feels like I'm missing out now that I don't have that extra ten minutes of time with her. Having a crush sucks. But she has a girlfriend, and I'm in the closet, so I don't know why I'm being such a baby. I spend the rest of the ride home pretending not to be jealous while Cesar and Jamal hold hands across the center console.

Maybe if Jamal and Cesar weren't so cupcakey, I wouldn't be so mopey. They're a weird couple, but a cute one. I don't ever walk in on them making out or anything, but I catch them doing other weird shit almost every day. Last time I walked in on them, they were trying and failing to bench-press each other. When I walk into Cesar's room after we get home, Jamal looks like a chipmunk sitting on the bed. His cheeks are completely stuffed with marshmallows, but that doesn't stop Cesar from shoving another one in his mouth. Jamal says something unintelligible, then starts laughing. He catches the marshmallows in his hand as he spits them out.

"Boo. That was ten," Cesar says.

"What is happening?" I interrupt. I have to acknowledge them, or I would be convinced I'm imagining things.

"We're playing chubby bunny. Want to play?" Jamal says after dropping the marshmallows into the trash and wiping his mouth.

"What the hell is chubby bunny?"

"You have to put marshmallows in your mouth and say 'chubby bunny.' Whoever fits the most wins," Cesar says.

I sit on the bed with them, next to Cesar. My options are whatever this is, working, or homework. It's not that hard of a decision.

They both have an unfair advantage because of sheer mouth size, but I try my best. By the time I get to six, Cesar claps my cheeks in his hands hard enough to send the marshmallows shooting out of my mouth. It almost happens in slow motion. Jamal's eyes get wide and his scream goes up two octaves. The marshmallows go flying right at him.

I'm choking so hard I can't even laugh.

Jamal springs off the bed like a cat from a snake. He wildly shakes off all his limbs and makes a gagging noise. Cesar slaps my back while I gasp for air, but he's laughing too hard to be any help.

When Jamal finds a soggy marshmallow stuck to his shirt, he screeches and flings it at Cesar. And that starts a war I want no part of, so I sneak back to my room while they throw hopefully uneaten marshmallows at each other.

They are the weirdest couple I've ever seen. I'm so jealous.

✦ ✦ ✦

When I go back to my room, I try to keep from checking my phone. Dad has taken over a week to "process," and I'm trying not to freak out about it. I guess he needs a little more time. It's fine, though. I'm fine.

My dad and I have gone longer than this without talking, but it's not like him not to respond at all. Usually it only takes a couple of days. I brainstorm all the logical reasons he might not have responded.

Maybe something happened to his phone, and he never got my text. Maybe he needs time to come up with a heartfelt response. Maybe I'm overreacting.

"Has anyone seen my phone?" Mom calls out much louder than she needs to.

"Nope!" I shout as her phone's screen goes black while I hold the power button and hide it in an old shoebox in my closet. One can hope, but I don't trust that I have the luxury of believing Dad's old promises of confidentiality. Maybe he's just busy, but maybe he hates me. At least now he won't be able to tell Mom.

I can't stand not knowing what he's thinking or if he even saw my text. I get out my phone to take a video on Marco Polo to send him.

"Hey, Papi . . . I don't know if you got my text before. I hope we're still good. I'm just having a hard time, and I miss you. Let me know. Love you."

I send it. Dad always told me to prepare for the worst and hope for the best.

I force myself to take a breath and think. The worst-case scenario would be getting kicked out. I wish I could talk about it with Cesar, but he's always with Jamal, and I don't want to bum them out, especially since it's exactly what Jamal's going through right now.

There's no time to be sad if I focus on logistics. Mom will think she lost her phone, and that'll buy me some time to figure out what to do if Dad wants to tell her about me being gay. Honestly, she's such a busy mess right now with work and jewelry stuff, she'll barely miss it.

If he does find a way to tell her, I'll deny it. It'll be his word against mine, and I have a fake boyfriend to back me up. But . . . in case that doesn't work, I should probably get another job as a backup plan. It's not like I can support myself with this jewelry stuff if Mom disowns me.

I shove my anxiety as far down as it'll go and focus on solutions. I need to start on job applications. Just in case. After a quick Google search, I figure out how to beef up my résumé and make myself sound a lot more experienced than I am. Apparently I'm a "social media and marketing manager" for my mom. Plus, I have creative, organizational, and time management skills from this jewelry job. That should get me in the door somewhere.

Jamal has more than overstayed the "few days" Mom gave him, but she hasn't made him leave yet. Even after a couple of weeks, she hasn't acknowledged it. At least not in front of me. But I don't think it'll last much longer, since Mom is definitely not looking to adopt another kid. I sometimes want to talk to Jamal about what happened when he got kicked out, but it's such a sensitive subject for him that I can't bring myself to ask. We're not close enough, and it's way out of my lane. I mind my own business, just like I want other people to mind theirs.

As far as Jamal knows, I'm just doing him and Cesar a favor. Pretending to be his girlfriend is actually a lot of fun. Probably because I know he isn't interested. It's good practice for me, too. And Cesar gets a little jealous of me, which adds to the appeal.

When Thanksgiving rolls around, Jamal's still with us. We have the rest of the week off, but since we don't celebrate the colonial holiday, it's just another couple of days off school.

Cesar wants to go get Takis, and Mom makes Jamal and me go, too, so we won't be in the house alone. It's a good opportunity for me to submit some applications in person, since no one has answered the online ones so far.

Mom sends us out with a container full of chilaquiles to drop by Doña Violeta's. Jamal and I hold hands as we walk out, then let go the minute we're out of my mom's sight. The breeze is actually pretty nice today, and the sun isn't quite bright enough to give me a foot tan through my chanclas. It's about time mother nature decided to give me a break from this heat.

Even though Jamal and I aren't holding hands anymore, Cesar and Jamal don't get to act any more couple-y in public than they do with my mom. There's the occasional car driving by, so I guess they can't be too careful. When we walk, the most they do is brush hands every once in a while. It's brief enough to look like an accident, but happens too often for it not to be on purpose.

I hold my breath when we pass Bianca's house. I don't want to run into her. I notice someone's put away our—her—flowerpots. They aren't outside anymore, so their front yard feels naked. She must have gotten rid of them after I ruined the flowers. Good.

We keep following the mariachi music, which blares louder and louder until we're at Doña Violeta's porch. Another family beat us to bringing her food today. There's already a good handful of people eating with her on her porch, so she doesn't need us.

From down the street, I see Bianca and her friends walking from the store we're headed to. Even from a distance, she looks pretty. I'm smart enough now to know it's not the kind of pretty you want to get close to. Bianca is pretty like *Snow White*'s evil queen. The scary kind of pretty. The kind of pretty that won't hesitate to poison you.

I briskly walk inside Doña Violeta's house to avoid having to walk past them. Cesar and Jamal say quick hellos to everyone, while I put the chilaquiles in the fridge and wait for Bianca to pass the house. I put my hand on my chest until my heart rate returns to normal, listening to the conversation outside to try to calm my nerves. It sounds like one of them is about to go off to college, so they're all talking about their futures. My heart slows to a normal pace once enough time has passed that I'm sure I won't cross paths with *her* on the way to the store. I walk out, acting like nothing out of the ordinary happened, and bless

Cesar and Jamal for going along with it. We keep walking.

"I don't think we've ever talked about it before. What's you guys' dream jobs?" Jamal asks, continuing the conversation from Doña Violeta's.

I shrug. I guess I don't really have one. Maybe if I had more supportive parents, I would be able to entertain these kinds of thoughts. I hate that the thought even crossed my mind. I don't *know* Dad isn't supportive yet. Mom, though—probably. So, I'm left scrambling to save enough money to move out if it comes down to it, all while licking the wound from my dad's new-found absence.

"What's the point of having a dream job when tomorrow's never guaranteed?" Cesar asks, and it surprises me a bit. It's kind of a morbid thought for Cesar. I think of Doña Violeta's husband. It's true that tomorrow is never guaranteed, but that's the opposite reason for why I don't have a dream job. For me, it's to plan *for* the unknowable tomorrow.

"Well, it's not guaranteed, but it's probable. We're still in high school. We most likely have tomorrow."

"You don't know that, though," Cesar mumbles.

"Just like you don't *know* you're gonna die tomorrow. So we might as well plan for it, right?" I say.

"Whatever." Cesar rolls his eyes, and I roll mine back.

Jamal must be trying to avoid a sibling argument, because he changes the subject quickly. "So, when are you gonna spread your wings and be gay with us, Yami?"

"You told him?" I glare at Cesar.

"There's no secrets here." Cesar gives Jamal these annoying big googly eyes. "He's my other me." Who knew "in lak'ech" would backfire on me?

"You say that about everyone," I say. I don't like that that's the excuse he's using to tell Jamal my business.

"Hey, you know you can trust Jamal, right?" Cesar says.

Jamal gives me an innocent toothy smile. I know he won't tell anyone, but that's not the point.

"Shit, Yami, I didn't think you would care," Cesar says when I don't answer. For Cesar, "shit, Yami" = "sorry," since he's incapable of that word.

"Well, I do. How would you like it if I went and told . . . Bo, or someone, about you?" Jamal hangs back and walks behind us, letting us have our argument.

"What? Are you and Bo—"

"No! It was just an example. Never mind."

"No, no, no, you can't fool me!"

"Cesar, *stop*," I say through gritted teeth.

"I knew it! You like Bo!"

"*¡Cállate!*" I throw my hand over his mouth, even though we're miles away from anyone who might know who Bo is. That little asshole licks my hand.

"Eugh!" I shudder and wipe my hand on my hip. He keeps going like nothing disgusting just went down.

"Hey, when you ask her out, I'll return the favor and be her fake boyfriend for you! We can go on double dates as two fake couples who are actually two real couples!" Cesar is practically jumping up and down, he's so excited. That would never work, though, considering Bo already *has* a girlfriend.

"I'm not asking her out! Stop!" I want to be mad, but my laugh betrays me.

"Okay, I'll stop." Cesar puts his hands up in defeat. "Back to Jamal's question, then. Be gay with us!"

"I thought you were bi?"

"Yeah, and I thought you were lesbian? But I don't hear you using that word either."

I'm a little stumped by that, actually. I never really thought about it.

"If 'gay rights' is supposed to include us, then we get to call ourselves gay. You don't hear nobody fighting for bisexual or lesbian marriage. Gay es un 'umbrella term.'" Cesar emphasizes his point by pushing my shoulder. "Stop dodging me, though!"

"Fine. I'll be gay with you when I move out, probably." Truth is, I'm not ready yet.

"Coward."

"If I'm a coward, you're a hypocrite! If it's so easy, why aren't you out, then, huh?"

"That's not what I meant. You don't have to be *out* out to be gay with us. You do have to talk to Bo, though." He sings Bo's name and pokes my belly. If he's trying to egg me on, it's not working. Jamal finally catches back up to us, and I can't argue anymore.

Cesar is right about me being a coward. Coming out is one thing, but admitting my feelings to Bo? I don't think I'll ever be ready to do something like that sober. Not after Bianca. Cesar has always been the brave one between the two of us.

There's a secret code somewhere that says you can't admit your sibling is right, though, so I flick both his and Jamal's ears instead.

"Hey! What'd *I* do?" Jamal cradles his ear.

"You probably deserved it." I shrug. If Jamal is going to be with my brother, that makes him family. And family gets flicked ears. It's a sign of affection.

We're almost at the corner store, but Doña Violeta's music is loud enough that we can still hear it. "Cielito Lindo" plays, and on instinct Cesar and I start singing as we walk. Cesar throws his arms around both me and Jamal and we belt the words in our best deep mariachi voices. Jamal quickly learns the "ay, ay, ay, ay" part, but that's it. He just laughs at us while we make fools of ourselves.

Then Cesar stops singing.

"Shit . . ." He stops walking, too.

"What?" I ask.

"I, uh, forgotmywallet." His words come out too fast.

"It's fine, I got you," Jamal says.

"No, I'm not hungry anymore." He's staring at a black truck in the corner store parking lot. "Let's just go back."

That's when I see them. Through the store window, six guys from Rover. I recognize a couple of them Cesar was always fighting. I never thought of Cesar as the type to avoid a fight, but he's already turning around. He doesn't want to be noticed right now.

"Okay, let's go," Jamal says when he sees them. But just

when we start to turn around, the store doors open and my gut pulls at the slur they call him.

"¡Oye, maricón!"

Cesar clenches his fists but keeps walking. I want to turn around and fight them for him, but I don't have the alcohol to give me the courage like I did at the party. Besides, there's too many. Even Cesar has to know he can't take all six, with or without me and Jamal helping. I secretly hope it doesn't come to that, because I don't know if I'd have the guts.

"Look, he's running away again!" They erupt in laughter.

I'm ready to hold Cesar back and convince him to drop it, but he doesn't turn to fight. He *runs*. Jamal and I take off with him. The secret code also states that when one of us runs, we're all gone. I chose the worst day to leave the house in chanclas. The Rover boys get into their truck, a couple of them hopping into the bed, and drive after us.

I'm not as fast as Cesar or Jamal, so the distance between us grows a little with every stride. Still, I run as fast as I can in freaking chanclas. The truck pulls one wheel onto the side-walk, like they're trying to run us over. My feet can't move any faster than they already are, but it doesn't stop me from trying. I pump my legs so hard my calves burn, but I'm still trailing behind Cesar and Jamal. There's an alley we can turn into up ahead, but I don't know how quickly I can get there. The truck gains on me. The fence on the other side of the sidewalk is impossible to avoid without running into the street. The horn honks less than a few yards behind me, pulling a sharp scream out of my throat. I almost fall forward, but I keep running. Cesar turns at the noise.

"Yami!" His eyes widen when he sees how close I am to getting run over. He stumbles and changes directions.

"Cesar, no!" Jamal turns around when Cesar does. Cesar runs back and pushes me into the fence hard enough so the truck is heading for him instead of me.

Just when my brother is about to be roadkill, the truck pulls back on the road and drives off. The laughter is almost as loud as the blasting music.

I yank off one of my chanclas and take a running start. I let out a strangled war screech and throw it at the truck. It hits the back window, but it doesn't give me the satisfaction I want. They laugh and drive away, and my chancla gets run over by another car. They could have just killed me. If Cesar hadn't pushed me out of the way . . .

"You okay, Yami?" Cesar asks, panting. I spin around and redirect my anger.

"Why would you do that?" I yell. He could have *died*.

He shrugs like it's no big deal. But it is a big deal. He didn't even think about risking his life for me. I want to push him into the fence. Instead, I hug him. He laughs an uncomfortable laugh.

"You're so dramatic."

I hold on tighter before letting go. When we turn to walk back home, Doña Violeta is standing at the edge of her house, like she's ready to rush over. On the other side of the street,

Bianca is staring at us with wide eyes while her friends keep walking. I almost think she's going to come check on us, but she turns around to catch up with her friends. After we calm down Doña Violeta and make her promise not to tell Mami, none of us talk about what happened the rest of the way home, or ever again.

13

THOU SHALT CONFESS THY SINS—SELECTIVELY

I made the mistake of posting a bunch of friendship bracelet pictures on Insta for Black Friday, so now we have a backlog of orders to catch up on. I can't complain, though. Even though I like the beadwork best as far as aesthetics go, the woven bracelets are my favorite to work on. I get into this rhythm when I make them. It's repetitive and predictable, and something about that is soothing, almost like braiding hair.

While I weave, I strategize about job hunting to keep from thinking about my dad. Am I starting to freak out over his lack of response? Yes. Yes, I am. But if I replace those thoughts with thoughts of job hunting, I won't have to deal with it, right? We'll go with that.

Finding a job is a lot harder than I thought it would be, and it seems like I've already exhausted all my options for work anywhere near our house. I've dropped off résumés for fast food, coffee shop, retail, and receptionist jobs and still nothing. Maybe I'll have better luck if I try closer to Slayton.

There's an apartment I have my eye on just in case. It only requires a one-month security deposit, and the rent is way cheaper than anything else in the area. If I can get a minimum-wage job, I can make it work. Granted, it's not the nicest apartment in the world—which explains why there are so many available units—but it'll do. Cesar and I could get a bunk bed or something. But we can't get the apartment if I can't get a *job*.

I can't stress too much if I stay focused. The winter mercado is in town soon, like it is every year on the second and third Saturdays of December. I'm hoping to catch up on orders so I can make extras to sell there. It'll be held at the plaza on Central for the next couple of Saturdays, and Mom said if I set it up on my own, I can keep all the money I make minus expenses for materials. At the rate I'm going, I'll catch up on all our existing orders by the weekend, and then I can go to the mercado the next two weekends to sell everything extra I've made.

Jamal walks into the living room. He sits next to me and watches my hands, like he's trying to figure out how it works. Cesar is helping my mom make dinner, so it's just the two of us here right now.

"These are really pretty. . . ." Jamal eyes my creations, and I take the opportunity to do so myself. The friendship bracelets all have different color palettes, from desert sunset to cotton candy to jungle flowers. The angular patterns feel like they belong in a Mexican calle being sold to anyone passing by.

"Thanks." The thought makes me grin. These look legit.

"Do you need any help?" Jamal asks.

I put down the strings I was tying and stretch out my cramped fingers. It would take me way too long to teach him how to make the friendship bracelets, but maybe he can help me make some extra things while I catch up.

"Can you start cutting these threads for me? Ten inches each." I try not to grin too hard when he picks up the ruler and gets right to work.

"Sorry about the other day," he says as he measures out a thread. "I thought you knew Cesar told me. I wasn't trying to make you feel bad for not being out."

"I don't feel bad," I say, too quickly. Almost defensively.

"Okay, that's good. You shouldn't. It's all on your own time-line." He stops for a moment to look up at me. There he goes again getting all serious. "And you're not a coward, okay? I don't think Cesar meant it like that. You're smart."

"What do you mean?"

"I mean you're smart for being guarded. I was stupid to come out."

I immediately feel bad for snapping at him. Here I am, sulking about the possibility of getting kicked out, while Jamal is living it.

"I'm so sorry. . . ." I don't know how else to comfort him. "If it makes you feel better, I'm not that smart. I came out to my dad."

"How'd he take it?"

"He still hasn't responded . . . if he tells my mom, I might get kicked out, too."

"Nah, let me stop you there. I don't know your dad, but your mom is *way* too nice. She wouldn't do that to you."

Except Jamal doesn't know that.

Before I can say anything else, Cesar squishes himself between us.

"Food's ready," he says, grinning proudly.

"That's my boy. I'm watching you two!" My mom points two fingers at her eyes, and then at me and Jamal. It's funny how completely wrong she is.

After dinner, Cesar reluctantly agrees to help me since Jamal wants to, and with the three of us working, I don't even have to stay up late to meet my productivity goal before school tomorrow.

On Monday, my luck seems to continue. We have a half day of classes to celebrate the sacrament of Confession. Once a year, almost the entire student body has to confess their sins to the priest. While some kids opt out, they still have to go to the assembly. Those kids get to sit in the back and don't actually have to do anything. My mom would die of a heart attack if she realized we opted out, so Cesar and I participate. The upperclassmen are the last to go to church, so we had shorter classes through the morning before getting let out.

My teeth chatter as I walk to the chapel, and I wish I'd gone for the pants instead of the skirt this morning. It's finally starting to get cold. Well, cold for the desert. It's the beginning of December and the leaves are barely starting to change colors. I'm always complaining about the heat, but I was definitely not built for cold weather. Hunter finds me right after class as everyone walks to the chapel and jogs over to me.

"Hey, Yamilet!" I pretend I don't hear and keep walking. He catches up to me, like I'm sure what happened at the party will catch up to me. I've been successfully avoiding him for weeks now. But I didn't see him coming this time.

"Are you avoiding me?" he asks.

"No." Lie. Obviously.

"Okay, good. Well . . . um . . . I wanted to talk about . . . um . . ." He throws an arm around my shoulder and starts whispering, "You know, what happened at the homecoming party . . ."

I squint at him.

"I know I promised you I wouldn't say anything, but—"

"Who did you tell?" I stop walking and shrug his arm off my shoulder. I knew I couldn't trust Hunter.

"No one! I was just gonna say, you know one of my secrets, too. And . . . I would really appreciate it if you also didn't tell."

"What?" My memory of that night is a little blurry.

"That I'm a . . . you know." He whispers the last word. "Virgin."

"Oh!" A grin pulls at my lips. He won't tell anyone about me because I have leverage on him. Not that I would ever tell anyone, but the fact that he thinks I might calms my nerves. It means I'm safe, at least from Hunter. I grab his arm and pull it back over my shoulder. I could use the extra warmth. "Yeah, I got you."

We sit next to each other in the chapel, and it doesn't feel like he's just being nice because I have potential blackmail material on him. It feels like he's being nice, period. Maybe I need to stop thinking of secrets as leverage. But it's hard to get out of that mindset when my biggest one was used against me.

Not just the gay thing, either. Bianca knew *everything* about me. Looking back, it was always a matter of time before she got mad and let it all slip. Bianca is a special breed of evil. The kind of evil that preys on trust, on vulnerability, on something real. The kind of evil that makes you love them first.

Bo catches my eye from the pew across from me. She widens her eyes and sticks out her tongue, making me giggle. Then I notice her backpack has a new pin on it. Next to her rainbow one is a heart-shaped pin with the lesbian flag's pink stripes. I can't believe I ever doubted she was gay. I wonder if Jamie got her that pin. God, I'm annoying *myself* with my fixation on Bo and Jamie.

For once I'm happy to hear the priest's confession spiel, because it distracts me from my thoughts, even though I'm not particularly looking forward to telling all my secrets to some old guy I don't know. Why does some priest have to be my middleman?

If there's a God, I would hope I could keep my business between the two of us. Still, I'd prefer not to be damned to hell just because I skip out of formally telling my sins to a priest to pass it on to the all-knowing entity he worships. I start thinking about all the sins I've committed since my last confession. Being gay. Drinking at a party. Flicking Cesar just because I feel like it . . . Being gay.

Mom has made us go twice a year ever since we were seven, but it's not like I can stop being gay after confession. I wonder how the rules work when your "sin" is a constant thing. If confession is supposed to absolve me, it's not working. The day after every confession, I'm always gay all over again. Based on the way the rules have been explained to me, that means the only way I can get into heaven is if I spontaneously die the moment the priest absolves me.

I guess I wasn't paying attention, because I somehow missed whatever the priest said that made Bo stand and argue with him. That's right. Bo is *arguing with a priest* in front of half the school. I knew she had balls, but damn.

"I just don't see why I have to apologize for being exactly the way God made me," she says.

"The sin lies in the action and the thoughts. Because sex outside of the sacrament of marriage is a sin."

"But gay marriage is legal. So it's not a sin if you're married then." She crosses her arms. Everyone's heads dart back and forth from Bo to the priest as they argue. I guess they're all as surprised as I am about this. I can feel Hunter's eyes on me every now and then, like he's trying to gauge my reaction. I look for Cesar in the crowd so we can have a little telepathic solidarity. I find him, and I almost laugh at how sweaty and pale he looks. He looks like he ate a moldy Rover chicken nugget. He didn't seem sick this morning, but he definitely looks it now.

"It may be legal in the eyes of the United States, but not in the eyes of God."

Cesar isn't looking back and forth between the priest and

Bo like everyone else, so I can't get him to make eye contact with me. His eyes are shut and his lips are moving as he silently mutters what I assume is a prayer. How he can find prayer more interesting than Bo telling off a priest is lost on me. He eventually crosses himself and opens his eyes, but he still looks miserable as hell. He really does buy into the whole religion thing. Good for him, I guess. I go back to watching Bo.

"Why?" she snaps.

The priest pauses for a minute.

"Because the Bible has written it so."

"Where? Don't cite the Old Testament at me, since our uniforms are made from mixed fabrics. Another sin, according to the Old Testament."

"Romans 1:26 and 1:27. 'For this reason God gave them—'"

"'Up to vile passions,' blah blah. I know the passage." Someone gasps when Bo interrupts. "It's about adultery, not homosexuality in the context of committed partners. You can't put us through a year of scripture class and expect us to learn only the convenient parts."

I wish Bo had a mic so she could drop it right there. I clap my hands for two seconds before I realize what I'm doing. Bo catches my eye and sucks in her lips like she's trying not to laugh. Then my stomach drops as I realize everyone's looking at *me* now. Hunter claps a few times, and I think since we're sitting so close people assumed it was him who clapped first. Bless Hunter. I've never wanted to hug someone more.

"Ms. Taylor, you have five seconds to sit down, or you'll be escorted to the principal's office," one of the teachers on the edge of Bo's pew scolds as he stands up.

"You don't have to escort me." Bo walks out of the church on her own.

"You okay?" Hunter whispers when the priest starts talking again.

I nod. I'm better than okay. Bo knows how to contextualize things for me. She's right. The Bible says a whole lot of things that the Catholic church kind of just ignores. Why get so hung up over this one detail? I can't explain why, but I feel like I'm floating.

We start lining up by the confessionals, one pew at a time. Some people leave looking relieved, and some leave crying, which is super intimidating. It tells me I'm not the only one here who's carried their body weight in shame. I'm done with that, though. When Cesar comes out, he looks like he's about to throw up, and I wonder if he's sick today. He hasn't been looking too hot since we got to the chapel.

When it's my turn to confess, my legs don't even shake as I walk inside the confessional.

"Bless me, Father, for I have sinned," I start. "This is my . . . um . . . I don't know how many confessions I've done. But it's a lot."

The priest chuckles and welcomes me to confess.

I think about telling him I'm gay. It's the first thing I always confess when I do this. Priests are among the few people I've ever uttered my secret to, since they're sworn to secrecy. But something in me tells me not to this time. I tell him about hurting Bo's feelings, and getting drunk. I confess all the things I feel guilty about.

But liking girls? I feel like I can be okay with that part of myself, or at least try to, even if others can't. There's no point in hating myself over it. Penance is to say a bunch of Hail Marys. I'm sure I'll get to that eventually.

After school, I rush outside to meet Bo and make sure to give her the hug she deserves. She stiffens up a little, so I back off and clasp my hands behind my back. She isn't much of a hugger, I guess.

"What was that for?" Her lips twitch like she's trying not to smile.

"Um . . . just because you're awesome." Unlike Bo, I don't try to hide my smile. I think we're about to have a "moment" when Cesar walks past us without saying anything. That's when I notice that Jamal's car is pulled up to the curb. I sigh. Jamal puts Cesar first so much that he's ditching the last half of school to pick us up. I already told him to stop leaving early to pick us up, but I'm not his mom, so I can't force him. Besides, he's got so much other shit going on right now that I can hardly blame him for not putting school first.

"I gotta go." I reach to give Bo another hug but stop myself, since she tensed up the first time. And now I don't know what to do with my outstretched hand. I blow her a kiss before I realize how gay that is. "Ciao!" I say, because straight Italian people blow kisses, right? God, I'm the worst.

I jog over to the car before I can embarrass myself any more.

"Things are going well with Bo, I see?" Jamal says as I climb into the back seat. He's discreet enough to wait for the door to close before letting out a laugh.

"Shut up."

"That's a yes, right?" Jamal looks to Cesar, who shrugs. He's not laughing. Not even smiling.

"Hey, you okay?" Jamal asks.

Cesar nods but doesn't say anything. He's usually the type to start making jokes when he's in a bad mood so no one knows he's upset. Quiet Cesar is new, even for me, and I don't know how to handle it. Apparently neither does Jamal, because we go the rest of the ride home without a word. Music is blasting to substitute for conversation, but it still feels awkward.

Cesar mumbles a thank-you to Jamal when we get to the house, and walks in on his own.

"Did something happen?" Jamal turns to me.

"We had confession today. Maybe he feels bad about making me spit marshmallows in your face." The truth is, I have no idea what's wrong with him. He'll probably bounce back in an hour. He always does.

Jamal laughs, but there's no heart in it. We go inside. I would go talk to Cesar, but it looks like Jamal's got that covered, since he goes straight for Cesar's room. I take the opportunity to get to work. I already finished my half of the orders, but I still want to make a few more earrings and necklaces before the mercado on Saturday. Being extra prepared helps with the nerves.

When Mom gets home, she starts stringing beads together

to fill her half of the orders. As cumbia plays softly in the background, she comments every now and then on how good the necklace I'm making is turning out. We make small talk about her job and the telenovela we've been watching. She doesn't even ask me a single question about Cesar. I'm starting to really enjoy doing this with her. So I try to push the thought aside that this will only last as long as she doesn't find out the truth about me.

She's due for a phone upgrade in a month, so she's waiting until then to get a new phone to replace the one I hid. I would feel guilty about stealing hers if it wasn't my saving grace right now. I'm desperately trying to scrounge up enough money to move out before she finds out and makes me. That way, if Dad tells her, I won't be caught off guard.

"So, Mami . . ." I take a breath to build up the courage to ask, "Have you talked to Papi lately?"

"Mhm." Her rhythm doesn't stutter. "We've been emailing."

"What?" I squeeze the bead I was holding so hard it flies across the room. She tsks and gets up to grab it.

They talked. Which kills all my hopeless theories about my dad being too busy to respond to *me*. Did I steal her phone for nothing? Does she already know?

"What did you guys . . . um, talk about?" My heart does a few roundhouse kicks against my chest, but I hold it together.

"Oh, just catching up."

"Did he have anything, like, *interesting* to say?"

"He never has anything interesting to say." She laughs, and I let out my breath. He didn't tell her. Not yet, at least. And if he's talking to Mom through email, maybe he still hasn't seen his phone? But then, if he's casually emailing my mom, why hasn't he emailed *me*? If his phone is broken and he never got my text, what's keeping him from contacting *me*?

The pit in my stomach tightens as I rack my brain, searching for something to make it make sense. My dad loves me. He always has. He's not religious like Mom. When he finally calls me, I can tell him how paranoid I was and we'll laugh about how ridiculous I'm being.

"What's wrong, mija?" She looks at me all concerned, and I realize my eyes are watering.

"I just miss him, I guess," is all I say.

"I miss him, too." She gives my hand a quick squeeze before going back to beading. "Have you not been talking lately?" she asks, all concerned.

"Um, no, we've been talking," I lie. If she doesn't know about what I told him, she doesn't need to know about the aftermath.

We don't talk much the rest of the evening. I bead faster to keep from thinking. I don't stop working when Mami's tired enough to go to bed.

I wake up with the worst crick in my neck, lying on the couch with a blanket over me. I guess I fell asleep working, and Mom must have tucked me in here. It takes a minute before I realize that Cesar and Jamal are talking by the front door. I'm too tired to get up and give them privacy, though. I'm probably half-sleep dreaming anyway.

"Can I hug you?" I hear Cesar ask, and he sounds like he's crying. Why would he ask to hug his boyfriend? I don't open my eyes, because I probably shouldn't be seeing this, or hearing it. I don't hear Jamal's answer, only the sound of two boys quietly whimpering for what feels like forever. Then the door closes, and Cesar goes back to his room.

I roll over, still not sure if I'm dreaming.

Cesar: Jamal left, if Mom asks.

"You good?" I ask Cesar while we both get ready for school in the bathroom.

"Why wouldn't I be?" he asks, then shoves his toothbrush into his mouth and starts brushing. A smart move, so he won't have to answer any questions coherently.

"You just seemed off yesterday, and with Jamal going back home and everything, I wanted to check. He can still come visit, right?"

Cesar gives a half-hearted grunt in response, but doesn't stop brushing until he's ready to spit.

"He didn't go home. He's"—spit—"staying with his cousin. In New Mexico."

"Oh, that sucks. . . . Are you guys okay?" I ask.

"We're spectacular." I don't believe that for one second, and I'm about to call him out on it but he gives me finger guns, flicking nasty toothbrush water in my eye.

"Gross!" I snatch his toothbrush from his hand and flick it

back at him, but he runs away to his room, cackling. I shudder and wipe his disgusting spit-water off my face. Part of me worries that he's hiding something about what happened with him and Jamal, but it doesn't seem to be bothering him too much. At least he's back to normal, somewhat.

When I go to tell Mami about Jamal leaving, she's wearing her post-crying sunglasses, sitting at the counter with her laptop open.

"Mami, what's wrong?" I ask. She turns her laptop to show me an email from Jamal. It looks like I won't have to break the news after all. He did it himself, with a lengthy goodbye email thanking all of us for letting him stay. Mom is such a sap.

"I'm going to miss that boy being here the last few weeks. Are you two going to be okay?" she asks.

"We're trying the long-distance thing," I say without thinking twice. Lying is starting to become second nature.

"Bueno. I'll pray for you two."

"It's not like he died," Cesar says as he walks into the kitchen, grabbing a piece of toast from the toaster.

"Don't be insensitive," she scolds before shuffling us into the car to head to school.

In art class, we have another creative freedom day.

I look around the room, thinking about what to do. David's and Hunter's portraits of each other from earlier this year are hanging up on the wall, along with some other student art projects. It's not lost on me that Bo still hasn't let me see the portrait she drew of me *months* ago. The only thing worse than knowing how she really sees me is *not* knowing.

Bo and I end up doing a joint drawing. I draw a little doodle with a dark brown colored pencil and hand it to her to add to it. We keep going back and forth like that most of class.

Bo sucks in her cheeks when she concentrates, and she has to keep brushing her hair behind her ear because it keeps falling in front of her face. The gay part of my brain wants to take my colita out of my braid and braid her hair so it behaves. After all, she needs her hair out of her eyes to art.

The practical part of my brain knows that at this rate, I'm gonna mess around and get caught sooner or later. Got to be more careful.

I might be staring hard enough for her to notice, because she glances up at me. I shoot my eyes back down at the page.

"Do you two need a room?" David asks. Hunter must assume that I think he told David about me, because his eyes go wide.

"I didn't say—" Hunter starts.

I cough to keep him from finishing the sentence, and he sucks his lips in. I must have been staring a little too longingly at the hair I want to brush behind Bo's ear. It's one thing for Bo to notice me looking, but David? Who else can see how blatantly gay I am? I open my mouth to defend myself, to make some kind of excuse, but my voice is lost. I don't want to say something shitty like last time.

"I was just kidding," he says when neither of us answer. Why would he joke about that? It's not cool, even if I wasn't just secretly fantasizing about braiding Bo's hair.

"She's straight, David," Bo says nonchalantly before she slides the page back over to me. I force a laugh and take the paper. Thank God for something less gay to concentrate on. It's starting to look almost like a face. There are two orbs that could be eyes, and I start coloring them. The patterns Bo drew around them give more depth, and they look like two black holes, attracting everything else toward them. I don't know if I was subconsciously thinking about Bo's magnetic eyes while I was drawing. But that's what we drew.

We get an A, obviously.

When the bell rings for lunch, I stay put instead of going to my normal spot in the cafeteria with Bo and David. I have more jewelry to make and not a lot of free time to make it, so I decide to take advantage of Ms. Felix's open-door policy. Since art is right before lunch anyway, it's convenient this way.

"You're not coming?" Bo asks when she and David notice that I don't get up after class.

"No, I think I'll stay and make some jewelry."

"Fun! You want some company?" Bo asks.

"Only if you let me put you to work," I say. It's only half a joke. I could use some extra hands. I learned from Jamal that making people help with the simple things saves me a ton of time.

We have a little assembly line going in the art room: Bo cuts the threads, David beads them, and I braid and tie them. By the time lunch is over, I have all the braided bead necklaces I'll need for this weekend.

14

MAKE UNTO THEE A FAT WALLET

On Saturday, I'm all set up at the mercado before it opens. Early as I am, there are already a few other vendors set up. The smells of fried dough and dulce de leche from the churro stand travel straight to my nose through the December wind, which makes me regret having skipped breakfast. There's plenty of food I could eat, but there's no point in being here just to eat all my potential earnings. All the tables are set up facing inward around the plaza, leaving space for the entrance. I'm lucky to have my assigned table right up front. That way I'll be one of the first and last stops, and I'll only have one table next to me—less direct competition. The lady next to me is selling champurrado and aguas frescas. Which is doubly great, since I won't have to compete with her for customers.

At this point I've done everything I could possibly do to prepare, so the rest is up to the universe. With every sale, I'll be one step closer to financial independence.

The first few hours are slow. I smile at everyone who walks

by, but most of them avoid my eyes, and my table. Guilting people over with a smile obviously isn't working, so I give up on that front.

The day is already halfway over by the time an older white guy actually stops for more than a few moments. We're outside in December, but he's sweating harder than I do in church. He rubs his chin and eyes everything individually for what feels like a century.

"Are you looking for anything specific?" I ask to break the silence.

"Forgot my anniversary. She likes purple."

I spring into action, picking up an intricate purple-and-green beadwork necklace with a flowerlike pattern. "She'll forgive you if you get this one! It's my mom's favorite!" I hold it to my neck so he can see it better.

"How much?"

"A hundred and ten dollars." I say it with as much confidence as I can.

"I'll take it for fifty." He inspects it like it's worth nothing more. I put the necklace back down and blink at him.

"I'm sorry, this one's a hundred and ten." Cutting the price even a dollar feels like an insult, and he wants less than half for it? The prices are already pretty low considering expenses for materials and how much time went into making them.

"Sixty. Final offer." He strokes the necklace, and I hold myself back from swatting his sweaty hands away from my art.

"One hundred," I offer. I hate hagglers, but I'm afraid I

won't sell anything if I don't budge with this guy. I suck it up because I don't want to be homeless if my mom kicks me out. I need this. Besides, he already contaminated it with his greasy sausage fingers.

"You know what? I'll come back." He starts to turn away. I've seen Mami do this enough to know that people don't come back.

"Wait!" I shout louder than I need to. "Sixty is fine." I hate the desperation that comes out in my voice.

He grins and gets out his wallet. I try not to let my eyes water as I bag up the necklace and accept his cash. Fifty dollars less than what I should be getting.

People start coming in droves around lunchtime, and thank God, because I need to make up for my lack of sales this morning. Normally being in a place so crowded by myself would be my worst nightmare, but I make my table my shield and the jewelry my weapons in order to face the oncoming traffic.

I prepare myself for the rush as several other tables start building up lines. A family of five walks to my table, and I smile at one of the adults. They smile back, but just as the family reaches my table, I spot Bianca and her mom at the entrance.

My heart jumps out of my chest and I can't think straight. All I know is I can't let them see me. I'm still holding back tears from Sausage Fingers, and if Bianca sees me upset, she'll know I'm failing at this, too.

"I'm so sorry, I need to take a break! Come back later?" The words sound desperate enough that the family doesn't get irritated. But I doubt they'll come back. I grab the blanket off the grass and throw it over my table, then duck underneath.

The champurrado lady gives me a curious look. I press a finger to my lips, so she shakes her head and goes back to minding her business.

My gut pulls at me to get up and make my money, but I can't. I can't see them. Tears press against my eyes. I hate how she can still make me cry. She didn't even have to do anything, and I'm hiding under a table, crying like a baby.

I sit for at least an hour before my back starts hurting. I check the time on my phone. I put it away as soon as I see it, since I don't want to look at my dad right now. He wants nothing to do with me, so why should I keep him as my wallpaper? I guess I just don't have the heart to change it, so I've been avoiding looking at the screen.

Okay, focus, Yami. There's only a couple of hours left before I'll have to pack up. I can't stay hiding all day.

I peek out from behind the blanket. They're gone.

I carefully pull the blanket off my table. I missed the rush, and there's barely anyone left anyway. All I manage to sell for the next two hours are a couple of friendship bracelets, so when I'm ready to pack up, I only have a hundred dollars to show for a full day of work.

I start packing my things like the failure I am, but a viejita and a boy around my age approach my table at the last minute. His arms are filled with a ton of home-brought shopping bags. They must be loaded if they spent so much money filling those bags. The viejita speed-walks over faster than she should be able to.

Without a word, she starts picking up bracelets, earrings, and necklaces and handing them to me. I'm frozen for a bit before I kick into gear and start bagging them up and doing the math in my head for how much all this will cost. I thank her every time she hands me something.

"Thank you." *A hundred.*

"Thank you." *Plus fifty.*

"Thank you." *Plus thirty-five.*

"Thank you." *Plus a hundred twenty.*

I lose count when the boy stops her from handing me a pair of earrings.

"Marisol and them have some like that already, welita."

"Ay, sí, this is why I bring you." She looks at me. "Getting ahead on Christmas shopping for mis nietos." I nod like it makes perfect sense to spend hundreds of dollars in one outing. This woman alone is going to make today worth it. The more stuff she hands me, the less sense the numbers make. I have to pull out my phone calculator to ground myself in reality. I tear up looking at the total.

"Thank you," I say one last time as I hand over her bag. I wipe my eyes, embarrassed. What kind of salesperson cries when they make their sale?

She smiles and kisses my cheek. I don't stop crying when she leaves.

I have enough for my security deposit.

On Monday, Bo is sick with some winter bug that's apparently going around. All I want to do is gush to her about how great the mercado went, but somehow interrupting Amber's and David's heart eyes at each other to talk about it just doesn't feel as exciting. The entire day goes sooooo slow without Bo. When I realize how miserable I am, it hits me that I'm way past catching feelings. Denial isn't as reliable of a coping mechanism as it used to be.

I should have seen this coming. This is how it started with Bianca. I can't go back to that.

The minute I realized I had feelings for Bianca, shit went downhill fast. I am not ready to fall for Bo. Especially because Bo already made her lack of feelings toward me painfully clear at not-homecoming. And she has a girlfriend, who I wish I wasn't jealous of. But pretending not to feel anything isn't working either.

I can't even pretend while I do homework. All I can think about is how screwed I am. I go to Cesar's room after failing to reason with myself.

"Cesar, *help!*" I flop facedown onto his bed while he sits at his desk doing homework.

"What happened?"

"You were right. I like Bo."

"Okay, so . . ."

"It's the worst."

"What? Why?" He puts his pen down and faces me.

I groan into the comforter. Hopefully that's enough to

telepathically communicate an answer. I don't have the energy to say it out loud. It's the worst because she doesn't like me, too. It's the worst because I want her to think I'm straight, but I also want her to like me. And she won't like me if she thinks I'm straight. And telling her how I feel could ruin her relationship. I secretly hope they already broke up but feel terrible about wishing that on someone I care about.

"Don't overthink it. You're supposed to be in the fun stage!" he says.

"How is it fun? I feel like I'm being crushed from all sides. Is that why it's called a crush? Because that's what it feels like." I roll over. "Seriously, tell me how it's supposed to be fun so I can stop wanting to die."

Cesar's expression changes to something unreadable.

"Sorry, I guess I shouldn't joke about that," I say.

He just shakes his head, like he's shaking away whatever thoughts just flew through his brain. "Anyway. You got to let go of any kind of expectation on the other person and enjoy the feeling, you know? Let the butterflies stick around. Eat it up whenever she does something cute, just because it's cute. It's a crush, it's supposed to be *fun*."

"How'd you get to be so mature, huh? Is Jamal that good an influence?"

"Nah, I'm just super mature." He grins, then glances at the promise ring on the nightstand, and the smile disappears.

"Are you guys okay?"

"Yeah," he answers quickly, shooting me an annoyed glare.

"Don't change the subject. What's happening with you and Bo?"

"There is no me and Bo. I like her, that's it. It's not gonna happen."

"Why not?"

"Because I'm not telling her. I already know she doesn't like me anyway. I think she has a girlfriend." I sigh, not mentioning the embarrassing fact that I told Bo I was straight.

"What do you mean, you think?"

"I mean, she told me she had one back at homecoming."

"Has she mentioned anything about her girlfriend since then?" Cesar asks.

"Well, no, but—"

"So it was probably just a quick thing. Bet you money she's single now."

I roll onto my side and rest my chin on my palm. "I feel like Bo would have said something if they broke up, though."

"People don't always have to talk about breakups, Yami. Shit happens."

"I guess." I'm not totally convinced. Wouldn't Bo have mentioned a breakup?

"Why are you so desperate to keep your feelings a secret? You already know she's gay, so if she doesn't feel the same, at least she'll understand. It's not like she'll go telling people."

"You don't know that! What if she tells everyone?"

"Why would she tell anyone?"

"I don't know, to embarrass me . . ." It sounds ridiculous when I say it out loud.

"I think you're just making excuses because you're scared."

"Aren't you scared?" I say. He has to be scared of Mom finding out about him, too.

"I meant about Bo."

"I'm not scared." I roll my eyes.

He smirks like he knows he's right. And he is, but I'm not admitting it to him. But I let him give me advice and ask me whatever questions he wants. It's all talk, because I'm going to do nothing about this crush until I eventually suck all the fun out of it and it goes away.

My phone beeps at me. I grab for it quicker than I should on the off chance it's my dad.

Bianca: I miss you . . .

I stare at the text, half expecting to blink and realize I'm seeing things. But the name on my screen doesn't change, no matter how many times I blink at it. A smile creeps onto my face.

"Ayy, that's her, huh?" Cesar says.

"Um, yeah." I know he means Bo, but I don't feel like explaining the situation. I still haven't told him what happened with Bianca. I can't deal with his questions right now, so I lie.

"All right, you can go now," he says, and I laugh.

"Are you kicking me out?"

"Yes. Go talk to your girl."

I grab my phone, rush back to my room, and sit on my bed, staring at the *I miss you* . . . on my screen.

I know it's not an apology. But it feels good. I'm not smiling because she texted me, I'm smiling because she *misses* me. I know she never felt the same way about me, but damn it feels good to know she's thinking about me. I feel like I won. Because she's thinking about me, and I'm thinking about someone else. Someone better.

I think I'll leave her hanging.

The dots show up on my screen that say she's typing again. I used to respond to her right away, so she's not used to waiting. It's a minute before another message shows up.

Bianca: *as a friend

I could give myself a migraine from rolling my eyes so hard. Why the fuck would she feel the need to add that? It's like throwing in my face that she's uncomfortable with the fact that I'm gay. I wasn't going to respond, but my fingers are already furiously typing away. The adrenaline rush is unreal.

Yami: First of all

Yami: bitch

The dots show up again, but I keep typing and send a few more messages before her response shows up.

Yami: I do not miss you

Yami: Second

Yami: Kindly, kiss my ass.

Yami: *as a friend

I block her number before she can respond.

15

THOU SHALT NOT ADULATE FALSE IDOLS

I spend the next week so focused on making jewelry for the second mercado that the last days of school before winter break fly by. I work on the mercado jewelry while Mom works on the Etsy orders. It's kind of perfect. I'm almost tempted to ask her to come with me to the mercado this time, but I know that would put her way behind. She won't have my help filling orders this weekend because of the mercado, so I really just need to suck it up and go without her. I keep my hands busy beading, not bothering to check my phone when it buzzes. Before, I would jump every time I heard it on the off chance it was my dad texting, but I've given up on that now. He's not talking to me . . . whatever. Maybe one day I'll process what that actually means for me, but for now all I have to keep me from breaking are distractions.

While the rest of Slayton is on break as of our last class earlier today, I'm working harder than ever. It's my last chance at the mercado, but I'm not optimistic about it. If it wasn't for that one viejita last time, I wouldn't have sold more than three things the whole day. Even though I barely slept, I'm still up when it reaches four a.m., stressing about the rest of the day.

Something falls in the living room, and I'm on my feet and grabbing at the metal bat hanging from the bathroom door before my brain processes what I'm doing. Our neighbors got robbed while they were out of town for the summer, but it takes a ballsy robber to break into a house that has a car parked outside. I creep into the hallway, gripping the bat so tight my hands hurt. Mami wouldn't want me putting myself out there like this, but I'm not trying to get robbed. Not when I need that jewelry for the mercado today. Having something to lose makes me braver. I get to the edge of the hallway, ready to swing at an intruder, when I hear a footstep right outside the hall. I wind up and jump out.

And swing right at my brother's head.

Cesar ducks out of the way just in time and falls on the floor. "Jesus, Yami!"

I drop the bat and clutch my chest in relief. "I thought you were a robber! Why are you out here so early?"

"Well, it's a good thing I'm not, since you swing slow as hell!" He laughs, but he's clutching his chest, too. "Couldn't sleep, I guess."

That boy really never sleeps, does he? I help him up, then realize he fell on top of some fallen jewelry. He must have knocked it over before, which explains the noise.

"Oh no . . ." I rush down on all fours to check if anything

is damaged. A necklace and a couple of the bracelets fell apart.

"Shit, Yami," Cesar says when he realizes that he broke something.

"It's fine." I sigh. It was my fault for swinging at him. It's annoying, but fixable. "It's not like they would have sold anyway. I'm the worst at this." I must look pathetic, so I stand back up. If I was Cesar, I'd have sold everything I have by now. If he can charm strangers the way he does my mom, it'd be a done deal. I gasp at the idea it gives me.

"Cesar, you have to come with me!"

"To the mercado? All day?" He looks at me with a *hell no* kind of face.

"I'll give you ten percent?" I plead, and his face immediately switches to a *hell yeah*.

I don't know where Cesar learned any of it from, but he does things a *lot* different than I do. First, we had to leave the house in our school uniforms so people will know we're kids and feel bad for us—leave it to Cesar to guilt people into buying things. Then he made us stop at Doña Violeta's to borrow her dog for the day—who knows why. And we had to set up the table differently this time.

Now we have only one of each piece displayed, so it looks like everything is one of a kind. (This one was my idea!) That way, if anyone wants to "come back," they'll be afraid of risking someone else buying the thing they want.

After I explain all the prices to Cesar, he makes me give him a play-by-play of last time so he knows what went wrong.

"Oh, sweet, sweet, Yami . . ." He shakes his head and tsks at me. I would flick him, but a little boy is pulling his mom over to us.

"Can I pet your dog?" he asks, and his mom gives us a *sorry about him* kind of look. Cesar plays with the kid, and the woman starts looking at our table to pass the time.

"How much for these?" She points at the traditional gold earrings.

Cesar cuts in before I can tell her sixty.

"They're usually eighty, but you get the cute kid discount. Seventy."

She laughs and *gets out her wallet.*

When she leaves, I'm seventy bucks richer. Well, sixty-three after I pay Cesar.

Cesar catches someone else eyeing the dog.

"You can pet her if you want!" he shouts, and they come over.

Rinse and repeat. He really is a genius.

We get a steady stream of customers throughout the day, mostly thanks to the dog or Cesar shouting compliments at people and telling them how good some bracelet or necklace or earrings would go with their skin tone. He's really hustling for that ten percent.

But by noon, he's about to fall asleep. It doesn't surprise me, since it seems like he pulled an all-nighter. We've already made almost twice what I made last week, so we call it a day and head back home.

With roughly a couple months' worth of rent and a security

deposit saved up, I'm less stressed about finding another job. I'll still need one, eventually, but the fact that no one wants to hire me doesn't sting as bad right now. I'm a jewelry-making, moneymaking machine!

I post about today's success on Insta, then start scrolling. Jamal posted recently, and I go to his profile, curious about how he's doing in New Mexico. I immediately recognize the Rover courtyard in the background of a recent picture. Taken yesterday! He's in town!

I wonder how long he'll be visiting for. If he doesn't come over to say hi, I'll drag him to the house myself. Suddenly a light bulb goes off in my head.

If Jamal comes over as my fake boyfriend, I might be able to reverse all the damage I did with my dad. If I send him a video of me and my "boyfriend," maybe he'll just forget about this whole gay thing.

I was wrong about wanting my dad to know. It's not worth it. Coming out to him was a mistake, but it's one I can fix. I call Jamal to see if he'll come over to take a video with me.

"Yami?" Jamal answers, sounding surprised.

"Hey, fake boyfriend, I need a favor."

"Is everything okay?"

"Yeah. How long are you in town for?" I ask eagerly.

"What are you talking about?"

"Before you leave, can you come over sometime and take a video with me? To send to my dad."

"Leave where? And, um, are you sure Cesar would be okay with that?" Jamal asks.

"Back to New Mexico? You're staying with your cousin, right?" I say slowly, second-guessing my entire life. What is going on? "Why wouldn't Cesar be okay with it?"

"New Mexico? Yami, I'm staying with my cousin in *Phoenix*. Cesar and I . . . we broke up. . . ." His voice cracks a little. "He didn't tell you?"

I open my mouth to answer, but all that comes out is a tiny croak. He most definitely did *not* tell me. Jamal never even left the state. I finally manage to choke out an apology, then hang up and go to Cesar's room. He's doing homework on his bed. He doesn't look up at me until I sit next to him.

"So . . . um, how are you?" I ask. I give him a look that is supposed to psychically tell him to just open up to me about what happened with Jamal.

"Good?" He squints at me. I squint back.

"What happened with you and Jamal?" I get to the point. If I don't, I'll grow a frickin' beard before we're done dancing in circles. I'm fully prepared to break our "only ask once" rule, but he actually gives me a straight answer.

"We broke up." He says it like it's no big deal.

"What? Why?" The whole day at the mercado and he didn't let on once. How freaking clueless can I be?

"Don't worry, you can still use him as your fake boyfriend." I can't tell if he's being sarcastic.

"Are you okay, though?"

"I'm fine. Are *you* okay?" He always does this. And I'm never prepared for him to turn it around on me. Let's see how he likes it when I double-whammy him.

"I'm fine, are *you* okay?"

"I'm fine, are *you* okay?" he asks again, grinning. We could go back and forth like this for ages. Maybe if I open up a little, it'll encourage him to open up, too?

"Have you heard from Dad?" I ask.

"Yeah, he sent me a video this morning, but I haven't watched it yet."

"Pull it up." I scoot closer so I can look at his phone over his shoulder.

Cesar opens the Marco Polo app and plays the video from Dad. Seeing his face makes me want to cry, I miss him so much.

"Hola, Peke! I gotta show you something." My dad is the only one Cesar lets call him "Peke," short for pequeño, because Cesar has always been short for his age, and skipping a grade makes him seem even smaller. The camera moves to face a lake in the middle of a plaza. He zooms in on a brown duck with a bunch of fuzz on its head. He's laughing. The camera goes back to his face. "Do you remember Canela? Doesn't she look just like her? I thought you might like that." He keeps laughing, and the video ends.

My throat contracts. Dad used to take Cesar and me to the park to feed the ducks when we were little. Canela was the only duck with a ball of fuzz perpetually stuck to her head, so she was our favorite. We "adopted" her and looked for her specifically every time we went to the park. I was there with them, but Dad only wanted to tell Cesar.

The video was sent this morning. Which confirms again that he could have responded to me but didn't. He could have responded to me a hundred times by now. And he's talking to Cesar about something I was involved in. I want to throw up.

There's no avoiding it anymore. My dad, my idol, who was once upon a time the most trusted person in my life, wants nothing to do with me.

It's such bullshit that there's a stigma around being closeted. We get shit for "living a lie" just because we want to survive. I don't want to keep losing everyone I'm close to. I don't want to get disowned and kicked out of my house. It's self-preservation, not dishonesty. I don't owe anyone the truth, and I'll take my damn time with talking about it. Maybe never a-fucking-gain.

It's not like I can come out once and be done with it, either. I came out six times already. To Bianca, Cesar, Hunter, Jamal, my dad, and Bo. Maybe Bo doesn't count, since I don't think she got the message. But if I'm "living a lie," then so is every straight person who's never "come out" to every single person in their life about their sexuality. I shouldn't have to talk about it if I don't want to. I don't want to *have* to tell everyone. Not after how Dad reacted. Or didn't.

"You good?" Cesar asks.

I shake my head and wipe my nose.

"You mad at him or something?"

I shake my head again and leave for my room before he sees me cry. Maybe this opening-up thing can wait.

Cesar and I are both quiet during dinner.

"You haven't mentioned Jamal lately. ¿Qué pasó?" Mom asks.

"Um . . ." I glance at Cesar. He stabs his enchilada with his fork and keeps his eyes on his food. He did say I could keep fake-dating him. . . .

"Nothing, we're fine," I say. "He's back in town now."

"I thought you guys broke up," Cesar says coldly, and I have to resist rolling my eyes at him—he's so fickle. He takes another jab at his plate with his fork without putting any food in his mouth. What does he want from me?

Mom almost chokes on her food. "¿Por qué?"

"I . . . um . . ." I don't even know the real reason Cesar and Jamal broke up, so I have no idea what to say. He cheated on me? I cheated on him? I don't love him anymore? Mom adds some questions of her own.

"Did he hurt you? Did he cheat?" She gasps, "He's gay, isn't he? I knew there was something wrong with that boy!" Okay, ouch. I clutch my silverware tighter.

"I hoped I was wrong, but I always suspected it. Such a shame, he was so cute, too. . . ." She tuts disapprovingly, then snaps her fingers like she just solved a mystery. "*That's* why he got kicked out of his house, ¿qué no? His folks must have found out. That makes more sense."

"Mom, no . . ." My voice comes out weak, and I hope she thinks it's because I'm upset about the breakup. Not that she just confirmed being gay was a disownable offense. "I don't want to talk about it, okay?" Cesar didn't want to talk about it either, so it's a realistic reaction.

"I have homework." Cesar takes his barely touched plate to

the sink, where he lets it drop loudly before storming off. I wish I could do the same.

"What's wrong with him?" Mom doesn't wait for him to be out of earshot.

Maybe he's mad because his mom is homophobic.

I shrug.

"It's good he left, because I have something I want to talk to you about," she whispers.

"Okay?"

"Since your brother's birthday is coming up, I thought we could do something special."

"Yeah?" Cesar's birthday is December 23. Mine's on February 12, so both of our birthdays are overshadowed by some other big holiday. At least Cesar gets double the presents.

"I've been saving up some money. I have enough to send the two of you over to your dad's for the winter break!" She shows me a printed-out itinerary, tearing up. We leave on Monday. I swallow down bile. She doesn't know Dad's not talking to me, and I can't tell her why without risking the same treatment from her. Or worse, since I kind of depend on her for survival.

"You wouldn't be coming?" I ask.

"I only have enough for two tickets, so no. It's okay, though. You spend every Christmas with me. You should get to spend one with your dad." She looks sad that she can't go, but so happy for me at the same time, I can't handle it.

"Mom . . ." Now we're both tearing up. If she had told me

this two months ago, they would have been tears of joy, which I'm sure Mom thinks they are.

"WHAT!" Cesar calls out from the hallway. He was probably eavesdropping to see if we would keep talking about Jamal. He rushes back to the table and sits down.

"We're going to see Dad?"

Mom throws her arms up in defeat. "You couldn't wait for me to surprise you?"

"Thank you, Mami! Thank you, thank you!" Cesar gives her a tight hug and kisses her on the cheek. They're talking back and forth, but I can't concentrate anymore.

"I can't go," I interrupt.

"¿Y por qué no?" She's using her scary voice now, and I can't help it. I break down into a teary, blubbering mess, and she ditches Cesar to hug me instead. Her scary voice completely vanishes. "Mija, what's wrong?"

I can't answer that, so I just sob into her chest. She doesn't say anything, just rubs my back while I cry. Her hand on my back coaxes the tears to calm, and I wish things could stay like this between us forever. I wipe my eyes. I have to get myself together enough to make an excuse.

"I'm just really stressed with homework. I have a huge project due after break, I have to stay and finish it."

"Okay, mija, it's okay." She strokes my hair.

"Mami, are you gonna take Yami's ticket and come with me?" Cesar asks. My throat contracts again. If she goes, and Dad tells her . . .

"And leave Yamilet here alone? I don't think so," she says, and I let out my breath.

"Um . . . But I'm still going, though, right?" Cesar asks, and Mami rubs her temple.

"Mijo, I don't want you flying out there by yourself."

"Are you kidding me? It's for my birthday! Suck it up and do your homework there, Yami!" he shouts.

"I can't . . . I can't . . ." My voice cracks. When both Cesar and I are in tears, Mami finally gives in.

"Okay, okay. But if I go, how do I know you're not going to burn my house down, huh?" she asks.

"I'm practically an adult. It'll be fine. Look at me! I'm giving up vacation with Dad to do *homework*." I sniffle, but I think I still sound convincing. "If that doesn't scream responsibility, I don't know what does."

Mami chews on her lip. "Well . . . I guess you are old enough. But if you're going to stay here, you need to focus on your project. No working or nothing like that, all right?"

"Really? But what about all our orders?" I ask.

"I handled this before you started helping me, and I'll handle it now. Focus on your homework. I'll take care of the rest on my own, con el favor de Dios."

"Okay, Mami."

She pulls me back into the hug. I love my mom. I'll enjoy her hugs for now, before she decides she wants nothing to do with me after hearing Dad's side of the story. He'll probably tell her when they visit. A selfish part of me wants to convince her not to go, but I know Cesar would never forgive me if I ruined this for him. Frankly, I wouldn't forgive myself.

I should probably warn Cesar. If he's going to be spending time with Dad, he should know how he really feels about people like us. I follow him to his room.

"Can I help you?" he says when he realizes I'm following him.

"I came out to Dad," I whisper as I walk in and close the door behind me.

"What? What'd he say?"

"Nothing. I texted him after the homecoming party. I still haven't heard from him."

"Oh . . ." He rubs his head. "Maybe he never got it?"

"He got it," I snap.

"How do you know?"

"Because I know! I sent him a video, too. And he hasn't said shit."

"Seriously, you can't convince me not to go, if that's what you're trying to do."

"I just want you to be careful. But why would you even *want* to go if you know he's homophobic? If he finds out about you, he won't treat you any different." I immediately feel bad for saying it, even though it's true.

"You're so dramatic! He probably just didn't see your text."

"Then why'd he send you a video and not me? Canela was my duck just as much as yours!" I'm crying again.

"Goddamn it, Yami, not everything is about you!" He hits his fist on his desk.

I step back. Cesar raising his voice at me is enough to make the tears stop, out of surprise more than anything.

"He's allowed to talk to me first sometimes! Dad sent me a video because he knew I was having a shit day. Can you just let me deal with my own shit for *one* day? I can't talk about this with you." He's shaking now.

"Well I'm having a shit day too! Why won't he talk to *me*?" I know I'm not being fair. It's not Cesar's fault that Dad hates me.

"Maybe because you don't know how to leave people the fuck alone! Not every problem is yours to fix! You're always in my business. With Jamal, football, and now with Dad . . . Just let me do what I want to do for once! He's *my* dad too!"

"What are you talking about? If I didn't cover for you—"

"I never *asked* you to cover for me! I never asked you to date Jamal or come to Slayton! You can't keep me away from Dad just because he doesn't want to talk to *you*."

I hate that I can't stop crying. And I hate that he's right.

"He won't *talk* to me. . . ." It finally hits me when I say it out loud. Another sob escapes.

Cesar sighs, and his voice softens. "Shit, Yami, he's probably busy or something."

I can't keep talking about Dad, or I won't be able to stop crying. I just leave.

Maybe I need to give Cesar some space. I need to deal with my own shit and let him deal with his. He's right about that, and if he wants me to leave him alone so bad, I will. But he's wrong about our dad.

+ + +

Bo's dad is calling me. Early. It's Sunday and I'm not really trying to be awake yet. I know I gave Bo's parents my number, but
I never expected them to actually call. I answer because I still
want to make a better impression on them—can't leave them
thinking I'm a drunken mess.

"Hello?"

"Hi, is this Yamilet?"

"Yeah, hi, Mr. Taylor," I say, trying to match his upbeat tone.

"Please, call me Rick."

"Okay, what's up?"

"I have a problem I think you can help solve." He sounds
like an infomercial, and it's hard not to laugh.

"Yeah?"

"I'm making some pies."

"Okay . . ."

"And there's no way Emma, Bo, and I will be able to eat
them all on our own. We need your help, Yamilet." His tone is
urgent, like he's dispatching me on an important mission.

"Dad! Stop calling my friends!" Bo shouts in the background.

"She's my friend too. Right, Yamilet?" I can hear the grin
on his face, and I laugh. There are sounds of a struggle on the
line, and then Bo's voice instead of her dad's. Her voice alone
gives me butterflies.

"Sorry about my dad. He's just . . . like that. He gets bored
and starts baking way too much sometimes. You don't have to
come if you don't want to. But there will be pie. A lot of it. If
you do want to."

"What kind of pie?"

Bo echoes my question to her dad, and he shouts out the answer loud enough for me to hear.

"Pumpkin, apple, cherry! You like something else, I'll make it!"

I laugh again. "That sounds awesome. I'll see if I can get a ride."

"Great! Cesar can come, too, if he wants!"

"I think he's busy." Lie. I've been avoiding him since our fight.

Amber is out of town for break, so it's just me and David going to Bo's. I'm relieved Hunter wasn't invited, too, because then I'd surely have to invite Cesar. Sometimes I forget Hunter isn't as close to Bo as me, David, and Amber. Today, I'm grateful for it.

My house is on the way to Bo's from David's place, so I get up the nerve to ask him for a ride. I feel okay about David knowing where I live, since I know he won't judge. It's not that I think Bo would judge me, it's just . . . different. David lives on the Navajo res. There aren't many Bo-sized houses there.

David honks when his old blue pickup truck pulls up outside my house. I hop into the passenger seat and close the door. It's a lighter door than I expected, so it shuts a little hard. David gasps.

"Be careful with Tootsie! She's too old to be getting her doors slammed." Apparently, his truck's name is Tootsie.

"Sorry . . . why Tootsie?"

"She just looks like a Tootsie, don't you think?" He smiles, patting the steering wheel endearingly.

"You know what, yeah, she does." I can't explain it, but it somehow makes sense.

We spend the ride listening to metalcore. Well, I'm more listening to David screaming and drumming on the steering wheel than the actual music. I have no idea how people get their voices to do that, but it's pretty impressive.

When we finally get to Bo's house, her dad opens the door and waves us both inside.

"Come on in!" He jogs back to the kitchen, leaving the door open for us.

"Hi! So nice to see you two!" Bo's mom flicks off the living room TV and hops off the couch to greet us.

"Bo! Our friends are here!" her dad calls from the kitchen.

"*My* friends, Dad!" Bo shouts from somewhere upstairs. It's only a few seconds before she comes scampering down the steps, wearing baggy denim overalls with one shoulder strap down. The white crop top underneath shows just a hint of skin on her sides. Exposed side torso skin = the sexiest part of the lesbian anatomy. Who the hell gave her permission to look this cute?

Bo's dad doesn't give me a chance to get all tongue-tied, since he immediately herds us toward the dining room table. After he sits us down, he dances his way into the kitchen, even though there's no music playing. My mom would never have people over with no music on, so it feels like something's missing.

"Don't worry, kids, Rick's pies are the best," Bo's mom says as we all sit.

"He's so embarrassing . . ." Bo covers her face, but she's laughing.

"Are you kidding? Your dad is the best!" David says.

Bo rolls her eyes, and her dad walks over, masterfully carrying three pies in his two arms.

The wait during the time it takes him to put down, cut, and serve the pies is excruciating. If it was my mom, we'd all be serving ourselves, which I prefer, since I can control when I stuff my face with beautiful pie. This is the "proper" way, though, apparently.

David, Bo, and I are shoveling pie into our mouths for a good minute before any of us are ready for civil conversation. While we're eating, all I can hear is the sound of pie being cut and silverware clinking on plates until Bo's dad breaks the silence.

"So, any plans for the rest of winter break?"

"I'll be helping my dad out with work," David says while chewing.

"That'll be fun, I'm sure," Bo's mom says.

"Tile installation. *Super* fun," he says with a smirk.

"What about you, Yamilet?" Bo's mom asks.

I take a big bite of pie instead of answering. Classy, I know. Not a good solution, since I eventually have to chew and swallow, and answer the question.

"Um, I'm not doing anything."

"What? No Christmas plans?" Bo's dad asks, and her mom steps on him under the table. He jumps a little. "Sorry, holiday plans?" It's refreshing, because they know we go to a Catholic school, but they still don't expect us to celebrate.

"No . . ." I don't have the energy to make up a lie, so I tell them. "My mom and Cesar are going to Mexico to visit my dad for Cesar's birthday, but I didn't want to go."

Bo's dad gasps out loud. "You'll be all by yourself for Christmas?" Another kick under the table.

"Yeah. We do celebrate Christmas, but . . ." I have to be mindful with my breathing in order to keep from choking up. I can't tell them about my dad without explaining everything. "I have a big project for chemistry, so I have to stay home and work on it."

Bo's head tilts like a confused puppy, and David looks at me like he knows I'm lying. Shit. They have the same teacher, so they know there's no big project. To their credit, they don't blow my cover.

"Oh, honey . . ." Bo's mom reaches over the table and grabs my hand. "You're more than welcome to spend break with us! I don't want you spending your break all alone."

"Really?" I look at Bo, not her parents. It's her I want to make sure is cool with this. I've never stayed at anyone's house for more than a weekend, and if she still has a girlfriend, things might be a little weird. I should probably ask about that at some point, but I'm afraid I'd sound gay about it. An unreadable expression flashes across Bo's face, and her cheeks flush before she smiles.

"Of course!" both her parents answer. I raise my eyebrows at Bo, urging an answer out of her. I would understand if she didn't want me at her house for two weeks straight.

"Yeah, it'll be fun!" she says, smiling again.

"Great! My mom will probably love that idea. She was worried about leaving me by myself." It does sound like a step up from spending the break wallowing in self-pity.

Taking Cesar and my mom to the airport is harder than I expected. I haven't been talking to Cesar much lately, which isn't fair. The only reason I'm not talking to him is because he's not talking to me. If he would just apologize, I'd forgive him in an instant. I know it's petty to hold a grudge, but what am I supposed to do? If I'm a petty bitch, so is Cesar. He didn't even cave to make some kind of joke about how I'm staying with Bo. I'm not good with conflict, but it's been too long to turn back now. Usually we get over our fights within a day. But there's something different about this one, and I don't know what it is. I hate that.

When she's not looking, I slip my mom's phone into her bag so she can find it later. There's no point in keeping it from her now if she's actually going to see Dad in person. She gives me the biggest hug I've gotten since probably ever. She's crying, and I feel nothing. I can't feel anything right now, or I'll break down. Mom looks at us expectantly, so Cesar gives me a half-assed side hug, and I return it. I don't cry until I turn around.

I walk straight to the parking lot and don't look back.

16

THOU SHALT NOT FOSTER PETTY GRUDGES

I'm glad for Bo's family to keep me from getting too far in my feelings, but maybe spending break with my crush was not the best idea. What if all this time alone with Bo is going to have me doing something very Yami-like, like outing myself . . . again. I could have stayed home, but I can't go back now, so here I am with Bo. Perfect Bo, who I avoid eye contact with because I can't look at her without getting lost. This should be interesting.

While they're gone, Mami sends me video updates on Marco Polo. Cesar is sometimes in them, but as a background voice. If she asks him to say hi, he waves, but doesn't say much. Dad isn't in the videos. If he told Mom why he doesn't want to talk to me, then she seems to be cool about the gay thing. But I'm guessing he hasn't. I'm not going to bring it up. If I do, and he really didn't tell her, then I'm screwed. If he did tell her and I bring it up, then what's the benefit of that? Just knowing? Nah, I don't need to know. I'm good, right here in the dark.

Half the time Mom sends videos, she's in the middle of visiting with Dad's family, so the calls are usually pretty short. I stare at the app for a while after Mom's video is over. It's not that I'm expecting anything to happen. Actually, I know nothing is going to happen, which is why I'm staring at it. I want to *make* something happen. I think I'm ready to talk to him. Not to my dad. I won't be ready to talk to my dad until he's ready to talk to me. If he ever is.

I start a video for Cesar.

"Hey . . . hi. We haven't talked in a while. I miss you. . . ." I'm rambling, but I don't want to stop talking, because I haven't talked to him in so long, and this is the closest I've been able to get to it. "How's Chiapas?" I pause as if waiting for an answer. "I don't know if you're still mad at me. But I'm not mad anymore. Actually, I was never mad. I just suck at human communication. I'll own that. Anyways, talk to me, if you don't hate me, please. Bye . . ." I hang up before saying the *I love you* part.

I end the video and let out a deep sigh. I don't want to be alone right now, so I go to find Bo. She's lying on the couch on her phone, a few hair wispies escaping her messy bun. She looks even cuter in a messy bun than I ever could have imagined. I picture her resting her messy bun-head in my lap while I tame the wispies for her. Even though she's right in front of me, the thought makes me feel lonely. I can't just go around playing with a taken girl's hair wispies.

It hits me then that *Bo's* been alone most of break so far

too. Maybe Cesar was right, and she doesn't have a girlfriend anymore? No, no, no, Bo would have told me if they broke up. She's not like Cesar. Maybe she hasn't invited her over because of me? I wonder if my being here would make it awkward to have her over.

"You should invite Jamie over." I sit on the other couch. Why am I encouraging this? I hate it, but maybe it'll help me get over Bo if I have to see her with her girlfriend. Then again, maybe they want their alone time. "I have my mom's car, so I can go somewhere and leave you guys alone. If you want." Bo's face drops, and she looks almost sad. Crap. Maybe she and Jamie did break up, and I've just reopened the wound.

She sighs. "Jamie's out of town to stay with her parents for break, unfortunately."

Oh. "I'm sorry. That sucks." For both of us.

Bo sinks into the couch, and I feel bad for bringing her down. I hate how weird this conversation feels now.

"So what's it like dating a college girl?" Part of me asks because I want to cheer her up, but the other part is just curious. I'm guessing Jamie is with her family over break instead of staying in the Arizona State dorms. I wonder if Bo is worried about what will happen with them when she graduates.

"She's only a year older, so it's not *that* weird."

"Oh, I didn't mean it like that! I was just curious."

"You're good."

Now we're sitting in awkward silence, and I can't figure out how to change the subject. Bo's whole mood changed when

I brought Jamie up. She must really miss her. I'm totally not jealous. The silence between me and Bo right now makes me completely *not* jealous of how she probably doesn't have awkward silences like this with Jamie. I miss my mom's cumbia music filling the quiet. I even miss Doña Violeta's weepy music. How am I supposed to cheer myself up if there's no music?

"Don't you guys ever listen to music?" I ask. Bo listens to her headphones sometimes, but there's never music playing out loud. I don't have headphones, so I sort of hate when she has them on instead of sharing her music with me.

"What? Of course we do."

"Do you have a rule against playing it in the house or something?" I'm not trying to be sarcastic. I genuinely don't know if there's some bigger reason they don't play it.

"Um, no?"

"Well then, do you have a speaker or something? I'm having withdrawals."

"Yeah! One sec." Bo hops off the couch and goes to her room. She comes back out with a Bluetooth speaker. She puts it on the table and sets it up with her phone. "What do you want to listen to?"

"You can pick. I just need some noise in here."

"You have to promise you won't make fun of me."

"Promise." I doubt her playlist could be cheesier than mine—a random mix of Disney music, reggaetón, cumbia, and musical soundtracks.

"Actually, you know what? If you can honestly tell me this

doesn't make you want to dance, then you can make fun of me. But that's not gonna happen," she says. I don't know how, but she got me feeling better before even starting the music.

She presses play and starts dancing. I don't know what I was expecting, but it wasn't *this*.

"Disco?"

"What's wrong with disco??"

"Nothing, it's just not what I expected."

"Fact: the fall of disco is the direct result of homophobia and racism. As a Gaysian, I take full offense to that." Bo flops on the floor in what looks like an attempt at a shablam to emphasize her point. Then she gets up and starts jumping and spinning in circles.

I don't know why I expected Bo to be a good dancer. She seems perfect in every way because she's such a badass at—I thought—everything. But this is one thing I definitely have her beat on. I'm not sure why she asked me not to make fun of her. She's clearly not afraid of my judgment.

She points at me as if to invite me to dance with her, but I'd rather watch. Then she swings a fake lasso and pretends to reel me in.

I have no choice.

I'm pulled off the couch against my will, and just like that, I'm bouncing and twirling around with her. I feel like we're in a nightclub in space—that's the vibe I get from disco. It seriously needs a revival.

Bo grabs my hands, and for some reason the music keeps

me from overthinking it. We start spinning around each other until everything but Bo seems to whirl around the room. Like she's the only constant thing around. She throws her head back in laughter and holds onto my hands tighter to compensate for the picked-up speed. Then I trip over a clump of air, sending both of us toppling in opposite directions, giggling hysterically over the music.

I like how Bo can make me forget about stuff. I don't have to worry about what other people think, and I can enjoy being around her without thinking about everything else going on. I don't think about my dad or Cesar until the sun goes down, when I check Marco Polo to find nothing. Cesar hasn't watched my video yet, so at least he didn't leave me on read like Dad did. I sent him another video for his birthday earlier today, but he didn't respond to that one either.

The sound of the garage door opening brings me out of my sulking. Bo and I go downstairs to say hi, but her mom doesn't look too happy.

"Rick, can you *please* do the dishes? I'm working all day and I don't appreciate coming home to a dirty sink."

I want to disappear. I feel like I shouldn't be witnessing any-one's family arguments, but they don't seem to mind that I'm here. Rick, who's watching TV in the living room, doesn't answer.

"Hello?? Did you not hear me?"

He still doesn't say anything, and this time Bo steps in. "Dad, Mom's calling you."

"Relax, babe, I'm on it," Rick finally calls out as he turns off the TV.

"You could at least answer me so I'm not talking to myself."

"Well, I'm so sorry I don't respond well to nagging."

Bo clears her throat, which seems to remind her parents that they have an audience. Bo's dad turns red and gives a quick apology and gets to the dishes while her mom seems to notice Bo for the first time since she got home. She holds her arms out for a hug, and Bo runs into it, holding her mom tight. It's not like a regular *hi, Mom* hug, but a real one, squeezing and everything. I always thought Bo wasn't really a hugger, but I guess she is? Maybe it's just with family. I haven't had a hug since Mom and Cesar left. I miss my mom's hugs. I might be touch-starved at the moment. Ugh. Guess I'm not done sulking.

It's sweet how much Bo's parents love her. And how much her dogs love her. And her friends. And me. She's a very loved person.

I guess I am, too, if I think about it. My mom loves me a lot. And even if Cesar is ignoring me, I know he still loves me. Somewhere deep, deep down. But with my mom, at least, it feels conditional. Like if I'm not exactly who she needs me to be, then I'm unlovable. Maybe she doesn't actually love me, but the person she thinks I am. The way Bianca did. And my dad. My own fucking dad.

I haven't been able to be really close with someone in a long time. The closest I can get is some kind of fake-Yami limited closeness. I know straight Yami is lovable. Sometimes I wonder about *me*, though. I always lose people when they find out. Except for Cesar. But maybe I lost him, too. I don't know.

Maybe I'm being dramatic. He's my brother. Siblings fight. It's probably not a big deal.

Still, there's a little bubble in my chest that's been growing the last couple of days since they left. I wonder if they're having fun right now. I wonder if they're having too great a time with each other to think about missing me. I wonder if they're all bonding over how much they hate me.

And if Mom knows now, I wonder if Cesar is okay.

17

REMEMBER THY ANCESTORS. KEEP THEM HOLY.

Bo's parents apparently have a no-presents rule for Christmas, but I still feel like I have to give them some kind of thank-you gift. They're giving me a place to stay and keeping me company all break. Christmas is tomorrow, so I don't have much time to figure it out. The least I can do is . . . something. I have no idea. They won't even let me do chores around the house, because I'm "the guest." I feel like a huge burden without being able to *do something.*

I can't wrap my head around why they're so kind to me. I definitely don't deserve it. Maybe I should go home to save them the trouble. But at the same time, I selfishly want the special treatment. When I go home from break, I'll have to face my mom. If she hasn't found out I'm gay yet, she probably will before I see her again. Staying here makes that problem feel so much more distant.

I still don't know what to do about money once that happens. Maybe if I drop out of school, finding a job will be easier since I could work full-time? I never thought about dropping out before, but I'll have to if I get kicked out. Honestly, I was never that great in school anyway.

Bo interrupts my thoughts by blasting "Take Me to Church" while she showers. She's been playing her music out loud more ever since I brought it up. That song seems to be a favorite of hers. She calls it the lesbian anthem. And she's definitely not afraid to belt it in the shower, where her voice echoes throughout the whole upper floor, muffled only by the flow of water. I would be mortified to let anyone hear me singing, let alone in the shower. But I guess that's another difference between me and Bo. She's not afraid of anything.

Sometimes I wish I was more like Bo. Unapologetic, proud, happy, supported. But I also wish I was less like her. I wish I didn't have to *want* to be unapologetic. I wish there was nothing for me to be unapologetic about.

I don't know what else to do, so I pray for the first time in a long time.

But it doesn't make me feel any better.

It's two in the morning and I've been lying in bed, staring at the ceiling, for the last two hours. It's officially Christmas. After working all day yesterday, I'm embarrassed with the present I came up with. I don't know what I was thinking. It's too personal. They'll probably think it's stupid. They'll know I did it because I couldn't afford to get them a real present.

Maybe I shouldn't have bothered. This isn't my family, and

this isn't my house. It's too perfect. Bo's parents are too nice to me, and they're all too happy. And I'm trying to be perfect and nice and happy, too, but I feel like an imposter, and I kind of just want to be miserable right now. There's no way I'll be able to sleep tonight, so I wander downstairs to get some chips or something.

When I pass by Bo's parents' room, the sound of them bickering throws me off a little. They're still awake? I plug my ears as I pass by, so as not to intrude on their argument. Just another reason I feel like I don't belong here. I open the pantry and grab a bag of chips when I hear my name. I stop where I stand and shamelessly eavesdrop. They seem to have calmed down and are just talking normally now, but if their previous argument had to do with me, it's my business.

"Why do you think she didn't go to Mexico with her family?" Rick's voice. The words tug on my gut. They know I lied about the school project? Maybe they know more about the curriculum than I thought. I should have kept up some kind of act and pretended to do homework. I get in my head and miss some of the conversation.

"Poor girl. No kid should have to live like that." Bo's mom.

Live like what? I don't know what assumptions they've made about me, but I'm doing just fine. I don't need their charity, or their pity. I don't deserve it. I back away and run up to the guest room. Without giving it another thought, I start packing my bag. It would be in everyone's favor if I left before they all woke up.

I sneak downstairs again. Just as I'm passing the kitchen,

water from the sink turns on, and I scream. So does Bo's dad. His plastic water cup falls to the ground.

He brushes himself off when he realizes it's me. "What are you doing up?" he asks. Then his eyes go to my bag. "Are you leaving?"

"Oh, I was . . . um . . ." I can't think of a good lie right now, and I can feel blood rushing to my face. I make myself meet his eyes. "I heard you guys talking about me."

"Oh, sweetie, I'm sorry." He looks surprised and a little confused, like he still doesn't get why I'm leaving.

"I don't want to be a burden on you," I say.

"Okay, I mean this in the nicest way possible, but what are you talking about?"

"I don't want to make you guys fight. And you don't have to take care of me out of pity." I cross my arms. I know it makes me look defensive, but it's more of a self-hug right now.

"Hon, I'm really sorry you had to hear us fighting again, but you have to know that kind of thing just happens. It has nothing to do with you, that's not what we were saying at all." His face softens.

"Then what were you saying?" I grip my suitcase in one hand to ground me, but also in case I want to bolt.

Rick sighs. "We wish you felt safe enough to tell us the truth about what's going on with your family, but I get that it's none of our business. We're just worried about you. We *care* about you, Yamilet. We *like* having you around. You're the furthest thing from a burden to us."

I open my mouth, but I can't find my words. I can't relax my shoulders. Tears sting at my lashes, and I can feel my lip start trembling.

"I hate the idea of you being alone for so long, especially over the holidays. But if that's really what you want, then I won't stop you. Is that what you want?"

"No!" I hate how the word comes out like a sob. He puts a hand on my shoulder, and the touch pulls the tears out of my eyes. I don't mean to, but I release my grip on the suitcase and fall into a hug. He flinches in surprise for a second before he starts rubbing my back.

"Hey, it's all right. It's all right," he repeats over and over until I pull away.

"I'm sorry, this is so embarrassing." I hide my face with my hands.

"Okay, I'm not an expert at this sort of thing, but it seems like there's something bigger going on here. Do you want to talk about it?" he asks.

I bite my bottom lip to keep it from trembling.

"I miss my dad," I whisper. I don't even know if he can hear me.

"Maybe we should sit." He walks over to the couch and sits, and I follow him.

"Being a teenager has got to be a really rough time for you. It's confusing, I'm sure. There's a lot you're figuring out about yourself, and not everyone is going to support you. But know you have me in your corner, all right? And Emma, too. We might fight sometimes, but that doesn't mean we don't love each other, or Bo, or you, okay?"

I can't tell if this is a generic "troubled teen" pep talk or if he's trying to insinuate something. Does he know I'm gay? He can't know. Does he suspect it? Am I overthinking it?

"Thank you" is all I can say. He smiles and nods at my suitcase.

"So hey, if you still want to leave, you can. But I'd love for you to stay for breakfast. I was about to make your favorite."

"How do you know what my favorite breakfast is?"

"Because you're about to tell me." He smiles. "So, what's for breakfast?"

"Chorizo burritos." I don't know why talking about my favorite breakfast food makes me tear up.

"You got it. If you still want to leave after I make you some bomb chorizo burritos, go ahead. But not without a proper goodbye, all right?"

"Okay. Thanks, Mr. Taylor." I wipe my eyes.

"Rick." He pulls me into another hug. "Now go get some sleep. It's too early for crying. Save that for the happy tears when you're eating the best chorizo burritos of your life."

I laugh. I doubt he can top my mom's. He gives me a pat on the back before sending me back upstairs.

Rick is a good cook. He's a great cook. But his burritos don't taste like the ones I'm used to. Don't get me wrong: they're amazing. They might even be up there with my mom's when it comes to the cooking itself. But I didn't just want a good chorizo burrito. I wanted my mom's cooking. I wanted my mom. Really, I want Cesar, too. And my dad. I want all of them, together.

It makes me feel like shit for not being grateful about the chorizo burritos I'm eating now. I eat them like they're exactly what I need. I smile and say thank you and have seconds. But it's not the same.

We gather around the tree for "presents." Which is basically all of us going around in a circle brainstorming things we can do together. Instead of giving gifts, the idea is to spend the day doing things we all want to do. The activities can take place anytime from today until New Year's. It's the first Christmas I've ever had that no one dragged me to church. It feels weird, but in a good way.

Bo's mom wants to watch a family movie at the house, which makes me nervous because I'm not sure if I'm supposed to be included, since she said "family" movie. Rick wants to go ice blocking, which I've only done once before when I was little. Bo and I both take longer to decide what we want to do.

"Maybe we can get culture passes at the library?" I ask. It's the only free thing that comes to mind. The library offers free "culture passes" for local events.

"That sounds like a great idea! I'll look up what they have available in the next few days." Bo's mom pulls out her phone and types away.

"For my present, can we eat at C-Fu?" Bo asks.

"Of course!" her dad responds. I've never been there, but

from what I heard, it's a fancy Chinese restaurant, and Bo's favorite.

"I'm looking at the culture passes now," Bo's mom says as she scrolls on her phone. "Looks like we can go to the science center, the Japanese friendship garden, and, oh! This looks fun! There's a ballet, oh, gosh, I'm going to butcher the pronunciation here, ballet folclórico festival on the twenty-eighth! Which do you want to go to, Yamilet?"

It's not a hard choice, but I'm hesitant to ask.

"Can we go to the baile folklórico show?" I barely hear my own voice. Since being at Slayton, I've been feeling a little culturally separated, not to mention super homesick right now. Going to a Mexican baile performance sounds like the perfect Band-Aid. Plus, I kind of want to share a little bit of who I am with Bo and her family. It's my way of opening up to them.

Bo's dad fist-pumps. "I was hoping you'd pick that one. So, today we can do a movie and go to C-Fu if it's not too busy. The festival on the twenty-eighth, and I think ice blocking will be a New Year's Eve outing!"

I know today will be fun, but I'm *so* ready for the twenty-eighth.

"So what movie should we watch?" Bo asks.

"You should pick, Yamilet! What's your favorite movie?" Bo's mom says to me. So I am allowed to join. Which I guess should have been obvious. It's not like they would have made me hide in the guest room or leave for them to watch a movie.

"You probably won't have it," I say. My favorite movie is

Selena, of course. It's almost a rite of passage for Mexican Americans to have seen it, but it's probably not mainstream enough for Bo's family to own.

"Maybe not, but if we don't have it, we'll buy it," Bo's mom says. I blink to keep from showing my surprise. It blows my mind that they can buy whatever movies they want whenever they have a craving to watch them.

"*Selena*." My neck retracts like a shy turtle when I say it. I don't know why being intentionally included in a family thing makes me so nervous. It's not as personal as going to a baile folklórico show, but sharing my favorite movie with them still feels like opening up.

"I'll get it right now!" Bo's mom says, and less than an hour later, we're all in the living room with popcorn and sodas.

Bo's mom and dad cuddle up on one couch, while Bo and I sit on the other. When they're not fighting, Bo's parents are pretty sweet with each other. Meanwhile, Bo's knee touches mine sometimes. So that's something.

Okay. Not just something. Maybe I'm more than a little touch-starved. When our knees scrape against each other, it feels like static electricity throughout my whole body. It makes the hairs on my arms stand up. Who gets butterflies from freaking knee touching? A burning sensation fills my face before I can enjoy the butterflies too much. I feel like everyone around me can tell when I have a gay-ish feeling, as if I'm radiating some kind of intensely gay aura, and that terrifies me. Bo shifts, leaving my knee all alone, like she's recoiling in disgust. But then she pulls her legs onto the couch and crosses them. Now our *thighs* are touching.

Suddenly it's hard to breathe. I'm afraid one of my standing arm hairs could prick her like a cactus needle, and she'll *know*. I hear Bianca's voice in my head telling me how gross I am. I fold my arms so the hairs lie flat, and cross my legs so our thighs don't touch. I spend the rest of the movie painfully aware of every inch of my body. How much space it takes up. How much distance there is between me and Bo at any given moment. Whether I come across as too comfortable, or not comfortable enough with her. How heavy my breathing is. No gay auras here. No *Selena*, either. I'm too focused on our not-touching.

I don't realize how hungry I am until Rick brings up C-Fu after the movie. When we get there, it's busy, but apparently not busy enough to go another day. While we wait for the food to come, Bo and I walk around the restaurant. She just seems so happy here with me, so I force my angsty self-conscious feelings deep down and let myself enjoy her contagious smile.

There are huge fish tanks in some of the walls, and Bo grabs my wrist to pull me toward the tanks. She hasn't stopped smiling since we got here. She is radiating some serious happy vibes. It almost makes me forget how hungry I am.

"Which one looks the yummiest?" she asks. I look around and notice a huge shriveled-up flaccid penis clam . . . thing. I point at it and grin.

"That one. The penis fish. Mmmm . . ."

"Yami*let!*" She chokes on her laugh and wheezes. I didn't

think it was *that* funny, but there's no way I'm complaining about making Bo laugh. Not when it looks and sounds like (chef's kiss) *that*.

"What about you?" I ask. She points to one of the bottom feeders.

"See that grumpy-looking guy? Rockfish. They're good in soup. Yours is a Pacific geoduck clam." Bo starts pointing at the different fish and explaining them to me. She's kind of rambling, but I've never seen her this joyful about anything, besides maybe disco. Bo is really knowledgeable about a lot of things, like disco and social justice, but I wasn't expecting her to be any kind of fish expert.

Fish don't particularly interest me, but Bo is so excited about them it's hard not to get into it. I find myself asking questions just to hear her talk. I can't get enough.

"How do you know so much about fish?" I ask when she's gone through all of them.

"I just really like this restaurant." She shrugs, but I feel like there's more to it. Before I can ask, she changes the subject.

"So . . . my dad told me you tried to leave." She says it casually, without looking away from the fish tank.

"Oh, um, yeah. I felt bad for intruding on your guys' Christmas, I guess."

"Oh my gosh. Please intrude more. It'd be so boring if you left!"

"Really?"

"Trust me, you're keeping my parents on their best behavior.

They fight way more when you're not here. And it's way more fun with you here." She turns her head away from the fish tank to give me an adorably crooked full-cheeked smile. "Besides, I'd miss you too much if you left."

"Really?" I say again, this time barely hiding the squeal that wants to escape.

"Of course! Wouldn't you miss me?"

Obviously I would, but I freeze up. Before I get the chance to answer, Rick calls us over when the food gets to the table. And it's a good thing, because I don't know if I could have told Bo that I would miss her without accidentally revealing all the gay-for-her feelings.

I let Bo pick my meal; she ordered me her favorite, crabmeat fish maw soup, with a boba drink. I start with the drink, since it's a bit tamer than the meal, and chew on the cool tapioca balls while I build up my confidence to eat the soup. Baby steps.

"You don't like the soup?" Bo asks when she notices I haven't touched it, and because I don't want to hurt her feelings, I make a show of taking a huge spoonful of it—then immediately spit it back out.

Not because I didn't like it, but because it's *hot*.

Bo and Rick laugh hysterically while Emma covers her mouth, looking almost as embarrassed as I feel. Luckily, I didn't get any on their food, just on myself.

"Maybe blow on it first," Bo says between laugh-wheezes. After wiping myself off, I go for round two. This time I take a smaller spoonful and blow it off before delicately dipping my tongue into the spoon. I immediately give Bo a thumbs-up, and she sighs in relief. I knew I liked crab but never thought to try it in a soup. The creamy, flaky texture of the crab is even softer in the thick soup it comes in, and I can't get enough. I blow on another spoonful and slurp it right up, and Bo does the same.

After stuffing ourselves with mango pudding for dessert, we head back to Bo's house, and everyone sits on the couches in the living room. They're laughing and talking about things I'm not paying attention to. I laugh along, even though I'm thinking about whether or not I should even give them my present. I know Bo's parents will want to go to bed soon, so if I'm going to give them my shitty gift, it should be now.

"Um, I know we're not doing presents, but I made something for you guys," I say as soon as there's a lull in the conversation. "It's not a Christmas present so much as, like, a thank-you? I really appreciate you guys. I don't know why you're all so nice to me when I haven't done anything to deserve it. So, thanks. A lot." I pull out a beaded family portrait of them from a folder in my bag and stretch out my hand for someone to take it away from me. It's small, about the size of a birthday card, since I didn't have enough material for something bigger. I'm embarrassed to even look at it, honestly. Bo's such a better artist than me. What was I thinking, doing art for them when Bo is good enough to go pro? And beadwork of all things? What if they think it's stupid?

"It's not good. I should have gotten a real present." I avoid eye contact with any of them as they look over the portrait.

Probably scrutinizing all the flaws and comparing it to Bo's perfect artistry.

"You got Gregory and Dante, too!" Bo hugs me, and I think it's the first time she's ever done that. I hugged her after confession, but this one is different. She's fully pressed against me with her cheek nestled against my neck. I shudder, hoping she can't feel the chill rushing up my spine.

I squeeze back, savoring the embrace for a moment before I realize her parents are right behind her. I clear my throat and take a step back.

"Oh, honey, this is beautiful! Thank you so much!" Bo's mom is tearing up.

"We can put it on the wall with the other family pictures! We have to frame this," Rick says.

"Yamilet, you know you're always welcome in our home, right?" Bo's mom hugs me. Rick joins in, and so does Bo. The group hug is tight enough that it's hard to breathe, but a good kind of breathless.

The hug lingers longer than most, but not long enough. I get a call. I pull my phone out of my pocket to see a phone number I don't recognize, so I don't answer it.

We all split off into our rooms for the night. I throw myself on the mattress, and Gregory hops on the bed with me so I can scratch his ear.

I get another call. Usually random numbers don't call twice, so I pick up.

"Hello?"

"How dare you not answer me the first time I call you?"

I sit up so fast I startle Gregory. "Cesar?"

"No, your other brother with this exact voice."

"Okay, well, you could have been a scammer trying to steal my identity. I don't know why you thought I would answer a random number in the first place."

"Well, obviously I'm not a scammer. I had to use a burner phone since mine broke." Of course his phone broke. That's why he hasn't seen any of my videos! I want to ask if Dad said anything to Mom, but I'm not sure I'm prepared for an honest answer.

"So, what'd you call me for?" I'm still not completely sure he's not mad, so I'm treading with caution.

"What, I can't call my sister on Christmas just to say hi?"

"Awwwwww, did you miss me?"

"Shut up." Despite Cesar's inability to be sentimental, I can hear his telepathic message. He totally missed me.

"I missed you too." I say it like I'm joking, but I'm really, really not. I can almost hear him smiling.

"So . . . I, um . . . I feel like I should . . . say sorry. For blowing up on you," Cesar says, and it takes me a while to process that he's actually apologizing.

"Thanks, Cesar." I feel myself tearing up.

"So, did you make a move on Bo yet?" He changes the subject as quickly as he brought it up. Sounds like things are back to normal.

"Cesar! *No!*" I whisper-yell, even though there's no way anyone could have heard him.

"Why not? You have the ideal situation here. You could go into her room and woo her right now."

"Woo her? Seriously, what century are we in?" I'm still whispering, just in case. I don't mention to Cesar that Bo does in fact still have a girlfriend. He's finally talking to me, and I don't want to ruin it by being a bummer.

"Listen, here's what you got to do." I can picture him leaning forward like it's a secret. "You make an excuse to go into her room. Lie and say you think you left your phone in there or something."

"I wasn't even in there to leave anything today. . . ."

"Hmm. Okay, then say you had a nightmare and you need her to hold you so you can sleep. And boom. You're cuddling."

I roll my eyes. "Okay, I'm officially not taking your advice."

Bo opens the door, and I reflexively throw my phone across the room as if it would somehow destroy the evidence that I was just talking about her. It scares Gregory off the bed, and Cesar and I both might have broken phones now. Bo stands in the doorway, laughing.

"Sorry, wasn't trying to scare you." She walks toward my phone and picks it up. "Luckily, it's not broken."

I can hear Cesar shouting through the phone from here. "IS THAT HER? YAMI, YOU KNOW WHAT TO DO!"

I leap out of bed and grab my phone from Bo. "Okay, bye, Cesar. Good night!" I hang up and let out an awkward laugh. "Sorry, ignore my brother, please."

"Okay . . . um, I came to see if my other shoe was in here. I think Gregory took it."

"Oh," I say as I check under the bed for the missing shoe. I try to ignore Cesar's voice in my head, telling me she's using an excuse not too far off from the one he gave me. There's no shoe under the bed. I hold my breath as if it will slow down my rapid heart rate. Will I get to see how Cesar's plan would have worked out from the other side of things?

"Hmm, I'll check downstairs," Bo says, and she leaves. I blow out my breath and fall back onto the bed. I guess she wasn't making an excuse to spend time with me, since she left right after not finding her shoe. I wonder how Cesar's plan would have ended if I actually did go into Bo's room looking for something that wasn't there. Was I supposed to just be like, *Oh, yeah, looks like my phone isn't in here. But hey, let's cuddle!* It . . . wouldn't work.

With Cesar giving me bad advice about dating, I'm just glad things are back to normal. Knowing he wasn't actually mad at me makes me even more homesick. As though he senses it, Gregory hops back on the bed with me and gives me all the cuddles I need.

When the date of the festival rolls around, I start to get nervous. I know it's for fun, but I kind of feel naked right now. Just going there will give Bo and her parents clues about my culture and upbringing. Revealing my layers isn't always wise. People are happy with the parts of me they can be comfortable with, but I can't be too brown or too gay or too anything I am to my core. It's exhausting. I know Bo and her family can handle my gay.

Obviously, since Bo is gay, it wouldn't be an issue. Her parents are great. But I don't want to find out they're not as great as I thought. Like maybe they're afraid of big loud groups of Mexicans or something.

We get to the festival, and Bo's parents are two of only a handful of white people. And for once, it's not my turn to be uncomfortable. I'm with my people now. It's not that I want them to be uncomfortable. Actually, I really don't want them to be uncomfortable. I'm just sick of being the one to shoulder the un-comfortability of every situation so other people can feel like everything is normal. This is *my* normal.

Everyone is smiling right now, and I can breathe. It's not like I need their approval, but it's nice to see Bo and her parents enjoying themselves. After everything they've done for me, I want to give something back. I want them to fall in love with the colors and the music and the clothes and the dancing the way I did when I was little.

I used to do baile folklórico. My mom signed me up when I was little, and I still regret quitting to this day. I don't think I was any good at it, but I was five, so no one was. I always felt so beautiful tapping my feet and swinging my skirt around my waist. That was how I learned to stand straight and smile and look presentable, which ironically is why some people used to tell me I "act white." But the people who taught me to dance are the same people who taught me about the cultures of our Indigenous ancestors.

I know a lot of baile folklórico came out of a mixture of

Spanish and Indigenous cultures and dances. I'm fully aware that the standing up straight and the smiling were probably more from the Spanish side. But baile folklórico isn't all about the posture and the smiles. It's about the music, the colors, the dance. It's a dance of Mexican pride. My people. My heart.

I may not know the languages of my ancestors. I may not know much about them at all. Colonization will do that to a people. But when I'm watching my people dance. When I see my own skin on the stage. There's something about the joy on their faces and in their bodies that feels ancient somehow. And I feel like my ancestors have been with me all along. I can almost see them here, dancing with us.

It's not something I can explain to Bo and her parents, though. All I can hope for is for them to have a good time while my spirit finds its way home to Mexico.

I check their expressions every so often to see if they look like they're having fun. Bo's parents smile and laugh and clap along, but Bo is a little harder to read. She doesn't take her eyes off the dancers except to occasionally glance at me, which makes me shoot my eyes back to the stage. Need to be less obvious about how much I look at her. Or just look at her less.

Impossible. I'll be less obvious.

I have to fight the urge to hold her hand. It just feels like a hand-holding moment. We're sitting right next to each other, and our hands are, like, an inch apart. It's a little cold. Closing the gap to warm up our fingers is the logical thing to do. Holding hands isn't even inherently gay. Bo held my and Amber's hands at the movies that one time, and that was friends holding hands. Maybe that's just a scary movie thing to do, though. Or a thing when you don't have a girlfriend with blue hair and cool piercings.

Before I can decide whether to hold Bo's hand, she pulls it away to take out her phone. I try to keep my eyes forward, but it kind of hurts my feelings that Bo's phone is more interesting than the performance. After a minute, she's still on it, so I glance over her shoulder out of curiosity. She's scrolling through Jenna's Instagram. My ears get hot even though it's cold out. I find myself jealous of both Jamie and Jenna at once, and angry with Bo at the same time. It sucks that she's doing this here, now. I can't tell if I'm overreacting because I'm jealous or if I'm justifiably hurt. But I'm also worried about Bo. Does she still have feelings for her Bianca? When Bo realizes I'm looking, she shoves her phone back in her pocket and blushes. I keep my hands to myself.

Bo's parents rave about the performances the whole way back, but Bo stays quiet. I wait until we get to the house to go to Bo's room and talk some sense into her. Jenna is a terrible, homophobic person who doesn't deserve one second of Bo's attention.

There's an easel and a canvas covered with a sheet by her desk.

"What are you working on?" I ask, taking my time with bringing up the Jenna thing.

She blushes for a second, then clears her throat. "It's a piece for the art show."

"Can I see it?"

"At the art show, yeah." She sounds a little off, so I drop it. She's been acting weird all day. The show isn't until March, so I'll be waiting for a while. I would tease her about it, but she doesn't look in the mood for jokes.

"You okay?" I ask. If I was still into Bianca, I know I wouldn't be.

"Um . . ." She goes to close the door before answering. "If I tell you something, you can't tell anyone, okay?"

"Okay, I promise I won't say anything." I sit cross-legged on her bed, hoping Bo will bring this Jenna thing up before I have to. This is my first time sitting on her bed, but I think we're at the bed-sitting friendship level by now. When she sits on the bed across from me, her weight sinks the mattress just enough to slide my knees toward hers so our knees bump into each other. I scoot back even though I don't want to. Can't ruin this conversation by feeling all flustered.

"Okay . . ." She's quiet for a while before saying anything else. "Don't get me wrong, I love my parents. But it's kind of weird, being surrounded by white people. I barely even know any other Chinese people." She's talking faster than usual and bouncing her knee up and down. This is not what I was expecting her to say, but it's important, so I wait for her to continue.

"I guess I got a little jealous of you tonight. You seemed so in your element. You just, *belonged*, you know? The closest thing I have to my culture is going to Chinese restaurants and having all these performative decorations and statues around that I had to research to know the meaning behind. I have to look up every little thing on my own because I don't have anyone to ask. That's why I know so much about freaking *fish*." She rolls her eyes at herself, takes a breath, and keeps going.

"Like, I know my parents are trying to help me feel connected to my roots, but it just feels weird because *they're* not connected. Like, I love them, and you can never tell them or *anyone* I said this, but . . . sometimes I feel like they're a little racist. Don't get me wrong, I know they mean well and it's just misguided, but still. It's super embarrassing. All the Chinese stuff they put everywhere feels forced, almost like I'm faking my heritage. It's all just Chinese decorations and Chinese aesthetics. Sometimes I feel like that stuff is more for them than me. Meanwhile I don't even really feel like I can claim being Chinese. And I feel guilty for feeling that way, like I'm throwing that part of myself away. But I also feel guilty for like, wishing I was more Chinese? If that makes sense. Because my parents are white. It's shitty. They've done everything for me and I'm complaining."

I never thought Bo would be jealous of *me*. I'm jealous of her all the time, because she can be herself openly without worrying about consequences. But I guess she feels that way about me, too.

"No, that makes a lot of sense," I say. "I think it's important to remember there's no one right way to be Chinese. Just like there's no right way to be queer or Catholic or *anything*. And I don't think you're being ungrateful. Just because your parents raised you doesn't mean you owe them anything. That's literally a parent's responsibility. It's okay to have conflicting feelings. I know what you mean about feeling guilty either way, though.

Have you ever talked to your parents about it?"

Bo stops bouncing her knee. "I'm scared to."

"Why?"

"I don't want it to start a fight. I just want them to understand, you know? Ugh, sorry for dumping this on you. I just don't know who else to talk about this with. I know if I ever said anything about it to my parents, it would hurt their feelings. And Amber wouldn't get it. I know you're not adopted or anything. I just felt like . . . I don't know . . ."

"No, I know what you mean. Is it because I'm not white?"

"Is that racist?" Bo covers her mouth to stifle a laugh.

"I don't think so. I'm not gonna understand everything because I'm not adopted, but I at least know what you mean. I know it's different, but sometimes I feel distant from my culture, too. My dad was the one who knew about all our history and stuff. . . ." I trail off. I'm not trying to talk about my dad right now.

Bo nods. "I get that. My birth parents died when I was just a baby, so I never really got to participate in my culture in an authentic way, you know?"

I shake my head. "Bo, any way you engage with your own culture is authentic, because it's *yours*." And damn, I kind of feel like I needed to hear that myself.

"Thanks. But it still kind of feels icky when the engagement comes through my white parents, you know? They just don't get it."

"Yeah, that makes sense. I think it's only natural to feel that cultural separation, and it sucks that your parents don't get that.

I think a lot of white people don't know what it feels like to be the only one, you know?"

"Exactly! They just don't know what it's like to not be white in a place full of white people! I kind of loved that about tonight. I feel like my parents felt how I always feel. I don't think they've ever been such a small minority before. It's not the same, though, since they just got to see all the fun stuff, and then go back home to their comfortable house where they never have to think about race. I can't really talk to my parents or Amber about this kind of thing."

"Or . . . Jenna?" I ask.

Bo sighs. "I was hoping you wouldn't bring that up. I don't know why I was looking at her Instagram. It's like I hate her so much I want to know what she's doing, you know? I don't know how to explain it."

"Do you still like her?" I ask, the question burning my throat.

"*No!* I . . . I have a girlfriend. I don't . . ." She buries her face in her hands. "I was just trying to get out of my own head, so I got on my phone, and I happened to see her picture, and then I just got mad and started angry-scrolling through her Instagram, you know? Ugh, I sound ridiculous. I should have just enjoyed the show, but I was jealous and I hated feeling that way about you, so I needed to distract myself."

"I get that," I say. I've definitely angry-scrolled through Bianca's Instagram more than once. "Are you still feeling that way?"

"Jealous?" Bo starts picking at her fingernails. "Not *really*. I know tonight was about you. I just haven't ever had *my* night, you know? I'm used to being the only one like me in any room."

"The only one who's Chinese?"

"Chinese, gay, et cetera."

In lak'ech.

"That must be hard." I *know* it's hard not being white or straight. But I can't tell her that.

She nods. "I feel like I'm always the elephant in the room no one wants to talk about. Do you know what I mean? I make people uncomfortable just by existing, but no one wants to acknowledge it. I know I have it easier than a lot of people because of my parents, and because I'm light-skinned, but I still feel like I'm invisible. I'm like Schrödinger's gay. I have to shout about being gay and Chinese to prove I actually exist."

"Is that why you wear the rainbow Vans? And the pins?" I ask.

"It helps not to have to come out to every new person all the time."

"That's smart. But aren't you ever afraid to like, come off too gay?" I know I would be.

"Yeah, sometimes . . ."

"Is that why you don't hug girls?"

"What?"

"I mean, you hug your parents a lot, and David sometimes. But hardly ever me and Amber. At first I thought you didn't like me, but Amber's your best friend, so maybe it's a girl thing?"

She's quiet for a while. "Well, yeah. I guess it is a girl thing.

I don't want to make you guys feel . . . uncomfortable, or anything."

I reach my arms out and open and close my hands to invite her to hug me. "I'm comfortable."

She smiles and accepts the offer. Her sweater makes it feel like I'm hugging a pillow, and I love it. Her hair smells like vanilla. I try not to savor the embrace too long, or else she'll be the one feeling uncomfortable.

"I love hugs, so you can hug me anytime you want, okay?" I say as I pull away so I don't get lost in that vanilla-smelling pillow.

"Thanks, Yamilet. It's nice having you here. I'm glad you came." Her smiling eyes are alluring as always, but I can't stop staring at her lips.

"Me too. Hey, if you want, you can call me Yami." I think she's earned the nickname. I get up to leave, because if I stay sitting on Bo's bed any longer, I won't be able to resist the urge to kiss her.

18

THOU SHALT NOT COMMIT ADULTING

I wake up in the morning with an insatiable need to dance. It's not enough to watch a performance. I want to *move*. I march into the living room, where Bo is already set up playing some fighting video game. Her speaker is sitting on the table, just asking to be used.

I can't bring myself to take it back to the room. Bo made me dance to her favorite music. It's only fair if I make her dance with me to mine, right?

"Everything okay?" Bo asks, and she pauses her game.

"Yeah. Um. Are you busy right now?" I'm making it awkward. Why wasn't it awkward when Bo wanted me to dance with her?

"Nope. What's up?" She puts the controller down.

"Remember when you made me dance to your favorite music?"

"Yeah." She's smiling.

"Want to hear mine?" I ask.

"Yeah!" She hops up, and I offer her my hand.

"Do you know how to cumbia?"

She shakes her head. I play "Baila Esta Cumbia" by Selena, and show her the moves. She follows my feet until she gets the basics, then we start messing around with turns and dips and all that fancy shit. When I pull Bo up from our first dip, she looks impressed. I grin, chin up. Yeah, I'm strong enough to dip her. To impress her, I twirl her and do it again. This time she comes up giggling, face red.

"Again!" she squeals, and I happily oblige. Then I take her hand above our heads to twirl her. This time she just keeps twirling. Of course it didn't take long for Bo to revert to her go-to move of spinning in circles. She has so much fun doing it that I start spinning with her. She giggles when I join her, and oh my God, her laugh. I could listen to her laugh all day.

I spend a good chunk of the next day sitting on the couch in the upstairs living room, hoping Bo will come out of her room to hang out with me. She's been in there all day, and I don't want to bother her unless she wants me to, so I just sit here waiting.

After what feels like forever but really is only about another hour, she finally comes out of her room. She marches over to the couch like she's on a mission. Instead of sitting down next to me, she towers over me.

"I'm gonna do it," she says, chest out.

"Do what?" I sit up straighter.

"Confront my parents. About what we talked about after

the baile folklórico show. But I need you to come with me. For moral support."

"Of course," I say, happily getting up off the couch.

She leads me downstairs, where her parents are sitting on the couch watching Netflix. Bo just stands there without saying anything until they pause the show.

"Everything okay, you two?" Rick asks.

Bo opens her mouth to speak, but nothing comes out. She sticks her shaking hand out to me, and I take it and squeeze. "I . . . um . . . I have something I want to say to you guys," Bo starts, voice uncertain.

"What is it?" Emma asks.

Then there's another uncomfortably long pause from Bo. "Okay, so . . . you know how you guys have all these Chinese decorations and stuff around the house?" she starts, squeezing my hand harder than when we watched that horror movie with Amber.

"Yeah . . . ," Rick says slowly, like he's waiting for Bo to continue.

"Well, I was thinking. Maybe I'd like it if you two kind of . . . took a step back from all of that, you know?"

Emma raises an eyebrow, and Rick gives Bo a sad look of surprise.

"Why do you say that, sweetie?" Emma asks.

Bo hesitates, and I give her hand a little squeeze.

You're doing great, my hand says.

Bo takes a deep breath, then finally goes on. "I guess it just kind of feels like, you two are exploring my culture for me, and I'm only kind of watching. I want to be the one to do the exploring for a while. Like even if it's just going to Chinese restaurants or watching C-dramas or whatever, I think it should be on my terms, you know?" She finally lets go of my hand and inhales, like it took her whole breath to say all that.

Bo's mom's covers her mouth with her hand. "Oh, honey, I'm so, so sorry we made you feel like that."

"We *never* wanted to hurt you, Bo. That was never why we did any of that. You know that, right?" Rick says.

"I know, I know. You guys love me and just wanted to help. But, like, intentions don't change the impact. And it took me a while to realize how I felt about it, anyway."

"Sit with us," Emma says, patting the space on the couch next to her.

I take a step back, suddenly realizing how awkward it is that I'm in the middle of this very intimate family discussion. Bo looks back at me, and I try to send a telepathic message, like I would to Cesar.

Do you want me to stay?

"You don't have to stick around for this part, Yami. Thanks." She reaches out to give my hand one final squeeze before sitting down with her parents. I'm almost too shocked that she actually got my message to leave, but I manage to give her a reassuring smile before heading upstairs to the guest room.

I could get used to being on vacation. I know I'll have to work twice as hard when I get back home, but that can be my New

Year's resolution. Mom and Cesar come home for New Year's tomorrow, so I have one more day to enjoy before I have to worry about working, and I intend to make the most of it. It's easier not to worry when my mom's not around. I feel guilty for thinking that, but it's true. Without her around to remind me what I have to lose, all I have to worry about is ice blocking.

Taking a big block of ice and riding it down a hill is already pretty fun as it is, but the Taylor family apparently takes it to the extreme. They even freeze ropes into the blocks to act as handles, so you can steer yourself.

We wait until around ten thirty at night to leave the house and head for the park, so we can be outside when the fireworks go off. Our ice sleds sit in two different chests, and we have to lug them all the way to the top of the hill above the lake when it's time.

I take the spot on the top of the hill where the grass looks shortest. It's better that way, since there's less traction. The first slide down is just to get a feel for the hill, but Bo happens to slide down at the same time as me, and I'm a competitive bitch. There's no way I'm letting her beat me to the bottom. We're neck and neck, but there's a lump in the ground up ahead. I yank my rope to the side, but go too far left and bump into Bo's sled. She's thrown off track for a second, but then she pulls her rope and bumps me right back. We're officially bumper sledding.

After a few hits, we both end up falling off our blocks before we make it to the bottom.

"Ha! I win!" Rick shouts as he speeds by us.

"We were racing?" Bo's mom calls out from the top of the hill.

Bo laughs and rolls her eyes, then hands me her phone.

"Yami, can you record this? I want to try something." I nod, and she runs up the hill with her ice. She stands on her block, hunching down low enough to reach the handles. "Okay, are you recording?"

I throw her a thumbs-up. She leans forward and starts ice block surfing down the hill. I don't know how she manages to look clumsy and badass at the same time. She's an enigma. She's surfing right toward me, and we both start screaming like we're about to die. I'm as frozen as her sled when she and her ice block tackle me to the ground.

It feels like that one scene in every rom-com ever, where the romantic interest and the main character knock into each other and end up in an awkward position on top of each other. Except it's somehow not awkward. We're both laughing so hard we can't breathe. If we were in a rom-com, I think this is where we're supposed to kiss.

It isn't until Bo's parents come to help us up that I remember they're here in the first place. It's almost like that first time we spun around together, when everything else was a blur but Bo. That's how it is with her sometimes. Dizzying and breathtaking, but she's right there when I come up for breath.

Bo starts recording us all the next time we slide down. For the camera, I decide to try something cool and slide down belly first for maximum aerodynamics. Bo chases me down the hill, recording and cheering me on. The farther down the hill I get, the faster I go. Since I'm on my belly, I don't stop sliding at the bottom of the hill. I'm about to slide right into the lake when Bo leaps forward and grabs my ankles to keep me in place. My ice block shoots out from under me and into the water.

I roll around when she lets go of my ankles.

"I GOT THAT ON CAMERA!" Bo hops up on her feet and wags her butt in a victory dance.

"You saved me!" I get up and tackle-hug her. We both fall to the ground laughing again. "Thanks for not letting me fall into the lake for views."

"Oh man, I didn't even think of that!" She sits up and snaps like she's disappointed. I laugh and curl up on my side. Adrenaline really drains you. Bo lies down next to me, and I swear I'm dreaming because the fireworks go off right when she looks at me. I watch them go off in her eyes for a second before I roll onto my back to see them for real. We just lie there, while rainbow matches light up the sky.

Bo's parents meet us at the bottom with blankets, hot chocolate, and Oreos. There are only two blankets, so Bo and I have one to share. I'm side-eyeing Rick super hard right now, since he totally could have brought more than two blankets for the four of us, but I'm not exactly complaining. It's cold enough outside for a straight girl to want to snuggle her friend-who-has-a-girlfriend to keep warm, right?

Bo leans her head on my shoulder, and I want to melt into the grass under me. Because she's not afraid of making me uncomfortable anymore. Because she's comfortable like this. Because her parents are right here with us and it's not weird. I respond by leaning my head on hers, so she knows I'm not being weird. And because I want to. Because I'm comfortable, too.

Even though I like her, it's not about that at all right now. I'm just happy to be this close with someone.

It's not long before Bo's parents start packing up.

"What? We're going home already?" Bo whines.

"No, *we're* going home already," Bo's mom says. "We're old, honey. You two enjoy the fireworks."

I don't need to hide my relief. This feels too intimate, and I don't want to ruin it by going back. Bo and I stay lying out on the grass.

"Is it weird if we cuddle?" Bo asks. Thank God, too, because I'm cold and gay.

"Not weird. It's cold." I throw the blanket Bo's parents left over both of us and hug Bo's arm like a body pillow. I can feel her shivering.

I hope she doesn't catch on to how badly I've been wanting to snuggle up to her ever since I dreamed about cuddling her after the homecoming party. But this is way better. We don't talk for a while. I used to think silence could only be awkward, but it's not. I'm just watching the fireworks and enjoying her company. No music necessary.

When the fireworks slow down a bit, I sit up to watch their sparkling reflections in the lake. I like how the reflection distorts the lights just enough that it feels like a dream.

"Yamilet. Have I ever told you how much I like that name?"

"You do?" I feel my cheeks darken, and I hope she thinks it's from the cold.

"Yeah. It's really pretty."

"Well, I really like your name, too."

She turns her head fast and gives me a skeptical look.

"What? Why's that hard to believe?" I ask.

"Because it's a weird name. It sounds like a dog name."

"Well, I like it. I'm allowed to like it, okay? It's cute. We both have weird names, but good names. I love my name. I just wish more people would say it right."

"Oh, shit, am I saying it wrong?" she asks.

"No, actually. A lot of people don't even try. It's not even that hard a name to pronounce, but people are always getting it wrong."

"That sucks. Everyone thinks Bo is a nickname, but no, it's my real name. At least no one ever mispronounces it." She laughs.

"What does it mean?" I ask.

"You first." She's blushing, for some reason.

"Uh, one second." I don't actually know what my name means, so I pull out my phone to look it up.

"Apparently it's the Spanish equivalent of Jamila. Which means 'beautiful.'"

"You're shitting me!" Bo slaps her hands on the ground. "That's what *my* name means!"

"Quit lying! Seriously?"

"YES! Technically it's misspelled French, but yeah."

I giggle. Bo. Bo-*nita*.

"It's fitting." I smile. This is the closest I can get to admitting how I feel. A coded message that I think she's beautiful.

She blushes again. "All right, we both have good names."

We're both quiet for a while. Every time I find out something new about Bo, it makes it harder to deny how into her I am. I'll admit it. Even if only to myself. I like her so much.

I think I'm more comfortable in the silence than she is, because she speaks up again after a few minutes.

"Can I ask you a personal question?"

"Sure. But I get to ask you one, too." I smile.

"Okay, you first."

I like the question game. I hear it's prime flirting material, but I just want to get to know Bo better. The first questions that come to mind are about Bo's coming-out process. Were her parents always this supportive? Were her friends? The next thing I want to ask about is her girlfriend. Is she happy? How serious are they? But then, it's probably best to stay away from gay stuff, in case it comes back to me somehow. I ask a safer question.

"What's your New Year's resolution?"

"To take things less personally." She answers quickly enough that it's obvious she's already thought about it. "What about you?"

"To get rich."

"No, seriously!" Bo laughs. "What's something you *really* want to do better?"

I was being serious, though, even if it's an exaggeration. I need to get rich enough to be financially independent. But I don't know if Bo would understand that, since she's already rich. Still, I look up at the sky and think. There are plenty of things I want to be better at besides making money.

"I guess I want to be more brave," I say. Brave like Bo.

"Okay. I'll work on taking things less personally, and you"— Bo holds out her pinky to me, and I take it—"will be brave."

Her eyes are so reflective in the moonlight that I can see myself in them. I could tell her how I feel right now. I could kiss her under the fireworks.

Be brave.

The thunder of the next firework shakes me back to my senses. It's a New Year's resolution. I can start on the bravery tomorrow.

"So my turn . . . What's the real reason you didn't go to Mexico with your family? Don't you want to see your dad?"

My smile drops, and when I don't answer, she continues.

"It's just . . . I've seen your wallpaper," Bo goes on. "You guys look really happy."

I think I could maybe tell her everything right now. That I'm gay. That my dad isn't cool with it. That he might tell my mom while she's over there.

But I'm not brave.

Not even brave enough to change my freaking wallpaper. It's like if I change it, I'm admitting he's never going to come around. And it's not that I don't trust Bo. I do. Other than Cesar, I trust her more than anyone right now. But . . . I'm not ready to tell her.

"Sorry, you don't have to answer that. I shouldn't have asked."

"It's okay. I just . . . I don't really get along with my dad anymore. But I don't want to talk about him." Even mentioning him makes me want to cry.

"That's fine, I understand."

"My turn." I want to get the focus off my dad as quick as possible. "Why do you adopt ugly animals?"

"They're not ugly!"

"They're a little ugly." I laugh, and she frowns at me. It's a playful frown, at first. Then her eyes wander to the lake and she chews on her lip.

"I guess I just want to take the animals other people would leave behind. All the cute animals have no problem getting rescued. But the ugly ones might eventually get put down, you know?"

I nod. "I never really thought of it that way," I say. Of course Bo would think of the well-being of all the "ugly" animals. "So, it's your turn," I say. She shifts her body to face me again.

"Okay, um . . ." She takes a minute. "Are you embarrassed for me to meet your mom?"

"You already met her at the homecoming game."

"I know, but that was in a group. Like, you never want me to go over to your house. And you take the light rail instead of letting me drop you off. But you let David pick you up when you guys came over. Maybe I'm overthinking it, but I thought maybe you didn't want your mom to know me too well. Because of the gay thing . . ." She starts fidgeting. "Sorry, I know, I'm already going against my resolution. I can get a little paranoid. Ignore me." She's wrong, but I hate how relatable that is right now. It's almost off-putting, because Bo usually comes across so confident.

"Why didn't you tell me you thought that?"

She shrugs. "I don't know. I guess I was scared to know the truth."

It seems like Bo has no problem calling out teachers and administrators and even priests, but when it comes to her friends, she holds it in. I think I get why. When it's someone you care about, you have more to lose. But is she really afraid of losing *me*?

"Well, I'm not embarrassed of you at all," I say. Even if my mom is homophobic, she'd never treat a guest poorly, no matter who it was. "Um . . . I'm actually a little embarrassed for you to know where I live."

"Why?"

"It's just . . . different from here." I turn to face the lake instead of her.

"Do you think I'll judge you or something?"

"I don't know . . ."

"I know most people don't have as much money as we do, and as much money as most people at Slayton do. I'm not that sheltered. I don't want to make you uncomfortable or anything, but you have nothing to be embarrassed about."

"Okay."

"Do you think you're ever going to let me drop you off at your actual house?"

I bite the inside of my cheek and think about it. "Probably not."

"Okay. That's fine, I guess. . . ." She looks away. I think I hurt her feelings.

I know she won't judge me, but maybe I'm not as ready for Bo to know me as I thought I was. I want her to know me in some ways. I want her to know the good stuff, like the way I think and what I like. I want her to know all the things we have in common. Well, *most* of the things we have in common.

I want her to know about how we both love animals, and how our names mean the same thing, and how we're both competitive, and like the same kinds of jokes. And maybe part of me even wants her to know I'm gay. I want to keep feeling like we're the same.

But we're not.

19

ADDENDUM: THOU *SHALT* COMMIT ADULTING

I know I can come back anytime I want, but I'm sad to leave Bo's place the next day. Time to go back to surviving. I swear Bo's mom is getting misty-eyed when I hug them all goodbye.

"It was so nice having you around, Yamilet. Drive safely!" she says.

"Mom, she's still my friend. It's not like you'll never see her again." Bo pushes her mom out of the way to hug me. "Seriously, I hope they didn't scare you out of ever coming back."

"No! I love you guys!" I surprise myself at how affectionate I'm being right now.

"We love *you*!" Bo's dad shouts, and makes a hand-heart.

I'll miss them, but when I get to the airport, I run to my mom and throw myself into a hug the minute I see her. I missed my mom's hugs. I missed my mom.

"Ay, mija, you're gonna break my back," she says, but she's squeezing me just as tight.

Cesar pretends to clear his throat, and I let go of my mom and hug him. I missed Cesar, too. A lot. I want to ask them about the trip, but I also don't want to hear about Dad, and I think Cesar gets my telepathic message. He hugs me back and talks about how he missed his bed.

And that reminds me how much I miss *my* bed.

The one in Bo's guest room is much comfier than mine, but right now, I don't want to be in any other bed but my own. As soon as we get home, I leap onto my mattress. It creaks at me to please not jump, but I don't listen. When I settle in, there's already cumbia music echoing through the house. I missed *this*.

After Cesar and I get plenty of time to soak up the feeling of being back in our beds, he comes into my room and sits at the foot of mine.

"Hey," I say, but he doesn't answer. Not for a while. I sit up and lean against the wall, waiting for whatever it is he needs to say.

"You were right."

"What?"

"About Dad. You were right." My stomach drops. Oh no . . .

"What do you mean?" I ask. Did Cesar come out??

"He just kept saying shit that pissed me off. I mean, I'm glad I went, I had a good time, you know? But I know why you didn't want me to go. And I get why you didn't want to." He rubs the back of his neck. This feels like another one of his almost-apologies.

I can't concentrate on anything besides that Dad "says shit," and I wonder if he said anything to Mom about me.

"What did he say?"

"Doesn't matter."

"What did he say?" I ask again. This time my voice is stern.

"He talked about you, all right?"

Of course he did. I want to be surprised, to cry, but I already knew. I was stupid to make excuses for him.

"What did he *say*, Cesar?" The pit in my stomach tightens. I know hearing the answer could ruin me, but I *have* to.

"Dad is a homophobic dickhead, okay? It doesn't matter what he thinks."

"That's not true and you know it. He's our *dad*." It does matter what he thinks, no matter how much I wish it didn't. I'll always care what he thinks.

"So? Just because he ejaculated in Mom doesn't mean it matters what he thinks."

"Gross, stop! Wait, did he tell her?" I'm gripping my knees so hard it hurts. I almost don't want to hear the answer. But I need to know.

He shakes his head. "He thinks you'll get over it. Said he doesn't want you out on the streets because of some 'phase.' He's not gonna tell her. He was kind of venting to me about it."

I don't know what I'm supposed to feel. Upset that Dad still refuses to talk to me, or relieved that he's trying to protect me from Mom? I rub my temples to soothe my aching brain.

"Anyways. What happened with you and Bo?" He winks. He always changes the subject before it gets too emotional. Right now, I'm glad for it.

"Nothing!" I hit him with my pillow.

"You better make a move on that girl. She's not going to wait around forever!"

"She has a girlfriend. If anything, I'm the one waiting around."

"I beg to differ!" He lifts his finger like we're debating politics. "She likes you."

"*I* beg to differ!" I lift my finger right back.

"You don't have to beg, just ask her out nicely!" He snickers, and I know he's trying to get under my skin. I push him off my bed.

"You know I'm right!" he says. I throw my pillow at him as he runs out of the room.

Getting used to being back at school is a trip. I liked the break life. No homework. I was with Bo and her rich parents. I could wear whatever I wanted. Now I'm doing a forty-minute commute to a school full of straight white kids who all wear the same thing as me. I look just like them, but I also don't.

It hasn't been long, but I'm excited to see Bo again, and the rest of our friends. I missed having friends. Not just since break, but since Bianca.

When I get to our lunch table, Amber is groaning with her head down on the surface, and David is patting her back.

"What's wrong?" I ask.

"She's having a fifth-life crisis," Bo says.

Amber looks up at me. "My cousin is going to college next year. She knows exactly what she's doing and why, and I still have no idea what I want to do with my life! I only have one more year to figure it out!"

"You'll be okay," I say.

"But how can you *know* that?" Amber asks.

"Because you don't have to figure it out in a year. That's what college is for, right?" It's not like she'll be put on the streets if it takes her a couple of years to find her calling.

"I don't even know what college I want to go to." Amber puts her head back down. I almost roll my eyes before I realize I'm being insensitive.

"That's good, though! You have choices, babe," David says, and I start to tune them out. People like Amber and Bo can do whatever they want with their lives after high school. Their parents will pay for them to figure it out. I'll probably have to get a full-time job I hate right out of school. That way me and Cesar can come out to Mom, and I'll be able to get a place for us if we get kicked out.

Honestly, as scared as Amber is, I'm terrified everyone besides me is going to be successful and leave me behind. I'll probably end up working at a call center and hating my life, like my mom. Actually, scratch that. She doesn't hate her life. Mom worships everything about this country, including her shitty job that has her barely living paycheck to paycheck, even with me helping. The best thing I can do for my future right now is save up, which would be a lot easier to do if I could find another *job*.

At this point I've applied everywhere I can possibly walk to from home or Slayton. Still nothing. I need a break and I don't even have a job yet. Job hunting is its own job, honestly.

I put my head down and join Amber in her sulking.

"What's wrong with you?" Bo asks.

"Now I'm bummed about money. I need a better-paying job."

"Have you tried the Taco Bell right here?" David suggests.

"I tried everywhere," I say without lifting my head.

"What about somewhere at the mall?" he says, still rubbing Amber's back.

I shake my head, since for some reason he thinks I haven't already thought of any of these ideas.

"Oh!" Bo slaps her hands on the table. "You should work for my mom! She's been looking for a secretary for all her lawyery stuff."

My head pops back up. That I did not think of. "How much does she pay?"

Bo shrugs. "I don't know. Call her after school and see."

Amber groans loudly again, and everyone goes back to comforting her.

As soon as I get home from school, I get to work filling orders and call Bo's mom while I work. If I'm weaving bracelets while I talk, maybe I'll be less nervous. I weave faster.

"Hey, Yamilet, what's up?" Rick answers the phone.

"Hi, Mr. Taylor." I'm trying to sound as professional as possible, since this might turn into a phone interview. "I've been looking for another job, and I heard Mrs. Taylor needs a secretary?"

"Oh, yeah! You want the job? Say the word and I'll fire her current secretary." He laughs. How can he laugh about firing someone?

"Oh, sorry, no, don't do that. I didn't know she already found someone."

"It's fine, I'll do it right now! You're fired!" A slight pause, then he's using a different voice. "Nooo! I have a family!"

"Um . . . okay . . ." He's so awkward sometimes, I don't know how else to respond.

"Sorry, sorry, bad joke, I know," he says after a little chuckle.

"Wait . . . does this mean I have the job?"

"Hold on. Emma! Phone!" he calls out, and there's a bit of shuffling before I hear Emma on the line.

"Hi, Yamilet. Sorry about that. Rick's been helping me out while I look for someone. So, you're looking for a job? Do you have any experience?"

"Yes! Right now I'm working as a social media and marketing manager for my mom's jewelry business. Bo told me you might need some help, and I'm interested in the position!" I don't mention that I spend 99 percent of my working time making jewelry. I'm guessing there won't be a lot of that in secretary work. "I know I'm still in high school, but I promise I'm a really hard worker!" I add desperately.

"No worries, Yamilet! This job is pretty simple. It's really just checking my emails and bookkeeping for me, so you should be able to handle it just fine with your current experience. Let's do a few days of a trial period. If you're a good fit, we'll make it a long-term position."

"Yay! I mean, thanks so much, Mrs. Taylor!"

She laughs. "You can call me Emma. Do you have a computer and Wi-Fi?"

"My laptop is pretty old, but it works. We have Wi-Fi." She doesn't need to know I share the laptop with Cesar and my mom. It'll work for now.

"Perfect. Let's start with weekends. I won't need more than about fifteen hours a week. Are you good with that? Can you start this Saturday?"

"I can do that. Thanks so much!" I have to hold back a squeal.

"See you then!"

"Perfect!" I can help Mom after school and work for Emma on weekends. I'll cram in homework on the light rail and while I wait for Cesar to get out of detention when he has it.

I'm so excited there's no way I can sleep tonight, so I keep making friendship bracelets. Before I get much done, my phone buzzes, and a selfie of Bo lights up the screen. She must have stolen my phone at some point and taken that picture, because I definitely didn't take it. She's sticking out her tongue with her eyes shut. I laugh and pick up the phone, holding it between my neck and shoulder so I have my hands free to weave.

"I can't believe you're gonna work for my mom," she says before I get a chance to speak.

"Hey, I needed a job, and no one else was calling me back!" It's an empty excuse. Working for Emma would have been my top choice.

"Well, if you decide to quit, you better not make it weird.

You should still come over and stuff." It's nice talking on the phone, because I can blush or smile or whatever and she'll have no idea.

"It'll definitely be weird, but I'll still come over."

"You better. I already miss you. This house feels so empty now."

"I miss you too," I admit, since I didn't say it back the last time. I kind of wish I could have been the first to say it, but Bo keeps beating me to the punch. There's some background music on the line that I can't make out. It almost sounds like . . . "What are you listening to?"

"Selena." She says it like the word isn't Cupid's arrow shooting me right in the heart. "I was waiting for you to notice. I've been listening to her a lot since you left. I totally get why you're obsessed."

"I'm so proud," I say, making my voice choke up. She laughs.

"Well, I have to do some homework. I'll see you later!"

"See you later," I say, trying not to sound disappointed. I could talk to her all night. Instead I keep my hands busy for hours. When the house goes dark, I rely on my phone flashlight since I don't want to wake anyone up by turning on the light. When the battery dies, my eyes adjust, and I work through heavy hands and heavy eyes through the night.

"Why are you still awake?" I don't realize it's the middle of the night until Cesar comes into the living room and calls me out for still working.

"Lost track of time, I guess." I yawn and finish up the last couple of beads on the necklace I'm making. Cesar sits down next to me.

"Why are *you* still awake?" I ask.

"Same reason as always."

"What's that?" I tilt my head, hands still moving on their own despite my sore fingers. I guess I knew he didn't sleep well, since he falls asleep in class so much, but I kind of assumed it was the extra homework or something keeping him up.

"I don't know. Brain won't shut up."

I nod, way too tired to process anything.

"You need help?" he asks.

"Sure."

He starts weaving a bracelet of his own. We sit there weaving in silence for a while. I'm about to fall asleep working when he talks again.

"I didn't mean what I said before. . . ."

"What?"

"I wasn't mad at you for covering for me. I was mad 'cause I didn't deserve it. You deserve better."

I look up and catch his eyes for the first time tonight. They're red and puffy, like he might have been crying.

"¿Qué te pasa? You okay?"

"I'm tired." He yawns. "Night, Yami." He leaves his half-finished thread on the couch and goes back to his room. Instead of following him with more questions, I get back to work.

✦ ✦ ✦

After I finish my trial period as Emma's assistant and officially get the job, I feel like my life is a broken record. If anything interesting is happening, I don't notice because I'm stuck on repeat. School. Homework. Work. Sleep. School. Homework. Work. Sleep. School. Work. Work. Work. School. Work. Work. Work. Work. Work . . .

Before I know it, it's been over a month, and I actually have a decent amount of money saved up. I spend less money now that I have it than I did when I was broke. I want to keep growing my cushion for when I'm on my own. Then I'll get a full-time job when I'm done with school. My conversation with Cesar told me one thing: even my dad thinks Mami will kick me out if she finds out. That knocks me into high gear.

The worst part about working so much is having to miss out on group hangouts and having to blow off Cesar when he wants to hang out or get Takis, which is almost every day. Lunch at school is the only time I get any social interaction anymore.

"Isn't your birthday this weekend? What are you gonna do?" Amber asks.

"I need the money, so I'll be working." I almost didn't realize it was coming up.

"But we have to celebrate!" Amber grabs my shoulders and shakes them. David and Bo chime in with a chorus of yeahs.

"Sorry! I have two jobs, and pretty much all my free time goes to homework." My birthday is on a Saturday this year, but I can't even celebrate it late during the week because I'm so behind on schoolwork.

They all frown. We share a moment of silence to mourn my social life.

"I have an idea," Amber says.

"I'm listening," I say.

"We can do something *during the day*."

"You mean like ditching?" David's eyes get wide.

"Yeah, I mean it's just one day. We'll do it on Monday! We can't let her not celebrate her birthday." Amber frowns at him.

"I think it's perfect! What do you think, Yami?" Bo smiles at me.

"Do you think Jamie would mind?" I ask, since Monday is Valentine's Day. "Maybe you can bring her?" Why would I *say* that? I don't want to celebrate my birthday with Bo's girlfriend.

"Who's Jamie?" Amber asks.

"My *girlfriend*." Bo widens her eyes at Amber. Why would Amber not know about Jamie? "Um, no. She wouldn't want to ditch class."

"Ohhhhhhh, right. *Jamie*. Silly me!" Amber says, laughing nervously. David tilts his head, all confused.

I just stare at them for a second. I can't believe it took me until now to figure it out.

Jamie isn't real.

This whole time I've been jealous of someone who doesn't exist. I don't know if I should be happy there's no Jamie, or mad that Bo lied about it. Why would she lie? Does she know I like her? Is it because she doesn't want to date *me*?

I shoo that thought away with a quickness. Bo doesn't know how I feel. She can't.

"So are we doing this?" Bo asks.

I shrug, trying to hide how much I'm freaking out. "When else am I going to get a chance to celebrate?" I have to admit I need a day off. Cesar can pick up my homework from my teachers so I won't be too behind.

"Come on, David, it'll be fun!" Amber bats her eyelashes at him and takes his hand.

"Aren't you worried we'll get in trouble?" He looks around at all of us. He's looking for someone else as scared as he is, because he has major FOMO. Fear of missing out is going to save my birthday.

"What's life without a little risk?" Bo says.

"Exactly. And we make sacrifices for our friends in this family." Amber pouts at David.

"Please? For my birthday?" I puff out my bottom lip at him. Bo and Amber add their own puppy faces, and with our combined cuteness power, David doesn't stand a chance.

"Okay, let's do it." He finally breaks.

"Great. I'll park my car in the back of the parking lot Monday morning, and whoever's getting dropped off at school can ride with me," Bo says.

"What's the plan?" I ask.

"It'll be a surprise!" Amber says.

"Okay. We better not see any horror movies, though."

Bo grins. "Deal."

·20·

THOU SHALT NOT
ADMIT IT'S A DATE

My mom gives me a hard time about working all day on my birthday, so after a lot of begging on her part, I let her take me and Cesar to a quick lunch. But I eat fast because I don't want to waste time. Sure, Emma offered me the day off for my birthday, but I need the money. Honestly, it's a bit of a waste of good pizza, since I don't have time to enjoy it. When we get back home, I take a second to check my phone before getting back to work on the computer. I don't expect anything from my dad, but the tiniest bit of hope dies when I don't get anything from him on my birthday of all days. Instead, I have birthday texts from Bo, Amber, and David.

And Bianca.

"Uh, Bianca said to tell you happy birthday," Cesar says as he walks into my room.

"Why are you texting Bianca?" I snap at him.

"Because she wanted me to tell you happy birthday? Do you have her number blocked or something?" Cesar asks.

"Yup. She can choke and die. Don't respond."

"Damn, still? What'd she do, anyway?" He raises an eyebrow.

I sigh. "She outed me last year."

"What the fuck? You never told me that."

"Didn't want to talk about it."

"Oh, okay. Do you want to now?" He lies down on my bed like he does when we're about to have a heart-to-heart. But I don't have time. I'm supposed to be working.

"Not really." I open Outlook and start going through Emma's emails and scheduling appointments for her.

"I'm bored. Come with me to get Takis?" He sits back up like he's ready to hop off the bed and go.

"We just ate, though."

"Okay, then let's go see Doña Violeta. She's been asking about you."

"Shit . . ." I haven't had any time to visit her lately with work and everything.

"And I'm still hungry. We can go to Doña Violeta's and then get Takis. Nothing wrong with Takis for dessert, right?"

"True, but I have to work right now. Sorry, Cesar. Tell her hi for me," I say without looking away from the computer.

"Okay, well, happy birthday."

"Thanks."

Cesar lingers for a moment, then sighs and walks out.

When Monday rolls around, I'm a little nervous. I have no idea what to expect. I get up extra early to get ready. I still have to wear my uniform, but I put extra love into doing my hair and makeup. Cesar comes into the bathroom, and he's even groggier than usual, with dark circles under his eyes.

"Couldn't sleep?" I ask as I put on some homemade earrings instead of my usual hoops. Beaded red heart earrings for Valentine's Day.

He shakes his head and splashes water on his face. He's probably bummed because it's Valentine's Day. Maybe he misses Jamal.

"I'm gonna ditch today with Bo and them," I whisper, even though Mom is in her shower and can't hear. Telling him what I'm doing is as good as an invite. He usually invites himself anyway, but he doesn't this time.

"Oh, fun," he says, then brushes his teeth and leaves me to finish my makeup.

The one time I *want* Cesar to invite himself, he doesn't care. It's Valentine's Day, and I'm afraid it might feel like a double date, since David and Amber are all cupcakey. I don't know how to feel about that.

As soon as Mom drops Cesar and me off at school, I walk straight to Bo's car in the back of the parking lot. It's already parked, so I hop into the passenger seat and wait for Amber and David to join us.

"So, what's the plan?" I ask.

"You'll seeee," she sings. "It will be fun, I promise."

We get a group text from Amber.

Amber: My mom has to gas up, so David and I are running late. Be there soon 💜

The longer we wait for them, the more likely we are to get caught. We're sitting ducks in the school parking lot, waiting for someone to notice we aren't going to class. Common sense should have told them to get here early so no one would try to stop them from meeting us.

When the first bell rings, our chances of getting caught rise exponentially. I send them a text.

Yami: Um, how late exactly?

The campus police officer sees us.

"Shit, we got to go," I say.

"It's fine, he probably thinks we just got here. He'll get distracted in a minute."

I sigh. Amber and David better hurry the hell up before we get caught.

The cop doesn't get distracted. He's walking toward us.

"Shit, shit, shit, GO!" I yell. Bo screams like she's being murdered instead of *driving*. I pull down the visors so we don't get recognized. The cop is only a few yards away when she finally slams on the gas. Now we're both screaming, because she's driving right toward him. He leaps out of the way. I can barely hear him yelling over the sounds of both of us shrieking. We race over all the speed bumps and somehow make it out of the lot in one piece.

Then we start dying laughing. Bo has to pull over so we don't crash.

"Oh my God, my heart!" She thumps her hand on her chest to show how fast her heart is beating.

"I can't believe you almost ran over a cop!"

"I'm sorry! I panicked!"

I laugh until it's nothing but a silent wheeze. My sides hurt and there are tears coming out of my eyes. Bo has one of those laugh-screams you can only have when you're laughing so hard it's bad for your health. She does this shriek thing on the inhale that just makes me laugh harder. Every time I think I'm done laughing, she makes that noise, and I fall right back in another laughing spell. We cackle for a solid five minutes before we finally calm down. We're both panting and crying, and I definitely got my ab workout in for the week.

I'm finally chilled out enough to check the texts Amber sent us.

Amber: Saw you guys try to run over Officer Jim! I laughed so hard we got caught trying to leave.

Amber: He made us go to class 😑 You should have run him over.

Amber: jk FBI if you're reading this it was a joke please don't arrest me

I laugh again and show Bo the texts.

"Looks like it's just us today," I say, sure that I'm sweating and my brain is malfunctioning.

Bo and me??? Alone??? Valentine's Day??? DATE???

"Sorry, is that okay?" she asks.

I clear my throat. "I mean, we kind of committed to ditching when you almost committed vehicular manslaughter."

"Shit. Do you think he took down my license plate? What if

he recognizes my car?"

"I think he was a little too busy trying not to get run over to take down your license plate."

"Okay, true. Anyway, if you're down to go without them, then I'm down. It's your late birthday, after all." She smiles.

"I'm down. It sucks they can't come, but I still want to do whatever you guys had planned for me. Which is . . . ?"

"First is breakfast." Bo pulls back onto the road.

We end up at a board game café. Bo wants me to pick the game, and I suck at deciding, so we pick randomly. We end up with Monopoly and Connect Four.

When the server comes to our table, he gives us a weird look.

"Shouldn't you kids be in school?"

Shit. We're still in our uniforms.

"Uhhh . . ." Bo is usually good with her words, but apparently improv isn't her thing.

"It's a late start today. We still need a minute to look at the menus," I say.

"Oh, all right . . ." He doesn't look like he's buying it. "I'll come back in a few."

He's talking to someone behind the bar, and I know it's probably nothing, but I'm picturing they're conspiring to get us sent back to school.

"Go, go, go, go, go!" Bo grabs my arm and pulls me away from the table. We run out of the café at full speed. It's fun to pretend like the stakes are much higher than they are. We're two secret agents on a mission. Can't blow our cover. We get into the car and retreat.

"We should go to my house and get some civilian clothes," Bo says in a super-sexy spy voice that makes me shudder.

"Won't your dad be home?" I ask, remembering that Rick is a stay-at-home dad.

"He usually goes to Starbucks in the morning, so he's probably not back yet. We'll have to make it quick, though."

We park a few houses down from Bo's. That way if her dad is home, he won't notice the car right away. Bo is the spy, and I'm the getaway driver.

She grabs her backpack, takes the house key off the keychain, and opens the car door, leaving the car on for me.

"If I'm not back in five minutes"—her voice almost cracks and she whispers the next part—"wait longer."

She's gone before I can answer. She's doing somersaults and army crawling, acting a complete fool getting inside in the most extra way possible. She eventually sneaks in through the side gate. I wait for her to be out of eyeshot before I put my hand on my chest and swoon. She had to go and do the spy thing.

I switch to the driver's seat and wait for her to come back. After a minute, she calls me.

"Did you get the clothes?" I ask.

"No, my dad's here." She's whispering. "I can't make it up to my room without blowing my cover. I'm going for plan B. I think there's some clothes in the laundry room."

She hangs up before I answer. Who does she think she is, Batman?

The front door opens, but Bo doesn't come outside. It's her

dad. He sits on the porch and starts reading a book. I send Bo a quick text letting her know he's out front, and I get a thumbs-up in response.

The side gate opens, and Bo starts army crawling along the side of the house. I roll the windows down. If I give her the opportunity, I'm hoping she'll do some badass leap through the window as I drive off. If she stays low enough, her dad might not notice her passing. But as soon as she reaches the porch, he puts his book down and looks right at her. She freezes. My heart is popping out of my chest, I'm so anxious for her. And for me.

Instead of getting up and trying to talk her way out of it, she bolts toward the car, screaming bloody murder the whole time. She doesn't slow down when she gets close, which means I'm about to see the sexy-car-chase window leap.

It's not as cool as I thought it would be. She gets stuck halfway through the window because of her backpack.

"Pull me in, pull me in!" she screams.

I grab her arms and pull, and she scrambles her way into the car. She would have gotten in a lot faster if she used the door. I hit the gas. Not too hard, though. This ain't my car and I'm not trying to wreck it. I see Rick in the rearview mirror, shaking his head and laughing. At least he's not mad.

"Woo!" I scream out the window, and laugh. I feel like we're on a high-speed chase even though I slowed down to five miles an hour to stick my head out the window. Bo doesn't laugh with me.

"I have some bad news. . . ."

"Shit. You couldn't get the clothes?"

"Oh, I got clothes, but . . ." She unzips her backpack. There's one pair of leggings, a huge pair of basketball shorts, and a huge T-shirt. The shorts and T-shirt are clearly Rick's.

"We'll make it work," I say, trying my best to match her drama.

We go to the gas station to change. I take the leggings and the T-shirt. The shirt goes halfway down my thighs. It looks like a dress. Bo wears the school uniform hoodie instead of the uniform shirt, and her dad's shorts. They're so big on her she has to tie them at the waist with a hair tie so they don't fall off. The outfits make us seem a lot shorter than we already are, and we're both looking a hot mess. But we're hot messes together.

I'm still hungry, since we didn't get to eat at the café, so the next stop is free samples at Costco. Since neither of us have memberships, we sneak in with another family, following them close enough that the lady up front thinks we're with them, but far enough that they aren't freaked out by us. It's the perfect plan.

We split up to cover more ground, and for maximum samples. After getting two of every sample around the warehouse, we meet back by the front, both our bags stuffed with free food.

"Let's send a selfie to Amber and David," Bo says. I get out my phone and we pose mischievously, showing off our full bags. The woman from up front walks toward us.

"Aww, happy Valentine's Day, you two!" Bo and I both jump at the unexpected interaction. I have a bad habit of throwing my phone on the ground when I'm startled. The world slows down as it flies through the air.

"NO!" I snatch at it, but it's no use. The sound when it hits the floor devastates all of us. Well, mostly me.

"Oh, I'm so sorry, I didn't mean to startle you." The woman picks up my phone for me—and the screen is cracked. Dammit.

"It's okay," I say, even though I'm screaming on the inside. I don't want her to think of me as a kid who's ditching school, so I put on my grown-up voice. "I could save the money from the phone bill anyways."

She smiles. It's working. "I just came over here to say, it's so nice seeing young couples like you around here. How long have you been together?"

I glance at Bo for an answer. She looks like she's about ready to run away screaming for the fourth time today, so I figure I'll handle this one before she bolts.

"A year next month." I give my sweetest smile, then grab Bo's hand and start walking. My heart is racing, but I play it cool. Bo probably would have either stayed frozen there or run away if I hadn't intervened. She is really not good at this whole secret-agent thing.

"Is this okay?" Bo whispers to me as we leave the store. Cheeks red, she looks down at our intertwined hands, and I realize how big a deal it is.

"Yeah," I say, surprising myself at how I didn't even have to think about it. "Better to stay in character. In case, like . . . she looks back at us, or something."

Bo smiles her crooked smile at me, and we hold hands all the way through the parking lot.

Once we're in the privacy of Bo's car, we empty our bags to

reveal the treasure. It's supposed to be an appetizer before we eat at the mall, but it's a decent amount of food and it's actually pretty filling.

"Sorry about your phone. Does it still work?" Bo asks.

"Doubt it." I get out my phone to show her. The screen is all kinds of messed-up colors. It almost looks pretty. Right now, though, I don't even care that it's broken. I won't have to worry about my mom's wrath until I get home. She'll kill me for ditching, but that's a problem for later. Now I'll worry about how someone just assumed I was in a relationship with Bo and I didn't self-destruct. She knew we were gay and it didn't even bother me at all. It was just a stranger, but I felt seen. And I *liked* it.

"I didn't even realize it was Valentine's Day," I say, even though I definitely did realize it. I immediately want to disappear into the seat, because I'm *wearing heart earrings*. Bo definitely knows I'm lying, but she doesn't say anything. Part of me actually wonders if David and Amber ditched us on purpose just to set us up. Amber has been trying to get Bo a girlfriend forever. And since Jamie doesn't exist . . . I wonder if Bo was in on it. Maybe this is all supposed to be a date?

"Yeah, that's why I asked if it was okay with you that it was just us. I didn't want to make it weird." Okay, so not a date then. Just two friends not being weird.

"Oh, okay. Yeah, I don't think it's weird. I do birthday stuff on Valentine's Day all the time." Lie. I do birthday stuff on my birthday.

Bo smiles at me with just her eyes, and I swear we're flirting right now. But maybe that's just me.

Next stop is the arcade at the outlet mall on my side of town. It's as close to my house as I've ever let Bo take me. It's hard to focus on playing games when I'm overthinking whether or not this is a date. I mean, I know it's not *supposed* to be a date. But I wonder if it feels like one to her. We do some date-like things. There's a lot of laughing and playful arm touching. She wins me a bunch of prizes from the games she plays. It's cheesy, but I have cosquillitas fluttering around in my belly the whole time. The day goes so fast with her.

When we sit to eat at the arcade restaurant for dinner she says something that makes my heart stop.

"Hey, do you want to be my girlfriend again?" she asks, while casually showing me the menu like she didn't just flip my whole world on its side.

"What?" I ask, to make sure I heard correctly. There's no way Bo just asked me out.

She points to the menu and laughs. There are bold letters saying they offer free ice cream on Valentine's Day to couples who buy any of the arcade food. I try not to visibly sink, because when I thought she was asking me out for real, I wasn't even scared.

"Oh!" I clear my throat. "Yes! For the ice cream."

We play up the assumption that we're together one more time. I'm nervous to do anything more than hold hands, since I don't want to make her uncomfortable. What gets me feeling some type of way about it is that we keep holding hands when no one is looking. I'm not going to be the one to let go, and apparently neither is she, so we leave still holding hands.

Ice cream cones in our free hands, we walk around the mall flaunting our fake relationship. Bo seems to have completely forgotten about her other fake girlfriend. She's an even worse liar than I am. The fear of looking "too gay" usually makes my stomach roll, but right now I'm too excited to think straight. I don't want to ruin this by thinking "straight."

Bo has this big smile on her face, and every now and then she starts swinging our arms like we're little kids. She's too cute sometimes. All the time. I feel like a child with her. I know I'm still technically a kid, but I already can't wait to retire. Because of all the work and homework and stress, I'm surprised I don't already have a full head of gray hair. It's different with Bo, though. I *feel* like a kid. Like anything is possible if I can imagine it.

Pretending with Bo is so different than pretending with Jamal. When Jamal held my hand, it didn't warm the rest of my body or make the hair on the back of my neck stand up. We never held hands longer than we had to. No one gave us weird looks like they are now. Somehow even that doesn't bother me.

I feel like I'm soaring, until I see the one person with the power to bring me crashing back down.

21

THOU SHALT STEP ON LEGOS, BITCH

Bianca.

We're walking right in her direction and it's too late to turn around. Instead of trying to hide, I hold Bo's hand tighter. I *want* Bianca to see this. Bo gives me a curious look, and all I can do is smile at her. Because fuck Bianca. I'm happy right now, and not even she can ruin that.

From the corner of my eye, I can tell by how far Bianca's jaw is hanging that she has very much noticed us by now. Is she jealous? It must be pretty earth-shattering for her to realize she isn't *still* the center of my universe. Not that she ever was. Bo and I walk right past her, and I don't even give her a second look.

"Yami?" Bianca calls out just when I think I'm in the clear. Bo turns her head, which kind of blows my whole pretending-Bianca-doesn't-exist cover. I keep walking.

"I think someone's calling you?" Bo says.

"Nope, didn't hear anything." I walk faster, pulling Bo along with me.

"Yami!" Bianca's voice is closer now, and before I know it, she's grabbing my shoulder.

I finally let go of Bo's hand and snatch at Bianca's.

"Oh, don't touch me," I say as I throw her hand off my shoulder. Seriously, how dare she?

"Sorry." Bianca puts her hands up. "It's been forever. . . . I'm glad you, um, moved on."

"Not that it's any of your business, but I moved on a *long* time ago," I say, and smile at Bo, just with my eyes. I'm not doing it because of Bianca, either. I guess I'm trying to tell Bo something right now. Maybe she can figure it all out right now, and maybe I want her to. I want this to be a sweet moment between us, but one of Bo's eyes is twitching and the other is about to pop out of its socket.

"Okay, well . . . good. That's good. I'm Bianca, by the way." She gives Bo a smug smile, like she's expecting Bo to be jealous, or to have at least heard of her, which she hasn't.

"I'm Bo." I'm relieved that Bo doesn't try to hold a conversation. She must have caught on to how much I absolutely hate our current company. "We're kind of in a hurry, but it was nice meeting you!" Bo says, then she offers me her hand. I take it, and we walk to the parking lot without looking back.

I'm sure Bianca's face is priceless, but I'd rather look at Bo.

"So . . . do you want to tell me what just happened?" Bo asks when we're out of Bianca's earshot.

"Not right now," I say. I won't let Bianca ruin my mood for one second. When we leave the mall, the sun's already been down for about an hour. We stand outside Bo's car for a minute, still holding hands.

"Can I drive you home?" she asks.

I hesitate. Not because I don't want her to, but because I do, and it's a big deal. So for the first time, I let Bo take me home.

I thought having Bo sitting outside my house would be embarrassing, but it's not. It's one of the many details about myself I've been sharing with her. In the past few months, I've gotten to know her so much better, and it only feels fair that she can know some things about me, too. I want to tell her other things, like how gay and into her I am, but I'll take it one step at a time.

I don't get out of the car when it stops. I don't want today to be over yet, and I'm hoping Bo doesn't, either. Jamal's car is in the driveway instead of my mom's, which means she's still at work, so I'm in no hurry to get inside. I'm happy that they've finally realized they are perfect for each other. If they're working things out right now, I don't want to interrupt.

"So, how did it feel to be gay for a day?" Bo laughs.

"What?" is all I can say, because I can't bring myself to admit to her I'm gay every day.

"Everyone thought we were a couple, because it's Valentine's Day?" she says, and I think me asking for clarification made it awkward. "Sorry, I hope that didn't make you uncomfortable."

I hate that she's scared of me being uncomfortable again. I thought we were past that. But I've been afraid of making her uncomfortable all day, so I can't blame her.

I'm feeling brave all of a sudden. Her hand is resting on the console, so I reach over and slip my hand into hers. Because I'm not uncomfortable with her. Not even a little.

"I'm comfortable," I whisper. "Are you?"

I don't know if I'm doing it of my own free will, or if Bo is just like a magnet because of those eyes of hers, but I'm leaning forward. And so is she.

Her forehead touches mine. I close my eyes. My breath stutters, and our faces are so close I'm sure she can feel the air from my mouth.

Be brave.

"Can I . . . ?" I start breathlessly.

"Please."

I stop resisting the magnetic pull and eagerly close the space between our lips. Kissing Bo is like being in a sensory deprivation tank. The world around us disappears, and the soft sensation of her lips on mine is the only thing tethering me to this plane of existence, keeping me from floating away to the clouds. I hold my breath as if doing so could stop time, keeping us right here in this moment. This moment where nothing else matters. None of the lies I've told can touch us, until I have to breathe again.

"I lied to you," I blurt out, pulling away. Maybe there's a good reason I tend to overthink things. I shouldn't have kissed her, but there's no turning back now. I brace myself for her anger. I trust Bo, but she trusted me, too. . . . I hear Bianca's voice in my head.

I trusted you . . . how could you do this to me?

"What?" Her eyes flutter open, like she needs a second to get back to reality and register what I said.

"About being straight . . ." I know the kiss probably tipped her off, but I need to say it. "I'm not."

"Yeah, I know." I'm not even surprised she knows. After what happened with Bianca today, how could she not? "I lied to you too. . . . I don't have a girlfriend."

"Yeah . . . I know," I say, smiling.

"So you're not mad?" we both ask at the same time.

"No." I laugh. I'm just relieved to hear that Bo is officially single.

"Me either," she says. She smiles and takes my hand. "Why aren't you mad, though? I lied to you."

"I lied to you, too."

"Yeah, but that wasn't about me. I know how hard it is to come out, especially when you go to Slayton. You were protecting yourself, like I was until last year." She squeezes my hand. "I get it."

"Thank you," I squeeze her hand back and close my eyes. *She gets it.*

"I want to be clear, though, that day you told me you were straight . . ."

"I still feel terrible about that. Um . . . You looked really pretty, and I felt like you could tell I thought that, so I panicked."

"*I* panicked!" Bo laughs. "That's why I told you I had a girlfriend! It kind of snowballed from there and I was too embarrassed to admit it. I thought you were being bitchy, but we were both just gay panicking."

"Definitely gay panicking."

She drops her head on my shoulder and laughs into it. I lean my head on hers and laugh along. We've been doing a lot of laughing today. I always do, with her. I feel like I've died and gone to heaven, because this can't be real. Before I can over-think the implications of today, and that kiss, my phone starts buzzing. Which I honestly didn't think was possible.

"Ugh . . . That's probably my mom." The screen lights up, but I can't see a name through the cracks, so I ignore it. I'm not sure it would work if I tried to answer anyway.

"Thanks for today. I had a really good time," I say.

"Me too. Maybe next time you'll let me come inside?"

"Next time, definitely," I say. She grabs my hand and kisses the back of it. She's so freaking cute, goddamn it.

My phone goes off again. "I better get that. . . ." I groan. Mom is going. To. Kill. Me.

"Mami, I can explain—" I start, but get interrupted.

"Where are you?" Jamal's voice is on the other end, almost yelling.

"Jamal?" I ask, taken aback. I glance at Bo, who looks surprised, hurt almost. She doesn't hold eye contact for long. Instead she looks out the driver's window. I guess to her, it probably looks bad that I'm talking to my "ex" on the phone instead of kissing her good night.

"Yami, where are you?" Something about the shake in his

voice makes my chest tighten. He's loud enough that I'm sure Bo can hear him, too.

"I just got home, why?" I unbuckle my seat belt.

Jamal's voice is quieter now. Broken almost.

"I'm here. I'm taking you to the hospital. It's Cesar."

My feet move on their own, and I'm running inside before I have a chance to think. I don't explain myself to Bo. I just run.

22

DROP THE COMMANDMENTS. LIVE BY THE CODE.

Cesar is suicidal and I had no idea.

He's already at the hospital with my mom. Thank God Jamal waited for me to get home so he could take me. I'm sure Mom made him.

"I'm sorry, I'm sorry," Jamal mutters, gripping the wheel tight enough for his veins to show. I'm not sure if he's talking to me or not. "I think I did the right thing? I don't know what else I was supposed to do." He's practically hyperventilating.

If Jamal hadn't been there . . .

"Tell me what happened. All of it," I manage to say. Jamal's already been through the story twice, but I can't seem to grasp onto the details. Everything after "Cesar is suicidal" just becomes a blur. I force myself to make sense of the words this time.

"He called me a while ago. He was crying really hard and it was kind of hard to understand him, but he just kept begging me to stop him. I didn't know what he was talking about, so I just came over." Jamal takes in a shaky breath before continuing. "He . . . he wanted to . . ." Jamal's voice catches like he's going to cry.

"He wanted to what?" I ask, even though I know the answer. I need to hear it out loud.

Jamal wipes a stream of tears from his cheek with one hand and sniffles. "To die, Yami. But he also must not have wanted to, or he wouldn't have called me, right?" Jamal sounds like he's trying to convince himself more than me. He looks at me with tears in his eyes. I nod, since words are escaping me.

"Wait, did he hurt himself?" I cover my mouth.

"No, I got there before he did anything. We called a hotline. I didn't know what else to do. He wasn't calming down, so they had us three-way call your mom and take him in. He didn't fight me on it. I think he knows he needs help." His voice shakes as he talks, and I can't bring myself to say anything back.

It should have been me. Why didn't he call *me*? I had no idea he needed help. He was doing great in school. He hasn't gotten in any fights. But clearly he wasn't as happy as he let on. I think back to the conversation between Cesar, Jamal, and me, walking to get Takis. Cesar said tomorrow wasn't guaranteed. I thought he was saying anyone could die at any moment, but no. He was saying *his* future wasn't guaranteed. I'm so angry with myself for not having figured it out then. He tried to tell me. . . . We're supposed to be able to read each other's minds. In lak'ech ala k'in. I should have known. *I should have known.*

Jamal's phone rings and he hands it to me. Mom starts yelling before I get a chance to say anything.

"What is wrong with you, child? You should have been there! But instead you're ditching to be with some boy for some *stupid* holiday while Jamal is over here picking up your slack."

"That's not why—" I start, but I can't argue. She's right. I should have been home with him. And *she* should be with him right now instead of yelling at me. "I'm almost there, so you can tell me how everything is my fault then."

I hang up. I want to cry, but I can't.

"It's not your fault, Yami," Jamal says as we pull up to the ER. "Keep me updated, okay?"

I nod and get out of the car. I have to sit in the waiting room instead of with my brother while I wait for my mom to take me to his room. All I hear is her voice yelling in my ear that I should have been there with him. *I should have been there with him.* But I was celebrating. I was having fun while my brother was . . .

I have no idea how long I'm waiting there before I hear her voice for real.

"He's okay, mi amor, he's okay," she says, but I can hear that she's sobbing. I'm guessing she's telling Papi what happened. I selfishly wonder if he'd be willing to talk to me right now, because of the intensity of the situation. But before I can ask to talk to him, Mami's already hung up, and she's hugging me. I didn't see her coming. She's crying, and I'm not. I can't. Not until I see my brother. She grabs my hand and leads me through several hallways. The hospital is a maze. Even with my mom guiding my hand, I feel so lost.

The door to Cesar's room is wide open. There's a stranger

in scrubs sitting in the corner of the room. She looks tired, but not as tired as Cesar. The room is completely empty besides the bed and her chair. Cesar's eyes are puffy, with bags under them that tell me he hasn't had a full night's sleep in days. How could I have missed the signs? He doesn't say anything when we walk in, just stares up at the ceiling instead of looking at either of us. The only noise in the room is Mami crying. She's clutching her rosary and whispering prayers in Spanish through her sobs.

"Mami, please stop crying," is all Cesar says before closing his eyes again. She doesn't.

I want to say something, but how can I comfort him right now? I want to ask if he's okay, but obviously he's not.

Two men walk in. One looks a lot younger than the other.

"Mrs. Flores, can we borrow you for a minute?" the older guy says without acknowledging Cesar or me at all.

"Don't worry, mijo, it's gonna be okay." Mom wipes her eyes. I think she's trying to convince herself more than anyone else. She steps out with the two men, leaving me, Cesar, and the rando lady in the corner. I glance over at her. I guess privacy is a luxury we can't afford.

"Hey," I say when Mom leaves. What else is there to say?

"Hey." It's not much, but at least he's talking.

"Who were those guys?"

"The mental health worker and his intern."

"Oh, cool." I've never had such a forced conversation with him. I feel so stiff and unnatural. It's not supposed to be like this. Not with Cesar.

"Why didn't you call me?" I shouldn't ask, not now, but it slips out.

He doesn't answer.

"I talked to Jamal . . . ," I say, hoping that'll get him talking.

"I like how you're still using him as your beard even though we broke up. That's real cool, Yami." His tone is cold.

"What? I'm not—he just told me you called him."

Cesar doesn't say anything.

"You know you can talk to me, right?"

Nothing.

"I'm serious. I'm here for you. Always . . ."

He clenches his jaw.

"Cesar, talk to me, *please*." My voice catches in my throat, and the "please" comes out like a whimper.

"I'm fine."

"You're obviously not fine, Cesar!" I don't mean to raise my voice.

"Oh, so now you notice?" he snaps back.

"How can I notice when you won't talk to me?"

"Seriously? You're the one who hasn't been talking to me!"

"You two need to calm down, please." The woman's tone is kind, but it has an edge to it—a warning.

"Sorry," we both mumble.

"I didn't call you because you wouldn't have answered. You never answer. You're always busy. And Mom, too. Jamal's always there. . . . You and Mom can't help me." The words cut deep and hollow me out.

I open my mouth, but nothing comes out. Maybe he's right. I've been so busy with work and school and Bo that I barely had a chance to worry about Cesar. I think about all the times recently that I blew him off. I had one job: look out for Cesar. And I didn't. I wipe my eyes before any tears get the chance to fall.

"I . . . I'm so sorry . . ." Of course I didn't see this coming. I've been too worried about work. "I'm glad you called *someone*. If you died, I would . . ." I don't know what I would do. Maybe I'd die too. "In lak'ech . . ." is all I can manage to say about it.

"Don't." His fists clench and his eyes shoot through me. "Drop it, okay? I don't want to talk about it."

"Okay, just . . . please promise me you won't hurt yourself?" My voice cracks.

"Yami, fucking stop!" He grasps the sheets tightly in his fists.

When I'm sure I'm about to get kicked out, Mom comes back with the suit guys. She goes right back to Cesar's side and holds his hand. The intern comes forward.

"Cesar, it was brave of you to ask for help. We're all glad you did. Luckily, we already have a bed for you at the Horizon Behavioral Health Facility. They specialize in helping kids like you."

"Mami, is that okay?" His voice is so low I can barely hear it. Mom and I both know what he actually means: *Can we afford that?*

"I'm sorry, but it's not exactly a choice, kid. Whether you

like it or not, this is the safest option for you." The mental health worker sounds rushed. It's not like Cesar needs any more convincing; he just needs a second.

"Mom?" Cesar looks scared for the first time since I got here.

"It's okay, mijo. I just want you to be safe. That's all that matters." She rubs the back of his hand with her thumb, and he squeezes hers.

"But—" Cesar starts to protest, but the mental health worker interrupts.

"Like I said, it's for your own safety. I'm not a fan of the whole involuntary detainment thing, but that's really your only other option." He sighs, as if thinking about what an inconvenience it would be to have to do it that way.

"Give him a minute, okay? Jesus . . . ," the nurse snaps. I want to hug her. I guess not *everyone* here is desensitized.

The mental health worker sighs. "Right, sorry. It's been a long day."

I want to punch him in his throat. My brother could have died tonight, but *he's* had a long day.

"It's gonna be all right, honey." The nurse's voice softens when she turns her attention to Cesar.

Cesar stares at the ceiling and shuts his eyes like he's having regrets. A couple of tears fall down his cheeks, and Mom wipes them for him.

"It's only three days of inpatient, as long as everything goes well. Then, if you're ready, you can go home for outpatient treatment, all right?" the intern says.

Cesar lets out a small whimper and doesn't answer.

The older guy cuts in again. "Listen, we really are just trying to help you here. And I'm afraid I've got a lot of other patients who need help too. So are we going nicely or the other way?"

I hate this guy so much. I hate him. I hate him.

After a long pause, Cesar answers. "I'll go, sir," he chokes out. It's the "sir" that kills me. It's fucked that he has to show that piece of shit respect to keep from getting threatened with "the other way." It's not like Cesar's being violent right now.

"Atta boy." He has the nerve to go and ruffle Cesar's hair.

"Don't touch him," I snap, because I know Cesar wants to say it but can't.

"Yamilet, you can go home now," Mom says, but I don't move. They're all staring at me. I want to help my brother, but I don't know how.

"It's okay, Yami, just go. I'll be fine," Cesar says, but I don't think he convinced either of us.

"Go home. I'll handle it." Mom hands me her keys. We're both crying. But I can't stay here forever, and I can't go to Horizon with Cesar. So I go home.

23

IN LAK'ECH ALA K'IN

The cracked mirror in my room mocks me. It zooms in on my runny nose and wet eyelashes. I slam my fist on the desk but don't feel it. All I feel is dizzy and mad. I grip the edges of the vanity for balance. I want to blame someone. I can't stop thinking about that doctor threatening Cesar. Or my parents being homophobic. Or Cesar wanting to . . .

The edges of my vision go black, and all I can see is my fractured reflection staring back at me. My mom's voice echoes in my head.

You should have been there!

I want to take back punching the mirror the first time, just so I can do it now.

You should have been there!

I punch it again anyway. And again. And again.

I can't hear myself bawling, or feel the blood dripping from my knuckles.

"You should have been there!" I scream out loud at what's left of my reflection.

I hit it until every bit of shattered glass falls from the vanity.

My knees are about to give out, so I stumble to the bathroom to wash the blood off my hands. I refuse to look at my face. I focus on the blood. So much blood on my hands. I can't stop them from shaking. From anger or blood loss, I don't know. They're already starting to swell.

I want to punch this mirror, too. But this one is *ours*. And I barely have the strength to pick out the leftover shards of glass from my knuckles.

I let the water run over my hands. I don't know how long I'm standing there. A few minutes, an hour, maybe. It doesn't matter.

Cesar has gauze and bandages under the sink. He hasn't had to use them all year. I thought that meant he was doing better, but maybe it just meant he lost the will to keep fighting. I should have been there. . . .

It takes me longer than it should to wrap my hands. They won't stay steady. When I'm finished, I look up. The Code of the Heart stares back at me: *In Lak'ech Ala K'in.*

I got blood on the poem.

My knees finally give out, and I sob on the bathroom floor until I fall asleep from exhaustion.

I wake up in my bed. Mom must have carried me here, which means she saw the glass on the carpet and didn't kill me. She turns on her bathroom shower, but I can still hear her wailing. When the sound of pouring water goes away, she cries louder.

Eventually I hear her footsteps, and light peeks through the crack of my door.

"Are you up, mija?" She sounds hoarse.

"Yeah."

She turns the light on and sits at the foot of my bed without mentioning the glass on the floor. She didn't bother putting on the sunglasses she always wears to hide her crying eyes. She's holding Cesar's phone.

"I have to tell you something. I'm so sorry."

"What?" I sit up so fast my vision goes white. I can't handle any more bad news.

"Mija, I don't know how to tell you this. . . ."

"Just *tell* me, Mami. You're scaring me." As much as I don't want any bad news, I don't want to be in the dark either.

"I think Jamal was cheating on you . . . with your brother."

"What?" This feels like a fever dream. Why would she be bringing this up now?

She shows me Cesar's phone, like she wants me to read some texts. I'd be pissed if Cesar read my texts, so I push the phone away. It's too big an invasion of privacy for me.

"You went through his phone?"

"I wanted to know what happened. Where I went wrong . . ." She's crying again. I'm surprised she's not blaming me. If I had any strength in my hands right now, I'd be reaching for hers.

"Don't cry, Mami. I'm sorry . . . what were you saying?"

She clears her throat. "Cesar and Jamal. They were together. Did you know this?"

I decide it's best to come clean and admit to it. I'm in a little too deep to play innocent right now.

"I knew."

She winces.

"I was trying to protect him. Like you told me to," I say.

"Protect him . . . from me?" She touches her quivering lips with her fingertips.

I nod cautiously, afraid I've crossed a line. But part of me doesn't care.

I want to tell her I'm gay, just to take some of the weight off Cesar. But I can't bring myself to say it. I'm a terrible person. I still have three days before Cesar gets back. I'll tell her before then.

"Where did I go wrong?" She cups her face in her palms. Telling her is going to be tough. But her disapproval only makes me want to tell her more. So Cesar won't have to deal with it alone. She pulls her rosary from her pocket, but I interrupt before she starts praying.

"There's nothing wrong with not being straight, Mom."

"But why would he want to . . ." Her voice cracks. "I don't know how I missed this."

"Me either . . ." I, of all people, should have seen the signs that he wasn't okay.

"I missed so much. Did you know he was never on the football team?"

I can't bring myself to answer.

"I thought he was doing so well." She wipes her face and walks out.

✦ ✦ ✦

I'm still awake when my alarm goes off the next day. I can't go to school. The second Bo asks me what's wrong, I know I'll lose it. I'm not trying to cry in public anytime soon. I don't move until my mom storms into my room, clapping her hands. She's really going to pretend everything's normal.

"Time to go! What are you doing in bed?"

"I'm sick . . . ," I say.

"Oh, no you're not. You don't get to ditch two days in a row, missy. You're going."

"No, I'm not."

"Yes, you are!" She's yelling now. "You missed yesterday, and look at where that got us!"

"What the hell is that supposed to mean?" I throw the covers off myself and sit up, even though she has a point. I don't know why I'm daring her to say it.

"You didn't come home with him! You were supposed to be *here*!" Her voice being hoarse from crying doesn't stop her from trying to scream at me. She's right, but she's just as much to blame.

"Oh, so this is *my* fault?" I know it is. But not just mine.

She throws her purse at me but misses.

"*YES!*" The scream doesn't sound like my mom. It comes out low and starved, like her real voice is trapped somewhere deep down.

"Fuck you!" I yell, ignoring the steam escaping her ears. "You're the one making gay jokes in front of us! You're the one who said there was something wrong with Jamal because you thought he was gay!"

Her lip trembles, and I don't know if it's because she's about to chew my ass out or if she's going to cry again. Her expression goes blank.

"Stay home, then. And clean this shit up." She stands straight while she walks over to grab her purse, then leaves. I hear the front door shut, the car starts, and she's gone.

I don't get out of bed for anything except to go to the bathroom. And I can't use the bathroom Cesar and I share. I can't look at that bloody poem. So I use my mom's bathroom instead. The landline rings, but I ignore it. I throw myself on my mom's bed. All I want to do is sleep, but the damn house phone keeps ringing. It's probably my mom calling to yell some more, so I pull a pillow over my head and pray for the ringing to stop.

When she calls a third time, I throw the pillow and stomp over to the kitchen to answer it.

"What do you want?" I shout.

"Yami, it's Jamal." He's crying. "Please tell me Cesar's okay. He's not answering his phone."

"He doesn't have it." I sniffle. I have no idea what to say. Because no, he's not okay. I don't know what Cesar would want me telling Jamal, either. Would he be mad if I told Jamal he went to Horizon? I kind of wish I did look at Cesar's phone now, so I'd have an idea of what to say to Jamal. But Jamal is the one Cesar called, not me.

"But he's okay? Is he in trouble? Is he *okay*?"

"He's alive," is all I can say. I find myself wandering into Cesar's room. It feels so empty. The whole house does. I see

Cesar's promise ring from Jamal on his nightstand. I'm surprised he still has it.

"Where is he? Can I talk to him?" Jamal sounds so desperate, I can't leave him in the dark.

"He's at the behavioral hospital, so he's only allowed to talk to family right now. I'm sorry."

"Can you just tell him I'm not mad at him? And I could never hate him. Tell him that for me, okay?"

I close my eyes, pushing out a small, dehydrated tear. "I'll tell him. Thanks, Jamal."

"And that I love him," he blurts out.

"Oh . . . I don't know if that'll help him right now. . . ." I want to tell Cesar that, but honestly, with where he's at, it might not be a good idea for him to be missing his ex right now.

"Just tell him the other stuff, then. Thank you, Yami." He hangs up.

I lie down on Cesar's bed, and finally fall asleep.

I don't want to test my luck with Mom, so I get up when my alarm goes off the next morning. I put on one of Cesar's oversize school hoodies so the sleeves hide my mutilated knuckles. I use eyedrops to make my eyes less red, and I take extra time doing my makeup. My hand shakes, but it has to be perfect. Perfect eye makeup is the only motivation I have to keep my eyes dry today. They look too good to ruin with tears.

Mom drives me to school, and neither of us acknowledge what happened yesterday. Or the day before.

Bo sits next to me in first hour, and I smile like everything is great, but she's looking at me all confused.

"Is everything okay?" she asks, and I instantly feel guilty.

"Mhm!" I smile again, avoiding her eyes and the subject. I feel like if she looks me in the eye, she'll just *know*. I can't deal with her brujería right now. I might be a little short with her, but it's only because I don't want to cry. I'm mostly tight-lipped smiles and nods today.

Hunter, David, and some of Cesar's other jock friends keep asking me where he is. I tell them he's sick. I get his homework from his teachers so he doesn't fall behind. Homework could keep him busy while he's at Horizon. The classes I have with Bo are the hardest. She's the only one who seems to notice that anything's off.

I stare at a blank canvas for most of art class.

"Hey, can we talk, Yami?" Bo touches my shoulder. She should know not to touch me when I'm about to cry, because all I want to do is turn around, get a hug, and sob. But I can't, so I smile and nod, like I've been doing all day.

She steps closer now, so only I can hear her.

"Are you avoiding me?"

I can't think about Bo's feelings right now. I can't deal with any more feelings. I know it looks bad. I know it looks like I'm ghosting her after our kiss. I know it looks like it has something to do with Jamal, my "ex." But I can't think about it. I can't think about Bo being mad at me on top of everything else.

"Yami." She touches my shoulder again, and I can't handle it. I shake her hand off and bolt. I grab my bag and run straight to the bathroom without asking Ms. Felix.

First thing I do when I get to the bathroom is take out my makeup.

"No, no, no . . ." My eyeliner is starting to drip. I get a paper towel and wipe the edge of my eye so it doesn't smear down my cheek. The door starts to open, so I rush into a stall and lock the door before anyone comes inside.

I see rainbow Vans under the stall door. It's Bo. An ugly sob escapes from the back of my throat against my will. I can't cry quietly anymore. I hear the stall door next to me open, and the sound of Bo sitting down. It feels like confession. But a priest could never absolve me of my guilt, and neither can Bo.

She reaches under the stall with a literal white flag in her hand: a wad of toilet paper, just like the first time I came in here crying. Of course it was Bo. It's always Bo. I want to laugh, but I can't stop crying. I take the toilet paper to blow my nose. Her stall door opens, and she knocks on mine.

I open the door and fall straight into her arms. She stumbles back a little but catches me.

"I'm here," she says. It's all I needed to hear. I'm tired of this double life, of the lies.

I finally let all the secrets pour out of me like a broken dam, and I can't stop until I'm rid of every last secret. I tell her about Cesar, and Jamal. About Bianca and my dad. All of it.

My knees give out, and she lowers me to the floor to sit. She rubs my back, and when I'm done, she lets me cry in her arms until the dam runs dry.

24

TÚ ERES MI OTRO YO

Bo comes with me to the library after school. I roll my eyes at Karen and her boyfriend, who are making out in the back corner. It's Wednesday, so Bo wants to take me home after we're done here. I could use the moral support. There's something I need to fix before Cesar gets home.

In the library, I retype the Code of the Heart and the poem. I switch the font about twelve times to get it exactly how Cesar had it. I don't want him knowing I got blood on this. When I finally get it right, I print it out and let Bo drive me home. Part of me feels guilty for still having feelings for her. But I also think Cesar would be pissed if I stopped talking to Bo because of what happened with him. He's been trying to convince me to go out with her all year.

I stare at the poem the whole ride without saying anything. I don't want to talk. Bo holds my hand, and I wince. I didn't realize how much hand holding could *hurt*.

She doesn't ask about the scabs on my fists. Instead, she pulls my hand to her lips and gently kisses my knuckles like she gets it. When we pull up to the house, I don't get out of the car. The driveway is empty, but it still feels too familiar. I don't want to go back into the house alone. I blink to clear my vision.

"Yami?" Bo looks concerned.

"Do you want to come inside?" I ask.

She smiles. "Are you sure?"

I nod.

She answers by getting out of the car and opening my door. I gently take her hand and lead her straight to the bathroom to show her the Code of the Heart. I tear off the old poem from the mirror. She helps me tape the new one on, exactly how it was before. I thought I'd feel weird about showing her the poem, but I'm relieved. More than anything, I don't want to be alone right now. And she's here.

"Do you want to talk about it?" she asks.

I shake my head.

"Is there anything I can—" I interrupt her by pulling her into a kiss.

She makes a startled noise, but then kisses me back. I don't know what I'm doing, but I know I don't want to talk. I want to feel something other than pain. And right now, I do.

I pull Bo closer and back up toward the bathroom door. I slide a hand behind me to open it. We stumble into my room, and I can't ignore the sound of glass cracking under our feet. I know Bo won't ignore it, either. A pathetic whimper slips out of my mouth without my permission. I don't realize my cheeks are wet until Bo pulls away.

Her eyes go from the glass on the carpet to my hands, then

back up to my eyes. I wipe them and look down to avoid look-ing at her. But down is where the glass is, and I don't want to look at that either.

"Sorry . . . I don't know what I'm doing," I say, shaking.

"You have nothing to be sorry about, Yami."

She couldn't be more wrong. I back away toward my bed without taking my eyes off the glass. I sit at the edge of the bed.

"Hey, it's okay. I'll be right back." Bo leaves, and I let her. I probably freaked her out, so I don't blame her. I kick my shoes off and curl into myself on the bed, but I don't hear the front door open. Instead, I hear water running from the kitchen sink. Bo comes back into my room with a glass.

"Where's your vacuum?" she asks, and hands me the cup. I stare at the water.

"You're not leaving?"

"Not unless you want me to," she says.

"Hall closet." I point, smiling despite the situation. "You don't have to clean this up for me. I can do it," I say, even though I know I won't until my mom makes me.

Bo ignores me and leaves to get the vacuum. I get up to help, but she kicks my shoes away so I can't put them on.

"Stay on the bed or you'll cut your feet!"

I laugh and finish the water while the glass disappears from the floor.

Bo leaves before my mom comes home, so I have some time to myself. I'm still pissed at my mom, but I'd almost rather be around her than be alone with my thoughts right now. I distract myself by pulling out my laptop and googling "how to support someone who is suicidal." It basically says I'm supposed to ask all these questions. I sigh and shut my laptop, because I just know Cesar would hate that. What does Google know, anyway? I guess I wanted Google to tell me something that made more sense than all of this.

When my mom gets here, she doesn't even come inside, just honks the horn for me to come out. We're visiting Cesar at Horizon today, but since we're still barely on speaking terms, we're both silent the entire ride until I make her stop at the gas station to get Takis for Cesar. When we go in to visit him, we do it individually, so Cesar doesn't have to deal with our tension while we're there.

They tell me I can share the Takis with Cesar, but he has to eat them during the visit. Mom goes first, so I sit in the waiting room until she comes back. I feel like the Takis are stale by the time she's finally ready to tag me in.

We have to meet in this community room where a few other patients are having visitors, too. There are a few nurses on the sides of the room, but they look more like security guards than nurses. On instinct I want to bust him out of here, but I have to remind myself he's here to get help. He needs help.

The circles under Cesar's eyes aren't as dark, so at least he's getting some sleep. It's weird seeing him without his cross and jaguar necklaces, though, but I guess they wouldn't allow that sort of thing here. I sit at a table across from him and put the Takis and his homework down as a peace offering.

"You know me so well. Thanks." But I don't know him that

well, apparently. I fake a laugh so he doesn't get uncomfortable. "I'm getting out tomorrow," he says with a grin.

His smile looks forced. I wonder if his smiles were always this forced and I didn't notice. Has it always been like this? Right now, his happiness seems undeniably fake.

I wish I knew how to help him. I think back to the article I read. I guess asking questions is worth a shot. "How long?" I ask, and Cesar just gives me a confused look. "How long have you been feeling this way?"

Cesar sighs. "Do we have to get into this now?"

I shake my head. I don't want to make him dig into any of his trauma if he doesn't want to. Not right now. No matter how badly I want to know.

He must see something desperate in my eyes, because he answers anyway. "A long time, okay? A long time." Before I can answer with an apology, he's changing the subject, like he does. "Yami, it's so boring in here, you don't even know."

"Yeah?"

"They don't let you do shit. It's just therapy and, like, coloring books all day."

"Do you think it's helping at all, though?" I ask.

He shifts in his seat and shrugs.

"How's therapy?" Cesar isn't usually one to talk about his feelings, but I let myself hope it's helping.

"Fine, I guess." I wait a second, but realize that's as much as he's planning on giving me.

"So, I should probably warn you . . . ," I say. He deserves a heads-up that Mom knows about Jamal.

"What?"

"Promise you won't freak out?"

"Just tell me." He fidgets with the bag of Takis. He still hasn't opened them.

"Um . . . Mom went through your phone."

"Fuck." He runs a hand through his hair. "What did she say?"

"Not much. She knows about Jamal, though. . . ."

Cesar covers his face. I'm only making things worse. I shouldn't have told him.

"But it's okay! I don't think she's mad at you, and I promise I'll come out to her before you get home. And I have a job and enough money saved up to put down for this apartment I'm looking at, so we can make it work if we need to." I'm talking so fast I don't know if I'm making any sense. I slow down. "I got you, okay?"

He's quiet for a while. I hate that the job is part of the reason I haven't been there for Cesar, but now more than ever, it helps to have a backup plan.

"You really have enough to get a place?" Cesar asks.

We'd be struggling, and I don't know the first thing about living independently as minors, but I nod. If I need to, I'll figure it out. I try to steady my hands so Cesar doesn't know how terrified I am.

"I guess I should say thanks." He doesn't force a smile. I do.

"I, um, I talked to Jamal, too." Maybe there's one thing that can make him feel better.

"Yeah?"

"He wanted to know if you're okay. He's not mad, and he doesn't hate you." Somehow the words don't feel as powerful coming from my mouth as they did from Jamal's.

"He should. . . ." Cesar's eyes are shiny, like he's about to cry.

"Why?"

"Because he did everything for me and I broke up with him right when he needed me. He didn't do nothing wrong, and I fucked him over. Here, I'm not hungry." He hands me the bag.

"It's okay. Feelings change. That's not your fault." I open the bag, hoping he might subconsciously start eating them if it's open. I don't know why I want him to eat them so bad. I just want to feel like some small part of this can still be normal.

"My feelings didn't change, though. I'm just a shit person."

"You're not a shit person."

He doesn't answer.

"So, why did you break up with him?"

He's quiet for a while. He draws in a slow breath, and his nails jab into his palms. It feels like a full minute passes before he says anything.

"Why did God make me like this if I'm not supposed to be like this, huh?" His chin quivers, and he wraps his arms around himself. I want to hug him, but I don't even know if that's allowed here.

"I don't know," I ask myself that all the time. "Is that why you broke up with Jamal? Because you want to be straight?"

It takes him a while to say anything. "It was my penance."

"Penance . . ." It takes me a minute to process what that

means. "Like from confession? The *priest* made you break up with him?" I never thought I could be so pissed at a priest in my life. What gives him the right to play God in people's lives like that?

"No one made me do anything. I just wanted to get right with God. . . . I thought I could get better. Date girls from now on. And I could be good with Dad, too."

"Better . . . as in straight?"

He doesn't answer.

"What about me then? Am I going to hell, too? Is Jamal?"

"In lak'ech . . ." He shrugs. Meaning, we're all going to hell. That's a fucking shitty way to use that phrase.

"Well, I don't believe that. There's nothing wrong with us. There's nothing to fix, besides your backward attitude."

There's a sting in his laugh. "Okay, so why are *you* still in the closet then?"

"Are you kidding me? I came out to Dad, to you, to Bo . . . it's a process. I'm getting there. It's not a one-and-done thing. It has nothing to do with shame. And if you're ashamed of yourself, then are you ashamed of me, too? And Jamal? Is that how you feel?"

"I'm not ashamed of you. . . ." His voice is softer now. I don't realize I'm crying until he reaches for my hand. He holds it gently and doesn't say anything about the scabs. "Yami, I'm not ashamed of you, okay?" I hate that even now, with him in a freaking hospital, he still feels like he has to comfort me, instead of the other way around.

"Then how can you be ashamed of yourself?"

He looks down and doesn't answer.

"You're the one who said it. In lak'ech. I know you know what it means. 'Tú eres mi otro yo.' I love you, so I love myself. I *love* myself! And I know you love me, too." I put my other hand on his so it's sandwiched between both of mine. "So, you don't get to say 'in lak'ech' to me and not mean it. You got to show yourself some love. If not for yourself, for me. Or Jamal. Or Mom."

Cesar lets his head fall down so his forehead is on the back of my hand, and he whimpers. I want to leap over the table and hug him, but I don't want to get kicked out. I know I can't take all that shame away from him. But I can start by showing him how much I'm not ashamed. Not only am I not ashamed, I'm *proud*. I can't make him love himself. The closest I can get is loving myself unapologetically right in front of him. Like Bo did in front of me. Maybe then he'll get it. He doesn't make any noise, but I feel my hand getting wet from his tears.

"I need to be able to see your hands, sweetheart," one of the nurses says.

Cesar puts his hands flat on the table without picking up his head. He's taking deep breaths, like he's trying to calm himself down. I get why, but I hate that we can't have our moment in peace right now. I glare at the nurse, even though I know it's not her fault. Why can't it be someone's fault? We're all just trying to keep him alive. Cesar wipes his eyes and nose.

"You want me to jump that nurse for you?" I say, because if Cesar isn't going to break the tension with his usual jokes, I will. He chokes on his laugh.

"No. I want you to tell me how you came out to Bo." He turns his head and takes a Taki from the bag. Things might not be back to normal anytime soon, but he's eating his favorite food and gossiping about my love life, so I know we're on the right track.

After our visit, Mom goes out for a long walk, and doesn't come back for another hour or so. I know she's just trying to avoid me. I want to keep away from her, too, but I told myself I would come out to her before Cesar got home. He said he'd be back tomorrow, so I should do it now.

"Siéntate, mija. I want to talk to you," she says right when she walks in the door.

"Me too," I say, trying not to let the lump in my throat downplay the fake confidence in my voice. I sit at the table and so does she. I start stroking my hair. She's the one who usually strokes my hair when I'm anxious, but I obviously can't ask her to do that right now.

We both speak at the same time.

"I'm sorry, mija—"

"I like girls—"

She closes her eyes. "What?"

I straighten up and speak with more confidence. "Mami, I'm lesbian."

I think it's the first time I ever used that word to describe myself, and I like how it feels.

"Okay." She pinches the bridge of her nose. I expect some kind of lecture, but she doesn't say anything.

"Are you, um . . . okay with that?"

"Mija, get me a glass of water, will you?"

A weird request, but I do it, then sit across from her. She drinks the whole glass before saying anything.

"Ay Dios mío, all of my children."

I shift in my chair.

"How long have you known this?" she asks.

"I don't know. A long time, I think." Maybe it hasn't been that long, but I don't want to say it's only been a couple of years and have her tell me it's a phase. I guess I figured it out with Bianca. "Look, I already found an apartment for me and Cesar. If you want us out, just tell me now so I know if I need to—"

"Mija . . ." Mom puts her hands on the table toward me, palms up. The gesture makes my eyes spicy. I take her hands and she squeezes mine. "Please don't leave. . . ." She doesn't bother wiping the tears falling from hers.

"Okay, Mami," I whisper. I don't wipe my own because it feels better to hold her hands. I'm so surprised I can't think straight. She wants us to stay. . . .

"I know I said some stupid shit to you and your brother over the years." She shakes her head and rubs the backs of my hands with her thumbs. "¿Sabes qué? I don't care if you're bisexual, gay, whatever. I just want you to *talk* to me. I didn't know. How could I have known when you don't talk to me? Neither of you. I have to find out from your brother after he almost . . ." She pulls a hand away from mine to cover her mouth. I can't believe how much I relate to her right now. I guess I understand why Cesar hasn't talked to me, if it feels anything like talking to Mami.

"I shouldn't have put that on you, Yamilet. What happened with your brother is not your fault, I know that, I hope you know that. I've been unfairly hard on you, and I'm sorry for that. I need you to know I appreciate everything you've done for us. It's more than anyone your age should have on their shoulders. I've been so worried about Cesar, and somehow still missed the signs. And look at your hands, mija, I—" she takes a sharp breath and lets it out shakily. "Just promise me you talk to me before you get to that point. I know I haven't made it easy, but please talk to me if you need anything, okay, mija?"

"Okay, Mami. Thank you," I say.

She wipes my eyes.

"So . . . you're okay with it?"

She cups my cheeks in her palms and kisses my forehead. "Mija, I love you. That's never going to change."

"I love you too, Mami." I scoot so I'm sitting next to her and slide my arms around her, letting all my muscles go weak. *She's okay with it.* She still loves me.

"You tell me if anyone gives you or your brother any trouble, okay?"

I take a deep breath and let it out measured. "Um, Dad did. . . ."

She slow blinks. "Excuse me?"

"I told Dad in October. He hasn't talked to me since then. That's why I didn't want to go see him."

She starts muttering profanities in Spanish I won't repeat, then pulls her phone out of her pocket and stomps out of the room.

Even with Mami on my side, being home still doesn't feel right without Cesar. I'm worried about him, but hopefully the worst is in the past. At school, I have Bo to make me feel better. Plus, Mom being supportive makes things a lot easier. I can't even put into words how nice that feels. I don't have to worry about getting kicked out and having to support Cesar, too. I have time to decide what I want to do with my life now that I'm not in a hurry to support myself. Not knowing what I'm going to do is the biggest weight off my shoulders I could have imagined. The uncertainty is exhilarating because now I have a choice.

When Mom picks me up from school on Thursday, we don't go straight home. Instead, we go get Cesar. Finally. I feel like he's been gone a year.

Mom must have been busy all day, because when we get home, there's decorative papel picado hanging from the ceiling. The intricate designs cut into the every-colored tissue paper looks like my mom did it herself. It's not Easter yet, but there's a bunch of colorful cascarones everywhere. There's also pan dulce with bread dyed pink, purple, and blue on the table. It takes me a minute to absorb it all.

"Um, what's the occasion?" Cesar asks.

"Es *gay*," Mom says with a huge grin on her face.

Cesar and I burst out laughing. The pan dulce is made up of

the bi flag colors, and the decorations are rainbow. Oh, Mom, she tries so hard. It's really sweet.

"Hey! I'm cool, okay? You wanna be gay, you go be your gay li'l selves!" She pulls us both into a hug. I know she's overcompensating, but it's still nice having someone besides ourselves to celebrate with and just tell us we're good.

"You didn't have to do all that." Cesar squirms out of the hug. I guess it makes sense that he's a little overwhelmed. Up until very recently, I thought Mom would disown us if she found out, and now she's all rainbows and gay pride. It's a little dizzying.

"I did. Because I love my gay children! I love you!" She pinches both of our cheeks and kisses Cesar's nose.

"Sure. What about the Bible?" He gives her a skeptical look.

"Mijo, if the Bible tells me I shouldn't love my kids, then the Bible is wrong."

Cesar and I share a telepathic look for *whaaaaat?* Mom has never said anything against her faith, ever.

"You're being weird, Mami . . . ," Cesar mumbles, and I don't blame him. I know what she's doing, though. She's trying to make up for what Dad did. At Cesar's comment, her smile disappears, and she looks into his eyes all sad, giving up the charade.

"Mijo, I've done a lot of praying about this. And the answer is clear to me now. How can I abandon my kids when they need me most? Now that I've seen what can happen"—she gets all choked up—"what can happen if I don't support you with everything I've got, how can I not celebrate my children to the fullest? I'm not saying screw the Bible. I'm just saying, I love you, both of you, and that's *never* going to change. The Bible also says to love everyone, and not to judge. And I believe God has a place in heaven for everyone with a good heart." She taps both of us on our chests.

I roll my eyes because it's so cheesy, but it still makes me tear up. I glance at Cesar and see that he's already accepted her answer and is stuffing his face with pan dulce. I can't let Mom's effort go to waste, so I stuff my face, too.

Happy times are a little hard to maintain when your brother is on watch. We all have to sleep with our doors open, just in case. Since my room is right by Cesar's, Mom wanted to switch with me to keep a better eye on him, but I refused. I like my room, and I imagine Cesar would rather have me lurking than Mami. Plus, I want to be there for him if he needs anything.

He's starting therapy soon, and hopefully that will help, but he doesn't seem too excited about it. Mami offered for me to go to therapy, too, but I don't think I'm ready for that yet. Cesar takes his antidepressants from a daily counter, so me and Mom can see if he's taking them and make sure he doesn't take too many. I don't even know where Mom keeps the pill bottle. She's the only one who refills the counter. I don't like feeling like I'm spying on Cesar, but it has to be done. Better to spy than to lose him.

I wake up early to the sound of an upbeat ranchera, then the smell of eggs and bacon. Mom never cooks breakfast for us on weekdays, with the exception of Cesar's game days, and this isn't her usual music. I follow my nose out into the hallway, and Cesar is already peeking out of his room. We wander into the kitchen, but Mom isn't in there. It's Doña Violeta. Her feet shift with the music as she flips bacon on the comal. She shushes us before we get a chance to make a noise.

"Your mom had a long night. Let her sleep before work, okay?"

Cesar and I rush into a tight hug.

"I missed you, Doña," I say, even though it hasn't been that long since we've seen her. I missed this. This is the Doña Violeta I know. Mom probably told her about what happened with Cesar. Maybe she needed someone to take care of, like she used to.

"Are you okay?" Cesar asks her. We haven't seen her leave her porch since her husband's funeral. She gives us a sad smile.

"Don't worry about me, mijo. Let me take care of you for a few days." She kisses his forehead and gets back to making breakfast.

Miracles like this only happen in what feels like the darkest moments. Doña Violeta stays home with Cesar so my mom doesn't have to take time off work and risk getting fired. Cesar wasn't ready to go back to school right away, and Mom didn't want to force him, so Doña Violeta came through. No matter what happens, my brother won't be alone.

On Saturday I would rather stay home with Cesar and work from there, but he would rather have the laptop than my company, so I leave to work at Bo's house to use their extra computer. I don't want to make Cesar feel babied, especially since his childhood babysitter is already tending to his every need. Mom lets me take the car for work, and she stays with him and Doña Violeta while I'm gone.

I have to admit I have really missed Rick and Emma. Work goes by a lot quicker when I'm here, too. On the downside, I'm a little less productive.

It's the first time I've been back in this house since winter break, and I notice that they've listened to Bo and taken down most of the Chinese decorations since then. I'm glad they're giving her the space to do her own exploring on her own terms.

Emma lets me use their study to work, and Bo sneaks in for some quick kisses every chance she gets. Her parents won't let her hang out in there with me, because they know I'll get distracted. But I don't think they know me and Bo like each other, so it's kind of fun sneaking kisses whenever they aren't looking. It feels like we're secret agents again, except this time the mission is to be cute and do couple things like kissing and holding hands. Sometimes all she has to do is give me this *look* when no one can see, and my insides turn to mush.

She never tries anything cute at school, though. She knows it's up to me when I come out there, so she's not trying to push it. I'm the one getting impatient with myself. Sneaky kisses and secret affections are exciting, but I'm ready to do it for real. I want to tell my mom, and Bo's parents, and the whole school, and *everyone* how into Bo I am. The reason I never wanted to be completely out before was self-preservation, but now that Mom and Dad know, the worst has already passed. I'm not getting kicked out or disowned. It sucks that my dad isn't talking to me, but that's the worst that could happen at this point. I know my friends will be fine with it, since they're fine with Bo.

I also want to prove to Cesar, and to Bo, that I'm not ashamed. I don't want Cesar to feel like he has to come out, but maybe me being out will make it easier on him when and if he decides to do it.

No one can hurt me the way my dad or Bianca did anymore. I'm ready.

As soon as I get home, I start plotting. It's decided. I'm going to ask her out. Officially. Not yet, but it's going to happen. I just have to figure out how to do it. Cesar is my go-to advice giver, and I'm too excited to wait for him to finish his homework.

"Yo, Cesar, you got a minute?" As soon as I walk in, he shoves something into his pocket, but I notice. "Uh, what's that?"

"What did you want to tell me?" He's a master subject changer, but I'm not falling for it. He also can't resist some good chisme, so I'll use his weaknesses against him.

"It has to do with Bo. . . ." I pause to gauge his reaction. He raises his eyebrows. He's taking the bait. "You first, though. What's in your pocket?"

He squints at me. "Oh, you're good. You're real good."

"I know. So what are you trying to hide?"

He sighs and pulls the ring Jamal gave him out of his pocket.

"I know I should give it back. . . ."

"You don't have to do it right away. You can wait until you're ready to face him," I say.

"It's been months, though."

"So what do you want to do?"

"I don't know. I feel like I don't deserve to keep this. I was too ashamed of myself to wear it when I had the chance." He fidgets with the ring in his hand. I get why he doesn't want to give it back. Giving the ring back means the relationship is really over. Jamal still loves him, and Cesar obviously still loves Jamal. He just has some self-acceptance to grow into.

"Are you still ashamed of yourself?" I ask, praying for an answer that doesn't hurt.

"I'm working on that." He shrugs. It's better than a flat-out yes, but it hurts to know he's struggling with that shame. "Anyways," Cesar says, "what happened with Bo?"

"Wait, first—are you okay?" Even though I want to talk about Bo, I don't want to let him deflect the conversation that easily. I sit on his bed and assume the heart-to-heart position, but he doesn't move from his desk.

"I will be." He's looking down at his notebook and clicking his pen like he'd rather do homework than talk about this. But I'm happy he's not lying and saying he's great. He *will* be okay.

"Can we talk about you and Bo now?" he asks. I know he's deflecting again, but I don't want to keep prying and push him away. He'll talk to me about it when he's ready.

"I'm gonna ask her out."

He whips his head around like an owl and almost falls out of his chair.

"When? How? Can I watch?"

"Oh my God, calm down!" I laugh. "I don't know yet. That's why I need your help."

He adjusts himself to face me so he's sitting backward in the chair. "You're the one all smitten and shit. What does she like?"

"Um . . ." I'm drawing a blank. She likes art, disco, and free samples from Costco. She likes ice cream. She likes . . . *oh!*

"That's perfect! Thanks!"

"You're welcome?" he says, and I go back to my room to formulate a plan.

I'm going to ask Bo to prom. And I know exactly how to do it.

25

SI TE HAGO DAÑO A TI, ME HAGO DAÑO A MÍ MISMO.

Just when I'm about to start getting ready for bed, I overhear my mom crying from her room. She's never been one to cry quietly, but it's still louder than usual. I step out of my room to find that Cesar had the same idea. We share a look that's telepathic code for *Do you know what's wrong?* and we both shrug. We wander down the hall to her room to cheer her up, but when I open the door, I immediately regret coming here with Cesar.

"He could have *died*, do you understand? And you won't even *talk* to him?!" Mami screams at her phone.

Cesar stops in his tracks. His chin quivers, and I can't bear to look at the pain in his eyes. He must have been in denial about Dad, like I was for the first couple of months he wasn't talking to me.

"Let me talk to him," I say, and march over to the side of my mom's bed.

"Face the consequences of your actions," Mami's voice comes out in a sob as she hands me her phone.

I stare deadpan at the phone as the words pour out of me. "You're out of our life for good. And that's my choice, not yours. What kind of asshole calls himself an activist but then won't speak to his own children when push comes to shove? We're better off without you, you pinche comemierda!"

Instead of lecturing me for cursing, Mami gets out of bed and stands next to me and starts cursing him out with me. "Fuck you, Emiliano! These kids are perfect and they don't need you for one second! I'll love them for the both of us, you pinche—"

She keeps yelling, but Cesar comes up behind us and butts in. "Yeah, fuck you, you ugly piece of shit! WE disown YOU, you got that? You're dead to ME!" he shouts, spit flying out of his mouth as he points to the phone as if Dad could see his taunts.

And we all go on like that for a solid minute, the three of us chewing him out at the same time in true Mexican fashion. It takes me a while to realize he's already hung up. Who knows how much of our yelling he actually heard, but it felt good to say it all out loud.

I drop my arm holding the phone to let Mami and Cesar know he's not listening anymore. Then I pull them both into a hug, and we all sink into it like it's the only thing keeping us from crumpling to the floor.

"I love you guys," Cesar says through a sniffle.

Mami holds us both tight.

I hug back harder. "I love you so much."

I can hear Cesar pacing in his room before my alarm goes off. It's his first day back at school after a week off, so he's probably nervous to face everyone. *I'm* nervous. I've done my best to keep rumors from spreading about why he was gone by telling everyone he had pneumonia, so he should be fine. Still, I don't blame him for being anxious.

He has his usual "everything is fine" act down perfectly when I check on him during lunch. After making sure he's good, Hunter and I go to the art room. The art show is finally happening at the end of this week, and I haven't made many pieces in class worth showcasing. I only have one piece that made it in, and I'm here to make another. Since it's something I could use some advice about, I made Hunter come along. I don't want to burden Cesar, and Hunter is the only other person at school I'm out to, besides Bo. And *she* definitely can't help me, for reasons.

"How's this?" I ask Hunter as I show him my fourth concept sketch.

"Ooh! I like that a lot! It looks great!" he says, giving me an encouraging slap on the back. He's said that about every other idea I've had. Hunter's a good dude, but he's completely useless for constructive feedback. I finally just let him go back to lunch.

Once he's gone, Ms. Felix stops grading our still-life art from last week and pulls up a seat across from me. I catch her staring at me, like she has something she wants to say. She's making me a little anxious. She definitely overheard me and Hunter talking about how I want to ask Bo to prom. She's always given me a really open-minded vibe, but what if I was wrong about her?

"What?" I ask, letting out a nervous laugh.

She smiles, but there's a sadness in her eyes. "I just wish I was as brave as you are, is all."

"What do you mean?"

She pauses for a while before saying anything else. "I'm only telling you this because I think it would have helped me a lot when I was your age if I'd had an adult in my life open up to me. But I need you to know you aren't alone."

I stare at her, wide-eyed. Is she . . . coming out to me?

"I'm not oblivious to what everyone says about me either. I know a lot of my students already suspect it. But I thought I'd let you know personally. I'm there with you."

"So . . . you're queer?" I know it's not the most tactful way of asking, but when have I ever been known for being tactful?

She nods. "And I'm not out. Not here. So let's keep this our little secret, okay?"

"Of course."

"If you ever need anything, to talk, or to just use my room, I'm here, all right?" She offers a warm smile.

"Thank you," I say. I don't know what else there is *to* say, but I just really hope my thank-you is enough to convey how much it means to me.

"I like this one." She points to one of the first concepts I drew. "It makes a statement."

I nod and get to work finalizing the sketch she picked. I was secretly hoping she'd pick that one. I'm a little more relaxed as I work, safe in the knowledge that Ms. Felix is right there with me, supporting me. By the time I've finished the sketch, she's almost as excited as I am about what I have planned. But not quite.

No, I'm definitely the most excited.

On Friday, Mom wants to hang out as a family before the art show, so Cesar and I help her make some jewelry at home after school. We used to do this together for fun when we were little, but it's been years. Even though my birthday was less than three weeks ago, so much has happened since then. It seems like we haven't hung out as a family in ages. At least, not in a good way. Now that I can relax around my mom, it's so different. It feels like exactly what we've been missing.

"What are you all smiley about?" Mom asks.

"I don't know. I missed you guys."

Mom reaches out and grabs one of my hands and one of Cesar's and squeezes. "I missed *this*."

I expect Cesar to get all embarrassed and change the subject, but he doesn't.

"Me too." He lays his head down on my mom's hand and closes his eyes, like her hand is a pillow. His lips turn up a little. Mom leans over the table to kiss his forehead, then kisses mine.

"I have something for you," she says to me as she pulls something out of her pocket. "It's not an iPhone, but I need to be able to get ahold of you." She hands me a dinosaur phone that matches Cesar's. The first thing I do with it is take a picture of the three of us to use as my new background. I tear up looking at it. I may not have my dad, but I have Mami and Cesar, and they're all I need.

We spend an hour using jewelry as an excuse to catch up. On small stuff, mostly. How Mom's work is going. How Cesar is catching up with schoolwork. How I like my job with Emma. But I'm a little distracted. By two things.

First, because of the art show, obviously. But also because of my parents. What is going to happen with them? Is Mami going to forgive Dad for what he did? Because I honestly don't know if I ever can.

I end up just blurting out the question, since I'm super over keeping things bottled up. "So what's going to happen with you and Papi?"

Mami hesitates before letting out a sigh. "Until he wants to have a relationship with his children, nothing."

"You're okay with that?" Cesar asks, incredulous.

I almost can't believe it. I didn't think my mom loved *anyone* more than my dad.

She squeezes his shoulder. "Listen. Your father has been the love of my life. But . . . I just don't know how to love someone who doesn't know how to love my children."

I like how she says "my" children. She's the only parent that matters.

"Anyways, enough sad talk. It's a big day, mija. Are you ready?" she asks me, wiping tears away and smiling.

"Nope!" I keep my eyes on the earrings. Honestly, that's a lie.

I'm using the art show to ask Bo to prom, and I couldn't be more ready. Getting approval from a teacher on the promposal makes it a lot less intimidating. No one at this school has tried to go as a gay couple before, even though there's no rule against it. I checked. Twice.

"She's lying. She's been ready for this since she *met* Bo." Cesar laughs, and I shoot him a look. But he's right.

As we talk, I find myself making earrings for Bo. I don't know if she even likes earrings, but it's fun making them with her in mind. They're cute enough that if she hates them, I'll keep them for myself. If she says yes, I'll give them to her before prom.

I look up to find Cesar staring at the bracelet he's not bothering to make.

"You okay, dude?" I slip in the "dude" to lighten the mood a little. Still, it takes him a while to answer. Mami and I have our eyes trained on him, waiting for whatever it is he might say, and I can see how this might be a little intimidating.

"Can I see a different therapist?" Cesar finally asks.

"Why?" Mom's hands stop moving, and I can tell she's trying to keep her voice calm.

"I'm not feelin' it."

"Well, maybe it takes a little getting used to." Her hand stutters, but she starts working again.

"I'm pretty sure I'm the only bi guy this lady has ever met.

I'd rather not spend my sessions educating her."

She looks at him and cups his face. "Okay. We'll find someone with more experience then."

"I already know who I want!" Cesar jogs over to his room and comes back with the laptop. It's opened to a search for therapists with an LGBTQ+ client focus. The therapist highlighted is an older Latina woman.

Mom scans the screen and frowns. "She doesn't accept our insurance, mijo."

"Oh." Cesar frowns.

"Do you think maybe it would help to join some kind of support group? Maybe something with kids your own age?" Mami asks tentatively.

"Nah. It's hard enough telling my shit to just one person," Cesar mumbles.

Jewelry making quickly turns into a therapist search. We all gather around the laptop and scroll together. Cesar has a few top choices by the time we have to go to the show. I'm just glad he told us about the problem instead of bottling it up. Right now, with Cesar smiling about therapy, I know we're getting somewhere.

Amber, David, and Bo and her parents are all waiting outside the auditorium for us when we get to the art show.

"Mr. and Mrs. Taylor, this is my mom." I sound a lot more formal than I usually do with them. Mom would be embarrassed if I used their first names or didn't formally introduce her.

"Nice to finally meet you! I'm Maria." Mom shakes their hands and hugs Bo, David, and Amber, even though she only met them all once before.

"Likewise!" Rick says.

All the art is set up in the gym, like a maze. There are makeshift hallways up so that you follow them and see each piece one by one. I pretend to be interested in everyone else's art. Really, I'm there for David's, Hunter's, and Bo's art . . . and mine, I guess. I'd rather not think about mine right now, though.

Bo and David both have several pieces scattered throughout the exhibit. I have two. One is a painting of the desert sunset. The second is the one I'm nervous for everyone to see, though. Ms. Felix told me she'd put that piece closer to the end, which makes me jittery walking past everyone else's work.

I stop walking when something catches my eye. It's me.

In class, Bo drew my portrait with pencil, but this one is painted over. She must have spent a lot of time finishing it up outside of class, because I never really saw her working on it after that day.

My mom walks up next to me and puts her hands on my shoulders. "Bo, you did this one?" She looks like she's about to cry.

"Yeah. Do you like it, Yami?" She looks nervous.

I think it's beautiful. She really captured that Selena vibe I'm always going for. She got my makeup looking exactly how I like to do it. The corners of my mouth are turned up a tiny bit, which I must have been doing subconsciously when I was modeling for her. She's made me look like I've figured out the meaning of life, and I'm keeping it a secret. She painted every piece of me I'm self-conscious about, and I love the way I look through her eyes. My square jaw, wide-set eyes, big mouth, and hooked nose couldn't look more perfect.

"You got my eyeliner right . . . ," I say while I wipe a tear from my eye. I knew I was pretty, but damn. She made me look like a goddess.

Bo laughs out a sigh of relief. "I was worried I wouldn't be able to do you justice."

Mom hugs Bo tight. "It's beautiful, mija!" Then she hugs me. "Just like my girl!"

I take a picture of the portrait so I can look at it when I'm feeling self-conscious. God, I love Bo.

Oh my God. *I love Bo.*

A few people are murmuring up ahead, which means they've probably seen my piece. We round the corner, and there it is. I focus on keeping my heart inside my chest, and make my way up slowly. It's not a masterpiece or anything. I threw rainbow colors of paint on a canvas over a bunch of tape. The tape came off to spell out *Prom?* in white over the rainbow splashes.

I didn't sign my name on the canvas, so no one knows it's mine, and no one is looking at me until I step up by my piece and start talking.

"Um . . . okay, I'm not really good at this sort of thing." I try not to fidget with my shirt, and I catch my mom's eye. She gives me an encouraging nod. I take a deep breath and look straight at Bo so everyone knows what's about to happen. There are a couple of gasps in the small, but growing crowd. Bo's covering her mouth with her hands, and I can tell from her eyes that she's smiling. The crowd gets bigger as more people make their way to my piece, but they go silent. I unfold the paper from my pocket because I know I'll forget the words I practiced if I don't read them. The paper shakes in my hand. I start reading and brace myself for the public booing.

"Bo, I know public demonstrations are more your thing than mine"—that gets a couple of chuckles—"but I want to be more like you. I don't want to apologize about who I am, or how I look, or what I feel. I think you're amazing, and inspiring, and beautiful, and I'm not even a little bit sorry about it. Will you go to prom with me?"

She doesn't give me any time to be anxious, because she's hugging me the second I'm done asking. No one boos. Silence.

"Is that a yes?" I ask. She nods, and then kisses me in front of everyone, and I kiss her back. Cesar is the first to start cheering, and I feel Bo's lips turn up while we kiss. Mine do the same. Someone else whistles, then a few others follow. I'm too happy to care what the rest of the crowd thinks.

"Okay, break it up, that's enough!" One of the other teachers shoos us away from my piece. I grab Bo's hand and we run outside the gym together like we're running from an explosion. Amber, David, and Cesar follow us.

When Mom and Bo's parents finally come out, I brace myself for their reaction. My mom already knew I was going to do this, but what if Bo's parents don't approve?

Emma reaches out and touches my shoulder, offering a warm smile. "I'm proud of you. What you did was really brave."

Once again, I find myself grateful for the brown skin that hides my blush. "Thanks."

"So how'd you convince this one to go to a school dance?" Rick asks me while he gently shakes Bo by her shoulders.

"It wasn't that hard." I laugh.

Ms. Felix and Principal Cappa walk out, and my fight-or-flight reflex kicks in. I try to ignore that I can hear them arguing as we walk away.

"Who wants ice cream?" I ask.

Bo and I hold hands the entire time, right in front of everyone.

After the regular morning prayers and pledge in language arts on Monday, the usual announcements play on the TV. One of the students is interviewing our principal. I was tuned out for most of it, but when he mentions prom, I'm fully listening.

"This is a reminder of the types of things that are appropriate during prom. We want to keep a wholesome environment, so inappropriate dancing will be given one warning, then you'll be asked to leave. Couples, make sure to leave room for the Holy Spirit—that means one foot of space! The dress code will be strictly enforced, and anyone not following the dress code will be turned away at the door.

"It has also come to my attention that there has been some

confusion around the rules. I want to be clear that Slayton Catholic does not endorse romantic same-sex couples for prom. We will be updating our code of conduct effective immediately to avoid any further . . . mishaps."

He keeps talking, but I can't hear anything else. Everyone is staring at me and Bo. Pretty much everyone already heard about what happened at the art show. My hands are shaking and I want to be anywhere but here. When the announcements are over, it's not Bo who speaks up. It's me.

"Well, I appreciate the subtlety of announcing to the whole school that Bo and I can't go to prom. That was *super* discreet and sensitive."

"Shouldn't have made a scene at the art show then," Karen says under her breath, but loud enough for everyone to hear.

"Excuse me?" I'm standing up now.

"Seriously? What is wrong with you?" Emily snaps at Karen, and the fact that someone other than me or Bo is saying something takes a lot of the pressure off.

"Sit down, Ms. Flores. Principal Cappa was simply stating the rules, like he does every year before prom," Mrs. Havens says.

"That's bullshit," Bo says. "Why didn't he say anything about same-sex couples last year? He literally said they *just* made that rule so we couldn't go."

"Language, Ms. Taylor."

Bo crosses her arms and sits back. Usually, she would be standing up and arguing at this point. I guess there comes a time when that gets exhausting. I'm not exhausted yet, though.

"He could have talked to the two of us about it instead of making a public announcement," I snap.

Everyone in the school knows that the announcement was about me and Bo.

"Sit down, Ms. Flores, or I'll have to ask you to go to the principal's office."

"You don't have to ask me," I say, and I grab my bag and head out. Two seconds later, the door opens again.

"Wait!" Bo's jogging to catch up with me.

We walk to the principal's office together, hand in hand.

26

SI TE AMO Y RESPETO . . .

I stand up straight and march like I'm proud, but I'm fucking terrified. I've never been sent to the principal's office in my entire life. This is a normal thing for Bo, but for me it feels like the end of the world.

One of the office ladies tells us we can go in to see Mr. Cappa, and we're still holding hands. I think Bo wants to prove a point, but I'm holding on for protection. It feels safer than going in alone. Mr. Cappa sighs when he sees us. He's sitting at his desk, and he gestures for us to sit.

"I was about to call you two in here. Do we have another problem?"

I use my best smart voice. "That announcement was in bad taste. It was humiliating, not to mention just completely wrong. Girls go to prom together as friends all the time." I want to keep going off and call this whole thing out as the bullshiterious miscarriage of justice that it is. I resist the urge so he'll take me seriously.

"If you two wanted to go to prom as friends, it wouldn't be an issue. There was an inappropriate public display of affection at the art show. Some of the students and parents were made to feel very uncomfortable. And as you know, this school operates by the laws of the Catholic faith. Homosexual activity is not permitted on this campus. I'm sorry, but that kind of inappropriate behavior can't go unpunished." He hands both of us a detention slip.

I laugh. It's easier to laugh than to cry right now.

"Do you want to be the one to tell my parents about this, or should I call them?" Bo says. This is why I like her parents. She knows they have her back. I can picture Emma raising hell over this.

"I will inform both of your parents of your behavior today."

"Great." Bo smiles sweetly, like this is a game. I, on the other hand, am not fucking smiling. I got *after-school detention* . . . As supportive as she is now, Mami is going to KILL me.

"You're free to go." He waves his hand toward the door as if to shoo us away. I thought arguing with the principal would be a lot more satisfying. Now I just feel sick.

For the rest of the day, Bo and I are practically celebrities. Well, we're admittedly not the most-liked celebrities. I'm not oblivious to the whispering when we walk by. It doesn't take long for news to travel here, and by second hour, everyone knows Bo and I got detention for my promposal. Bo smiles when she sees me between classes, like this is normal. Like we're not being punished and publicly humiliated for something I wanted to celebrate Friday night. I force myself to smile back.

People I barely know approach me all day to tell me how brave I am, or that they support me and Bo, or that they have a gay cousin, or whatever. The only person who actually makes me feel better is Cesar. He and Hunter sit with us at lunch today.

"So, are you guys still gonna go to prom, or . . .?" David asks.

"No," Bo says, and I swear my heart shrinks a little. I try not to let my body visibly slump. Because I was really looking forward to prom. With Bo. Even if we had to pretend to be going platonically. I was so excited for this.

"Respect," Cesar says. "Nobody cares about prom anyway. We should boycott."

"Boycott prom? Hell yeah," Emily says as she puts her tray down between Amber and Hunter. "Is it okay if I sit here?" she asks, and we nod, so she sits down.

"Karen, Jenna, and I are no longer friends. . . ." She sounds sad but doesn't look it. "I didn't know where else to sit."

"Thank God. I was waiting for you to dump them," Amber says.

"It's been a long time coming, trust me," Emily sighs. Then they all go back to discussing the prom boycott.

I think they all expect me to be happy about boycotting, but I'm not. I wanted to have a cheesy fairy-tale prom like everyone else. I just want to be salty for a minute. So I keep my mouth shut the rest of lunch. I get it. They want to stay energized, and boycotting prom makes sense after what happened. I just really wanted to go. Of all the worries I had leading up to the showcase, I never once thought I'd get in trouble for it. I didn't think I'd get *detention*.

The one time I have detention after school, Cesar doesn't. I take my time walking to my locker before I'll have to go to the cafeteria and sit in silence for an hour. When I get there, Amber is standing in front of it, blocking my way. She doesn't move aside when I step closer.

"What's going on?" I ask.

"Nothing! Nothing to see here!" She gives me the world's fakest smile, back firm against my locker. "Do you have notes from religion? I totally forgot to take notes," she rambles on.

"Amber," I say, trying to keep my voice steady.

"I completely blanked, you know? And there's that test on Thursday. . . ."

"What happened to my locker?" Did someone do something to it? This feels so unreal. I look around to see if anyone is watching me for a reaction. I feel like *everyone's* staring at me, like they have been all day.

"You don't have to look. I'll clean it off," Amber says.

"I can handle it." I expect resistance when I go to push her out of the way, but she steps aside before I can.

UGLY DYKE

My jaw clenches, but other than that, I don't let any emotions show on my face. I won't give anyone the satisfaction of seeing me react. I open the locker and toss my books inside like I didn't see shit.

"There you guys are!" Bo comes up to us, and I shut the door so she can see. Her eyes go wide for a second, then they start snapping around the courtyard, daring anyone looking at us to mind their business.

"No, let them watch," I say, and then I reach for her hand and kiss it to piss off whoever did this.

"Are you okay?" Bo asks. Her face is a little red.

"I'm fine." I hold her hand like a lifeline. My cheeks and ears are on fire, but I know whoever did this is watching, and I won't let them win.

Bo lets go to unzip her bag and take out a Sharpie. She scribbles out the word UGLY and replaces it with PRETTY, and circles it with a heart. I laugh much harder than the situation calls for.

"Don't worry," she says, taking my hand. "They get bored quick if you don't let it get to you."

She squeezes my hand, and we walk to detention together.

After Bo and me, there's a steady stream of students flowing into detention. Much more than usual. Bo and I have to sit at separate tables, so she sits at one facing me so we can still see each other. They don't allow anyone to sit directly next to each other in detention, so we all spread out at the tables across the cafeteria.

But the flow of students walking in doesn't seem to stop. I look around and find Cesar, Hunter, David, Amber, Emily, and a ton of other people in the cafeteria who I *know* don't have detention. Within a couple of minutes, there's at least forty kids milling around the room.

David and Amber take their seats as close to me and Bo as they're allowed, and before we know it, the tables have filled up. Everyone starts standing against the walls. They're orchestrating a sit-in for me and Bo. I meet eyes with Cesar from across the room, and he gives me a thumbs-up. I want to cry, because after everything that's happened with him recently, he's still in here supporting me. That's just how we are with each other. I'm there for him, and he's there for me, no matter what.

At first I think Bo is behind this whole sit-in thing, but she looks as surprised as I am. No one gets out any homework. They sit silently with those of us who actually have detention. It's so quiet we can all hear Bo's sniffle. I look over at her and see her wiping her cheeks. I want so badly to go over and hug her. God knows I need one too. But we're not allowed to talk or move, except to go to the bathroom. She looks at me and smiles, which is a relief. She's happy crying.

I smile back. Maybe we can't go to prom, and maybe some people here will always hate us, but it's not just me and Bo saying this is wrong anymore. Everyone in here has our backs. I feel like we made progress today. I feel like we won.

I hold my breath most of the car ride home, waiting for Mom to kill me. Any second now.

Or not.

She doesn't bring it up the whole ride. I know she was sort of in on the whole promposal plan, but she's not the most consistent person in the world. Especially when it comes to me getting in trouble. It keeps me on my toes.

She doesn't say anything about detention in the car. Or when we get home. Or during dinner. I finally ask her because I can't stand the suspense.

"Mami . . . did you talk to Mr. Cappa?"

"I did. I had some words for that man, let me tell you."

"What?" I want to ask if he told her about me getting sent to the office, but I don't want to get myself in trouble if I don't have to. Maybe she's talking about a different Mr. Cappa?

"Sorry about prom, mija." She puts a hand on my shoulder and squeezes. "Mr. Caca ain't shit, all right?"

I let out a snort at my mom calling the principal "Mr. *Caca*." "Thanks."

"Damn, Mom's a thug!" Cesar says.

"Why are you so surprised, huh?" She clicks her tongue.

"I thought I would be in trouble," I say.

"For what? You didn't do nothing wrong. You followed the rules and then they changed them. That's not right." She shakes her head, then grabs our empty plates and walks to the kitchen. She only takes our plates for us when she's proud of us or mad at us. For the latter, she doesn't wait for us to finish.

The stares and whispers don't stop on Tuesday. I can't tell who's on my side or not, and it's infuriating. I wish I could read their minds so I know who to shoot with my laser vision and who to bless with my smile. I wonder how long this will last. Was Bo a celebrity too when she first came out? She probably got even more attention, since she was the only one at the time. Then again, shippers gonna ship, so people are all excited that there's a gay couple at their very own Catholic school.

At lunch, Bo, Amber, and Emily are whispering to each other.

"What are you being all secretive about?" David asks.

Instead of answering, Bo stands up on the table and pulls a freaking megaphone from her backpack.

"Can I have your attention, please?" she shouts, and the room goes quiet.

"As some of you may have noticed, I won't be attending prom anymore. I know I'm not the only one here who doesn't agree with the rules. So, this is for anyone who feels disenfranchised by this school or the code of conduct, or if you want to be able to wear what you want, and dance without leaving room for Jesus. I'm going to be hosting anti-prom at my house. Same time as regular prom. And one more thing." She hops off the table and puts the megaphone down. She gets on her knee and takes my hand. Everyone goes dead silent so they can hear what she says next. "Yami, will you go to anti-prom with me?"

I can't stop smiling. People are cheering so loud I'm sure she can't even hear my "yes." I nod so she can be sure. We hug, and people are whistling and shouting for us to kiss. We don't. Because I don't want to kiss for them, and I don't want to get in trouble. But we hug again.

"Your parents are okay with that?" I say over the cheering.

"It was their idea! They wanted to raise hell about it, but I told them that would just embarrass me, so this was the next best solution." She laughs.

The support from the other students is exhilarating. I

thought they'd be booing and throwing food.

The cheerers are actually the minority, but they're the loudest, so I'm grateful for that. Plenty of others are giving us judgy looks. Some people are sitting awkwardly, and some are clapping because that's what they think they're supposed to do. I'm sure most of them don't actually care, but it's drama, and this school can get pretty boring sometimes, so I get it.

The hype doesn't die down all week. About half the promposals over the next couple of weeks are for anti-prom. Two of them are even gay. So we're trendsetters, I guess. I don't know if they're straight and proving a point or if they actually like each other, but I'll take it as a win either way. People are even starting to call it gay prom.

With only a few days to spare, I go dress shopping with Amber, because Bo says she wants to be surprised by how beautiful I look. Amber is the middle-girl for us. Her job is to advise both of us about what to wear based on the other's choices. With Amber's help, I end up choosing a purple dress that's short in the front and long in the back. The sleeves are long, mesh, and sparkly. I think it makes me look like a fairy princess, and I spend the next few days feeling giddy about it.

On the morning of prom, I wake up at five a.m. I don't need to be up this early, but I can't sleep. Cesar's up early, too; I can hear him pacing his room. I knock on his already open door to get his attention. He nods at me but doesn't stop pacing. I walk in and sit on his bed, and just wait for a minute in case he stops pacing anytime soon, but he doesn't.

"What are you doing?" I finally say.

"Exercise."

I raise an eyebrow.

"They said it's good to move around if I start feeling . . . you know, KMS-y." Cesar admitting he's feeling suicidal right now is like a punch straight to the gut. I didn't expect him to completely heal overnight, but it's hard to hear he's still feeling . . . like that.

"Do you want to talk about it?" I ask.

He slows his pace a bit.

"Um . . . maybe?" He stops walking.

"What's going on?"

"Look, I'm not gonna do it, all right? I just get really down on myself sometimes. I don't know how to turn it off."

"What are down on yourself over?"

He finally sits down and lets out a breath.

"Don't take this the wrong way, okay?"

"Okay . . ."

"I'm happy for you and Bo . . . I really am. Like, super happy. But at the same time, it kind of sucks. I feel like an asshole . . . because of Jamal. He was my person, you know? He took me seriously, even when I tried to cover everything up with jokes. He always took me serious. I fucked that up. And here you are being super proud and out with Bo, but I couldn't even put on that ring. I feel like a fucking coward."

"You're not a coward. Jamal knew you wouldn't put it on right away. It was always on *your* timeline when you wanted to come out. I only did it because *I* felt ready. And you shouldn't feel like you have to come out just because I did. Or because of Jamal, or anyone but you. It has nothing to do with how brave you are."

"I'm not scared to come out, it's just . . . I don't know how to explain it."

"You're ashamed . . . ?"

"I don't know!" he shouts. "I mean, I'm not ashamed of *you*. Or Jamal, or Bo, or anyone else. It's personal. But I can't be with Jamal without making *him* feel it too, you know? It's a hard feeling to break away from. I'm trying, though. *Really* hard."

"I know."

It's a while before he says anything else.

"I invited Jamal to gay prom. He said yes. I think . . . I'll wear the ring."

"Really?" I know it's a serious moment, but I have to purse my lips hard to fight back a squeal.

He laughs. "Go ahead, Yami."

"Ahhhh, I'm so happy!" I let it out. "We can finally double-date! We don't even have to fake-relationship double-date!" I hug him. He lets me but doesn't hug back.

"I don't think he wants to be my boyfriend anymore. I want to be with him, but I don't know if we're ready to jump back into it. For now, it's just gay prom. As friends."

"Friends who are in love with each other?"

"Yup." Cesar chuckles, but I can tell it's forced. "I guess we'll see where things go, eventually."

"Well, it's probably good to take it slow. Gives you some time to take care of yourself first. Because you really need to take care of yourself, Cesar."

"I just want to take it back. I let that priest get to me, you know? I couldn't stop thinking about what he said when he was arguing with Bo. And when he told me to break up with Jamal, I felt like it was my only option."

"I actually got something totally different out of that argument." I almost laugh. "Bo was reciting Bible verses, too. Just because she's not a priest doesn't mean she's wrong. Honestly, that was when I decided I could be okay with it, you know?"

Cesar laughs. "How'd we hear the exact same conversation and get totally opposite things from it? I thought we were supposed to be the same."

"We're really different, actually." I smile.

"What ever happened to in lak'ech? You're shattering my whole motto here."

I laugh. "In lak'ech doesn't have to mean we're the same. It's like . . . we *see* each other, you know? I get you."

"Yeah. I get you." He gives me a half smile, which is good enough for me right now.

"Well, I'm going to go start getting ready now."

"What? We don't have to leave until tonight!"

"Exactly! No time to waste!" I say, and turn toward the door.

"Wait—" Cesar starts, and I turn around, met with a hug that knocks the air out of me.

I hug back, hard.

"Thank you, Yami." He doesn't let go for a while, and I don't either.

"For what?"

He sighs, then pulls away. "Everything. You just do . . . so much for me. I know I don't deserve it—"

"Yes, you do. . . ."

"—but you should know I appreciate it. A lot. So, thanks . . . ," he says, looking down at his feet. "Now go fix your hair. You look like a chupacabra."

"Don't you ever insult the chupacabra like that ever again!" I say to get a laugh out of him, and I do. I'll admit my hair is a damn mess right now. I haven't touched it since waking up. "Love you, 'manito," I say, giving him another quick hug before finally leaving to get ready.

It takes me almost all day to do my hair and makeup. I do and redo my face three times before I'm satisfied. I'm wearing purple eye shadow and purple lipstick to match my dress. I'm usually pretty confident in how I do my makeup, but today I only care about if *Bo* thinks I look good. God, she better, after all the effort I'm putting in.

I have to help Cesar get ready, even though he only has to worry about putting on a suit and shoes. He spends almost as long as I do on his hair. He's mostly checking himself out in the mirror, though. Eye roll.

Gay prom is at seven, so Bo is going to pick up me, Cesar,

and Jamal at four thirty for dinner. If anyone is late, it can't be me and Bo, since Bo is the host.

Mom takes about a million pictures of us before there's a knock at the door. I look through the peephole and see Jamal fidgeting with the sleeve on his suit. I drag Cesar to the door.

"It's for you!" I whisper so Jamal can't hear me, then I push him to the door and leave so they can have a moment.

Mom doesn't give them any time. She's right behind Cesar, and she pulls Jamal inside to bombard him with pictures. He's a little stiff, and clearly nervous because he hasn't seen my mom since he and I were pretending to be together.

"You look handsome," she says instead of lecturing him about lying, then hugs him. "I missed you, mijo."

"I missed you too, Mrs. Flores." He gives her a squeeze before she pulls him over to Cesar for pictures. It takes Jamal a few minutes before he notices the ring on Cesar's finger.

He pulls Cesar into a hug that almost looks painful, but Cesar's hugging back. Jamal takes Cesar's hand and kisses the ring. I swear I want to melt, they're so cute. I hope Mom captured that on camera.

When Bo knocks at the door, I grab the earrings I made and rush to answer before my mom can interfere. I close the door behind me so Mom can't give her the same treatment as Jamal. I hold the earrings behind my back. She's wearing purple heels and a fitted suit with a purple bustier under it. I think I'm in love. Seriously. I think I might be drooling a little.

Her hand brushes against my neck, and she rests it behind

my head and gives me the softest kiss of my life. I can't breathe until she pulls away.

"I wanted a little bit of that lipstick." She smacks her lips together. "Also, you look gorgeous."

I giggle. It's not like we haven't kissed before, so I don't know why I'm so giddy right now.

"I made you something." I show her the earrings. Hoops with purple Chinese knots inside the holes. "I hope this isn't weird. But I thought it would be nice to make a cultural present, since we're both sort of trying to reconnect. It's hoops because, um, hoops are kind of my thing. And purple is your thing. And the Chinese knot is for good luck! And purple is the color of . . . um . . . romance . . . I'm just realizing how cheesy this is."

"No! They're perfect, I love it! Thank you." She blushes and pulls her hair back to expose her ears. "Put them on me."

I barely have time to put them on before my mom opens the door and pulls us inside for more pictures. She gushes over how beautiful we all are. She takes some of me and Bo, and some of the four of us together. Jamal and I take a couple of funny fake-dating pictures, too. This is why we needed the safety net of leaving at four thirty instead of five. Because my mom doesn't know how to do things quickly. After a whole lot of prodding, we finally get out of the house and head to dinner. Since it's anti-prom, we go to the least fancy place we know: McDonald's. But the McDonald's on the north side is weirdly classy as hell. There's a freaking water fountain on one of the walls. What business does McDonald's have trying to be a five-star restaurant?

Amber and David meet us there. They look surprised to see Jamal, and I realize they still think he's my ex.

"Jamal's not really my ex," I say to clear the air.

"What?" Amber and David say at the same time. Bo just chews her food.

"Yeah . . . it's kind of a funny story," Cesar says, and everyone stares at us for the answer. Cesar lets them wait in anticipation while he eats. He's an asshole like that.

"Yami was covering for me because I'm, uh, I'm bi. And she was pretending my boyfriend was her boyfriend so he could come over and stuff." He says it so casually, despite it being a huge deal, saying it out loud. I can't blame him. It's not much better than me impulsively shouting *I'M GAY* at anyone I want to come out to.

"So, you two are together, then?" Amber asks Cesar and Jamal. Cesar looks down and runs his hand through his hair.

"Uh . . . ," Jamal starts. His eyes cut to the side, like he's trying to gauge Cesar's reaction. Nothing. "We were, yeah."

David sucks in a breath through his teeth, and it's awkward again. I want to smack Cesar on the back of his head. Why isn't he *saying* anything?

"That's cool that you're still friends, though," Amber says.

"Yeah, it's cool," Jamal says, and I hurry up and change the subject before the poor boy implodes.

We get to Bo's house at six thirty, which is nice, because I want a little bit of chill time before people start showing up. All the furniture is moved outside to make room for dancing in the living room, and there's a bunch of tables and chairs for people to chill at out on the patio. Bo and I go off to the study upstairs and leave everyone else behind.

Don't get me wrong, I'm super stoked about gay prom, but all I want to do right now is be alone with Bo. I want to savor the time we have until people get here. Then we can dance all night. If my mom was here, she'd scold us for being in a room alone. But she's not here, and it's not like we're having sex or anything. I'm not even close to being there yet. Right now, just holding her hand sends lightning shooting through my nervous system.

"How are you doing?" Bo asks. It feels a little awkward to ask such a small-talk question. But I'm on cloud nine, so I tell her just that.

"I'm great. So great, you don't even know."

"I think I know a little bit." She smiles and slides her hand into mine. Right when she does, I feel my whole body relax. Like she sucked all the tension right out of me. I don't know how she does that. She's like a sorceress. I'm about to slip up and blurt out that I think I'm in love with her when I literally get saved by the bell.

27

. . . ME AMO Y RESPETO YO

It's barely seven, and someone's already ringing the doorbell. Why anyone wants to come to anti-prom right on time, I'll never understand. In the five seconds after the bell rings, everyone gets to their stations. Bo and I go back downstairs. David puts on some music. He volunteered to be the "DJ" for the night, which pretty much means setting up his playlist. Bo goes to block off the stairway with a dog fence to keep everyone else downstairs. Her parents are hiding upstairs with the dogs because "teenagers are scary." I go for the door.

Hell. No.

Jenna and Karen are standing in the doorway. I start to close the door on them, but Jenna stops me.

"Wait! We just wanted to say sorry. Can we talk to Bo?" she asks.

"No," I say, and start pushing the door closed, but Karen pushes it open.

"We just want to talk to her, then we're going to prom."

"Go to prom then! Say sorry at school if you want to so bad," I say. Karen tries to push past me. I push back. Who cares if they're trying to apologize? They don't get to insert themselves into *our* night to clear their guilty consciences. They don't get to make tonight about them.

When I push back against Karen, she grabs my arm, pulling me out with her.

"Just let us talk to her!" Karen shouts, and the crisp sound of tearing satin shouts back. I'm being pulled one way by Karen, and the other by my dress, which is stuck behind the now-closed door. Karen lets go of my arm as soon as she sees what she's done, and I fall to my hands and knees. I don't know if it was the loss of contact, or if my knees went weak from the rip.

"Yami, I'm so sorry," Jenna pleads, wide-eyed.

"GO AWAY!" I scream. And they do. They run back to their car and drive off.

One night. They couldn't let us have one night.

Bo comes rushing outside a few seconds later. She must have heard me yelling at them.

"Oh my gosh, Yami. What happened?" She's staring at my dress, then at Jenna's car driving off. "Is that Jenna?"

I start blinking really fast to keep tears from coming out. My dress is ruined, I can't ruin my makeup, too.

"I didn't let them in," I say. Bo squats down next to me and takes my hand.

"Thank you," she says. "Let's get you changed."

I maneuver myself so I can see the rip. I'm showing my whole ass.

"Oh my God!" I jump up so fast I'm dizzy, and pull the fabric behind me as best I can in case anyone drives up. I'm in a thong, so Bo just saw my *entire bare ass*. I should be mortified, but a laugh escapes from somewhere deep in my lungs. Bo cracks up with me, and we hurry upstairs to her room before anyone else gets the privilege of seeing the goods.

Bo doesn't have any dresses, so my options are pretty limited. I end up grabbing a sad pair of leggings and a floral T-shirt. It's hard not to cry, staring at myself in the bathroom mirror. My hair and face are all done up, but from the neck down, I look like I'm going to bed. At least Bo got to see me in my princesa dress before it got ruined. I step back into her room to find her also wearing leggings and a T-shirt.

"You look beautiful." She smiles and kisses me on my cheek.

"So do you." I giggle.

The bell rings again.

After the first few guests, people start rolling in pretty consistently. We eventually put a sign on the door so people stop ringing the bell and just come in. Seeing who decided to come to gay prom versus regular prom is kind of surprising. Hunter and Emily show up with an entourage of about twenty kids, mostly jocks.

Emily comes in for a hug right away. "Love your makeup!"

"Thanks!" I hug her back, relieved that I at least have *something* to show off.

Even with all these people, Cesar and Jamal are the only ones on the dance floor. Usually no one wants to be the first, especially not a queer couple at a dance full of Catholic school students, but they don't seem to care. They may not be back together, but they seem to be on the right track. Cesar definitely seems happier, at least. I take a video on my phone to show them later. They're going rounds, showing off for each other.

"Yeeesssss! Go, Cesar!" I shout when Cesar gets on the floor and spins on his butt.

A few people form a circle around them and I lose my view. Everyone is clapping and cheering them on. Bo and I go up to the circle for a better look. After a couple of rounds, Cesar notices me.

"Sorry, Yami!" Jamal says, as they both grab my arms and pull me into the middle of the cypher. He and Cesar must have coordinated an attack. They run away, and I'm frozen. I like dancing, but I don't know how to freestyle on the spot like them. I pull Bo in so I'm not alone, and she happily joins me.

With a completely straight face, she starts waving her limbs around like one of those inflatable arm-flailing tube-man thingies. I have to admire it for a minute before I can move, because she's too cute. I can't leave her hanging, so I shrug and flail my limbs around with her. We're not trying to dance well, and it's much more fun this way. There's something exhilarating about letting go and spinning around and flailing your arms and shit. Movement can be messy and wild and *free*. We're the only two people in the world for a minute. Until Amber and David flail their arms, too. Before we know it, we're surrounded by inflatable arm-flailing tube people. We started a Thing. Nice.

After a few arm-flaily songs, my sides are on fire. Apparently, being an inflatable dude is hard work. If I do that once a week, I'll be set for life.

"I need a break," I wheeze, hunched over. Bo laughs and leads me outside to get some water. We grab some chips too, and go to sit down. Even though a lot of people are dancing inside, outside is packed, too. Almost all the chairs are filled, so we sit out on the grass, at a spot a little removed from all the chairs.

There's at least a hundred people here. I wouldn't be surprised if every single person of color who goes to Slayton is in Bo's house right now. All twenty-three of us.

Bo is leaning back on her palms, and I put a hand on top of hers. She leans her head on my shoulder.

"I can't believe you asked me to prom," Bo says.

"I can't believe you asked me to anti-prom." I kiss the top of her head. I can't see her face, but I hope she's blushing. We sit in a perfect silence for a few minutes until Jamal comes over.

"Where's Cesar?" Bo asks.

"Probably still dancing. I don't know, it got crowded and I lost him."

"Want to sit with us?" I let go of Bo's hand and pat the ground next to me so he doesn't feel like a third wheel.

He lies down instead of sitting.

"You okay?" I ask.

"I'm out of shape," he says.

"I feel that." I laugh and lie down, too. Bo does the same. I could fall asleep right now. I haven't had a lick of alcohol, but I'm exhausted. I woke up so early, and I've been more than a little emotionally drained lately. I close my eyes.

My two-second nap is ruined by Cesar dogpiling on all three of us. Bo and Jamal both make cute little yelp noises, but Cesar's elbow got my side, so the noise that comes out of me is more like a donkey getting kicked in the balls. Cesar and Bo laugh like it's the funniest thing in the world.

"Okay, if y'all are done making fun of my pain now, I'm gonna go inside." I start to sit up, but Bo grabs my hand.

"We're not making fun of you! It was cute!" She's still laughing.

"Nope, I'm definitely making fun of you," Cesar says. I shoot him a mean look. Bo, too.

"I'm sorry! I'm sorry, it was funny, okay?" Bo gives my palm little kisses between phrases, and it makes it hard for me to pretend to be mad.

Cesar crawls between me and Jamal so he's sandwiched in between us. "I love you guys. I don't know you that much, Bo, but if Yami loves you, so do I."

My head whips to the side. I haven't told Bo I love her yet. I haven't even told Cesar! He wasn't supposed to know that.

"I mean . . . uhhhhh . . . Jamal, let's get a drink!" Cesar grabs Jamal's arm and they run away so fast they're stumbling over each other. It reminds me of how Bo and I ran away from all the sticky situations we've been in. I laugh. And then I remember why they ran. *Ooh*, I'll get him back for that.

"Um, ignore my brother," I say.

"Okay." I don't know if she was blushing before, but she definitely is now.

"Sorry. He's just—"

"I love you, too," Bo blurts out.

"What?"

"I love you," she says again. This time she holds my hand.

I gasp out loud. "Shut up! I love *you*!" I surprise myself at how easily I'm able to say it. My hand goes over my mouth to cover my huge smile. Bo kisses the back of my hand while it's still over my mouth. Then she gently pulls it away and kisses me again. I'm laughing between kisses because I can't believe she just said that. We both fall back on the ground, kissing and laughing.

Bo rolls over and spoons me, and talks to me softly.

"In case you didn't know, I think you're amazing and inspiring and beautiful, too." She kisses my ear, and I straight-up giggle.

I never understood the appeal of kissing before Bo. I didn't get kissing on the mouth, or on the hand, on the freaking ear. But I've never been kissed by anyone like Bo. It's different with her. She does something to me I can't explain. Kissing her is relaxing and intense and just . . . happy? It's nice. I don't even care that people can see us.

The music is loud enough that a few people are dancing outside. When the next song comes on, I'm on my feet in a split second. "Dreaming of You" by Selena. It's like David played this one just for me. It's slow, but I'm buzzing with excitement. Next thing I know, Cesar is jumping on my back, belting the lyrics in my ear. Maybe David meant for this to be a slow-dance song, but that is probably not going to happen. There will be other chances for slow dancing. Besides, we're outside, so it's not like we're ruining anyone's romantic vibes inside.

Cesar and I hold hands and belt out the words as loud as we can. Bo lifts her phone in the air like it's a light and sways her arm back and forth. I don't know if she knows the song, but she's excellent backup for us right now. After the first verse, Jamal steals Cesar away from me, and Bo turns me around and puts her hands on my hips. I guess our dates weren't so entertained by our foolishness.

But nothing can keep me from jamming out to Selena. Not even Bo. I start singing to her instead of Cesar. Loudly and badly, and it's great. She's laughing the whole time. I know it started as a joke, but this song is kind of perfect for me and Bo.

"*. . . and I still can't belieeeve, that you came up to me and said, I love you!*—Ahhh, YOU said that!—*I love you too!*—OH MY GOD IT'S OUR SONG!!!! —*Now I'm dreeeeeamin' . . .*"

Bo buries her face in my neck and I can feel her laughing. I grab both of her hands and lift our arms in the air while I serenade her. I twirl and dip her, then try to kiss her in the dip like I saw in some dance movie somewhere, but I'm not very strong. We stumble through it, somehow ending up on the ground, but she doesn't pull away, and she laughs at me through the kiss. Usually I'd be embarrassed about people seeing that, but I only see Bo right now, and I don't feel embarrassed about anything with her.

I look across the yard to see Cesar by the door, introducing

Jamal to Hunter. Cesar looks nervous, but Hunter hugs both him and Jamal, and Cesar relaxes his shoulders. Hunter was always closer to my brother than he was to me, so I'm glad Cesar finally got the chance to be himself around him.

When the song changes, Bo and I don't bother getting up off the grass. Instead, we wrap our arms around each other on the ground. Somehow I'm immune to the itchiness, and all I feel is warm. I could fall asleep like this. I guess it's the safety of it, and that Bo's whole vibe is so soothing. I open my eyes and see that hers are closed. She's so goddamn beautiful right now. And all the time, but especially right now. She looks like a friggin' angel.

She's sweaty, and her hair is a mess, and the lipstick from our kiss is smeared, and she looks so gorgeous I can't breathe. Looking at her, I realize I'm not surviving anymore. I'm dancing, and laughing, and *living*.

I love her. It feels so good to *know* that with so much confidence. No more second-guessing. No more double life. My cover is blown and it was my choice. I couldn't be happier.

She opens her eyes and blushes at me staring. I look into those beautiful black holes and wonder why I was ever scared of getting pulled in. I snuggle closer and kiss her nose.

"What are you thinking?" she asks.

I'm thinking that I'm not afraid of anything anymore. I'm not afraid of being like Bo. I'm not afraid to let her see me, and I'm not afraid of seeing myself. I'm not afraid to tell her.

"Tú eres mi otro yo."

ACKNOWLEDGMENTS

One of my favorite things to do is read with my mom. Many of the books we read together over the years inspired me to write my own, and the moment I told her I finished writing one, she asked me to read it aloud to her as if it was just another one of the published books we would read all the time.

I almost gave her a heart attack with the first line.

She gasped through every curse word, but never wavered in her support for me and this book. Ever since I wrote my first half-baked story at eight years old, she has been my biggest supporter. She always made sure I believed in myself, that I could make this dream happen, and for that, Mami, I can't thank you enough. Because of you I never once questioned if I would be able to become a published author, only when. And can you believe it? It's when!

While this book was such a joy to write, life brought me some of my darkest moments while writing and revising it, and I really need to thank Gabi, Erica, and my parents for always supporting me through those times and helping me see the light at the end of the tunnel. I wouldn't be here without you all. Thank you.

To my cousin Ally, who helped me come up with a title I'm obsessed with and let me brainstorm about every little revision until I knew exactly how to execute it. To Emery and Jonny for keeping me humble by roasting me 24/7 (Seriously though, thank you, Emery, for all your help from marketing to brainstorming!). To Adelle and Ana for always being there. To Alaysia for kicking my butt and actually making me write when I want to be lazy. And to all my beta readers who helped me whip this book into shape.

Huge thank you to my amazing agent, Alexandra Levick, who saw something special in Yami's story and became her champion. When we had our first phone call and I heard your ideas for revisions, I could feel how much more special this book would become with your help. Thank you so much for your support and for being there when I need a cheerleader. I really can't express how much it means.

I also want to thank my lovely editor, Alessandra Balzer, who believed in Yami and me enough to make this all possible. Thank you so much for giving me a chance to share her story with the world. Thank you, thank you, thank you.

And to my copyeditors, Laura Harshberger and Valerie Shea, and proofreader, Vivian Lee. To Jessie Gang for designing such a stunning cover and Be Fernández for bringing it to life. To the wonderful team at HarperCollins, and everyone who touched and will touch this book on its journey to finding readers, Caitlin Johnson, Andrea Pappenheimer, Kerry Moynagh, Kathy Faber, Nellie Kurtzman, Shannon Cox, Lauren Levite, Patty Rosati, Mimi Rankin, and Katie Dutton, thank you!

And finally, to all the teenage mes out there. To the queer kids, the Brown kids, the kids who don't quite fit the mold. Your voice matters. You matter. You're doing amazing and I love you.